_____

A young woman's body is discovered near a deserted highway—with the Nameless Detective's calling card in her purse. Nameless is puzzled. He wonders where she got his card. He also wonders where his next job is coming from. So when a well-to-do woman from affluent Sea Cliff hires him to protect her troublesome brother for a hefty fee, Nameless becomes one happy bodyguard.

The job seems easy enough—until the man he is guarding becomes the prime suspect in a murder case. Even Nameless couldn't have guessed that these first t⸍ are related. Soon he is followi⸍ trail of corpses, investigating a and fighting for his own life waters of the Pacific.

# BOOKS BY BILL PRONZINI

THE "NAMELESS DETECTIVE"

# LABYRINTH

•

## BILL PRONZINI

**KNIGHTSBRIDGE PUBLISHING COMPANY**
NEW YORK

This paperback edition of LABYRINTH and BONES first published in 1990 by Knightsbridge Publishing.

LABYRINTH originally published by St. Martin's Press in 1980.

Published by PaperJacks Ltd. in 1987.

BONES originally published by St. Martin's Press in 1985.

Published by PaperJacks Ltd. in 1986.

Published in the United States by
Knightsbridge Publishing Company
255 East 49th Street
New York, New York 10017

1-877961-92-2

10  9  8  7  6  5  4  3  2  1

First Edition

---

Thirty-five years ago, Harmon Crane, famous writer of detective pulps, took his own life. Now his son, who never met him, wants to know why. It's just the kind of job Nameless knows he should turn down . . . but doesn't.

As he tracks the dead man through his last days around San Francisco and the Bay Area, a complicated puzzle emerges and Nameless learns things about his idol he doesn't want to know. When an earthquake opens an old grave, Nameless finds himself involved in a world of deceit, intrigue, and murder reminiscent of old Crane's most sinister and puzzling stories.

# BOOKS BY BILL PRONZINI

"Nameless Detective" Novels:
*Deadfall*
*Bones*
*Double* (with Marcia Muller)
*Nightshades*
*Quicksilver*
*Bindlestiff*
*Casefile* (collection)
*Dragonfire*
*Scattershot*
*Hoodwink*
*Labyrinth*
*Twospot* (with Collin Wilcox)
*Blowback*
*Undercurrent*
*The Vanished*
*The Snatch*

OTHER NOVELS:

*Quincannon*
*The Eye* (with John Lutz)
*Starvation Camp*
*The Gallows Land*
*Masques*
*The Cambodia File* (with Jack Anderson)
*Prose Bowl* (with Barry N. Malzberg)
*Night Screams* (with Barry N. Malzberg)
*Acts of Mercy* (with Barry N. Malzberg)
*Games*
*The Running of Beasts* (with Barry N. Malzberg)
*Snowbound*
*Panic!*
*The Stalker*

NONFICTION:

*Gun in Cheek*

THE "NAMELESS DETECTIVE"

# BONES

## BILL PRONZINI

**KNIGHTSBRIDGE PUBLISHING COMPANY**
NEW YORK

For Ed McBain, a name to be reckoned with in the detective field—a novel about a detective in the field who reckons without a name

My love, she sleeps! Oh, may her sleep
As it is lasting, so be deep!
Soft may the worms about her creep!
—Edgar Allan Poe<br>The Sleeper


The evil that men do lives after them;
The good is oft interred with their bones.
—Shakespeare<br>Julius Caesar

# BONES

·

# ► ONE ◄

The house was in one of San Francisco's secluded residential neighborhoods, so neatly tucked away on top of a hill that most of the city's inhabitants would have had to consult a map to find it. I hadn't needed a map, but that was only because I had received explicit directions from the owner of the house, a man named Michael Kiskadon, who wanted to hire me. He had been vague about what he wanted to hire me to do—"It's not something I can explain very easily on the phone," he'd said. Then he said, "But I can guarantee it's a job you'll find interesting, one you're well suited for. Can you come here so we can talk? I've had some medical problems and my doctor keeps me housebound these days."

So here I was, up at the top of Twelfth Avenue across from Golden Gate Heights Park. It was eleven o'clock on a Monday morning, the sun was shining, there wasn't much wind—all in all, a pleasant October day—but hardly anybody was out on the tennis courts or the children's playground or on the wide green that paralleled the street for more than a block. It was a nice park, with big trees and picnic facilities and woody hillside paths; and from its west end you would have a sweeping view of the ocean. But its seclusion probably meant it was used more or less exclusively by the people in the neighborhood. Lucky for them, too bad for everybody else.

Not that this was a particularly affluent area. The houses lining the uphill curve of Twelfth Avenue to the east, and those back down the hill on Cragmont, were middle-class and well kept up, but mostly plain and on the smallish side. The one I wanted was opposite the park green—a semi-detached place that resembled a cottage more than anything else. It was painted blue. Behind a picket fence was a yard full of shrubs and acid-blue hydrangeas and a walkway that blended into a covered side porch.

I parked next to the green and got out. The air smelled of bay laurel, which is a good spicy smell, and I found myself smiling a little as I crossed the street. I was in pretty high spirits today, for no reason other than the balmy weather and maybe the fact that Kerry and I had spent the night together, doing what people do when they spend the night together. Kerry is my lady and a joy to be with, in or out of bed—most of the time, anyway. This morning I loved her even more than usual. This morning I loved everybody, even my partner Eberhardt and his stupid blond fiancée, Wanda.

There was a gate in the picket fence; I unlatched

it and went along the path to the porch and rang the bell. The guy who opened the door was in his mid-to-late thirties, long and lean and intense-looking. He had a clump of dry black hair that drooped down on both sides of his narrow face like a bush that had died for lack of nourishment. His skin had a whitish pallor, there were the vestiges of pain in his eyes, and he carried a cane in his left hand—testimony to the truth of his statement that he'd been ill.

He said, "You're the detective?" and I said I was and he said, "I'm Michael Kiskadon, please come in."

I went in. A big family room opened off the entryway, across the rear of the house; Kiskadon led me in there, moving slowly with the aid of his cane, favoring his left leg. Windows with rattan blinds rolled up at their tops let you see Twin Peaks straight ahead and, off to the left, the ugly science-fictional skeleton of the Sutro telecommunications tower. Incoming sunlight made streaks and splashes across some nondescript furniture and a row of potted ferns and Wandering Jews set inside wicker stands.

"Some coffee?" Kiskadon asked. "My wife made a fresh pot before she went shopping."

"Thanks, but I've already had plenty."

He nodded. "Well—thank you for coming. As you can see, I'm not really fit for travel yet."

"Medical problems, you said?"

"Yes. I'm a diabetic—diabetes mellitus. Do you know what that is?"

"I've heard of it."

"Well, I have a severe form of the disease, a disorder of carbohydrate metabolism. Hyperglycemia, glycosuria—you name it, I had it or still have it. I was in the hospital for a month." He gave me a wry, mirthless smile. "I damn near died," he said.

What can you say to that? I said inadequately, "But it's under control now?"

"More or less, assuming there aren't any more complications." He sank down on the arm of an overstuffed Naugahyde couch. "Look, I'm not after sympathy or pity. My medical problems don't have anything to do with why I want a detective. Except that they helped me make up my mind to call you. I've been thinking about it for some time."

"I don't understand, Mr. Kiskadon."

"I almost died, as I said. I could still die before my time. There are some things I have to know before that happens, things that are important to me."

"Yes?"

"About my father. I never knew him, you see. He and my mother separated a month or so after I was conceived, and she moved back to Philadelphia, where her people were. She refused to tell my father she was pregnant."

"Why?"

"She was very bitter about the split; it was my father's idea to end their marriage, not hers. She had always wanted a child and he'd been against

it. I was a planned accident on her part, I think."
But he seemed not to have inherited any of his
mother's bitterness toward his father; in his voice
now was a kind of intense yearning; for what, I
couldn't gauge yet.

I asked, "Did she tell him after you were born?"

"She never had the chance. She died giving birth
to me."

"I see."

"I was raised by my mother's sister and her
husband," Kiskadon said. "They legally adopted
me, gave me their name. My aunt hated my father,
even blamed him for my mother's death; she also
vowed not to tell him about me. He died without
ever knowing he had fathered a son."

"So it's not that you don't know who he was," I
said. That was what I'd begun to think he was
leading up to: a search for his roots, for the iden-
tity of his old man.

"No, it's not that at all. Uncle Ned told me the
truth two years ago, after my aunt died. He said
he didn't think it was right that I go through the
rest of my life believing my natural father was
killed in Korea, which was what I'd always been
told."

"Did you make any effort to contact him, once
you knew?"

The wry, mirthless smile again. "It was far too
late by then," he said. "But a few months later I
had a job offer in San Francisco and I accepted it.
It took me a while after I was settled, but I managed to make contact with my father's widow, the

woman he married after his divorce from my mother. I also located the man who'd been his attorney. Neither of them could or would tell me what I need to know."

"And that is?"

"Why he shot himself," Kiskadon said.

"Suicide?"

"Yes. With a handgun."

"Where was this?"

"At his home here in the city."

"How long ago?"

"In 1949, when I was four years old."

I stared at him. "Nineteen . . . did you say *forty-nine?*"

"That's right. December 10, 1949."

Well, Christ, I thought. I didn't say anything.

"I'm aware it might be impossible to find out the truth after thirty-five years," he said, "but I have to try. It's important to me—I told you that. It's . . . oh hell, I might as well admit it: it's become an obsession. I *have* to know why he killed himself."

I still didn't say anything.

"I'll pay you well," he said. "I'm a design engineer for Bechtel; I make seventy-five thousand dollars a year when I'm working full-time."

"I'm not thinking about money, Mr. Kiskadon," I said. "The kind of job you want done . . . it's an exercise in futility and I'd be a liar if I told you otherwise. I can understand why you want to go ahead with it but I don't think I'm the right man to—"

"But you are the right man," he said. He stood up again and made an emphatic gesture with his cane. "You're *exactly* the right man."

"I don't understand."

"Come into my office. I want you to see something."

I shrugged and let him lead me into an adjacent room that had an L-shaped desk covered with computer equipment, a recliner chair, a table with a rack of pipes on it, and a big, glass-fronted bookcase along one wall. What was in the bookcase caught my eye immediately. I glanced at Kiskadon, and he said, "Go ahead, take a look," so I went over there and opened the glass doors and took a look.

Pulp magazines, upwards of two hundred of them. Mostly detective and mystery, with a sprinkling of adventure and Western titles. A pile of slick magazines, the top one a browning issue of *Collier's* from 1944. A shelf of books, hardcovers and paperbacks both, with the same author's name on the spines—a name I recognized. And a photograph in a silver frame, black and white and several years old, of a tall, angular man wearing horn-rimmed glasses and bearing a resemblance to Kiskadon, standing on somebody's lawn with a drink upraised in one hand. I turned to Kiskadon again.

"Yes," he said. "My father was Harmon Crane."

Harmon Crane. A name on the covers of scores of pulps in the thirties and forties; a name that sold magazines back then and was still selling them, to collectors such as myself. One of the best writers of pulp fiction, whose blend of hard-boiled action and whacky humor had been rivaled only by Norbert Davis among the unsung heroes of the pulps. But Harmon Crane hadn't remained unsung because he hadn't remained a pulpster. He had graduated to such slicks as *Collier's, American Magazine,* and *The Saturday Evening Post;* and even more importantly, as far as aficionados of crime fiction were concerned, he had taken one of his pulp detectives, a screwball private eye named Johnny Axe, and fleshed him out and made him the hero of half a dozen novels that had sold remarkably well during the forties and that had been in print off and on ever since. Their titles, all of which were clever and outrageous puns, marched across the shelf behind me in their various editions: *Axe Marks the Spot, The Axe-Raye Murders, Axe for Trouble, Axe of Mercy, Don't Axe Me, Axe and Pains.*

I'd known that Crane had been a Bay Area resident since his college days at UC-Berkeley, and that he'd died here by his own hand around 1950; I had a vague memory of reading about his suicide in the papers back then, paying attention to it because of my interest in the pulps in general and his work in particular. But details about his personal life had been sketchy. I had always wondered what led such a successful writer to take his own life.

Crane was still one of my favorites; I read and collected his pulp work avidly. Which made things difficult as far as Michael Kiskadon was concerned. If his father had been anyone else I would have stuck to my guns and turned down his job offer. But because he had been sired by Harmon Crane, I could feel myself weakening. The prospect of poking around in Crane's life, even though he had been dead thirty-five years, held perverse appeal. For some damn reason, the private lives of authors are endlessly fascinating to people like me who read their work.

Kiskadon was watching me in his intense way. "I started collecting his work as soon as I found out who he was," he said. "It took time and quite a lot of money, but I have just about everything now; I'm only missing a dozen or so pulps. He wrote close to two hundred and fifty stories for the pulp market, you know."

I nodded. "Sold his first to *Black Mask* in 1933, while he was still at Berkeley."

"Yes. He was pre-med at the time." The intensity in Kiskadon's expression had been joined by eagerness: he was pretty sure he had me now. "I knew you'd remember him. A well-known detective who collects pulp magazines . . . well, now you see what I meant when I said you're exactly the right man for the job."

"Uh-huh."

"Will you take it, then?"

"I'm leaning that way." I glanced again at the photograph of Harmon Crane—the first I'd ever seen of him. He didn't look anything like the mental image I had formulated; he looked like a schoolteacher, or maybe an accountant. "Let's go sit down and talk. I've got a lot of questions."

We went back into the family room. Kiskadon sat on the couch and I sat in the closest chair, a creaky rocker that made me feel like an old fart in a retirement facility—the California Home for the Curmudgeonly, Kerry might have said. I watched Kiskadon light up a pipe. His tobacco smelled like chicken droppings; Eberhardt would have loved it.

I said, "First of all, what do you know about the suicide?"

"Very little. Just what my uncle told me, what I read in old newspapers at the library, and what I was able to find out from his lawyer. His widow wouldn't talk about it at all."

"He shot himself in his house, you said?"

"Yes. In his office."

"Where was he living at the time?"

"North Beach. Up near Coit Tower."

"Is the house still there?"

"No. There's an apartment building on the site now."

"What time of day did it happen?"

"Sometime around eight P.M."

"Was anybody else in the house at the time?"

"No. His wife was out to dinner with a friend."

"Just the two of them lived there?"

"Yes. My father had no other children."

"Who found his body?"

"His wife, her friend, and the lawyer."

"How did the lawyer happen to be there?"

"My father called him and asked him to come over. He arrived just as Mrs. Crane and the friend returned home."

"This friend—what's his name?"

"Adam Porter. He was Mrs. Crane's art teacher."

"Is he still alive?"

"No. He died in 1971."

"And the lawyer's name?"

"Thomas Yankowski."

Ah Christ, I thought, old Yank-'Em-Out.

Kiskadon said, "You look as if you know him."

"I know him, all right," I said. "We've had a few dealings in the past."

"You don't like him?"

"Not one bit."

"Neither did I. A sour old bastard."

"Yeah." Yank-'Em-Out Yankowski, the scourge of the legal profession and the bosom buddy of every slum landlord within a fifty-mile radius of San Francisco. He was retired now, but in his day he had specialized in landlord-tenant relationships, usually working for the landlords but occasionally playing the other side when there was enough money involved. He had boasted publicly that there wasn't a lease written he couldn't break, or a tenant he couldn't evict. The name Yank-'Em-Out had been tacked onto him as a pejorative, but he had taken a liking to it and used it as a kind of unofficial slogan. "How did he happen to be Harmon Crane's lawyer?"

"I don't know."

"Did he give you any hint what sort of legal service he might have been providing?"

"No."

"Did he say what Crane wanted to see him about the night of the suicide?"

"Only that my father seemed distraught, that he wanted someone to talk to."

"Were the two of them also friends?"

"That's what I gathered."

"But your father *didn't* wait to talk to Yankowski?"

"No. He . . . was drunk that night. Maybe that explains it."

"Maybe. Did he leave a note?"

"Yes. They found it in his typewriter when they broke in."

"Broke in?"

"The office door was locked from the inside," Kiskadon said. "His office was on the second floor, so they couldn't get in any other way."

"Were the windows locked too?"

"I don't know. Does it matter?"

"I suppose not. What did the suicide note say?"

"Nothing specific. Just that he felt he'd be better off dead. It was only a few lines long."

"He'd been despondent, then?"

"For several weeks. He'd been drinking heavily."

"Any clues as to why?"

"According to Yankowski, my father wouldn't discuss it with anyone. Yankowski thinks it was some sort of writer's block; my father wrote almost nothing during the last six weeks of his life.

But I find that theory difficult to believe, considering how much fiction he produced. And how much writing meant to him—others have told me that." Kiskadon's pipe had gone out; he paused to relight it. "In any case, his motive had to have been personal."

"Why do you say that?"

"Well, I don't see how it could have been financial. He had contracts for two new Johnny Axe novels, and there was a film deal in the works. There was also talk of doing a Johnny Axe radio show."

"Uh-huh. Well, if anyone knows the reason, it's his widow. Maybe I can pry it out of her. Where does she live?"

"In Berkeley. With her niece, a woman named Marilyn Dubek." He gave me the address from memory and I wrote it down in my notebook.

"Is her name still Crane?"

"Yes. Amanda Crane. She never remarried."

"Was your father her first husband?"

"Yes."

"How long were they married?"

"Two years. The split with my mother wasn't over her, if that's what you're thinking. They didn't even know each other at the time of the separation."

"What did cause the split with your mother?"

"She had extravagant ways; that was the main reason. She was a social animal—parties, nightclubs, that sort of thing—and my father liked his privacy. They just weren't very well matched, I guess."

"How long were *they* married?"

"Four years."

"Your father's first marriage?"

"No. His second."

"Who was his first wife?"

"A woman named Ellen Corneal. He married her while they were both in college. It didn't last very long."

"Why not?"

"I'm not sure. Incompatibility again, I think."

"Do you know what happened to her?"

"No."

"Back to Yankowski. Where did you talk to him?"

"At his home. He lives in St. Francis Wood."

"How willing was he to see you?"

"Willing enough," Kiskadon said. "I called and explained who I was, and he invited me over. He was a little standoffish in person, but he answered all my questions."

"Can you give me the names of any of your father's friends in 1949?"

"He apparently didn't have any close friends."

"What about other writers?"

"Well, he wasn't a joiner but he did know some of the other writers in the Bay Area. I managed to track down a couple who knew him casually, but they weren't any help. They only saw him at an occasional literary function."

"You might as well give me their names anyway."

He did and I wrote them down. One was familiar; the other wasn't. Neither had written for the pulps, unless the unfamiliar guy had cranked out stories under a pseudonym. I asked Kiskadon about that, and he said no, the man had written confession stories and fact articles for more than thirty years and was now retired and living on Social Security.

Be a writer, I thought, make big money and secure your future.

I spent the next five minutes settling with Kiskadon on my fee and the size of my retainer, and filling out the standard contract form I'd brought with me. He signed the form, and was working on a check when I heard the sound of a key in the front door lock. A moment later a woman came inside.

She stopped when she saw me and said, "Oh," but not as if she were startled. She was a few years younger than Kiskadon, brown-haired, on the slender side except for flaring hips encased in a pair of too-tight jeans. Why women with big bottoms persist in wearing tight pants is a riddle of human nature the Sphinx couldn't answer, so I didn't even bother to try. Otherwise she was pretty enough in a Bonnie Bedelia sort of way.

Kiskadon said, "Lynn, hi. This is the detective I told you about." He gave her my name, which impressed her about as much as if he'd given her a carpet tack. "He's going to take on the job."

She gave me a doubtful look. Then she said, "Good. That's fine, dear," in that tone of voice wives use when they're humoring their spouses.

"He'll get to the truth if anyone can," Kiskadon said.

She didn't answer that; instead she looked up at me again. "How much are you charging?"

Practical lady. I told her, and she thought about it, biting her lip, and seemed to decide that I wasn't being *too* greedy. She nodded and said to him, "I'll get the groceries out of the car. We'll have lunch pretty soon."

"Good, I'm starved."

She asked me, "Will you be joining us?"

"Thanks, but I'd better get to work."

"You're perfectly welcome to stay. . . ."

"No. Thanks, anyway."

"Well," she said, and shrugged, and turned and went out with her rear end wiggling and waggling. You could almost hear the stretched threads creaking in the seams of her jeans.

Kiskadon gave me his check and his hand and an eager smile; he looked better than he had when I'd arrived—color in his cheeks, a kind of zest in his movements, as if my agreeing to investigate for him had worked like a rejuvenating medicine. I thought: That's me, the Good Samaritan. But I had taken the job as much for me as for him: so much for virtue and the milk of human kindness.

When I got outside, Mrs. Kiskadon was hefting an armload of Safeway sacks out of the trunk of a newish green Ford Escort parked in the driveway.

She seemed to want to say something to me as I passed by, but whatever she saw when she glanced toward the porch changed her mind for her. All I got was a sober nod, which I returned in kind. I looked back at the porch myself as I opened the gate; she was on her way there carrying the grocery sacks, and Kiskadon was standing out in plain sight, leaning on his cane and looking past her at me, still smiling.

He waved as I went through the gate, but I didn't wave back. I'm not sure why.

# ◂ TWO ◂

St. Francis Wood was only a ten-minute drive, so I went there to see Yank-'Em-Out Yankowski first. Unlike Golden Gate Heights, the Wood is one of the city's ritzy neighborhoods, spread out along the lower, westward slope of Mt. Davidson and full of old money and the old codgers who'd accumulated it. Some of the houses in there had fine views of the ocean a couple of miles distant, but Yankowski's wasn't one of them. It was a Spanish-style job built down off San Juanito Way, bordered on one side by a high cypress hedge and on the other by a woody lot overgrown with eucalyptus trees; half-hidden by flowering bushes, more cypress, and a tangle of other vegetation. Either Yankowski was a bucolic at heart, which I doubted, or he liked plenty of privacy.

I parked at the curb in front and went down a set of curving stone stairs and onto a tile-floored porch. The front door looked like the one that barred the entrance to the castle in every B-grade horror film ever made: aged black wood, iron-bound, with nail studs and an ornate latch. There wasn't any bell; I lifted a huge black-iron knocker and let it make a bang like a gun going off.

Immediately a dog began barking inside. It was a big dog, and it sounded mad as hell at having been disturbed. But it didn't bark for long; when the noise stopped I heard it moving, heard the click and scrape of his nails on stone or tile, and then it slammed into the door snarling and growling and burbling like Lewis Carroll's jabberwock. It probably had eyes of flame, too, and its drooling jaws would no doubt have enjoyed making a snicker-snack of my throat. If I'd been a burglar I would have run like hell. As it was I backed off a couple of paces. I am not crazy about dogs, especially vicious dogs like whatever monstrosity Yankowski kept in there.

It went right on snarling and burbling. Nobody came and told it to shut up; nobody opened the door, either, for which I was properly grateful. I debated leaving one of my business cards, and decided against it; when I saw Yank-'Em-Out I wanted to catch him unprepared, just in case he *hadn't* told Michael Kiskadon everything he knew about Harmon Crane's suicide.

The thing in the house lunged against the door again, making it quiver and creak in protest. I said, "Stupid goddamn beast," but I said it under my breath while I was going back up the stairs.

Berkeley used to be a quiet, sleepy little college town, with tree-shaded side streets and big old houses as its main non-academic attraction. But its image had changed in the sixties, as a result of the flower children and radical politics fomented by the senseless war in Vietnam. In the seventies, Patty Hearst and the Symbionese Liberation Army had added a bizarre new dimension, which the media and the right-wingers had mushroomed into a silly reputation for Berkeley as the home of every left-wing nut group in the country. And in the eighties, it seemed to have become a magnet for a variety of criminals and the lunatic fringe: drug dealers, muggers, purse snatchers, burglars, pimps, panhandlers, bag ladies, bag men, flashers, acidheads, religious cultists, and just plain weirdos. Nowadays it had one of the highest crime rates in the Bay Area. And the downtown area centering on Telegraph Avenue near the university was a free daily freakshow. You could get high on marijuana just walking the sidewalks; and you were liable to see just about anything on a given day. The last time I'd been there I had seen, within the space of a single block, a filth-encrusted kid with bombed-out eyes reciting passages from the *Rubaiyat*; a guy dressed up like an Oriental potentate sitting cross-legged on the sidewalk with a myna bird perched on his shoulder, plucking out Willie Nelson tunes on a sitar; and a jolly old fellow in a yarmulke selling half a kilo of grass to an aging hippie couple, the female member of which was carrying an infant in a shoulder sling.

No more sleepy little college town: Berkeley had graduated to the big time. Welcome to America, babycakes.

Still, the old, saner Berkeley continued to exist in pockets up in the hills and down on the flats. The Cal campus was pretty much the same as it had always been, and the kids who went there were mostly good kids with their priorities on straight. Most of the residents were good people too, no matter what their politics happened to be. And the tree-shaded side streets and big old houses were still there, with the only difference being that now the houses had alarm systems, bars on their windows, triple locks on their doors, and maybe a handgun or a shotgun strategically placed inside. Driving along one of those old-Berkeley streets, you could almost believe things were as simple and uncomplicated as they had been in the days when this was just another college town. Almost.

The street Amanda Crane lived on was like that: it seemed a long, long way from the Telegraph Avenue freakshow, even though only a couple of miles separated them. It was off Ashby Avenue up near fashionable Claremont Hotel: Linden Street, named after the ferny trees that lined it and that, here and there along its length, joined overhead to create a tunnel effect. The number Michael Kiskadon had given me was down toward the far end—a brown-shingled place at least half a century old, with a brick-and-dark-wood porch that had splashes of red bougainvillea growing over it. A massive willow and a couple of kumquat trees grew in the front yard, providing plenty of shade.

A woman was sitting on an old-fashioned swing on the porch. But it wasn't until I parked the car and started along the walk that I had a good look at her: silver-haired, elderly, holding a magazine in her lap so that it was illuminated by dappled sunlight filtering down through the leaves of the willow tree.

She lifted her head and smiled at me as I came up onto the porch. I returned the smile, moving over to stand near her with my back to the porch railing. Inside the house, a vacuum cleaner was making a high-pitched screeching noise that would probably have done things to my nerves if I had been any closer to it.

The woman on the swing was in her mid-sixties, small, delicate, with pale and finely wrinkled skin that made you think of a fragile piece of bone china that had been webbed with tiny cracks. She had never been beautiful, but I thought that once, thirty-five years ago, she would have been quite striking. She was still striking, but in a different sort of way. There was a certain serenity in her expression and in her faded blue eyes, the kind of look you sometimes see on the faces of the ultra-devout—the look of complete inner peace. She was wearing an old-fashioned blue summer dress buttoned to the throat. A pair of rimless spectacles were tilted forward on a tiny nose dusted with powder to dull if not hide the freckles.

"Hello," she said, smiling.

"Hello. Mrs. Crane—Amanda Crane?"

"Why, yes. Do I know you?"

"No, ma'am."

"You're not a salesman, are you? This is my niece's house and she can't abide salesmen."

"No, I'm not a salesman. I'm here to see you."

"Really? About what?"

"Harmon Crane."

"Oh," she said in a pleased way. "You're a fan, then."

"Fan?"

"Of Harmon's writing. His fans come to see me once in a while; one of them even wrote an article about me for some little magazine. You *are* one of his fans, aren't you?"

"Yes, I am," I said truthfully. "Your husband was a very good writer."

"Oh yes, so everyone says."

"Don't you think so?"

"Well," she said, and shrugged delicately, and closed her magazine—*Ladies' Home Journal*—and took off her glasses. "Harmon had a rather risqué sense of humor, you know."

"Yes, I know."

"Yes," she said.

"You *did* read his fiction, though?"

"Some of it. His magazine stories . . . some of those were nice. There was one about a young couple on vacation in Yosemite, I think it was in *The Saturday Evening Post*. Do you remember that story?"

"No, I'm afraid I don't."

"It was very funny. Not at all risqué. I can't seem to remember the title."

"Was your husband funny in person too?"

"Funny? Oh, yes, he liked to make people laugh."

"Would you say he was basically a happy man?"

"Yes, I would."

"And you and he were happy together?"

"Quite happy. We had a lovely marriage. He was devoted to me, you know. And I to him."

"No problems of any kind between you?"

"Oh no. No."

"But he did have other problems," I said gently. "Would you know what they were?"

"Problems?" she said.

"That led him to take his own life."

She sat motionless, still smiling slightly; she might not have heard me. "I think it was 'Never Argue with a Woman,' " she said at length.

"Pardon?"

"The story of Harmon's that I liked in *The Saturday Evening Post*. Yes, it must have been 'Never Argue with a Woman.' "

"Mrs. Crane, do you know why your husband shot himself?"

Silence. A little brown-and-yellow bird swooped down out of one of the kumquat trees and landed on the porch railing; she watched as it hopped along, chittering softly to itself, its head darting from side to side. Her hands, folded together just under her breasts, had a poised, suspended look.

"Mrs. Crane?"

I moved when I spoke, startling the bird; it went away. The last of her smile went away with it. She blinked, and her hands settled on top of the copy of *Ladies' Home Journal*. Unconsciously she began to twist the small diamond ring on the third finger of her left hand.

"No," she said. "No."

"You don't know why?"

"I won't talk about that. Not about that."

"It's important, Mrs. Crane. If you could just give me some idea. . . ."

"No," she said. Then she said, "Oh, wait, I was wrong. It *wasn't* 'Never Argue with a Woman' that I liked so much. Of course it wasn't. It was 'The Almost Perfect Vacation.' How silly of me to have got the two mixed up."

She smiled at me again, but it was a different kind of smile this time; her eyes seemed to be saying, "Please don't talk about this anymore, please don't hurt me." I felt her pain—that had always been one of my problems, too much empathy—and it made me feel like one of the sleazy types that prowled Telegraph Avenue.

But I didn't quit probing at her, not just yet. I might not like myself sometimes, but that had never stopped me from doing my job. If it had I would have gone out of business years ago.

I said, "I'm sorry, Mrs. Crane. I won't bring that up again. Is it all right if I ask you some different questions?"

"Well . . ."

"Do you still see any old friends of your husband's?"

She bit her lip. "We didn't have many friends,"

she said. "We had each other, but . . . it wasn't . . ." The words trailed off into silence.

"There's no one you're still in touch with?"

"Only Stephen. He still comes to see me sometimes."

"Stephen?"

"Stephen Porter."

"Would he be any relation to Adam Porter?"

"Why, yes—Adam's brother. Did you know Adam?"

"No, ma'am. He was mentioned to me as a friend of your husband's."

"More my friend than Harmon's, I must say."

"Adam, you mean?"

"Yes. He was my art teacher. He was a painter, you know."

"No, I didn't know."

"A very good painter. Oils. I was much better with watercolors. Still life, mostly. Fruit and such."

"Do you still paint?"

"Oh no, not in years and years."

"Is Stephen Porter also a painter?"

"No, he's a sculptor. He teaches, too; it's very difficult for sculptors to make a living these days unless they also teach. I imagine that's the case with most artists, don't you?"

"Yes, ma'am. Does he have a studio?"

"Oh, of course."

"In what city?"

"In San Francisco."

"Could you tell me the address?"

"Are you going to see Stephen?"

"I'd like to, yes."

"Well, you tell him it's been quite a while since he came to visit. Months, now. Will you tell him that?"

"I will."

"North Beach," she said.

"Ma'am?"

"Stephen's studio. It's in North Beach." She smiled reminiscently. "Harmon and I used to live in North Beach—a lovely old house near Coit Tower, with trees all around. He so loved his privacy."

"Yes, ma'am."

"It's gone now. Torn down long ago."

"Can you tell me the address of Stephen's studio?"

"I don't believe I remember it," she said. "But I'm sure it's in the telephone directory."

Inside the house, the vacuum cleaner stopped its screeching; there was a hushed quality to the silence that followed. I broke it by saying, "I understand Thomas Yankowski was also a friend of your husband's."

"Well, he was Harmon's attorney."

"Did your husband have any special reason to need a lawyer?"

"Well, a woman tried to sue him once, for plagiarism. It was a silly thing, one of those . . . what do you call them?"

"Nuisance suits?"

"Yes. A nuisance suit. He met Thomas somewhere, while he was doing legal research for one of his books, I think it was, and Thomas handled the matter for him."

"Were they also friends?"

"I suppose they were. Although we seldom saw Thomas socially."

"Does he ever come to visit you now?"

"Thomas? No, not since I refused him."

"How do you mean, 'refused him'?"

"When he asked me to marry him."

"When was this?"

"Not long after . . . well, a long time ago."

"And you turned him down?"

"Oh yes," she said. "Harmon was the only man I ever loved. I've never remarried; I never could."

"You and Mr. Crane had no children, is that right?"

She said demurely, "We weren't blessed in that way, no."

"But your husband did have a son by a previous marriage."

"Michael," she said, and nodded. "I was quite surprised when he came to see me. I never knew Harmon had a son. Michael never knew it either. Michael . . . I can't seem to recall his last name . . ."

"Kiskadon."

"Yes. An odd name. I wish he'd come back for another visit; he was only here that one time. Such a nice boy. Harmon would have been proud of him, I'm sure."

"Did you know Michael's mother?"

"No. Harmon was already divorced from her when I met him."

"Did you know his first wife?"

"First wife?"

"Ellen Corneal."

"No, you're mistaken," she said. "Harmon was never married to a woman named Ellen."

"But he was. While they were attending UC . . ."

"No," she said positively. "He was only married once before we took our vows. To Michael's mother, Susan. Only once."

"Is that what he told you?"

She didn't have a chance to answer my question. The front door opened just then and a woman came out—a dumpy woman in her forties, with dyed black hair bound up with a bandanna and a face like Petunia Pig. She said, "I thought I heard voices out here," and gave me a suspicious look. "Who are you? What are you doing here?"

"We've been talking about Harmon," Mrs. Crane said.

"Yes," I said, "we have," and let it go at that.

"God, another one of *those*," the dumpy woman said. "You haven't been upsetting her, have you? You fan types always upset her."

"I don't think so, no."

She turned to Mrs. Crane. "Auntie? *Has* he been upsetting you?"

"No, Marilyn. Do I look upset, dear?"

"Well, I think you'd better come inside now."

"I don't want to come inside, dear."

"We'll have some tea. Earl Grey's."

"Well, tea *would* be nice. Perhaps the gentle-man . . ."

"The gentleman can come back some other time," Petunia Pig said. She was looking at me as she spoke and her expression said: I'm lying for her benefit. Go away and don't come back.

"But he might want to ask me some more questions. . . ."

"No more questions. Not today."

Mrs. Crane smiled up at me. "It has been very nice talking to you," she said.

"Same here. I appreciate your time, Mrs. Crane."

"Not at all. I enjoy talking about Harmon."

"Of course you do, Auntie," Petunia Pig said, "but you know it isn't good for you when it goes on too long. Come along, now. Upsy-daisy."

She helped Mrs. Crane up off the swing, putting an arm protectively around her shoulders, and Mrs. Crane smiled at her and then smiled at me and said, "Marilyn takes such good care of me," and all of a sudden I realized, with a profound sense of shock, that her air of serenity did not come from inner peace at all; it and her smile both were the product of a mental illness.

The niece, Marilyn, glared at me over her shoulder as she walked Mrs. Crane to the door. I moved quickly to the stairs, went down them, and when I looked back they were gone inside. The door banged shut behind them.

I sat in the car for a couple of minutes, a little shaken, staring up at the house and remembering

Mrs. Crane's smile and the pain that had come into her eyes when I pressed her about her husband's suicide. That must have been what did it to her, what unsettled her mind and made her unable to care for herself. And that meant she had been like this for thirty-five years. Thirty-five *years!*

I felt like a horse's ass.

No. I felt like its droppings.

# ▸ THREE ◂

As I drove away from there, back down Ashby, I
cursed Michael Kiskadon. Why the hell hadn't he
told me about his stepmother's condition? But
the anger didn't last long. Pretty soon I thought:
Quit jumping to conclusions; maybe *he* never
realized it at all. She looked and sounded normal
enough; it was only when you analyzed what she
said and the way she said it that you understood
how off-key it was. Look how long it had taken
me to realize the truth, and at that I might not
have tumbled if it hadn't been for the way the
niece treated her.

Some detective I was. There were times when I
couldn't detect a fart in a Skid Row beanery.

It was almost one-thirty when I came back
across the Bay Bridge into San Francisco. I took
the Broadway exit that leads to North Beach,
stopped at the first service station off the freeway,
and looked up Stephen Porter in the public telephone directory. Only one listed—and just the
number, no street address. I fished up a dime and
dialed the number. Nobody answered.

Yeah, I thought, *that* figures.

The prospect of food had no appeal, but my stomach was rumbling and it seemed a wise idea to fill the empty spaces; I hadn't had anything to eat all day except for an orange with my breakfast coffee at eight A.M. I drove on through the Broadway tunnel and stopped at a place on Polk, where I managed to swallow a tuna-fish-on-rye and a glass of iced tea. I wanted a beer instead of the iced tea, but I was on short rations again where the suds were concerned; after losing a lot of weight earlier in the year I had started to pork up a little again, and I was damned if I was going to get reacquainted with my old nemisis, the beer belly. So it was one bottle of Lite per day now—and the way this day was progressing, I was going to need my one bottle even more later than I did now.

From the restaurant I went down to Civic Center, wasted fifteen minutes looking for a place to park, and finally got into the microfilm room at the main library. Kiskadon had told me the date of his father's death was December 10, 1949. San Francisco had had four newspapers back then—*News*, *Call-Bulletin*, *Chronicle*, and *Examiner*; I requested the issues of December 11 and 12, 1949, from all four. Then I sat down at one of the magnifying machines and proceeded to abuse my eyes and give myself a headache squinting at page after page of blurry newsprint.

The facts of Harmon Crane's suicide—or at least the facts that had been made public—were pretty much as Kiskadon had given them to me. On the night of December 10, Amanda Crane had gone out to dinner on Fisherman's Wharf with Adam Porter; Harmon Crane had been invited but had declined to accompany them. According to Porter, Crane had seemed withdrawn and depressed and had been drinking steadily all day. "I had no inkling that he might be contemplating suicide," Porter was quoted as saying. "Harmon just never struck me as the suicidal type."

Porter and Mrs. Crane had returned to the secluded North Beach house at 8:45. Thomas Yankowski arrived just after they entered the premises; he had been summoned by a call from Crane, who had "sounded desperate and not altogether coherent," and had rushed right over. Alarmed by this, Mrs. Crane began calling her husband's name. When he didn't respond, Yankowski and Porter ran upstairs, where they found the door to Crane's office locked from the inside. Their concern was great enough by this time to warrant breaking in. And inside they had found Crane slumped over his desk, dead of a gunshot wound to the right temple.

The weapon, a .22 caliber Browning target automatic, was clenched in his hand. It was his gun, legally registered to him; he had been fond of target shooting and owned three such small-caliber firearms. A typed note "spattered with the writer's blood," according to some yellow journalist on the *Call*, lay on top of Crane's typewriter. It said: "I can't go on any longer. Can't sleep, can't eat, can't work. I think I'm losing my mind. Life terrifies me more than death. I will be better off dead and Mandy will be better off without me."

There were no quotes from Amanda Crane in any of the news stories; she was said to be in seclusion, under a doctor's care—which usually indicated severe trauma. Yankowski and Porter both expressed shock and dismay at the suicide. Porter said, "Harmon hadn't been himself lately— withdrawn and drinking too much. We thought it was some sort of a slump, perhaps writer's block. We never believed it would come to this." Yankowski said, "The only explanation I can find is that he ran out of words. Writing meant more to Harmon than anything else in this world. Not being able to write would be a living death to a man of his temperament."

No one else who knew Crane had any better guesses to make. He had been closemouthed about whatever was troubling him, and evidently confided in no one at all. As far as anyone knew, his reasons for embracing death had died with him.

So how was I supposed to find out what they were, thirty-five years later? What did it matter, really, why he had knocked himself off? We all die sooner or later, some with cause, some without. Ashes to ashes, dust to dust, and who the hell cares in the long run?

Amanda Crane cared. Michael Kiskadon cared. And maybe I cared too, a little: there's always some damn fool like me to care about things that don't matter in the long run.

I left the library, picked up my car and the overtime parking ticket flapping under the windshield wiper, said a few words out loud about the way the city of San Francisco treats its citizens, and drove back up Van Ness to O'Farrell Street. The office I share with Eberhardt is on O'Farrell, not far from Van Ness, and in the next block is a parking garage that by comparison with the garages farther downtown offers a dirt-cheap monthly rate. I put the car in my allotted space on the ground floor and walked back to my building.

The place doesn't look like much from the outside: bland and respectable in a shabby sort of way. It doesn't look like much on the inside either. The ground floor belongs to a real estate company, the second floor belongs to an outfit that makes custom shirts ("The Slim-Taper Look is the Right Look"), and the third and top floor belongs to Eberhardt and me. That floor is a converted loft that once housed an art school, which is why it has a skylight in the ceiling. Very classy, an office with a skylight—except when it rains. Then the noise the rain makes beating down on the glass is so loud you have to yell when you're talking on the telephone.

Eberhardt was talking on the telephone when I came in—settled back in his chair with his feet up on his desk—but he wasn't yelling; he was crooning and cooing into the receiver like a constipated dove. Which meant that he was talking to Wanda. He always crooned and cooed when he talked to Wanda—a man fifty-five years old, divorced, a tough ex-cop. It was pretty disgusting to see and hear.

But he was in love, or thought he was. Wanda Jaworski, an employee of the downtown branch of Macy's—the footwear department. They had met in a supermarket a couple of months ago, when he dropped a package of chicken parts on her foot. This highly romantic beginning had evolved into a whirlwind courtship and a (probably drunken) proposal of marriage. They hadn't set a definite date yet; Wanda was still assembling her trousseau. Or "truss-o," as she put it, which sounded like some kind of device for people with hernias. Wanda was not long on brains. Nor was Wanda long on sophistication; Wanda, in fact, was coarse, silly, and an incessant babbler. Nor was she long on looks, unless you happen to covet overweight forty-five-year-old women with double chins and big behinds and the kind of bright yellow hair that looks as if it belongs on a Raggedy Ann doll. What Wanda *was* long on was chest. She had the biggest chest I have ever seen, a chest that would have dwarfed Mamie Van Doren's, a chest that would have shamed Dolly Parton's, a chest among chests.

It was Kerry's considered opinion that Eberhardt was not in love with Wanda so much as he was in love with Wanda's chest. He was fascinated by it— or them. Whenever he and Wanda were together he seemed unable to take his eyes off it—or them

It was also Kerry's considered opinion that if he married her, he would be making a monumental mistake.

"What he's doing," she'd said to me in her typically caustic way on the occasion of our first meeting Wanda, "is make a molehill out of a couple of mountains."

I tended to agree, but there wasn't much I could do about it. You don't tell your business partner, your best friend for more than thirty years, that he is contemplating marriage to a pea-brained twit. You don't tell him that he can't see the forest for the chest. You don't tell him anything; you just keep your mouth shut and hope that he comes to his senses before it's too late.

He waggled a hand at me as I crossed to my desk. I didn't feel like doing any waggling in return, so I nodded at him and then made a slight detour when I saw that he had a pot of coffee on the hot plate. I poured myself a cup and sat down with it and tried calling Stephen Porter's number again. Still no answer. So then I just sat there, sipping coffee and waiting for Eberhardt to come back to the real world.

The office was big, about twenty feet square; otherwise it wasn't anything to get excited about. The walls and the carpet we'd put down ourselves were a funny beige color that clashed with some hideous mustard yellow fiberboard file cabinets Eberhardt had bought on a whim and refused to repaint. The furnishings consisted of our two desks, some chairs, my file cabinets and his, and

an old-fashioned water cooler with a bottle of
Alhambra on it that we used to make the coffee.
And suspended from the middle of the ceiling was
a light fixture that resembled nothing so much as
a bunch of brass testicles soldered onto a grap-
pling hook, which someday I was going to tear
down and hurl out a window. Not the window
behind Eberhardt's desk, which looked out on the
blank brick wall of the building next door; the
one behind my desk, which had a splendid view
of the backside of the Federal Building down on
Golden Gate Avenue, not to mention the green
copper dome of City Hall farther downhill at
Civic Center.

Spade and Archer, I thought, circa 1929. Only
there was no black bird and no Joel Cairo or
Caspar Gutman or Brigid O'Shaughnessy in *our*
lives. There was only Wanda the Footwear Queen,
and some poor bastard of a writer who had gotten
into the Christmas spirit one December night
three and a half decades ago by putting a bullet
through his brain.

Eberhardt muttered something into the telephone receiver, cupped his hand over it, and poked
his jowly, graying head in my direction. "Hey,
paisan," he said, "you got anything on for tomorrow night?"

"I don't know, I don't think so. Why?"

"How about the four of us going out to dinner?
Wanda knows this great little out-of-the-way
place."

I hesitated. The last thing I wanted to do tomorrow night was to have dinner with Wanda. The last thing Kerry would want to do *ever* was to have dinner with Wanda; Kerry disliked the Footwear Queen even more than I did, and was not always careful to hide her feelings. The four of us had had dinner together once, not long after Eberhardt had found true love via a package of Foster Farms drumsticks, and it had not been a memorable evening. "The only thing bigger than that woman's tits," Kerry had said later, "is her mouth. I wonder if she talks the whole time they're in bed together too?" Which was something I still didn't want to think about.

I said lamely, "Uh, well, I don't know, Eb . . ."

"Kerry's free, isn't she?"

"Well, I'm not sure . . ."

"You said last Friday she'd be free all this week. How about it, paisan? We'll make a night of it."

A night of it, I thought. I said No, no, *no!* inside my head, but my mouth said, "Sure, okay, if Kerry's not doing anything." It was a mistake; I knew it was a mistake and that I would pay for it when I told Kerry, but I hadn't wanted to offend him. He got grumpy when he was offended and there was something I needed him to do for me.

He said, "All set, then," and did a little more crooning and cooing to Wanda. I half expected him to play kissy-face with her when the conversation finally ended, a spectacle that would have made me throw up, but it didn't happen. I think he said, "Bye-bye, sugar," which was bad enough.

Then he took his feet down and gave me a sappy, lovestruck grin.

"That was Wanda," he said.

"Yeah," I said.

"What a peach," he said.

What a pair, I thought. Wanda's chest and him. I asked him, "Anything happen today?"

"Nah, it's been quiet. Some woman called for you; wouldn't leave her name, wouldn't say what she wanted. Said it was a private matter and she'd call back."

"Uh-huh."

"Only other call was from that asshole runs the credit company out in Daly City."

"Dennison? What did he want?"

"Another repo job. A new Jaguar, can you believe it?"

"I can believe it. You take the job?"

"Sure I took it."

"That's good."

"I never drove a Jag before," he said. "That's the only reason." He shook his head. "Repossessing cars. For Christ's sake, what kind of job is that for a detective?"

"The bread-and-butter kind."

"Nickels and dimes, you mean. Hell, I don't want Wanda to have to work after we're married. I want to buy her the kind of things she deserves."

Like a tent for her chest and a sack for her face, I thought, and immediately felt guilty. He was in love with her, after all. Maybe she had her good

points. Maybe underneath all that chest there beat
a heart of pure gold.

Maybe the Pope is Jewish, I thought.

Eberhardt said, "So how'd it go with you? The
guy up on Twelfth Avenue?"

"I took him on," I said, and explained what
kind of job it was and what I'd been doing all day.

"A nut case," he said, grimacing. "You better
make sure his check doesn't bounce before you
do any more work."

"It won't bounce."

"It's the pulp angle, right? That's why you took
it on."

"In the beginning. Now it's more than that."

"It always is with you." Another headshake.
"Nut cases and car repos—what a hell of a glam-
orous business we got going for us here."

"You want glamour? Go to work for the Pinker-
tons."

"Yeah, sure, and wind up a security guard in a
bank."

"Then don't bitch."

He sighed, rummaged around among the clutter
on his desk, found one of his pipes, took it apart,
and ran a pipe cleaner through the stem. "Old
Yank-'Em-Out Yankowski," he said musingly.
"What a miserable son of a bitch *he* was, in and
out of court."

"He probably still is."

"You ever have dealings with him?"

"Some."

"Me too. A goddamn bloodsucker. You know, I

thought he was dead. Didn't he have a heart attack or something a couple of years ago?"

"I don't know, did he?"

"Seems I heard he did. Too bad he survived."

"Bad karma, Eb."

"Huh?"

"Never mind. Listen, how far back do the Department's files go? Would they still have the inspector's report on a routine suicide in 1949?"

"Probably. Never get rid of anything—that was the policy before I retired." Eb had taken an early retirement from the cops less than a year ago—he was a year older than me, fifty-five—and he'd been my partner for about six months. He still had plenty of friends in the Department, plenty of old favors to call in; there wasn't much going on at the Hall of Justice that he didn't know about and nothing much in the way of official documentation that he couldn't lay hands on. "I suppose you want a look at the Crane report."

"Right."

"Why bother? It won't tell you any more than the newspaper stories."

"It might. Could be something in it, some hint of Crane's motive, that the reporters didn't get."

He shrugged. "Okay, I'll get it for you—if it hasn't been lost, stolen, or misfiled. Thirty-five years is a long time."

"Don't I know it. How soon?"

"Tomorrow sometime."

I nodded. My watch said it was almost four-thirty; I finished my coffee and lifted myself out of the chair. "I'd better get moving. You mind hanging around until five and locking up?"

"No problem. Where you off to?"

"A talk with Yank-'Em-Out, if he's home by now. And then dinner with Kerry."

"Dinner, yeah," he said. "Don't forget tomorrow night."

"I won't forget," I said. "Kerry won't let me."

And that was the truth in more ways than one.

# ▸ FOUR ▸

This time when I rang the bell at the Yankowski house, there was somebody home besides the fire-breathing jabberwock. The thing started up in there again, whiffling and burbling, but the noise came distantly, from the back of the place, and never got any closer. Pretty soon the door opened on a chain and a white female face topped by frizzy gray hair appeared in the opening. It said suspiciously, "Yes? What is it?"

"I'd like to see Mr. Yankowski."

"Is he expecting you?"

"No, but I think he'll see me. Just tell him it concerns Harmon Crane and his son."

"Your name?"

I held up one of my business cards. A chubby white arm slithered out through the door opening, snatched the card, and then disappeared with it. The face said, "Wait, please," after which it, too, disappeared and the door snicked shut.

I stood there. A thin breeze off the ocean carried the smells of eucalyptus and jasmine; it was that kind of early evening. Inside the house, the jabberwock continued to make a lot of distant noise, including a couple of thumps and a faint hollow crash. Probably eating some furniture, I thought. Or maybe eating the housekeeper, if that was who owned the white face and the white arm and the frizzy gray hair; as far as I knew, Yankowski had never been married.

But no, the door opened again finally, still on its chain, and there she was. She said, "He'll see you. You can go on around back."

"Around back?"

"He's in the garden."

There were some stepping stones that led away from the tile porch, through jasmine shrubs and dwarf cypress pruned into eccentric shapes. All the windows of the house had iron bars bolted across them, I noticed: an added precaution to ease the usual city dweller's paranoia. In Yankowski's case, though, there was probably more to it than that. There must have been a couple of thousand people in the Bay Area with just cause to break into his house and murder him in his bed.

At the rear I found a high fence with a gate in it. From the top of the fence, another six feet or so of clear molded plastic curved up and then back to the house wall; the effect was of a kind of bubble that would enclose and also secure the garden within. I tried the gate latch, found it unlocked, and walked in.

The garden contained a twenty-foot square of well-barbered lawn, bordered on three sides by rose bushes and on the fourth by the rear staircase and a path leading from it to the gate. On the lawn were a Weber barbecue and some pieces of redwood outdoor furniture. And on one of the chairs was old Yank-'Em-Out himself, sitting comfortably with his legs crossed, a drink in one hand and a fat green cigar in the other.

"Flip the lock on the gate when you close it," he said. "I unlocked it for you."

Yeah, I thought, paranoia. I shut the gate, flipped the lock, and went to where he was sitting. The rear of the house faced west and the sun was starting to set now over the Pacific; the glare of it coming through that plastic bubble overhead gave the enclosure an odd reddish tinge, as if it were artificially lighted. The glow made Yankowski look gnomish and feral, like a retired troll who had moved out from under his bridge to a house in the city. Which was a fanciful thought, but one that pleased me just the same.

My business card lay all by itself on a redwood table next to him; he tapped it with a crooked forefinger, not quite hard enough to knock the long gray ash off his cigar. "I'm honored," he said. "It isn't every day a famous private eye comes calling on me."

There was no irony or sarcasm in his voice. I didn't let any come into mine, either, when I said, "It isn't every day that I get to pay a call on a distinguished member of the legal profession."

"An honor for both of us, then. But we've met

before, haven't we? I seem to recall that you worked for me once a few years ago."

"Just once. After that I worked for your opponents."

He thought that was funny; he had a fine sense of humor, Yank-'Em-Out did. He also had his own teeth, the bastard, and a fine head of dark brown hair with only a little gray at the temples—Grecian Formula, I thought; has to be—and a strong, lean body and not many more wrinkles than I've got. He had to be at least seventy, but he looked ten years younger than that. He looked prosperous and content and healthy as hell.

But he lived in a house with bars on its windows and a vicious dog prowling its rooms, and sat in a garden with a plastic bubble over it, and told guests to be sure to lock the gate after they entered. Whether he admitted it to himself or not, he lived in fear—and that is a damned poor way for any man to live.

He swallowed some of his drink, put the glass down on top of my card—deliberately, I thought—and pointed his cigar at me. "Annie says you're here about Harmon Crane."

"That's right."

"Michael Kiskadon hired you, I assume."

"Yes."

"I'm not surprised. Well, sit down. I don't mind talking to you, although I don't see what you or Michael hope to accomplish this long after the fact."

I stayed where I was; I liked the idea of looking

down at him. "He wants to know why his father committed suicide," I said.

"Of course he does. So do I."

"I understand your theory is that Crane shot himself because he was no longer able to write."

"Yes. But obviously I have no proof."

"Did he ever communicate to you that he had writer's block?"

"Not in so many words," Yankowski said. "But he hadn't written anything in weeks and it was plain to anyone who knew him that he was despondent about it."

"Did he ever mention suicide?"

"Not to me. Nor to anyone else I know of."

"So you were surprised when you found him dead that night."

"Surprised? Yes and no. I told you, he was despondent and we were all worried about him."

"This despondence . . . it came on all of a sudden, didn't it?"

"No, it was a gradual thing. Did someone tell you otherwise?"

"Kiskadon seems to think his father was all right up until a few weeks before his death."

"Nonsense," Yankowski said. "Who told him that?"

"He didn't say."

"Well, it wasn't that way at all. I told you, Harmon's mental deterioration was gradual. He'd been having trouble working for more than three months."

"Had he been drinking heavily for that long?"

"More or less. Harmon was always fond of liquor, and he always turned to it when there was a crisis in his life. The writer's favorite crutch. Or it was in those days, before drugs became fashionable."

"You seem pretty positive about all this, Counselor." He shrugged, and I said, "Do you also have a clear memory of the night of Crane's suicide?"

The question didn't faze him. "As clear as anyone's memory can be of a thirty-five-year-old incident," he said. "Do I strike you as senile?"

"On the contrary."

He favored me with a lopsided grin. "Aren't you going to sit down?"

"I'd rather stand. Aren't you going to offer me a drink or one of your cigars?"

"Certainly not."

We watched each other like a couple of old pit bulls. I knew what he was thinking and he knew what I was thinking and yet here we were, putting on polite conventions for each other, pretending to be civilized while we sniffed around and nipped at each other's heels. It was a game he'd play for a while, but not indefinitely. If you cornered him, or if you just bothered him a little too much, he would go straight for your throat.

I said, "About the night of the suicide. Crane called and asked you to come to his house, is that right?"

"It is."

"And he was very upset, barely coherent."

"That's right."

"Drunk?"

"Very."

"What did he say, exactly?"

"Words to the effect that he needed to talk."

"He didn't say about what?"

"No."

"Did he sound suicidal?"

"No. If he had I would have called the police."

"Instead you went over there."

"I did."

"And met Mrs. Crane and Adam Porter."

"Yes. They had just returned from dinner."

"Did they seem worried about Crane?"

"Not unduly. Not until I'd told them of his call."

"Then he hadn't given either of them any indication he might be considering suicide?"

"No."

"What happened after you told Porter and Mrs. Crane about the call?"

"She became upset and called Crane's name. When there was no answer we all went upstairs and found the door to his office locked. We shouted his name several times, and when there was still no response we broke in."

"You and Porter."

"Yes."

"Whose idea was it, to break in?"

"Adam's, I think. Does it matter?"

"I suppose not. Was there anything unusual about the office?"

"Unusual? The man was lying dead across his desk."

"I think you know what I mean, Counselor. Anything that struck you *after* you looked at the body and found the suicide note."

He sighed elaborately. He had put on his court-room manner like a sweater; I might have been a jury, or maybe a judge. "We were all quite distraught; Amanda, in fact, was close to hysterics. The only thing I remember noticing was that the room reeked of whiskey, which was hardly unusual."

"Had Crane been dead long?"

"Less than an hour," Yankowski said, "according to the best estimate of the police coroner. He must have shot himself within minutes after he telephoned me."

"Why do you suppose he'd call you to come talk to him and then almost immediately shoot himself?"

He gave me a reproachful look. "You've been a detective almost as many years as I practiced law," he said. "Suicides are unstable personalities, prone to all manner of unpredictable behavior. You know that as well as I do."

"Uh-huh. Were you a close friend of Crane's, Counselor?"

"Not really. Our relationship was mostly professional."

"Then why did he call *you* that night? Why not someone close to him?"

Yankowski shrugged. "Harmon had no close

friends; he was an intensely private man. I think he called me because I represented stability—an authority figure, the voice of reason. I think he wanted to be talked out of killing himself. But his personal demons, coupled with whiskey, drove him to it anyway. He simply couldn't make himself wait."

There wasn't anything to say to that; it sounded reasonable enough. So I said, "I understand you met Crane while he was researching a book."

"That's right. He sat through a narcotics trial at which I was assistant defense counsel—a similar case to one in a novel he was writing at the time—and we struck up an acquaintance."

"How did you happen to become his attorney?"

"A short time after we met, a woman in Menlo Park began harassing him, claiming he had stolen her idea for one of his early Johnny Axe novels—I don't remember which one. Nothing came of it; I persuaded her to drop her notion of a plagiarism suit."

"I'll bet you did. What was her name, do you remember?"

"Tinklehoff. Maude Tinklehoff. No one could forget a name like that."

"Did she make any other trouble for Crane?"

"I hardly think so. She was in her late sixties and suffering from cancer; I believe she died a short time after my dealings with her."

"How long before his suicide was this plagiarism business?"

"At least two years. Perhaps three."

"Did you ever do any other legal work for him?"

"I drew up his will."

"Uh-huh. Who got the bulk of his estate?"

"His wife, of course."

"You mean Amanda Crane."

"Certainly."

"Did he happen to leave *you* anything?"

This question didn't faze him either. "Nothing at all."

"Did he leave anything to either of his ex-wives?"

"No. He wasn't on speaking terms with Michael's mother, Susan, and he had long since fallen out of touch with his first wife."

"Ellen Corneal."

"I believe that was her name, yes."

"Did you know her?"

"No. Nor Susan, if that's your next question."

"Do you know what happened to Ellen Corneal?"

"I have no idea."

"Amanda Crane seems to think her husband was married just once before her," I said, "to Kiskadon's mother. Why do you suppose that is?"

He frowned at me around the nub of his cigar. "How do you know what Amanda Crane thinks?"

"I spoke to her this morning in Berkeley."

For some reason that made him angry. He came bouncing up out of his chair and leaned his face to within a couple of inches of mine and breathed the odors of bourbon and tobacco at me. I stood my ground; I wasn't about to back down from the likes of Yank-'Em-Out Yankowski, bad breath or no bad breath.

"I don't like the idea of you bothering her," he said.

"Why should my seeing Mrs. Crane concern you?"

"She's a sick woman. Mentally disturbed."

"So I gathered. But if you're so worried about her, how come *you* haven't been to see her in years?"

"That is my business."

"The reason wouldn't be that she turned you down when you proposed to her, would it?"

His eyes went all funny, hot and cold at the same time, like flames frozen in ice. He put his free hand against my chest and shoved, hard enough to stagger me a little. "Get out of here," he said in a low, dangerous voice. "And don't come back."

I stayed where I was for a time. I was afraid if I moved it would be in his direction, and taking a poke at a seventy-year-old shyster lawyer in his own back yard would be a prize-winning act of stupidity.

"I told you to get off my property. *Now!*"

"My pleasure, Counselor."

I put my back to him and went out through the gate, leaving it wide open behind me. Inside the house I could hear the dog making growling noises, but they weren't as vicious as the ones I'd just heard from Yankowski. Pit bull—yeah. Sniff around, sniff around, and then right for the throat.

Whatever that thing in the house was, its master was a far nastier son of a bitch.

# ▶ FIVE ◀

Kerry and I were having dinner when the earthquake happened.

It was a little after six-thirty and we were in a cozy Italian place that we both liked—Piombo's, out on Taraval near Nineteenth Avenue. San Francisco's best restaurants aren't downtown or at Fisherman's Wharf or in any of the other districts that cater to tourists; where you find them is in the neighborhoods, residential and otherwise. The chef at Piombo's makes eggplant parmigiana and veal saltimbocca to rival any in North Beach, and at two bucks less a plate.

We had just ordered—the eggplant for Kerry, the veal for me—and we were working on our drinks and I was telling her about my new case. I hadn't told her yet about dinner tomorrow night with Eberhardt and Wanda; I was waiting until her stomach was full, because I figured then she'd be less inclined to throw something at me. As it was, she was in a twitchy mood: one of those days in the advertising business—she worked as a copywriter for the Bates and Carpenter agency—that "make you want to get up on a table and start screaming," as she'd put it.

Her drink was a martini, which was a good indicator of just how wired she was; she seldom drank anything stronger than white wine. She had already knocked most of it back, to good effect: she wasn't nervously toying with her olive anymore and her face looked less tense in the candlelight. Piombo's is an old-fashioned place with big, dim chandeliers and gilt-framed mirrors and one stone-faced wall full of niches stuffed with wine bottles; the candles are not only romantic but necessary if you want to see what you're eating.

Candlelight does nice things for most people's features, and it does especially nice things for Kerry's. Puts little fiery glints in her auburn hair. Makes her chameleon green eyes shine darkly and her mouth look even softer and sexier than it is. Subtracts ten years from her age, not that forty is an unattractive age and not that she needs those years subtracted. Handsome lady, my lady. I wouldn't have traded her for five Hollywood starlets, Princess Diana, and a beauty queen to be named later.

She was sitting with one elbow on the table and her chin propped on that hand, giving me her rapt attention. My business always interested her—too damned much sometimes, as I had cause to rue—and she found the Harmon Crane matter particularly intriguing because of the pulp angle. Like Crane, both of her parents had been pulp writers. Ivan Wade had written horror stories—still did—

and as far as I was concerned, was something of a
horror himself. Cybil Wade, surprisingly enough
for an angelic little woman with a sweet smile,
had produced a substantial number of very good
*Black Mask*-style private eye yarns under the
male pseudonym of Samuel Leatherman.

So there we were, Kerry with her martini and
me with my one allotted beer, discussing Harmon
Crane while we waited for our minestrone. I was
just about to ask her if she thought her folks
might have known Crane—and then the shaking
started.

It wasn't much at the beginning; and my first
thought was that one of the big Muni Metro trains
was rumbling by outside, because Piombo's is on
the L Taraval streetcar line and you can sometimes feel the vibrations of the Metros' passage.
But instead of diminishing after a couple of seconds, the tremors gathered intensity. Kerry said,
"Earthquake?" and I said, "Yeah," and we just sat
there. So did everybody else in the room, all of us
poised, diners at their tables, a few people on
stools at the bar, the barman and the waiters and
waitresses in various freeze-frame poses—waiting.

The tremors went on and on, still sharpening.
Ten seconds, fifteen—each second stretched out
so that it seemed like a full minute. Silverware
clattered on the tables; glasses hopped, spilling
beer out of mine and knocking somebody else's
off onto the floor with a dull crash. The chandeliers were swaying; the gilt mirrors quivered and
leaned drunkenly; the wine bottles in their wall

niches made jumpy rattling noises. The flickering of the candle flames gave the room an eerie, unstable look, as if we were all inside a giant box that was being rocked from side to side.

But this was a very San Francisco crowd: natives and long-time residents who had been through earthquakes before and were conditioned to them. Nobody panicked, nobody went charging out into the streets yelling like Chicken Little. The people sitting under the chandeliers and in the shadows of the mirrors got up and backed off; the rest of us just sat still, waiting, not saying anything. Except for the rattling and rumbling of inanimate objects, it was as still as a tomb in there.

What seemed like a long time passed before the tremors began to subside; I had no idea how long until the media announced it later. I thought the biggest of the mirrors was going to break loose and fall, and it might have if the quake had gone on any longer; as it was, nothing fell off the walls or off the tables except that one glass. When the tremors finally quit altogether, a kind of rippling sigh went through the room—a release of tension that was both audible and palpable. The people who were on their feet sat down again. The barman moved; the waiters and waitresses moved. A woman laughed nervously. Everybody began talking at once, not just among their own little groups but to others in the room. A man said in a loud voice, "Big one—five point five at least," and the mustachioed barman called back in jovial tones,

"*Voto contrario, signore! Sei à cinque!* Six point five!" It was as if we were all old friends at some sort of festive party. An earthquake has that effect on strangers in public places: it creates the same kind of brief camaraderie, in a small way at least, that the survivors of the London Blitz must have felt.

Kerry said, "Wow," and drank the rest of her martini. But she didn't look unnerved; if anything, the quake seemed to have put an end to her twitchiness and given her a subdued aspect. I didn't feel unnerved either. That is another thing about earthquakes: when you've experienced enough of them, even the bigger ones like this no longer frighten you. All you feel while they're happening is a kind of numb helplessness, because in your mind is the thought that maybe this is the Big One, the one that knocks down buildings and kills hundreds if not thousands of people. And when they end, and you and your surroundings are still in one piece, you find yourself thinking, No big deal, just another quake, and all you feel then is relief. There is little or no lingering worry. Worrying about earthquakes is like worrying about some damn-fool politician starting a nuclear war: all it does is make you a little crazy.

The guy at the next table asked me if I thought there'd be any aftershocks and I said I didn't know. The barman already had the TV over the back bar turned on and was flipping channels to catch the first news reports—epicenter of the quake, the damage it had done, how high it had

measured on the Richter scale at the Berkeley
seismology lab. Two guys across the room were
making bets, one saying it had been over six and
the other wagering under six. That sort of thing
seemed a little ghoulish at this point, with the
severity of the quake still in doubt, but it was
understandable enough: a right of survival.

Kerry and I talked a little, not much, while
things got back to normal around us; the thirty-
five-year-old suicide of a pulp writer didn't seem
quite so interesting or important at the moment.
One of the waitresses brought our minestrone.
The shakeup hadn't had any effect on my appetite, except maybe to sharpen it. The same was
true with Kerry, and apparently with everyone
else in Piombo's. We put the minestrone away
with gusto, along with a couple of slices of bread
each, even though I hadn't been going to have any
bread on account of my semi-diet, and our entrees
were being served when the barman called out to
someone in the kitchen, "Hey, Dino! *Sei à due!
Minuto secondo trenta-sette.* I told you, didn't I?"
and then turned up the volume on the TV set.

We all looked up at the screen. A newscaster
was repeating the facts that the quake had measured 6.2 on the Richter scale and had lasted for
thirty-seven seconds. Its epicenter was down
around Morgan Hill, near San Jose, and it had been
felt as far north as Fort Bragg, as far east as Lake
Tahoe. There were scattered reports of property
damage, of earth fissures, but no one had been
reported killed or badly injured and no structures

had collapsed anywhere. There had been three aftershocks, none above three-point and none felt in San Francisco. A minor quake, really, despite its original magnitude. Nothing to fret about. The Big One was still somewhere in the future, the newscaster said, smiling.

Yeah, I thought. Like that other Big One, death itself.

Which was a morbid thought and I put it out of my head and attacked my veal saltimbocca. It was as good as ever. I had a second beer with it, the hell with my semi-diet, and Kerry had some wine with her eggplant. Neither of us wanted coffee or dessert. All we wanted now was to get out of there, to be alone somewhere; the feeling of camaraderie had evaporated and Piombo's was again a place full of strangers.

On the sidewalk outside Kerry said, "My apartment, okay? If I know Cybil she's already called at least three times. She'll be frantic if I don't phone and tell her I'm all right."

"How come? They have earthquakes in L.A. too."

"Bigger than up here. But she subscribes to the theory that one of these days San Francisco is going to disappear into the Pacific."

"The country would be better off if it was L.A. that disappeared into the Pacific," I said. "Think of all the lousy movies and TV shows that would never get made."

"Hollywood can go," she said, "but not Pasadena." Pasadena was where Cybil and Ivan the

Terrible lived. "Come on, we'll make a fire. It's a good night for a fire."

Her apartment is on Diamond Heights, a fashionable newer section of the city whose main attraction is a sweeping view of San Francisco, the Bay, and the East Bay communities. Less than ten seconds after we came in, the telephone rang. "See?" she said. "Cybil—I'll bet you five dollars."

"No bet. When you get done, let me talk to her."

"Why?"

"I want to ask her about Harmon Crane."

She lifted the receiver on the fourth ring, and it was Cybil, all right. Kerry spent the better part of ten minutes reassuring her mother that the earthquake hadn't done her or her possessions any harm. I suppose that was how the conversation went, anyway; I quit paying much attention after the first fifteen seconds. I considered turning on the TV, to see if there were other news bulletins, and decided I didn't really want to hear any more tonight about the quake. Instead I went and got a Pine Mountain log and put it on the grate in the fireplace. I was hunting around for some matches when Kerry finished talking and called me to the phone.

Cybil was in one of her manic, chatty moods; it took me a couple of minutes to introduce the topic of Harmon Crane, to ask her if she'd known him.

"Not really," she said. "I met him once, at a publishing party in New York—the late forties, I think. Why on earth are you asking about Harmon Crane? He's been dead . . . my God, it must be more than thirty years."

"Thirty-five years," I said. "He committed suicide."

"Yes, that's right. He shot himself."

"You wouldn't have any idea why, would you?"

"The usual reasons writers do away with themselves, I suppose," she said wryly. "Why are you so interested?"

I told her about Michael Kiskadon and the reason he'd hired me. Then I asked, "Would Ivan have known Crane any better than you?"

"I doubt it. Do you want me to put him on?"

"Uh, no, that's all right." Ivan and I didn't get along; in fact, we hated each other a little. He thought I was too old and too coarse for Kerry, and in a dangerous and unstable and slightly shady profession. I thought he was a pompous, overbearing jerk. A conversation with him, even on the telephone, was liable to degenerate into a sniping match, if not something worse, and that would only get Kerry upset. "Do you know anyone who might have been friendly with Crane back in 1949? Any other pulp writer, for instance?"

"Well . . . have you talked to Russ Dancer?"

"Dancer? He didn't move to California until 1950, did he?"

"Not permanently. But he lived in San Francisco off and on during 1949—I'm sure he did. He's still living up there somewhere, isn't he?"

"Redwood City. As of last Christmas, anyway."

"Well, he might have known Crane. I can't think of anyone else. Ivan and I didn't know many people in the San Francisco area back then."

"Just out of curiosity—what was your impression of Crane the one time you met him?"

"Oh, I liked him. He was funny in a silly sort of way, very much like his books and pulp stories. He drank a lot, but then we all did in those days."

I thanked her and we said our good-byes. Dancer, huh? I thought as I put the receiver back into its cradle. I had crossed paths with Russell Dancer twice in the past six years, once on a case in Cypress Bay down the coast and once here in San Francisco, at the same pulp magazine convention where I'd met Kerry and her parents. Dancer had managed to get himself arrested for murder at that convention, and I had proved him innocent and earned his slavish and undying gratitude. Or so he'd claimed when the police let him out of jail. That had been two years ago and I hadn't seen him since; had only had a couple of scrawled Christmas cards, one from Santa Cruz and the other from Redwood City, some twenty-five miles down the Peninsula.

The prospect of seeing Dancer again was not a particularly pleasing one, which was the reason I hadn't bothered to look *him* up. Dancer was a wasted talent, a gifted writer who had taken the easy road into hackwork thirty-odd years ago and who still cranked out pulp for the current paperback markets—adult Westerns, as of our last meeting. He was also a self-hating alcoholic with a penchant for trouble and a deep, bitter, and unrequited love for Cybil Wade. A little of him went a long way. Still, if there was a chance he had known Harmon Crane, it would be worth getting in touch with him. Assuming I could find him, in Redwood City or elsewhere: he moved around a lot, mostly to keep ahead of the IRS and his creditors.

I swung away from the telephone table. Kerry was standing by the sliding glass doors to the balcony, her arms folded under her breasts, looking out at the lights of the city and the East Bay. I said her name, but she didn't turn right away. And when she did turn she gazed at me for a few seconds, an odd expression on her face, before she spoke.

"It's cold in here," she said.

"Is it? Well, I'll light the fire—"

"No, don't."

"Why not?"

"Let's go to bed," she said.

"Bed? It's not even nine o'clock. . . ."

"Don't be dense," she said.

"Oh," I said.

"Now. Right away."

"Big hurry, huh?"

She came over and took hold of my arm. Her eyes were bright with the sudden urgency. "Right *now*," she said, and pulled me toward the bedroom.

It wasn't that she was hot for me; it wasn't even sex, really. It was a belated reaction to the quake—

a need to be close to someone, to reaffirm life, after having faced all that potentially destructive force. Earthquakes have that effect on people too, sometimes.

## ◂ SIX ▸

The morning *Chronicle* was full of quake news, not that that was surprising. I seldom read the papers anymore—I have to deal with enough bad news on a daily basis without compounding it—but my curiosity got the better of me in this case; so I skimmed through the various reports while I was having coffee and waiting for Kerry to get dressed.

There was more damage than originally esti-mated, though none of it involving major loss or casualties. Some mobile homes had been knocked off their foundations down in Morgan Hill, and a freeway overpass in San Ramon had suffered some structural ruin. Out along the coast, especially in West Marin, several earth cracks had been opened up, one of them fifty yards long and three feet wide on a cattle graze belonging to an Olema dairy rancher. He claimed one of his cows had been swallowed up by the break, even though it wasn't very deep and there was no physical evidence to support his contention. "For all I know," he was quoted as saying, "that cow's all the way over in China by now."

I got a chuckle out of that, and so did Kerry when I read it to her. The lighter side of a grim subject.

Before we left her apartment, I girded myself and told her about dinner with Eberhardt and Wanda. She didn't say anything for fifteen seconds or so, just looked at me the way she does, and I was certain I was in for a little verbal abuse; but Kerry is nothing if not unpredictable. She just sighed and said, "What time?"

"I don't know yet. I'll call you after I talk to Eb."

"God, the things I do for you."

"Come on, babe, it won't be so bad."

"That's what you said last time."

"Was last time really so bad?"

"Was the Spanish Inquisition really so bad?"

"Well, I admit it did rack up a few people."

She glared at me, cracked me on the arm, said, "You and your puns," and then burst out laughing. Another potential disaster averted.

I followed her Mustang down off Twin Peaks and then detoured up Franklin and over to my flat on Pacific Heights. In a burst of energy last weekend, Kerry had forced me to help her clean the place up; it was spic and span, no dust mice nesting under the furniture, no dust clinging chummily to my shelved collection of some 6,500 pulps, which covered two full walls. It didn't look right and it didn't feel right. The home of an unrepentant slob ought to have some *dust* in it, for God's sake, if not a scatter of dirty dishes. Neatness depresses me.

I went over to the secretary desk in the corner and rummaged around in one of the drawers until I found the box full of old Christmas cards. Dancer's was on the bottom, naturally. I copied down his Redwood City address, guessing at one numeral and a couple of letters in the street name—Dancer had never won any awards for penmanship. In the bedroom I pawed through the bookcase where I keep my modest collection of hardcovers and paperbacks. I used to pile them up in the closet, on the shelves and on the floor, but they fell over on me one day when I opened the door, in a kind of Fibber McGee chain reaction; when I got done cursing I went out and bought the bookcase. It takes me a long time to learn a lesson sometimes, but then it damned well stays learned.

I had only two of Harmon Crane's Johnny Axe novels—the first, *Axe Marks the Spot*, and *Axe of Mercy*. It had been a while since I'd read either one, and it seemed like a good idea to refamiliarize myself with his work when time permitted. I tucked the two books under my arm and went back into the nice, neat living room. And right out of it again. It was lonely in there, now that Kerry had murdered all my old friends, the dust mice.

Eberhardt wasn't in yet when I got to the office; he seldom shows up before nine-thirty and sometimes not until ten. I opened the window behind

his desk to get rid of the stale smell of his pipe,
after which I filled the coffeepot from the bottle
of Alhambra water and put it on the hotplate.
Morning ritual. I completed it by checking the
answering machine and discovering—lo!—that
there weren't any messages.

I sat down and rang up San Mateo County
information and asked the operator if there was a
listing for Russell Dancer. There wasn't. Damn.
Now I would have to drive all the way down to
Redwood City, on what might well be a wild goose
chase. The way Dancer moved around, one hop
and two skips ahead of his creditors and the IRS,
he could be somewhere else in California by now.
Like in an alcoholic ward, or maybe even in jail.
With Dancer, anything was possible.

Well, I had one other lead to follow up first:
Stephen Porter, Amanda Crane's friend. I dialed
the number I'd copied out of the directory yesterday, and this time I got an answer. The right one,
too, for a change. A scratchy male voice, punctuated by coughs and wheezes, informed me that
yes, he was Adam Porter's brother and yes, he
would be willing to talk to me, either before
eleven or possibly after three, though he might be
busy then, because he had classes between those
two times, not to mention lunch, heh, heh (which
was either a feeble chuckle or some sort of nasal
gasp). I said I could come over right away and he
said fine and gave me the address. After which he
hacked again in my ear, loud enough to make me
wince, and hung up.

The telephone rang almost immediately after I cradled the handset. Michael Kiskadon, bubbling over with eagerness and curiosity. How was my investigation going? Had I found out anything yet? Who had I talked to? Who was I going to talk to? I gave him a brief verbal report, assured him I would be in touch as soon as I had something definite to report, and told him I had an appointment to get him off the line. But I had a feeling I'd be hearing from him again before long. He was that kind of client, and clients like that can be a pain in the ass.

Eberhardt breezed in just as I was about to leave. He was all smiles this morning, chipper and cheerful and whistling a spritely tune. "Coffee," he said, sniffing. "Man, can I use some of that."

"Big night, huh?"

"Yeah, well," he said, and smirked at me.

"You not only got laid last night," I said, "you got laid this morning. Not more than an hour ago, in fact. You had to hurry getting dressed so you wouldn't be any later than you usually are."

He gawped at me. "How the hell did you deduce all of that, Sherlock?"

"Your fly's still open," I said.


North Beach used to be a quiet, predominately Indian neighborhood, the place you went when you wanted pasta, Chianti, a game of bocce, conversation about *la dolce vita* and *il patria d'Italia*, the company of mustachioed waiters in gondolier costumes singing arias from operas by Puccini and Verdi. Not anymore. There are still Italians in North Beach, and you can still get the pasta and Chianti and conversation, if not the bocce and the singing waiters; but their turf has been reduced to a mere pocket, and the vitality and Old World atmosphere are little more than memories.

The Chinese are partly responsible, having gobbled up North Beach real estate when Chinatown, to the west, began to burst its boundaries. Another culprit is the so-called beatnik or Bohemian element that took over upper Grant Avenue in the fifties, paving the way for the hippies and the introduction of drugs in the sixties, which in turn paved the way for the jolly current mix of motorcycle toughs, aging hippies, coke and hash dealers, and the pimps and small-time crooks who work the flesh palaces along lower Broadway. Those topless and bottomless "Silicone Alley" nightclubs, made famous by Carol Doda in the late sixties, also share responsibility: they had added a smutty leer to the gaiety of North Beach and turned the heart of it into a ghetto.

Parts of the neighborhood, particularly those up around Coit Tower, where the Cranes had once lived, are still desirable, and in the shrunken Italian pocket you can still get a sense of what it was like in the old days. But most of the flavor is gone. North Beach is tasteless now, and hard and vague and unpleasant—like a week-old mostaccioli made without spices or garlic. And that is another thing that is all but gone: twenty-five years ago you couldn't get within a thousand yards of North

Beach without picking up the fine, rich fragrance of garlic. Nowadays, you're much more likely to smell fried egg roll and the sour stench of somebody's garbage.

Stephen Porter's studio was on Vallejo Street, half a block off upper Grant. It was an old building, the entrance to which was down a narrow alleyway plastered with No Parking signs. A hand-lettered card over the topmost of three bells read: *1A—Stephen Porter, Sculptor.* And below that: *Lessons Available.*

I rang the bell and pretty soon the door lock buzzed. I went into a dark hallway with a set of stairs on the right and a cat sitting on the bottom step giving me the once-over. I said, "Hello, cat," and it said, "Maurrr," politely, and began to lick its shoulder. The hallway ran past the stairs, deeper into the building; at the far end of it, a door opened and a man poked his head out. "Down here," he said.

I went down there. "Mr. Porter?"

"Yes, that's right. You're the gentleman who called? The detective?"

I said I was, and he bobbed his head, coughed, wheezed a little, and let me come in. He was about sixty, a little guy with not much hair and delicate, almost womanish hands. The hands were spotted with dried clay; so was the green smock he wore. There was even a spot of clay on the knot of his spiffy red bow tie.

The room he led me into was a single, cavernous enclosure, brightly lit by fluorescent ceiling tubes, that looked as if it had been formed by knocking out some walls. Along one side was a raised platform piled high with finished sculptures, most of them fanciful animals and birds. At the rear was a curtained-off area, probably Porter's living quarters. The rest of the space was cluttered with clay-smeared tables, a trio of potter's wheels complete with foot treadles, drums full of pre-mixed clay, and some wooden scaffolding to hold newly formed figures while they dried. Spread out and bunched up on the floor were several pieces of canvas, all of them caked with dried spatters of clay. But they hadn't caught all of the droppings, not by any means: what I could see of the bare wood underneath was likewise splotched.

"There aren't any chairs out here, I'm afraid," Porter said. "We can go in back, if you prefer. . . ."

"This is fine. I won't take up much of your time."

"Well," he said, and then turned away abruptly and did some more coughing and hacking, followed by a series of squeaky wheezes. When he had his breath back he said, "Emphysema." And immediately produced a package of Camels from the pocket of his smock and fired up.

I stared at him. "If you've got emphysema," I said, "why not quit smoking?"

"Too late for that," he said with a sort of philosophical resignation. "My lungs are already gone. I'll probably be dead in another year or two anyway."

The words gave me a chill. A few years back,

when I was a two-pack-a-day smoker myself, I had developed a lesion on one lung and spent too many sleepless nights worrying that maybe *I'd* be dead in another year or two. The lesion had turned out to be benign, but I still hadn't had a cigarette since. It was a pact I'd made with whatever forces controlled the universe; and so far they had kept their end of the bargain by allowing me to go on living without medical complications.

I said, "I'm sorry, Mr. Porter," and I meant it.

He shrugged. "Weak lungs and frail bodies run in my family," he said. "My brother Adam died of lung cancer, you know."

"No, I didn't know."

"Yes. He was only fifty-four." Porter sucked in smoke, coughed it out, and said wheezily, "You're interested in Harmon Crane. May I ask why?"

"His son hired me to find out why he shot himself."

"His son? I didn't know Harmon had a son."

"Neither did he." I went on to explain about Michael Kiskadon and his purpose in hiring me.

Porter said, "I see. Well, I don't know that I can help you. Adam knew Harmon much better than I did."

"But you *were* acquainted with him?"

"Oh yes. I was very young and impressed by his success. I used to badger Adam to take me along whenever he got together with the Cranes."

"How did Crane feel about that?"

"He didn't seem to mind. At least, not until the

last few weeks of his life. Then he wouldn't deal with anyone."

"Do you have any idea what caused his depression?"

"Not really. But it was right after he returned from Tomales Bay that we all noticed it."

"Oh? What was he doing at Tomales Bay?"

"He had a little retreat, a cabin; he went there when he was having trouble working in the city."

"Went there alone, you mean?"

"Yes. He liked solitude."

"How long did he usually stay?"

"Oh, a couple of weeks at the most."

"How long was he there that last time?"

"I'm not sure. A week or so, I think. He came back the day after the earthquake."

"Earthquake?"

Porter nodded. "I might have forgotten about that, if it hadn't been for the one last night. The quake in '49 was just about as severe, centered somewhere up north, and it did some minor damage in the Tomales Bay area. Harmon had a terror of earthquakes; he used to say that was the only thing he hated about living in San Francisco. Adam thought the quake might have had something to do with Harmon's depression, but I don't see how that's possible."

"Neither do I. Did Crane say anything about his experience out at Tomales?"

"Not to my knowledge."

"Not even to his wife? Didn't she talk to him after it happened? On the telephone, I mean."

"Well, he did call her briefly to tell her he was all right. But that was all. And he wouldn't talk about it after he returned to the city."

"How did Mrs. Crane feel about his trips to Tomales? Didn't she mind him going away alone like that?"

"No. Amanda was always very . . . passive, I suppose is the word. Whatever Harmon did was fine with her." Porter paused, fought down another cough, and ground out his cigarette in a hollowed-out lump of clay. "You've talked to her? Amanda?"

"For a few minutes yesterday."

"About Harmon's death?"

"No. She wouldn't discuss it."

"It's just as well. She . . . well, she had a severe breakdown, you know, after Adam and that shyster, Yankowski, found the body. She hasn't been right in the head since."

"So I gathered. She asked about you, Mr. Porter."

"Did she?" A kind of softness came into his face; he smiled faintly. "I suppose she wonders why I haven't been to see her the past few months."

"Yes. She said she'd like to see you again."

He sighed, and it turned into another cough. "Well, I suppose I'll have to go then. I stopped the visits because they depress me. Seeing her the way she is . . ." He shook his head. "She was such a vital woman before the shooting. An attractive, vital, happy woman."

He was in love with her too, I thought. At least a little. She must have been quite a woman before the night of December 10, 1949.

I said, "Crane's little retreat at Tomales—do you recall where it was?"

"No, not exactly. I never went there. Adam did, once, at Harmon's invitation; it seems to me he said it was on the east shore. But I can't be sure."

"Did Crane own the place?"

"I believe he leased it."

"Would you have any idea who from?"

"Well, as a matter of fact, I would. An Italian fellow in Tomales. The town, I mean. Harmon used his name in one of his Johnny Axe books, made him the villain. He liked to do things like that—inside jokes, he called them. He had a puckish sense of humor."

"Was the Italian a realtor?"

"No, I don't think so. A private party."

"What was his name?"

Porter did some cudgeling of his memory. But then he shook his head again and said, "I just don't remember."

"The title of the book?"

"Nor that. I read all of them when they were published, but I haven't looked at one in years. I believe I stored them away with Adam's books after he died." Porter paused again, musingly this time. "You know," he said, "there was a box of Harmon's papers among my brother's effects."

"Papers?"

"Literary papers—manuscripts, letters, and so

on. I don't know how Adam came to have them; probably through Amanda. If you think they might be of help, I'll see if I can find the box. It's somewhere down in the basement."

"I'd appreciate that, Mr. Porter. You never know what might prove useful."

"I'll start looking this evening."

"Can you give me the names of any other friends of Crane's I should talk to?"

"I didn't really know any of Harmon's friends," he said. "I don't believe he had many. He spent most of his time writing or researching. Have you talked to Yankowski yet?"

"Yes. He wasn't very helpful."

"I'm not surprised. An unpleasant sort. I don't know why Harmon dealt with him."

"How did your brother feel about Yankowski?"

"The same as I do. He found him overbearing. And the way he pestered poor Amanda after Harmon's death . . ."

"Pestered her how?"

"He wanted to marry her. That was before he found out her mind was permanently damaged, of course."

"He left her alone after he found out?"

"Fortunately, yes."

There didn't seem to be anything more to ask Porter; I waited while he lighted another Camel and got done coughing, thanked him for his time, and started for the door. But he wasn't quite ready to let go of *me* yet. He tagged along, with his face scrunched up thoughtfully again and his breath making funny little rattling noises in his throat.

When we got to the door he said, "There is one thing. I don't know that I ought to bring it up, after all this time, but . . . well, it's something that has bothered me for thirty-five years. Bothered Adam, too, while he was alive."

"What is it, Mr. Porter?"

"The circumstances of Harmon's death. They just didn't seem right."

"How do you mean?"

"Well . . . in the first place, it's very hard to believe that he would have killed himself, even in a state of severe depression. If you'd known Harmon you'd understand. He wasn't a courageous man; he feared death more than most of us."

I frowned at him. "Are you suggesting his death might not have been suicide?"

"I'm suggesting that it is a possibility."

"Who had reason to want him dead?"

"No one that I know of. Or that Adam knew of. That was one of the reasons the police discounted the idea when Adam broached it to them."

"What were the other reasons?"

"The main one was the locked office door. They said there was no way anyone but Harmon could have locked it from the inside. But that door was exactly what bothered us the most."

"Why?"

"Harmon never locked doors, not even the front door to his house; he was a trusting man and he was forever misplacing things like keys. Besides, he was alone in the house that night. Why would a man alone in his home lock his office door, even if he *did* intend to take his own life?"

I didn't say anything.

"You see?" Porter said. "It *could* have been murder, couldn't it?"

## ► SEVEN ◄

When I left North Beach I drove over to the foot of Clay Street and got onto the freeway interchange, heading south for Redwood City. As I drove I mulled over what Porter had told me. Not suicide—murder. Well, it was a possibility, as he'd said; and it would make an intriguing mystery out of Crane's death. But the police had determined that there was no way for a locked-room gimmick to have been worked, and I had a healthy respect for the SFPD Homicide Detail; I knew a lot of the men who'd been on it over the years, from my own days on the cops and from my friendship with Eberhardt, who had worked that detail for a decade and a half as inspector and then lieutenant. No, if they'd felt Crane's death was suicide, then it must have been suicide. And never mind why he decided to lock the office door before he put his .22 Browning against his temple and pulled the trigger. He'd been drunk at the time, depressed and overwrought; a man in that condition is liable to commit any sort of irrational act.

Sure, I thought, sure. But all the same I wanted a look at the police report—if it still existed and if Eberhardt could find it. Even the best of cops makes mistakes now and then, just like the rest of us.

It was a little past noon when I reached the Redwood City exit off 101. For the San Mateo county seat, it's a quiet little town sprawled out on both sides of El Camino Real and the Southern Pacific Railroad tracks. Not nearly as affluent as Atherton and Palo Alto to the south, or Burlingame and Hillsborough to the north. Just a town like a lot of other towns, with a fair amount of low-income housing along tree-shaded streets. A few writers had lived there over the years, some of whom had written for the pulps. I wondered if any of those were still alive and if Russ Dancer knew them. And if he did, if he had anything in common with them after all these years.

I pulled into a Chevron station near Broadway, the main downtown arterial. And pumped my own gas while a fat, indolent teenager looked on, waiting to take my money. Self-service at gas stations is one of my pet peeves. High prices, and you do all the work yourself. What the hell did attendants like this one do to earn their salary? Not much, that was for damned sure. Instead of walking over to where he was, I got back into the car so that *he* had to move his fat in order to get paid. Small satisfaction, but you take your satisfactions where you can these days.

I took another one by sitting there at the pump

for an extra couple of minutes while I dug a
Redwood City street map out of the bag of maps
in the glove compartment and looked up Stambough Street, Dancer's last known address. Only
it *wasn't* Stambough, it was Stambaugh: I had
mistaken an *a* for an *o* in the scrawled return
address on Dancer's Christmas envelope. Stambaugh Street was only a few blocks from where I
was, not far off Broadway—more or less downtown
and more or less close to the SP tracks.

But I didn't go there directly after I left the
nonservice station. I stopped instead on Broadway
and went into the first café I saw to eat lunch. I
was hungry, and Dancer isn't somebody you want
to deal with on an empty stomach.

I took my copies of *Axe Marks the Spot* and *Axe
of Mercy* with me, and skimmed through them
while I ate. Neither one had an Italian villain in
it. I couldn't recall which of the others did have;
it had been too long since I'd read them. I would
have to go see Kiskadon later on and check
through his copies.

With a cheese omelette and a glass of iced tea
under my belt, I drove to Stambaugh Street. The
number I wanted turned out to be a somewhat
seedy rooming house near a block-long thrift
store: a sprawling, two-story Victorian with tur-
rets and gables and brick chimneys, all badly in
need of paint and general repair. Two sickly palm
trees grew in a front yard enclosed by a picket
fence with a fourth of the pickets broken or missing altogether. Nice place. Every time I crossed

paths with Dancer, he seemed to have tumbled a little farther downhill.

I parked in front and went through the gate and up onto the creaky front porch. There was only one entrance and no marked mailboxes to identify who lived there. Just a doorbell button and a small card above it that said ROOM FOR RENT—SEE MANAGER. I tried the door, found it locked, and pushed the bell. Pretty soon somebody buzzed me into a dark hallway that smelled of Lysol and, curiously, popcorn. The somebody—a woman—was leaning out of a doorway beyond a flight of stairs, giving me a squint-eyed look.

I went over to her. The door was marked MANAGER and the woman was about fifty, gray-haired, wearing sequin-rimmed glasses. She had a face like something in an old, discolored wallpaper pattern—the gargoyle kind.

"Something I can do for you?" Brillo-pad voice, like Lauren Bacall with a sore throat.

"I'm looking for a man named Russell Dancer."

Her mouth got all quirky with what I took to be disgust. "Him," she said. "You wouldn't be a cop, would you?"

"I wouldn't. Why?"

"You look like a cop. Dancer's been in jail before."

"In Redwood City, you mean?"

"Sure. He been in jail somewhere else too?"

He had, but I wasn't about to tell her that. "What was he arrested for?"

"Drunk and disorderly, what else? You a bill collector?"

"No."

"Process server?"

"No. He *does* still live here?"

"Yeah, he lives here. But he won't much longer if he don't start payin his rent on time. He's just like my ex—a deadbeat and a bum. This was *my* house, I'd throw him out on the fuckin street."

"Uh-huh."

"Right out on the fuckin street," she said.

"What's his room number?"

"Six. Upstairs."

"He in now?"

She shrugged. "Who knows? If he ain't you can probly find him at Mama Luz's, over on Main. That's where he does his drinkin when he don't do it here."

"Thanks."

"Don't mention it. You a friend of his?"

"Religious advisor."

"What?"

"His religious advisor. I'm teaching him how to love his neighbor. Maybe you'd like a few lessons too."

"Fuckin wise guy," she said, and shut the door in my face.

I went upstairs, found the door with the numeral 6 on it, and whacked it a couple of times with the heel of my hand. Nobody answered. On impulse I tried the knob: Dancer had forgotten to lock it, or just hadn't bothered. I poked my head

inside. Just a room, not much in the way of furnishings; clothing strewn around, an empty half-
gallon jug of Lucky Stores generic bourbon, a
scatter of secondhand paperbacks that had probably come out of the thrift store nearby. I didn't
see any sign of a typewriter or a manuscript or
anything else that a professional writer ought to
have lying around.

I shut the door and went back downstairs and
out into the warm sunshine. It was a nice day
down here, cloudless, with not much wind; the
Peninsula is usually ten to twenty degrees warmer
than San Francisco and this day was no exception.
I left my car where it was and hoofed it along
Stambaugh to Main Street. Mama Luz's wasn't
hard to find. It was half a block to the west, and
its full name, spelled out on a garish neon sign,
was Mama Luz's Pink Flamingo Tavern. Some
moniker for a sleazy neighborhood bar. I crossed
the street, shook my head at the scrawny pink
flamingo painted on the front wall, and went
through an honest-to-God set of batwing doors.

The interior wasn't any better than the exterior.
The usual bar arrangement, some warping wooden
booths, a snooker table with a drop light over it,
and a mangled jukebox that looked as if it had
been mugged: broken glass top, caved-in side, and
a big hole punched or kicked in its midsection. I
would not have liked to meet the guy who had
done all that damage, even if he'd been justified.

There were four people in the place, including

an enormous female bartender. Two of the customers were blue-collar types nursing beers; the third was Dancer, down at the far end, draped over a newspaper with a cigarette hanging out of his face and a glass of something that was probably bourbon close at hand. He was reading with his nose about ten inches from the newsprint, squinting through the cigarette smoke as if he might have gone myopic; he was the type who would go on denying that he needed glasses right up to the day he went blind. He didn't notice me at first, as engrossed as he was, so I had a chance to take stock of him a little.

He had changed in the two years since I'd last seen him, and none of it for the better. He was about sixty-five now and looked every year of it: sagging jowls, heavy lines and wrinkles and age spots on his face and neck, a lot more ruptured blood vessels in his cheeks, and a rum-blossom nose W. C. Fields would have admired. There wasn't much left of his dust-colored hair; age spots littered his naked scalp as well. He looked dissipated and rheumy and too thin for his big frame, as if the flesh were hanging on his bones like a scarecrow's tattered clothing. The thought came to me that he was going to die pretty soon, and it gave me a sharp twinge of pity and compassion. He'd screwed up his own life—we all do to one extent or another—but he hadn't had many breaks, either, and very little luck. At sixty-five he deserved better than a furnished room near a thrift shop, a stool in Mama Luz's Pink Flamingo

Tavern, and death staring at him from the bottom of a whiskey glass.

"Hello, Russ," I said.

His head came up and he peered at me blankly for a couple of seconds. Then recognition animated his features, split his mouth into a bleary grin, and he said, "Well, if it isn't the dago shamus! What you doing here?"

"Looking for you."

"Yeah? Christ, it's been what, two years?" He stood up, more or less steadily—he'd had a few but he wasn't drunk—and punched my arm. He seemed genuinely glad to see me. "You lost some weight, paisano. Looking good."

"So are you," I lied.

"Bullshit. Listen, sit down, sit down, have a drink. You've got time for a drink, haven't you?"

"Sure. If you've got time to talk."

"Anything for you, pal, after what you did for me. Hey, Mama Luz! Drag your fat ass down here and meet an old friend of mine."

The enormous female behind the bar waddled our way. She was Mexican; she must have weighed at least three hundred pounds, all of it encased in a tentlike muumuu thing emblazoned with pink flamingos; and she wore so much powder and rouge and makeup that she resembled a mime. She might have been one, too: she didn't say a word, even when Dancer told her who I was. All she did was nod and stand there waiting.

"So what'll you have?" Dancer asked me. "You still just a beer man?"

"Always. Miller Lite, I guess."

"Miller Lite, Mama. Cold one, huh? Give me another jolt too." She went away to get the drinks and Dancer said, "So how'd you track me down?"

"Card you sent me last Christmas."

"Social call or you working?"

"Working. You might be able to help."

"Me? How so?"

"The job has to do with a pulp writer named Harmon Crane. Cybil Wade told me you might have known him."

A corner of his mouth twitched. "Little Sweet-eyes," he said. He was talking about Cybil, not Crane. "How is she?"

"Fine."

"And that son of a bitch she's married to? Tell me he dropped dead of a coronary, make my day."

"No such luck."

"He'll outlive us all—like Nixon. You still see-ing her daughter?"

"We're engaged, more or less."

"Good for you. Tell Sweeteyes I said hello, next time you talk to her. Hell, give her my love." He grinned lopsidedly and drained what was left in his glass. Still carrying the torch, I thought. He'd carry it right into the grave with him.

"About Harmon Crane, Russ. *Did* you know him?"

"Old Harmie—sure, I knew him. Met him at a writers' lunch the first time I came out here from New York. I'd read his stuff, he'd read mine. We hit it off."

"That was early 1949?"

"Spring, I think. I hadn't made up my mind to move to California yet, but I figured I would if I could find a place I liked. Tried L.A. first; forget it. So I came up to Frisco."

"You get to know Crane well?"

"We palled around a little, got drunk together a couple of times. Even tried collaborating on a pulp story, but that didn't work out. Too much ego on both sides; believe it or not, I had one back then."

"You had reason. You know what I think of Rex Hannigan."

"Yeah. But Hannigan was a second-rate pulp private eye compared to Johnny Axe. You remember the Axe series?"

"I remember."

Dancer chuckled, as if something funny had just tickled his memory. "Harmie had a hell of a sense of humor. Always good for a laugh. Last book he wrote, Axe gets framed for a murder of a guy that owns a soup company, see, so Harmie called it *Axe-Tailed Soup*. Perfect title, right? But his editor wouldn't let him use it. Too suggestive, she said; some bluenose out in the Bible Belt might read a dirty double meaning into it and raise a stink. The editor, this shriveled-up old maid named Bangs, Christ you should have seen her, this Bangs broad wants him to come up with another title quick because the production department and the art department are all set to move. So Harmie waits a couple of days and then sends the new title by collect wire, no comment or anything, just one line. What do you think it was?"

"I don't know, what?"

" 'How about *A Piece of Axe,*' " Dancer said, and burst out laughing. I laughed with him. "Man, Bangs almost had a shit hemorrhage and Harmie almost got thrown out on his ear. But he figured it was worth it."

"Uh-huh."

"I remember another time," he said, "we were kidding around with titles for mystery novels— you know, trying to see which of us could come up with the worst one using the word *death*. Things like *Death Plays Pattycake* and *Death Gets a Dose of the Clap.* But Harmie won hands down. Best title for a tough-guy mystery I ever heard."

"What was it?"

*"Fuck You, Death."*

That didn't strike me quite so funny, considering the way Harmon Crane had died, and I didn't laugh much. Not that Dancer noticed; he was too busy reaching for the fresh highball Mama Luz had set in front of him. He suggested we take our drinks to one of the booths, and we did that.

He said as he lit another cigarette, "How come you're interested in Harmie? Christ, he's been dead what . . . thirty-five years? He did the Dutch, you know."

"I know. That's why I'm interested." I explained it to him briefly. "Were you still in San Francisco when it happened?"

"No. I went back to New York the end of September, to tie up some loose ends. I'd finally made up my mind to settle out here, but I didn't make it back to California until early the next year."

"Were you surprised when you heard about Crane's suicide?"

"Yeah, I was. I never figured him for the kind who'd do the Dutch. I mean, he was one funny guy. But then I knew he had problems, a whole pack of 'em."

"What kind of problems?"

"His marriage. That was the big one."

"Oh? I thought he was happily married."

"Who told you that?"

"His widow."

"Yeah, that figures. She always did pretend she was Cinderella and Harmie was some poor schmuck of a Prince Charming."

"What was the trouble between them?"

"They weren't fucking," Dancer said. Leave it to him to choose the most delicate phrasing whenever possible.

"Why not?"

"She didn't like it. An iceberg in the sack."

"Oh," I said.

"Yeah," he said.

"Were they doing anything about it?"

"You mean was she seeing a shrink?"

"Yes."

"Uh-uh. She wouldn't go. Wouldn't discuss the deed with *Harmie*, let alone some stranger."

"No sex at all between them?"

"Not in close to a year, when I knew him."

"Did he talk much about it?"

"Some. When he was looped."

"Was he seeing other women?"

"Harmie? Nah, I doubt it. He wasn't the type."

"A year is a long time to do without sex," I said.

"I used to think so too. Not anymore."

I let that pass. "He must have loved her quite a bit, to put up with that kind of relationship."

"I guess he did." Dancer showed me another of his lopsided grins. "Love does crazy things to people. Always has, always will."

"What other problems did Crane have?"

"The booze, for one; he put it away like water. And one of his ex-wives was bugging him."

That was news. I asked, "Which one?"

"Some broad he married when he was in college, I forget her name."

"Ellen Corneal."

"If you say so."

"What was she bugging him about?"

"Money, what else? She was broke, she'd heard how well Harmie was doing, she figured he'd float her a loan for past services." Dancer laughed sardonically. "He sure knew how to pick his women."

"Did Crane give her the money?"

"No. Told her to bugger off. But she kept pestering him anyway."

"Was she living in San Francisco at the time?"

"He didn't say. But if she wasn't, she was close by."

"You know anything about her? What she did for a living, whether she was remarried—like that?"

"Nothing. Harmie didn't say much about her."

"How upset was he that she'd shown up in his life again?"

"Not nearly as upset as he was about not getting laid."

"He seem depressed the last time you saw him?"

"Not that I remember."

"Were you in touch with him after you went back to New York?"

"Nah. Dropped him a note but he didn't answer it. Next thing I knew, he was dead."

"You get to know any of his friends while you were out here?"

"Don't recall any."

"But you did meet some of them."

"One or two, I guess."

"His lawyer, Thomas Yankowski?"

"Name doesn't ring a bell."

"Adam Porter? Stephen Porter?"

"No bells there either."

I had run out of questions to ask. I drank some of my beer while Dancer lit yet another cigarette; then I said it had been good talking to him again and that I appreciated his help, and started to slide out of the booth. But he reached over and caught hold of my arm.

"Hey, come on, don't rush off," he said. "You didn't finish your beer."

"I'm working, Russ, remember?"

"Sure, sure, but you've got time for one more, haven't you? For old times' sake? Hell, it's been two years. Who knows how long it'll be till we hoist another one together."

He was a little drunk now, and inclined toward the maudlin; but there was also a kind of pathetic quality in his voice and manner—a tacit reaching out for a little companionship, a little kindness, that I couldn't bring myself to ignore. He was a lot of things, Dancer was, and one of them was lonely. And maybe another was afraid.

I said, "All right—one more. And I'll buy."

I spent another twenty minutes with him, talking about this and that—a rehash of the pulp convention two years ago, mostly, and how grateful he was to me for clearing him of the murder charge. Just before I left him I asked how he was doing these days, how things were in the writing business.

"Hack business, you mean," he said. The sardonic grin again. "It's lousy. Worst I've ever seen it. Too many hacks and not enough free-lance work; they're lined up around the block trying to get an assignment."

"I thought you had a deal to do a bunch of adult Westerns."

"I did but it blew up. Wrote one and the editor hated it, said I had my history screwed up and didn't know anything about life in the Old West. Some twenty-two-year-old cunt from Bryn Mawr, never been west of Philadelphia, she says *I* don't know anything about the Old West. Jesus Christ, I was writing horse opera before she was born."

"You pick up any other assignments since?"

". . . Not yet, no."

"Then how are you surviving?"

"Social Security. I hit the magic sixty-five a few months ago. It's not much, but it pays the rent and keeps me in booze and cigarettes."

"You're still writing, though?"

"Sure. Always at the mill. Got a few proposals with my agent, a few irons in the fire. And I'm working up an idea for a big paperback suspense thing that might have a shot. It's just that the market is so goddamned tight right now." Shrugging, he lifted his glass and stared into it. "You know how it is," he said.

I thought about his furnished room over on Stambaugh Street, the empty bottle of generic bourbon and the absence of a typewriter or any other tool of the writer's trade. And I thought about what we both knew was staring back at him from the bottom of his glass.

"Yeah," I said. "I know just how it is."

# ► EIGHT ◄

Eberhardt was out when I got back to the office a little past four. But he had left me a note, as he sometimes did; it was lying on top of a manila envelope on my desk blotter. His typing is almost as bad as his handwriting, what with strikeovers and misspellings and a smeary ribbon on his old Remington, but it's at least decipherable.

3 P.M.

Here's the report on the Crane suicide. Not much there, it was cut and dried.

Woman called for you three times, same one as yesterday. Still wouldn't leave her name or tell me what she wanted, just kept saying she'd call back. Does Kerry know about this?

I'm going out on that repo job for Dennison. In case I don't make it back before you leave the name of the restaurant is Il Roccaforte. 2621 San Bruno Ave. Wanda says 7:30 if that's okay with you and Kerry.

I'll be counting the minutes, Eb, I thought, and sighed, and put the note in my pocket. Il Roccaforte. The Stronghold. Some name for a restaurant. It sounded more like an outfit that rented you storage space, or maybe one of those S&M leather bars over on Folsom. Leave it to Wanda to pick a place called Il Roccaforte—and an Italian place, to boot. Rich Italian food two nights in a row. Kerry was going to love that almost as much as renewing her acquaintance with the Footwear Queen herself.

Eberhardt had remembered to switch on the answering machine. But he might as well not have bothered: one hangup call, followed by the usual screeching mechanical noise that sounds as if somebody is strangling a duck. A wrong number, maybe. Or my mysterious lady caller, whoever *she* was.

I sat down and opened the manila envelope. As Eberhardt had noted, there wasn't much to the report—no essentials that hadn't been in the newspaper stories or that I hadn't found out the past two days. Except, possibly, for one item: Harmon Crane had drawn $2,000 out of his savings account on November 6, the month before his death, and nobody seemed to know why. The money hadn't turned up anywhere among his effects, nor was there any record of what he might have done with it. Yankowski speculated that he might have lost it gambling—Crane had liked to play poker and the horses now and then—and that its loss had only deepened his depression. Nobody could say for sure if Crane *had* done any gambling during that last month of his life.

The police interrogation of Crane's neighbors had turned up nothing of a suspicious nature; no one had been seen entering or leaving the Crane house around the approximate time of death. Not that that had to mean much either way, though, since the house had been in a wooded area and was somewhat secluded from those near it. Likewise the results of a paraffin test—they were still using it back then—administered to determine if Crane *had* fired the shot that killed him: it had proved inconclusive. Which was the reason why police labs around the country had eventually stopped using paraffin tests; they were notoriously unreliable. As for the coroner's report, it confirmed that Crane had died of a single contact gunshot wound to the left temple and that he had been legally intoxicated at the time of death. And the lab technicians had found nothing questionable in Crane's office, no hint that the shooting might have been anything but a suicide.

Both windows had been latched, fine films of dust on their sills hadn't been disturbed, and nobody could have got in or out that way in any case because the office was on the second floor and there was nothing outside either window to hang on to; a ladder was out of the question because down below was a garden, it had rained heavily that afternoon, and there were no indentations or footprints or other marks in the muddy ground.

The office door had definitely been locked from the inside. The key was still in the latch when Yankowski and Adam Porter broke in, a fact corroborated by both men; the door fit tightly into its frame, making it a physical impossibility for anyone to turn the key from outside by means of string or some other device; and even though the bolt-plate had been torn from the jamb by the forced entry, and both it and the bolt had been damaged, neither had been tampered with beforehand. As far as I could see, the only way it could have been murder was through collusion between Yankowski and Porter—a set-piece carefully arranged before the police were called. But the inspector in charge of the investigation, a man named Gates, had ruled that out. From all I had learned at this late date, I agreed with him. Yankowski and Adam Porter had been anything but bosom pals. Besides which, why would *both* of them have wanted Harmon Crane dead badly enough to conspire to kill him? And for another thing, the circumstances of that night were such that Amanda Crane would also have had to be party to such a plot, and that made no sense at all.

Suicide, all right, I thought. Has to be.

I checked through the list of people Gates and his men had interrogated, looking for someone who had known Crane well enough to offer a theory about the nature of his depression. Aside from Yankowski and the Porters, there wasn't anyone. I wrote down the names of a few people, those who, like Dancer, had been in the same profession and/or who might have been occasional drinking companions. But it seemed a dead-end prospect. On the list were the two writers Kiskadon had spoken to and who hadn't been able to enlighten him; and the rest figured to be long gone from San Francisco or dead by now.

I put the report back in the manila envelope, hauled the phone over, and dialed Stephen Porter's number. I wanted to ask him about Crane's first wife, Ellen Corneal; if he knew what might have become of her. I also wanted to ask his opinion as to why Crane had withdrawn that $2,000 from his savings account. But talking to him again would have to wait: there was no answer. Late afternoons seemed to be a bad time to try to reach him.

I called Bates and Carpenter. Kerry was on another line; I sat there for five minutes, listening to myself on hold, before she came on. I told her where we were going tonight, and what time, and she said, "Italian *again*? I might have known it. I *hate* that woman, I really do."

"Just grin and bear it, okay?"

"If you promise me this is the last time."

"You know I can't promise you that."

"Oh, all right. The last time for a good long while, then. At least that."

"Deal. How's your day been?"

"Shitty. So my evening better not be."

"It won't," I said, and hoped I wasn't lying in my teeth.

We settled on what time I would pick her up, at

which point she had another call and had to ring off. "I should be so popular," I said, but she was already gone.

I swiveled around to the typewriter stand and hammered out a brief report for Michael Kiskadon. I intended to go see him later, so I could check through his Johnny Axe novels; but clients like to have written as well as verbal reports. Words more or less neatly typed on agency stationery reassure them that I'm a sober, industrious, and conscientious detective and give them a feeling of security.

When I was done I dialed Kiskadon's number. Lynn Kiskadon answered. I asked for her husband, and she said, "He's sleeping. Who is this?" Her response when I told her came in a much lower voice, almost a whisper, so I could barely hear her: "Oh, good, I'm glad you called. I've been trying to reach you for two days."

"So you're the woman who's called my office several times."

"Yes."

"Why didn't you leave your name?"

"I didn't want you ringing up here and asking for me if Michael answered."

"Why not?"

"Because I don't want him to know I've gotten in touch with you. I think we need to talk "

"What about?"

"Michael and his father. The job he hired you to do. Can we meet somewhere? Right away?"

"Well . . . I was going to ask your husband if I could stop by."

"Here? Why?"

"I need to look at his father's novels."

"What on earth for?"

"To find a name. Look, Mrs. Kiskadon—"

"We could meet in the park," she said, "the one across the street. Just for a few minutes, before you see Michael. Please, it's important."

". . . All right. Where in the park?"

"There's a circle with benches around it, straight across the green from our house and along the first path you come to. You can't miss it. How long will you be?"

"Twenty-five minutes or so."

"I'll be waiting," she said.

The wind off the ocean was pretty stiff today, bending the trees in Golden Gate Heights Park and making humming and rattling noises in their foliage. Nobody was out on the green; the only people I saw anywhere were a couple of kids on the playground equipment on the north side. I parked the car where I had yesterday, across from the Kiskadon house, and crossed the lawn with my head down: the wind slapped at my face and made my eyes water.

I found the path with no trouble, and Mrs. Kiskadon a few seconds later. Huddled inside a white alpaca coat, a bright blue scarf over her short hair, she was sitting on one of the benches at the near end of the circle, opposite a big cedar that grew in its center. She looked cold and solemn and worried.

"Thanks for coming," she said as I sat down beside her. Then she shivered and said, "God, that wind is like ice."

"We could go sit in my car."

"No. Michael was still sleeping when I left, but I don't want to take the chance."

"Why should it matter if he sees you talking to me?"

"He'll figure out why, if he does. Then he'll make trouble for me later on."

"Trouble?"

"He yells," she said, "he says things he doesn't mean. Or maybe he does mean them, I don't know. Then he'll ignore me for days, pretend I'm not even there."

"I don't understand, Mrs. Kiskadon."

"It's his illness," she said. "And his obsession with finding out about his father."

"Suppose you start with the illness."

"Did he tell you what it was? That he almost died from it?"

"He did, yes. Diabetes."

"But I'll bet he didn't tell you what it did to him psychologically. I'm not even sure *he* knows. He used to be optimistic, cheerful . . . normal. Now he has severe mood swings, periods of deep depression. His whole personality has changed."

"That's understandable, given the circumstances."

"That's what his doctor says too. But the doctor

doesn't have to live with Michael and I do. He can be . . . well, almost unbearable at times."

"He doesn't get violent, does he?"

"No, no, not toward me. But his depression gets so bad sometimes I think . . ." She broke off and made a fluttery, frustrated gesture with one gloved hand. "He has a gun," she said.

"Gun?"

"A pistol. He keeps it locked up in his den."

"Has he always had it, this pistol?"

"No. He bought it after he came home from the hospital."

"Why?"

"There were reports of prowlers in the neighborhood, a burglary down on Cragmont. He said the gun was for protection."

"But you don't think so?"

"I don't know what to think."

"Has he ever threatened to use it on himself?"

"No. But I don't like the idea of it in the house. You can't blame me, can you?"

I didn't say anything. It wasn't a question I could answer.

"Then, there's this obsession with his father," Mrs. Kiskadon said. "It's just not healthy."

"Why do you say that?"

"Because it isn't. It's all he talks about lately, all that seems to interest him. He spent close to two thousand dollars collecting all of his father's writings, and now he wants to spend God-knows-how-much more on a private investigation. We're

not rich, you know. We're not even well off anymore."

I had nothing to say to that either.

She said, "You're not even *getting* anywhere, are
you? How could you after all those years?"

"I might be," I said carefully.

"I don't care if you are. What does it matter
why Harmon Crane shot himself? It's Michael I
care about. It's *me*. Don't think my life hasn't
been hell this past year because it has."

"So you want me to quit my investigation."

"Yes. It's foolish and it's only feeding his obsession."

"My quitting wouldn't do any good," I said. "As
determined as he is, he'd only hire someone else.
Someone not as scrupulous as I am, maybe; someone who'd cost him, and you, a lot more money
in the long run."

"I didn't mean to imply that you were dishon-
est. . . ." She broke off again and stared up at the
big cedar, as if she thought insight and sympathy
might be hiding among its branches. "I don't
know what to do," she said in a small voice.

"Have you tried to get him into counseling?"

"A head doctor? He'd never go."

"But have you tried?"

"I mentioned it once. He threw a fit."

"Then I'm sorry, Mrs. Kiskadon, but that's the
only advice I can give you."

"You're going to go right on investigating," she
said with some bitterness.

"I have to; I made a commitment to your husband. If he asks me to quit, then I will; but it's got to be him. Meanwhile there's a chance, given enough time, that I'll come up with an answer that will satisfy him."

"How much time?"

"I can't answer that yet."

"More than a week?"

"Probably not."

She gnawed flecks of lipstick off her lower lip; one fleck stuck to her front tooth like a dark red cavity. "I suppose you're right," she said at length. The bitterness was gone; she sounded resigned now.

I said, "Why don't you talk to his doctor? A physician might be able to convince him that counseling is a good idea."

"Yes, I'll do that."

I got up on my feet. "You want me to go over first?"

"Please. I'll come in later; he'll think I've been out for a walk."

I left her sitting there, huddled and feeling sorry for herself, and went back along the path and across the green to Twelfth Avenue. Lynn Kiskadon struck me as a self-centered and self-pitying woman, at least as concerned with her own difficulties as she was with her husband's; but I still felt sorry for her. There was no question that she'd had a rough time of it since Kiskadon's illness was diagnosed, and she had stood by him throughout. It would have been nice to do something for her, or refuse payment for services rendered. But I wasn't feeling particularly noble these days. Besides which, I like to eat and to pay my bills.

It took Kiskadon almost a minute to answer the doorbell, but he didn't look as if he'd been asleep. He'd been eating something with mustard on it, if the little yellow blob on his chin was any indication. As soon as he saw me his eyes got bright with anticipation. He said, squirming a little, "Come in, come in. Have you found out something?"

"Not exactly, Mr. Kiskadon."

"Then why . . . ?"

"I'll explain inside."

He let me in, still eager, and limped with me into the big family room. I told him what I'd been doing since we last talked, and why I was here now, and watched him hang on every word as if I had just brought news of a possible miracle cure for his medical condition.

"You're making progress," he said. "I knew you would, I knew it. I'll check the Axe books, you wait right here."

"I can do it. . . ."

"No, no, I think I know which one it is," and he thumped out on his cane, moving more quickly than he had on my last visit here. When he came back after a couple of minutes he said, "It's the last book he wrote, *Axe and Pains*. I was pretty sure it was. The murderer's name is Bertolucci, Angelo Bertolucci."

He handed me the book and I opened it to the last chapter to check the spelling of the name.

Kiskadon watched me, rumpling his already tou-
sled clump of black hair.

I asked him, "Does the name mean anything to
you?"

"No, nothing."

"No one you talked to mentioned it?"

"I'm sure I'd remember if they had. Are you
going out to Tomales now?"

"Not tonight. Tomorrow morning."

"And then what?"

"That depends on what I find out in Tomales."

He had other questions for me, pointless questions that I answered with more patience than I
felt. I wanted to get away from there; it was almost
six-thirty, and I was picking Kerry up at seven. But
that wasn't the only reason. After my talk with
Mrs. Kiskadon, the house and Kiskadon's pathetic
eagerness were having a depressing effect on me.

I managed to extricate myself with a promise
to call him tomorrow, as soon as I returned from
Tomales. He insisted on shaking my hand at the
door; his palm was damp and a little clammy, and
I had to resist the impulse to wipe my own on my
coat when I let go.

Outside, there was no sign of Mrs. Kiskadon. I
wondered if she'd slipped into the house while I
was there; I hadn't heard her, if so. Or maybe she
was still over on that bench in the park, looking
for answers to her problems in the branches of the
big cedar tree.

## NINE

Dinner that evening was more of a disaster than the previous night's earthquake. And I don't mean that metaphorically.

To begin with, I should have known from its location what Il Roccaforte would be like. San Bruno Avenue is not exactly one of the city's ritzier neighborhoods, adjoining as it does the Southern Freeway interchange and the Hunters Point ghetto. I know a guy who lives in that area and he says it's not bad—blue-collar residential, mostly. But it's one of the last places you'd go looking for *haute cuisine* and an elegant, atmospheric dining experience.

The owners of Il Roccaforte had never heard of either *haute cuisine* or elegance. But the place was definitely atmospheric—in the same way a condemned waterfront pier is atmospheric. And without a doubt eating there was one hell of an experience.

It was in a building all its own, so old and creaky-looking it might have been a survivor of the 1906 earthquake, sandwiched between a laundromat and a country-and-western bar called the Bull's Buns. Kerry said, "My God!" in a horrified voice as we drove up, and I couldn't tell if she meant Il Roccaforte or the Bull's Buns or both. She didn't have anything else to say. She had been conspicuously silent since I'd picked her up, which was always a storm warning with her: it was plain she'd had a *very* bad day in the advertising business, running ideas up flagpoles and seeing if they saluted, or whatever the current Madison Avenue slang expression was, and that she was in no mood for what awaited us inside Il Roccaforte.

Please, Lord, I thought, let it be an uneventful evening. Not a good one, not even a companionable one—just uneventful.

But He wasn't listening.

We got out of the car and went inside. The motif, if you could call it that, was early Depression: some dusty Chianti bottles on shelves here and there, the corpses of three houseplants of dubious origin, a cracked and discolored painting of a peasant woman stomping grapes, tables with linen cloths on them that had not been white since the Truman Administration, and the smells of grease, garlic, and sour wine. Some people might have called the place funky, but none of that type had discovered it yet. The people like myself who called it a relic and a probable health hazard were the ones who, having taken one good look at it, no doubt stayed away in droves. The only customers at the moment, aside from a

waiter who looked as if he might have been stuffed
and left there for decoration, were Eberhardt and
Wanda, tucked up together at a table in one corner.

"Hi, people," Wanda said when we got over
there. She beamed at us from under a pair of false
eyelashes as big as daddy longlegs and fluffed her
gaudy yellow hair and stuck out her chest the way
she does, as if anybody but a blind person could
miss seeing it. "Say, that's a real cute dress, Kerry.
You didn't get that dress at Macy's, did you?"

"No, I didn't."

"Gee, it looks just like one we had on sale last
week in the bargain basement."

Kerry smiled with her teeth, like a wolf smiling
at a piece of meat, and sat down. There was a
carafe of red wine on the table; she picked it up
immediately and poured herself a full glass, which
she proceeded to sip in a determined way.

I said something to Eberhardt by way of greeting, but he didn't answer. As usual, all his attention was focused on Wanda's chest. Tonight the
chest was encased in a white silk blouse with the
top three buttons undone, so that most of it, very
white and bulging, was visible to the naked eye.
Eberhardt's naked eye was full of gleams and
glints; I felt like leaning over and telling him to
wipe the drool off his chin.

As soon as we were settled, Wanda set the tone
for the evening by telling a pair of jokes. Wanda
liked to tell jokes, most of which were dumb and

a few of which were in bad taste. Sort of like a female Bob Hope.

Wanda: "What's the definition of foreplay in a Jewish marriage?"

Eberhardt: "I dunno, what?"

Wanda: "Thirty minutes of begging."

Eberhardt broke up. I managed a polite chuckle. Kerry just sat there sipping her wine.

Wanda (giggling): "So what's foreplay in an *Italian* marriage?"

Eberhardt: "I dunno, what?"

Wanda: "Guy nudges his wife and says, 'Hey, you ready?'"

Eberhardt broke up again. I managed a polite smile this time, without the chuckle. Kerry just sat there sipping her wine.

"I hear lots of jokes like that down at Macy's," Wanda said. "I could tell jokes like that all night long."

Kerry rolled her eyes and gnashed her teeth a little. Neither Wanda nor Eberhardt noticed. Wanda was still giggling and he was watching her chest and grinning fatuously.

The waiter finally showed up with some menus. He was an older Italian guy dressed up in a shiny, rumpled tuxedo that looked as if it belonged on a corpse. He had a long, sad, creased face, ears that had big tufts of hair growing out of them, and a toupee so false and loose-fitting that it invited my attention the way Wanda's chest invited Eberhardt's. Every time the waiter leaned over the table, the hairpiece moved a little like something alive was clinging evilly to the top of his head. If he had heard Wanda's dumb Jewish and Italian jokes, he gave no indication of it. Nor did he bother to adjust his hair. Either he didn't notice it was so loose or he had a lot more faith in its ability to stay put than I did.

He went away and Wanda told us about her day at Macy's. Then she told us another dumb joke. Then she lit up a Tareyton and blew smoke that made Kerry cough and glare and pour more wine. Eberhardt stared at Wanda's chest, still looking both fatuous and horny. I didn't say much. Kerry didn't say anything at all.

The waiter brought us a loaf of bread. I would have eaten some of it, because I was hungry, but if I'd tried I would have broken every tooth in my mouth. It was so old and so hard you couldn't have cut it with a hatchet, much less a knife. It had gone beyond bread and become a whole new and powerful substance. It ought to have been donated to the Giants to use as a fungo bat.

Wanda told us about one of her ex-husbands, the one who had driven a garbage truck; she had two or three, I'm not sure which. One of the things she told us was a long and involved anecdote about his underwear that had no point and wasn't funny but she concluded it with a shriek of laughter so shrill I thought it might shatter the water glasses.

Nobody else came into the place—fortunately for them.

The waiter again, this time to take our orders. I

decided his hairpiece looked even more like a
spider than Wanda's false eyelashes—a deformed
and wicked spider. I almost said, "I'll have the
spider, please." Instead I said, "I'll have the scallopini, please." Eberhardt and Wanda both ordered
the veal piccata because Wanda said, "They really
know how to do it here, Ebbie, you never tasted
veal like this before, believe me."

I believed her.

Kerry said, "I'm not very hungry. I guess I'll just
have a small salad."

"What's the matter, honey?" Wanda asked her.
"Don't you like Italian food?"

"Yes," Kerry said, "but we ate Italian last night.
And I'm just not very hungry."

"You sick or something? Getting your period?
Sometimes I don't feel like eating much when I'm
getting mine."

Kerry buried her nose in her wineglass and sat
there looking at the Chianti bottle on the shelf
above Wanda's head, as if she wished there would
suddenly be another earthquake.

The waiter brought a tureen of soup. When he
leaned over to set it on the table I thought for sure
his hair was going to fall into the tureen. It didn't,
which was something of a disappointment. I
*wanted* that damned thing to fall off. We all have
our perverse moments, and under the circumstances I felt I was justified in having one of mine.

Wanda told us about the time she went to Ti-
juana and saw a bullfight. She told us about the
highest game she'd ever bowled, "a two-ten, I had

*five* strikes in a row, my God I thought I was going to wet my pants." She told us about the time she got drunk at a party and threw up into the heating register. "The place stank for *weeks* after that," she said. "I mean, you just can't get all that stuff *out* of there."

I tried to eat my soup. Minestrone, the waiter had said, lying through his teeth. Maybe it was just the power of suggestion, but what it tasted like was what Wanda had once upchucked into the heating register.

Still no other damn fools came into the place.

Wanda told us about the time she'd had a varicose vein removed from her leg and how painful it was. Then she told us about the time she'd broken her arm roller-skating and how painful that was. Then she told us about the first time she'd had sex and how painful *that* was. "I didn't start to enjoy it until my fifth or sixth time. How about you, honey?" she asked Kerry. "You like it the first time you got poked?"

Kerry said something that sounded like "Nrrr." After which she said between her teeth, "I don't remember."

"Oh, sure you do. Everybody remembers their first time. How old were you?"

Silence.

"I was fourteen," Wanda said. "The guy lived across the street, he was fifteen, we did it under the laundry sink in his basement—I mean, it had to be down there because his parents were home, you know? Boy, was I scared. Fourteen's pretty young, I guess, but I was a curious kid. How about you, Ebbie? How old were you?"

"Eighteen," Eberhardt said, staring at her chest.

She looked at me, but I got spared having to answer by the reappearance of the waiter and his wicked hair. The thing had slid down over his left ear and seemed to be hanging onto the edge of it. Fall, you furry bastard, I thought. Fall! But it didn't.

What the waiter brought this time was a bowl of spaghetti in marinara sauce. Or what he *said* was spaghetti in marinara sauce. The minestrone, which had been made out of three carrots, half a potato, some stringy celery, and a gallon of peppered water, had had more consistency and more flavor. But Wanda ate the spaghetti with gusto and half a pound of parmesan cheese. So did Eberhardt. I ate one strand and a tiny bit of marinara sauce, or whatever the hell the red stuff was, and decided that was enough of a risk for a man my age. Kerry finished what was left in the wine carafe and ordered a refill.

Wanda talked about her youth in Watsonville, where her father had been a grower of artichokes. "We never had much money," she said, "but we had all the artichokes we could eat. I ate artichokes until they were coming out of my ears. I can't eat them anymore. Just the smell of them makes me puke."

The main course arrived just then—perfect timing, I thought, considering Wanda's last comment—and the bowl of spaghetti in marinara sauce got transferred to a sideboard. I was not sorry to see it go. My scallopini had not been made with veal; it had not been made with any sort of animal that had been either young or alive in years. It was so tough you could have used it to make a baseball glove, also for donation to the Giants, a team that needs all the help it can get.

Wanda thought her veal dish was "scrumptious." Eberhardt thought her chest was scrumptious. Kerry took one look at her salad, pushed it away, and poured another glass of wine from the refilled carafe.

Between bites, Wanda talked about another of her ex-husbands, this one a dock worker who used to knock her around when he got drunk. Eberhardt said gallantly that he'd kill any son of a bitch who ever touched her. She rubbed her chest against his arm and batted her eyelashes at him and said, "Oh, Ebbie, you're such a *man!*" If he'd been on the floor at the time he would have rolled over on his back with his tongue lolling out so she could scratch his belly.

The waiter and his pet spider showed up again to ask if we wanted any dessert. Wanda asked him what they had, and he said, "Apple cobbler and zabaglione. But I wouldn't recommend the zabaglione."

"No? Why not?"

"I just wouldn't recommend it," he said ominously.

"Oh. Well, I'll have the apple cobbler then."

None of the rest of us wanted any apple cobbler

and definitely not any zabaglione. The waiter went away. Wanda talked. Eberhardt lusted. I fidgeted. Kerry drank. The waiter came back and put a dish of something in front of Wanda and went away again. Eberhardt took his eyes off Wanda's chest long enough to look at the dish.

"Say," he said, "isn't cobbler supposed to have crust?"

"It's got crust," Wanda said.

"Where?"

"There. See? Right there."

Eberhardt looked. I looked too. What she was pointing at was a little piece of something floating upside down in a brownish goop, like the corpse of some small creature floating on its back in a bog. Then Wanda, the ghoul, proceeded to eat it.

When she was finished she fired up another Tareyton, covered us all with a haze of smoke, and told us about her sister in Minneapolis who was a hairdresser and who worked with "a bunch of faggots, they even got 'em back *there*." Then she gave us her opinion of homosexuality, which was not very high. "You ask me," she said, "that Anita Bryant had the right idea. There oughta be laws against fruits. I mean, the whole idea of them sticking their things into each other—"

"Wanda," Kerry said.

Wanda looked at her. So did I. It was the first word she'd spoken in twenty minutes.

"Why don't you shut up, Wanda," Kerry said.

Wanda said incredulously, "What?"

"Shut up. You know, put your fat lips together so no sound comes out."

Eberhardt said incredulously, "What?"

"You've got diarrhea of the mouth, Wanda."

I said incredulously, "What?"

Everything stopped for a few seconds, like a freeze frame in a movie. We all sat there staring at Kerry. She was sitting stiff and straight, very calm and self-possessed, but her eyes said she was crocked. I also knew her well enough to understand that she was seething inside. Her kettle, as the saying goes, had finally boiled over.

Wanda made a wounded noise, shuffled around in her chair to break the tableau, and said like a siren going off, "You can't talk to me like that! Ebbie, tell her she can't talk to me like that!"

Eberhardt glowered at Kerry. "What's the idea? What's the matter with you?"

"Nothing's the matter with me. The matter is with your fiancée and her big mouth."

"Listen, I don't like that kind of talk—"

"Oh, why don't *you* shut up too, Ebbie."

I tried kicking her under the table, but she squirmed her legs out of the way. "Come on, folks," I said like a cheerful idiot, "why don't we all just relax? Kerry didn't mean what she said. She's just—"

"Fed up." Kerry said. "That's what I'm just. And the hell I didn't mean it. I meant every *word* of it."

Wanda pointed a trembly finger at her. "You

never liked me. I knew you never liked me right from the first."

"Bingo," Kerry said.

"Well, I never liked you either. You're nothing but a . . . a . . . cold fish. A *scrawny* cold fish."

Kerry's face took on a mottled hue. "Cold fish?" she said. "Scrawny?" she said.

"That's right—scrawny!"

"I'd rather be scrawny than a top-heavy blimp like you."

"Oh, so I'm a blimp, am I? Well, men like big boobs on a woman, not a couple of fried eggs like you got."

Kerry sat absolutely still for maybe three seconds. Then she scraped back her chair and stood up. The rest of us popped up too, like a bunch of jack-in-the-boxes, but Kerry was already moving by then, out away from the table. My first thought was that she was about to stalk off in a huff, but I should have known better; Kerry isn't the type of woman who stalks off in a huff. When I realized what she was really going to do I yelled her name and lunged at her. Too late.

She caught up the bowl of soggy spaghetti from the sideboard and dumped it over Wanda's head.

Wanda let out a screech that rattled the windows. Then she scrunched up her face and segued into wailing hysterics. A strand of spaghetti slid off her nose like a fat red and white worm, dropped onto one enormous breast, and wriggled down its ski-run length, gathering momentum as it went. Some more strands dangled off her ears and around her neck like so much art-deco jewelry. All that spaghetti and all that dripping sauce and all those tears gave her the look of a comic foil in an old Marx Brothers movie. I managed, just barely, to repress an insane urge to giggle.

Eberhardt was pawing at her with a napkin and his hands, trying to clean her off; all he succeeded in doing was pushing some of the spaghetti down inside her blouse, which only made her yowl the louder. He murdered Kerry with his eyes. Then he murdered me with his eyes. Then he smeared some more marinara sauce into Wanda's chest.

Kerry seemed sobered and a little awed by what she'd done. She said to me in subdued tones, "I think we'd better go. I'll be out in the car." She caught up her purse and off she went, leaving me there to deal with the wreckage alone.

I dealt with it by fumbling my wallet out, throwing a couple of twenties on the table, and saying stupidly, "I'm sorry, Eb. I'll pay for dinner . . ."

"Take your money," he said, snarling the words, "and shove it up your fat ass."

The waiter had come over and was trying to help clean up the mess. His hair had shifted to the right side of his head and was hanging there at a wickedly jaunty angle. I swear he winked at me just before I fled.

## ► TEN ◄

Eberhardt didn't show up at the office next morning. I hung around waiting for him, fidgeting a little. I had an apology speech all worked out, all about how much I regretted what had happened at Il Roccaforte and how contrite Kerry was. Which was the truth: once she'd sobered up last night, and had absorbed the full impact of what she'd done, she had been pretty hangdog about the whole thing. She had tried to call Eberhardt and Wanda, first at his house and then at her apartment, but nobody answered at either number. So she was planning to go over to Macy's today on her lunch break and apologize to Wanda personally, and then come here to the office and apologize to Eberhardt personally. She had already apologized to *me* personally. I let her do it, but I wasn't really mad at her. I pretended to be, a little, and I pretended to be shocked by such a public loss of control, but secretly I was kind of pleased about it. I kept having mental images of Wanda standing there bawling, with the marinara sauce dripping onto her chest and the spaghetti crawling over her head, and they weren't unpleasant at all. A product of the same sort of perversity that had made me yearn for the waiter's hair to fall off into the soup, with maybe a pinch of malice added.

Wanda was a twit and she'd *deserved* it, by God.

The only thing I was worried about was Eberhardt's reaction. What he'd said to me before I left might have been just words, flung out in the heat of anger; but on the other hand, he was something of a grudge-holder. The last thing I wanted was an episode like last night's putting a damper on our friendship and a strain on our working relationship. Fatmouth Wanda's feelings weren't worth that. And neither was what I found myself thinking of as the Great Spaghetti Assault.

So I stayed there in the office, waiting for him, instead of getting an early start to follow up on the Angelo Bertolucci lead. Keeping busy wasn't much of a problem at first. I called Stephen Porter's number again, found him in, and had a ten-minute talk with him that didn't enlighten me much. In the first place, he hadn't found the box of Harmon Crane's papers yet, even though he was sure they were around "somewhere." And in the second place, while he knew Crane's first wife had been Ellen Corneal, and that they had been married in Reno—an elopement, he said—in 1932, he didn't know what had happened to her after their divorce; nor had he had any idea she'd been pestering Crane for money not long before his suicide.

"Harmon never mentioned her to me," he said. "It was Adam who told me about her."

"Did your brother know if their divorce was amicable or not?"

"He seemed to think it wasn't. One of those brief, youthful marriages that end unhappily when all the passion is spent. I gathered they didn't get on well at all."

"Do you know if she had a profession?"

He paused to think, or maybe just to catch his breath; his coughing and wheezing sounded severe this morning. "No, I can't recall Adam mentioning it, if she did."

"Would you have any idea what she studied at UC?"

"No. You might be able to find that out through the registrar's office, though."

"Might be worth a try. Did you know Russell Dancer?"

"I don't believe I ever met him. The name isn't familiar. You say he knew Harmon fairly well?"

"They were drinking companions for a while."

"Yes, well, people tell each other things when they've been drinking that they wouldn't discuss sober. Or so I'm told. I wish I was a drinking man; I might have got to know Harmon much better than I did. But I haven't much tolerance for alcohol. Two glasses of wine make me light-headed."

"You're probably lucky," I said, thinking of Kerry last night.

When I hung up I dragged the San Francisco telephone directory out of the desk and just for

the hell of it looked up Ellen Corneal's name. No
listing. I checked my copy of the directory of city
addresses, just in case she had an unlisted number. Nothing. So then I called information for the
various Bay Area counties; but if Ellen Corneal
was still alive and still living in this area, she
didn't have a listed phone under that name. Which
left me with the Department of Motor Vehicles, a
TRW credit check, and the obit file at the *Chronicle.* I put in calls to Harry Fletcher at the DMV,
Tom Winters, who was part owner of a leasing
company and who had pulled TRWs for me before,
and Joe DeFalco at the newspaper office—all of
whom promised to get back to me before the day
was out. I decided to forgo a check with the
registrar's office at UC until I saw what turned up
on the other fronts. Likewise a research trip to the
Bureau of Vital Statistics, on the possibility that
Ellen Corneal might have remarried here in the
city.

Ten-fifteen by this time and still no Eberhardt.

I called his house in Noe Valley. No answer. I
went over to his desk and looked up Wanda's home
number in his Rolodex and called that. No answer.
I called Macy's downtown, and was told that Ms.
Jaworski was out ill today.

Well, hell, I thought.

I waited until ten-thirty. Then I scribbled a note
that said, *I'm sorry about last night, Eb—we'll
talk*, put it on his desk, and left for Tomales. A
long drive in the country was just what I needed
to soothe my twitchy nerves.

*  *  *

Tomales is a village of maybe two hundred people, clustered among some low foothills along the two-lane Shoreline Highway, sixty miles or so north of San Francisco. But there isn't any shoreline in the immediate vicinity: the village is situated above Tomales Bay and a few miles inland from the ocean. Sheep and dairy ranches surround it, and out where the bay merges with the Pacific there is Dillon Beach and a bunch of summer cottages and new retirement homes called Lawson's Landing. The town itself has a post office, a school, a service station, a general store, a café, the William Tell House restaurant, a church, a graveyard, and thirty or forty scattered houses.

It was well past noon when I got there. The sun was shining, which is something of an uncommon event in the Tomales Bay area, but there was a strong, blustery wind off the ocean that kept the day from being warm. There hadn't been much traffic on the road out from Petaluma, and there wasn't much in Tomales either. What little activity there was in the place was pretty much confined to weekends.

The general store seemed the best place to ask my questions about Angelo Bertolucci; I pulled up in front and went inside. It was an old country store, the kind you don't see much anymore. Uneven wood floor, long rows of tightly packed shelves, even a big wheel of cheddar cheese on the counter. There weren't any pickle or cracker barrels and there wasn't any pot-bellied stove, but they were about all that was missing. With its smells of old wood, old groceries, fresh bread, and deli meats, the place gave me a faint pang of nostalgia for my long-vanished youth.

Behind the counter was a dark-haired girl of about twenty; she was the only other person in the store. I spent a quarter on a package of Dentyne, and asked her if she lived in Tomales. She said she did. So I asked her if she knew anyone locally named Bertolucci.

"Oh sure," she said. "Old Mr. Bertolucci."

"Old? He's lived here a long time, then?"

"All his life, I guess."

"Would his first name be Angelo?"

"That's right. Do you know him?"

"No. I'd like to talk to him about a business matter."

"Oh," she said, "you want something stuffed."

"Stuffed?"

"A deer or something."

"I don't . . . you mean he's a taxidermist?"

"Didn't you know? He's got all kinds of animals and birds and things in his house. I was there once to deliver groceries when my dad had the flu." A mock shiver. "Creepy," she said.

"How do you mean?"

"All those poor dead things with their eyes looking at you. And Mr. Bertolucci . . . well, if you've ever met him . . ."

"No, I haven't."

"You'll see when you do."

"Is he creepy too?"

"He's kind of, you know—" and she tapped one temple with the tip of her forefinger. "My mother says he's been like that for years. 'Tetched,' she says."

"How old is he?"

"I don't know, seventy or more."

"In what way is he tetched?"

"He hardly ever leaves his house. Everything he wants he has delivered. He's always shooting off his shotgun too. Some kids got in his yard once and he came out with it and threatened to shoot *them*."

"Maybe he just likes his privacy," I said.

"Sure," she said dubiously, "if you say so."

I asked her where Bertolucci lived, and she said on Hill Street and told me the number and how to get there: it was all of three blocks away, off Dillon Beach Road. I thanked her, went out, got into my car, and drove to Hill Street. Some street. An unpaved, rutted dead-end scarcely a block long, with four houses flanking it at wide intervals, two on each side. The first one I passed had a Confederate flag acting as a curtain over its front window; the second one, opposite—a sagging, once-white 1920s frame—was half-hidden by a wild tangle of lilac shrubs and climbing primroses. The second one belonged to Bertolucci.

An unpainted stake fence enclosed the yard; I bumped along and parked in front of its gate. On the gate was a warped sign that said TAXIDERMY in dull black letters. I put a hand against the sign, shoved the gate open, and went along an overgrown path to the porch. Another sign hanging from a nail on the front door invited, *Ring Bell and Come In*. I followed instructions.

The girl at the general store hadn't been exaggerating: the room I walked into was definitely creepy. For one thing it was dim and full of shadows; all the curtains were drawn and the only illumination came from a floor lamp in one corner. There was just enough light so the dozens of glass eyes arranged throughout caught and reflected it in faint, dark glints that made them seem alive. Half a dozen deer heads, one sporting an impressive set of six-point antlers. An elk's head mounted on a massive wooden shield. A game fish of some sort on another shield. On one table, a fat raccoon sitting up on its hind paws, holding an oyster shell between its forepaws. On another table, an owl with its wings spread and its taloned claws hooked around the remains of a rabbit. Dusty glass display cases bulging with rodents—squirrels, chipmunks, something that might have been a packrat. Two chicken hawks mounted on pedestals, wings half-unfolded and beaks open, glinty eyes staring malevolently at each other, as if they were about to fly into bloody combat. All of that, and a farrago of ancient furniture and just plain junk thrown about in no order whatsoever so that the effect of the place—and the smell that went with it—was of somebody's musty, disused attic.

I was standing there taking it all in when the old man came through a doorway at the rear. He

was slat-thin and so stoop-shouldered he seemed
to be walking at a low, forward tilt. Thick, knob-
knuckled hands, a puff of fuzzy, reddish gray hair
like dyed cotton, a nose that resembled the beaks
of the two chicken hawks. Dressed in a pair of
faded overalls and a tattered gray sweater worn
through at both elbows. He was a perfect fit with
the rest of the place: old, dusty, frail, and riddled
with slow decay.

Or so it seemed until he spoke. When he said,
"Yes?" his voice spoiled the impression. It was
strong, clear, and more irascible than friendly.

"Mr. Bertolucci?"

"That's right. Help you with something?"

"Possibly. I'd like to—"

"Don't do deer anymore," he said. "Nor elk nor
moose nor anything else big. Too much work, too
much trouble."

"I'm not here about—"

"Birds," he said, "that's my specialty. Hawks,
owls—predators. Nobody does 'em better. Never
have, never will."

"I'm not here to have something stuffed and
mounted, Mr. Bertolucci. I'd like to ask you a few
questions."

"Questions?" He moved closer to me in that
crabbed way of his and peered up at my face. His
own was swarthy and heavily creased; the lines
bracketing his mouth were so deep they looked
like incisions that had not yet begun to bleed. His
rheumy old eyes were full of suspicion now, as

glass-glinty as those of the stuffed animals and birds. "What questions?"

"About a man named Harmon Crane, a writer who died back in 1949. I wonder if you knew him."

Silence for a time—a long enough time so that it seemed he might not answer at all. His gaze remained fixed on my face. There was a slight puckering of his mouth around badly fitting dentures; otherwise he was expressionless.

"How come?" he said finally.

"How come what, Mr. Bertolucci?"

"How come you're interested in Harmon Crane?"

"You did know him, then?"

"I knew him. Been dead a hell of a long time."

"Yes sir. I'm trying to find out why he killed himself."

"What for, after all these years?"

I explained about Michael Kiskadon. Bertolucci listened with the same lack of expression; when I was done he swung around without speaking, went over to the table with the owl on it, and began to stroke the thing's feathers as if it were alive and a pet. "Ask your questions," he said.

"Did you know Crane well?"

"Well enough not to like him."

"Why is that?"

"Stuck-up. Big-city writer, always tellin people what to do and how to do it. Thought we was all hicks up here."

"You did get along with him, though?"

"We was civil to each other."

"Did you know he used your name in one of his books?"

"Heard it. Didn't much like it."

"But you didn't do anything about it."

"Like what? Sue him? Lawyers cost money."

"You rented Crane a cabin, is that right?"

"Stupidest thing I ever done," he said.

"Why do you say that?"

"Told you. I didn't like him."

"Where was this cabin?"

"Not far. Five miles, maybe," Bertolucci said. Slowly, as if he were reluctant to let go of either the words or the information. "End of the big peninsula south of Nick's Cove."

"The cabin still there?"

"Long gone."

"Do you still own the property?"

"No. Sold it to an oyster company in '53, but they went out of business. Man named Corda bought it twenty years ago. Dairy rancher. Still owns it."

The smell in there was beginning to get to me— a musty, gamy mixture of dust, fog-damp, old cooking odors, and the carcasses of all the dead things strewn around. Even breathing through my mouth didn't quite block it out. Another fifteen minutes in there and I'd be ready for stuffing myself.

I asked him, "Do you remember the last time Crane was up here, about six weeks before his suicide?"

Bertolucci gave me a sidewise look. "Why?"

"There was an earthquake while he was here. About as strong as the one the other night."

He didn't say anything at all this time. Just stood there looking at me, still stroking the owl.

"You did see him then, didn't you?"

"No," Bertolucci said.

"Why not?"

"Only time I ever saw him was when he come to town to pay me his rent."

"Then you don't know if anything happened while he was staying at the cabin that last time."

"Happened? What's that mean?"

"Just what I said. Something that depressed him, started him brooding and drinking too much when he went back to San Francisco."

Silence.

I said, "Do you have *any* idea why he killed himself, Mr. Bertolucci?"

More silence. He turned away from the owl, gave me one more expressionless look, and shuffled through the doorway at the rear—gone, just like that.

"Mr. Bertolucci?"

No answer.

I called his name again, and this time a door slammed somewhere at the rear. Ten seconds after that, as I was on my way out, there was a booming explosion from the yard outside, the unmistakable hollow thunder of a shotgun. I reversed direction, shoved through the litter of stuffed animals and furniture, and hauled back the blind that covered one of the side-wall windows. Bertolucci was thirty feet from the house, stooped over in a meager vegetable patch, a big .12-gauge tucked under one arm. When he straightened I saw what he had in his other hand: the bloody, mangled remains of a crow.

I walked to the front door and out to my car. Through the windshield I could see him still standing back there, shotgun in one hand and the dead crow in the other, peering my way.

The girl at the general store hadn't exaggerated him either, I thought. Angelo Bertolucci was every damn bit as creepy as his surroundings.

## ELEVEN

I drove south on Shoreline Highway, following the eastern rim of Tomales Bay. The bay is some sixteen miles long and maybe a mile at its widest, sheltered from the rough Pacific storms by a spine of foothills called Inverness Ridge that rises above the western shore. The village of Inverness lies over there, along the water and spreading up into the hills; and beyond the ridge are the white-chalk cliffs, barren cattle graze, and wind-battered beaches of the Point Reyes National Seashore. On this side are a sprinkling of dairy ranches and fishermen's cottages, a few oyster beds, a boat-works, a couple of seafood restaurants, the tiny hamlet of Marshall, and not much else except more wooded hills and copses of eucalyptus planted as windbreaks. It's a pretty area, rustic, essentially untarnished by the whims of man— one of the last sections of unspoiled country within easy driving distance of San Francisco. That *wouldn't* be the case if it weren't for the weather; developers would have bought up huge chunks of prime bayfront property years ago and built tracts and retirement communities and ersatz-quaint villages, the way they had farther up the coast at Bodega Bay. But down here the fog lingers for days on end, so that everything seems shrouded in a misty, chilly gray. Even on those rare days like this one when the sun shines, the sea wind is almost always blustery and cold; right now, gusting across the bay, it had built whitecaps like rows of lace ruffles on the water, was tossing anchored fishing boats around as if they were toys, and now and then smacked the car hard enough to make it reel a little on the turns. Out on the National Seashore, I thought, it would be blowing up a small gale.

Bad weather doesn't bother me much, though; I come out to Tomales Bay now and then for a picnic, a visit to the Point Reyes lighthouse, fried oysters at Nick's Cove or one of the other seafood restaurants. The bad weather hadn't bothered Harmon Crane, either. It didn't bother the people who lived out here now, nor would it bother the people living elsewhere who could be induced to move here when one or another gambling developer finally pulled the right strings and the inevitable rape of Tomales Bay began. Onward and upward in the name of progress, good old screw-'em-all free enterprise, and the almighty dollar.

Bleak thoughts, a product of the mood Eberhardt's no-show and my unorthodox meeting with Angelo Bertolucci had put me in. Gloom and doom. It was too bad the sun was out; a dripping gray pall of fog would have been just the right backdrop for a nice, extended mope.

When I passed Nick's Cove I began looking for the peninsula Bertolucci had mentioned. It came up a mile or so farther on: a wide, humpbacked strip of grassland, dotted with scrub oak, that extended out some two hundred yards into the bay. A dirt road snaked up onto it off the highway, vanishing over the crest of the hump; but there was a gate across the road a short ways in and a barbed-wire fence stretching away on both sides. Bushes and a morass of high grass and tall anise blocked my view of the terrain beyond the rise.

Not far away, on the inland side of the highway, was a cluster of ranch buildings surrounded by hilly pastures full of dairy cattle. I drove that way. A lane lined with eucalyptus connected the ranch buildings with the county road, and a sign on one gatepost said CORDA DAIRY RANCH—CLOVER BRAND. I turned into the tunnel formed by the trees, which led me to an old gabled house ringed by bright pink iceplant. A couple of hounds came rushing toward the car, but their tails were in motion and their barks had a welcoming note. One of them jumped up and tried to lick my face when I got out, and a woman's voice called sharply, "Dickens! Down, you! Get down!" She had come out through the front door of the house and was starting toward me. The dog obeyed her, allowing me to go and meet her halfway.

She was in her mid-fifties, pleasant-featured and graying—Mrs. Corda, she said. I showed her the photostat of my investigator's license and told her what I was doing here. Then I asked her if she'd known Harmon Crane.

"No, I'm sorry," she said. "My husband and I are both from Petaluma. We bought this ranch in 1963."

"You do know there was once a cabin out on that peninsula?"

"Yes, but there's almost nothing left of it now. Nor of the oyster company that owned the land before us."

"Would you mind if I had a look around anyway?"

"Whatever for?"

I wasn't sure myself. If I had been a mystic I might have felt I could establish some sort of psychic connection by standing on the same ground Harmon Crane had stood on thirty-five years ago. But I wasn't a mystic. Hell, chalk it up to the fact that I was nosy. It also gave me something to do, now that I was here.

"*Do* you mind, Mrs. Corda?"

"Well, I don't know," she said. "The earthquake the other night opened up some cracks out there. It might be dangerous."

"I'll be careful."

She considered, and I could see her thinking, the way people do nowadays: What if he falls into one of the cracks and breaks a leg or something? What if he sues us? "I don't know," she said again. "You'd better ask my husband."

"Is he here now?"

"No, as a matter of fact he's over on that section. Mending fence that the quake knocked down. He had to take thirty head of cattle off there yesterday."

I thanked her, took the car back out to the highway and up to the dirt road, and turned it along there, stopping nose up to the gate. The wind almost knocked me over when I got out. The gate wasn't locked; I swung it aside and trudged up the incline, bent forward against the force of the wind, the smells of salt water and tideflats sharp in my nostrils. Ahead on my left as I neared the crest I could see the first of the fissures that the earthquake had opened up—a narrow wound maybe three inches wide and several feet long.

From atop the hump I had a clear look at the rest of the peninsula spread out below, sloping downward to the water's edge. A sea of grass and wild mustard, rippling and swaying in odd restless patterns, with one gnarled oak flourishing in the middle of it all like a satisfied hermit. More fissures showed dark brown among the green, half a dozen of them, one at least a foot wide in places, another some fifty feet long. They made me think of the old apocryphal tales of a tremored earth yawning wide and swallowing people, houses, entire towns. They made me wonder if maybe those tales weren't so apocryphal after all.

There were some other things to see from up there: a newish Ford pickup parked on the road below, and two men off to one side of it, working with hammer and nails, wire and timber, and a post-hole digger to repair a toppled section of fence. They hadn't noticed me yet, and didn't until I got down near the pickup and hailed them. Then they stopped working and watched me warily as I approached.

One of the men was about the same age as the woman down at the ranch—lean, balding, with the kind of face that looks as if somebody had been working on it with an etching tool. The other was more of the same, only at half the age and with all of his hair. Father and son, I thought. Which proved to be the case: the first generation was Emil Corda and the second generation was Gene Corda.

They were friendly enough when I finished showing them my license and telling them what it was I wanted. Emil was, anyway; his son was the taciturn sort and didn't seem overly bright. Emil, in fact, seemed downright pleased with me, as if he welcomed a break in the drudgery of fence-mending. Or as if meeting a private detective who wanted to poke around on his land made this something of a red-letter day for him.

"Guess I don't have any objections to you having a look," he said. "But I'll come along, if it's all the same to you."

"Fine."

"All those cracks—you see 'em out there. Got to watch your step."

I nodded. "Some quake, wasn't it?"

"Yeah it was. Gave us a hell of a scare."

"Me too."

"Next time we get a big one, this whole section's liable to break right off and float on over to Waikiki Beach," he said, and then grinned to show me he was kidding. "Fellow down at Olema claims one of his heifers disappeared into a crack, didn't leave a trace. You believe that?"

"Do you?"

"No sir," Corda said. "I've seen cows break a leg in one, I've seen 'em get stuck in one. But swallowed up? Publicity stunt, that's all. Fellow wanted to get his name in the papers." He sounded disappointed as well as disapproving, as if he wished he'd thought of it himself so he would have gotten *his* name in the papers.

I said, "Will you show me where the cabin used to stand, Mr. Corda?"

"Sure thing." He looked at his son. "Gene, you dig another half dozen holes. When I come back we'll anchor those new posts."

The younger Corda mumbled something agreeable, and Emil and I set off toward the far end of the peninsula. The road wasn't much along here, just a couple of grassy ruts, and long before we neared the water it petered out into a cow track. One of the fissures cut a jagged line across it in one place, disappearing into a cluster of poppies.

The outer rim of the peninsula was maybe a hundred feet wide, squared off, with a thin strip of pebbled beach and a couple of acres of mudflats beyond, visible now that the tide was out. The flats weren't being used as oyster beds anymore;

at least there was no sign of the poles that are used to fence off most beds. All that was out there was a dozen or so pilings, canted up out of the mud at oblique angles, like a bunch of rotting teeth. I asked Corda about them.

"Oyster company dock," he said. "Big storm broke it up fifteen, sixteen years ago. We managed to salvage some of the lumber."

"Was there also a pier that went with the cabin?"

"Not so far as I know." He gestured to the north, beyond a fan of decaying oyster shells that was half-obliterated by grass. "Cabin was over that way. You can still see part of the foundation."

We went in that direction, up into a little hollow where the remains of a stone foundation rose out of more thick grass and wild mustard. There wasn't anything else in the hollow, not even a scrap of driftwood.

"What happened to the cabin?" I asked.

"Burned down, so I heard."

"Accident?"

He shrugged. "Couldn't tell you."

"Do you know when it happened?"

"Long time ago. Before the oyster outfit bought the land."

I nodded and moved back to stand on the little strip of beach. Two-thirds of the distance across the bay was an island a few hundred yards in circumference, thickly wooded, with a baby islet alongside it. On the larger island, visible from where I stood now, were the remains of a building—somebody's once-substantial house. Those remains had been there a long time and had always fascinated me. Who would live on a little island in the middle of a fogbound bay?

Not for the first time, I wondered if *I* could do it. Well, maybe. For a while, anyhow. Buy an island like that, build a house on it, wrap myself in solitude and peace. Never mind the wind and fog; all you'd need when the fog rolled in was a hot fire, a good book, and a wicked woman. For that matter, throw in some beer and food and you had all you needed on *any* kind of day.

A seagull came swooping down over the tide-flats, screeching the way gulls do. The only other sound was the humming of the wind, punctuated now and then by little wails and moans as it gusted. It had begun to chill me; I could feel goosebumps along my arms and across my shoulders. But I was reluctant to leave just yet. There was something about this place, a sense of isolation that wasn't at all unpleasant. I could understand why Harmon Crane had come here to be by himself. I could understand why he found it a place that stirred his creative juices.

When I turned after a minute or two I saw that Emil Corda had wandered off to the south, following one of the bigger earth fissures through the rippling grass. I walked over to the fan of oyster shells. As I neared them my foot snagged on something hidden in the grass; I squatted and probed around and came up with part of an old wooden sign, its lettering element-erased to the point where I had to squint at it close up to make out the words: EAST SHORE OYSTER COMPANY. Oddly, it made me think of a marker at a forgotten gravesite.

I straightened, and the wind gusted again and made me shiver, and from forty or fifty yards away Emil Corda let out a shout. I swung around, saw him beckoning to me, and hurried over to where he was, watching my step as I went. He was standing alongside the fissure he'd been following at a place where it was close to a foot wide. There was an odd look on his seamed face, a mixture of puzzlement, awe, and excitement.

"Found something," he said, as if he still didn't quite believe it. "First time I been down this far since the quake."

"Found what?"

"Look for yourself. Down in the crack. This beats that Olema fellow's cow story all to hell. Man, I guess it does!"

I moved over alongside him and bent to peer into the crack. The hairs went up on the back of my neck; a little puzzlement and excitement kindled in me too. Along with a feeling of dark things moving, shifting, building tremors of violence under the surface of what until now had been a routine investigation.

Down at the bottom of that crack were bones, a jumble of old gray bones. The remains of a human skeleton, complete with grinning skull.

# ▸ TWELVE ◂

Emil Corda and his son drove back to their ranch to call the county sheriff's office. I sat in my car, off to one side of the dirt road, and brooded a little. Those bones out there didn't have to have anything to do with Harmon Crane; they didn't have to be related to his severe depression during those last few months of 1949 and to his eventual suicide. But they were *old* bones, there was no mistake about that. And they looked about the way bones would look if they had lain buried beneath the earth for more than three decades.

No, they didn't have to have anything to do with Harmon Crane. But they did. I knew that, sitting there, as surely as I knew that this was a bad day in October. I felt it in *my* bones.

Corda came back pretty soon, without his son, and I went over and sat in his pickup and talked some. The way he figured it, only the top layers of that fissure were newly split ground; the bottom layers were an old seam, the product of another quake many years ago, that had been gradually sutured and healed and hidden by nature. However the bones had gotten into the original crack, it must have happened while the fissure was still fresh, not too long after the quake that had caused it.

Yeah, I thought. Thirty-five years ago, the quake of October 1949. And maybe it wasn't only nature that had sutured and hid the part of it containing the bones.

A couple of deputy sheriffs arrived within a half hour, and we took them out and showed them what we'd found. One of them got down on his belly, poked around a little, and said, "Some other stuff down here."

"What stuff?" the second deputy asked.

"Dunno yet. Something that looks like . . . hell, I don't know, a cigarette case, maybe. Few other things too. It's all pretty dirty and corroded."

"Better leave it be until San Rafael gets here."

The one deputy got up and we all trooped back out by the highway, playing question-and-answer on the way. I told the deputies why I was there and let them draw their own conclusions, not that either of them seemed particularly interested. Old bones didn't excite them much. New bones, on the other hand, would probably have had them in a dither.

It was another twenty minutes before "San Rafael"—a reference to the Marin county seat—arrived in the person of a plainclothes investigator named Chet DeKalb and a technician with a portable field kit. We went through the same routine of going out to look at the bones, of Corda and me explaining how we'd found them and what my business there was. DeKalb seemed a little more interested than the two deputies, but not much. He was in his forties, thin and houndish, with a face that looked as if it would crack wide open if he ever decided to smile. He was the unflappable type. A room full of corpses might have thrilled him a little; bones, old or new, didn't even raise an eyebrow.

He and the lab guy began to fish out the bones and bone fragments and other objects from the fissure, with the technician bagging and labeling them. The rest of us stood around and watched and shivered in the icy wind. I moved up for a look at the other items as they came out; as near as I could tell, they included a cigarette case or large woman's compact, some keys, a lump of something that might have been jewelry—a brooch, maybe—and a couple of rusted things that appeared to be buckles. I also took a close look at the skull when DeKalb handed it up to the lab man. It was badly crushed in a couple of places, probably as a result of its internment in the fissure. It would take a forensic expert to determine if any damage had been done to the skull or any of the other bones prior to burial.

When he was satisfied they'd got everything out of the crack, DeKalb led the parade back to where the cars were parked. He took down my address and telephone number, asked a few more questions about Harmon Crane, and said he might want to talk to me again later on. Then he and the technician went away with the bones and other stuff, and the two deputies disappeared, and Corda said he'd better get back home, his wife and son were waiting and besides, it wasn't every day somebody found a bunch of human bones on his property and maybe a reporter from one of the newspapers would want to contact him about it. From the look in his eyes, if a reporter *didn't* contact him pretty soon he'd go ahead and contact a reporter.

Before long I was standing there alone, shivering in the wind and watching sunset colors seep into the sky above Inverness Ridge. For no reason I walked up on top of the hump again and looked out over the peninsula, out over the bay to the wooded island, its ruins dark now with the first shadows of twilight.

Maybe I wouldn't want to live out there after all, I thought. Or maybe it's just that I wouldn't want to die out there, all alone in the cold and the fog and that endless wind.

Six o'clock had come and gone when I got back to San Francisco. I went to the office first, found it still locked up as I'd left it. Eberhardt hadn't come in; the note I'd written him was right where I had put it on his desk blotter. I checked the answering machine: three calls, all from the contacts I had phoned earlier and all negative. No one named Ellen Corneal had died in San Francisco during the past thirty-five years; but neither was anyone named Ellen Corneal registered with the

BONES                    153

DMV, or the owner of any of the dozens of available credit cards.

For a time I stood looking at my phone, thinking that I ought to call Michael Kiskadon. But I didn't do it. What could I tell him? Maybe his father had perpetrated or been involved in some sort of criminal activity and maybe he hadn't been; maybe those bones were why he'd shot himself and maybe they weren't. Not enough facts yet. And Kiskadon had too many problems as it was without compounding them for no good reason.

The office, after Eberhardt's continued absence, and with darkness pressing at the windows, only added to the funk I was in. I shut off the lights, locked the door again, and went away from there.


Kerry said, "Where can he be, for God's sake? I must have tried calling him half a dozen times today and tonight."

She was talking about Eberhardt, of course. We were sitting in the front room of my flat; she had been waiting for me there, working on the glass of wine and her own funk, rereading one of her mother's Samuel Leatherman stories in an old issue of *Midnight Detective*. She did that sometimes—came by on her own initiative, to wait for me. We practically shared the place anyway, just as we shared her apartment on Diamond Heights. She had put a roast in the oven and the smell of it was making my mouth water and my stomach rumble. I drank some more of my beer to quiet the inner man until the roast could do the job right and proper.

"I called Wanda too," Kerry said. "Somebody at Macy's told me she was home sick, but she hasn't answered her phone all day. The two of them must have gone off somewhere together."

"Probably."

"But where? Where would they go?"

"The mountains, up or down the coast—who knows?"

"Just because of what I did to Wanda?"

I shrugged. "Maybe they decided to elope."

She looked at me over the rim of her wineglass. I had said it as a joke, but she wasn't laughing. For that matter, neither was I.

"You really think they'd do that?" she asked.

"No," I lied.

"God, I can't imagine Eberhardt married to that woman."

"Neither can I. I don't even want to try. Let's talk about something else. That roast out there, for instance."

"Ten more minutes. Tell me some more about the bones you found."

"There's nothing more to tell. All I know right now is that they're human. And *I* didn't find them; Emil Corda did."

"Well, he wouldn't have if you hadn't been there," she said. "What are the chances the Marin authorities can identify them?"

"Hard to say. Modern technology isn't infallible."

"Can't they do it through dental charts and things like that?"

"Maybe. It all depends."

"On what?"

"On how long ago the victim was buried. On how much dental work he or she had done. On whether or not the dentist is still alive and can be found. On a whole lot of other factors."

"Victim," Kerry said. "Uh-huh."

"What?"

"You used the word *victim*. You think it was murder, don't you?"

"Not necessarily."

"It *has* to be murder," she said. "People don't bury bodies in convenient earth fissures unless they're trying to cover up a homicide."

"By 'people' I suppose you mean Harmon Crane."

"Who else? He killed some woman up there, that's obvious."

"Is it? Why do you think it was a woman?"

"He had a frigid wife, didn't he? Besides, there's that cigarette case—"

"Men also carried cigarette cases back then, you know."

"—*and* the brooch. Men didn't wear brooches back then."

"If it was a brooch."

"Of course it was. The brooch and the cigarette case and the keys and other items must have been in her purse. He buried the purse with her and it rotted away to nothing, leaving the buckles. Simple."

I sighed. Kerry fancies herself a budding detective; and ever since she'd had some success along those lines—as a buttinsky on a case of mine in Shasta County this past spring, at considerable peril to her life and my sanity—she had been slightly insufferable where her supposed deductive abilities were concerned. It was a bone of contention between us, but I didn't feel like worrying about it anymore right now. The only bone I wanted to worry about tonight was the one in that roast in the oven.

"Go check on dinner, will you?" I said. "I'm starving here."

"You're always starving," she said, but she got up and carried her empty wineglass into the kitchen with her. She was just the slightest bit sloshed again tonight, a state to which she was entitled considering how hard she'd been working and her futile efforts to soothe her conscience about last night's fiasco. Not to mention her ex-husband, Ray Dunston, who had given up his law practice a while back to join a Southern California religious cult and who was pestering her to "re-mate" with him in a new life of communal bliss and daily prayer chants. But if being sloshed again was an omen of things to come, I didn't like it much. I had already had a demonstration of Kerry's impulsive behavior while under the influence, and one demonstration was all I wanted to witness, thank you.

I wandered over to the nearest shelf of my pulps and browsed through a few issues at random. I was in the mood for pulp tonight. *Bad* pulp. Something by Robert Leslie Bellem from *Spicy Detective*, for instance. I found a 1935 issue with two stories by Bellem—one, under a pseudonym, called "The Fall of Frisco Freddie"—and took it back to the couch. But I couldn't concentrate yet. That damned roast . . .

I got up again and lumbered into the kitchen. Kerry had the roast out; but she said, "Five more minutes," and started to push it back into the oven again. I said, "Give me that thing, I don't care if it's done or not," and grabbed a carving knife out of the rack and hacked off an end and stuffed it into my mouth.

Kerry said, "Barbarian."

I said, "Mmmmff."

It was a good roast. It was so good, in fact, that it put an end to my funk, allowed me to enjoy "The Fall of Frisco Freddie" a little while later, and to bring about the Lay of Kerry Wade a little while after that.

The lay kept her from inhaling any more wine, which was my primary intention, of course. The things I do to maintain harmony in my life. . . .

# ► THIRTEEN ◄

On Thursday morning, without stopping at the office, I drove back across the Bay to Berkeley. I was not about to make a habit of hanging around waiting for Eberhardt to get over his mad and come back to work. Or of worrying that he wouldn't do either one. If the Il Roccaforte incident loomed large enough for him to bust up both our friendship and our partnership, then he was a damn fool and there was no use making myself crazy over the fact. I had enough trouble trying to shepherd one damn fool through life—me—without fretting and stewing about another one.

Some mood I was in again this morning. And for no particular reason I could figure out, except that the fog had come in during the night and the day was gray and bleak. Even in normally sunny Berkeley it was gray and bleak, which would make Telegraph Avenue even harder to take than usual.

But the first place I went was to Linden Street, to the house where Amanda Crane lived with her niece. Not to see Mrs. Crane this time; it was the niece I wanted a conversation with—if I could break through her defenses long enough to get one. She must know the full story of what had happened back in 1949 and she might have picked up something from Mrs. Crane, or from some other source, that would be of help.

Moot possibility for now, though: neither she nor Amanda Crane was home. Or if they were, they weren't answering the doorbell for the likes of me.

I drove downtown via Shattuck, found a place to park on Channing Way, walked back to Telegraph, and turned north toward the Bancroft gate to the UC campus. The sidewalks were crowded with the usual admixture of students, shoppers, hustlers, dope peddlers and buyers, musicians, street artists selling everything from cheap jewelry to hand-carved hash pipes, and assorted misfits. A girl wearing a poncho and half a pound of brass bracelets, rings, earrings, and neck adornments leaned against an empty storefront and sang Joan Baez protest songs to her own guitar accompaniment; a red-and-white emblem on the base part of the guitar said *Death to the Warmongers*. A young-old paraplegic rumbled past me in a motorized wheelchair, going somewhere in a hurry, or maybe going nowhere at all. You see a lot of paraplegics on the streets of Berkeley—some born that way, others the wasted and forgotten residue of Vietnam. Three different kids tried to panhandle me in the two blocks to Bancroft, one of them stoned on some sort of controlled substance that gave him the vacuous, drooling expression of an idiot. A bag lady dressed in black knelt in the gutter to pry loose a crushed Coca-Cola can that was wedged in a sewer grating. A man carrying a Bible in one hand and a stack of leaflets in the other told me God was angry, God would not contain His wrath much longer, and handed me a leaflet that bore a pair of headlines in bold black type: THE END IS NEAR—BE PREPARED! THERE IS NO ESCAPING JUDGMENT DAY!

Go tell it on a mountain, brother, I thought. Maybe then someone will listen.

The street depressed me; it always did. The ugliness, the pervasive sense of hopelessness. The waste. And we were all to blame—mankind was to blame. We had all created the Telegraph Avenues of this world just as surely as we had created war and nurtured greed and applauded the actions of fools and knaves these past eighty-odd years. Some century, the twentieth. The age of enlightenment, understanding, wisdom, and compassion.

Cynical philosophy on a cold, bleak October morning. Maybe I ought to stand next to the guy with the leaflets, I thought, and shout it out for all to hear. Then passersby could laugh at me too: just another freak in the Telegraph Avenue sideshow.

The UC campus was something of an antidote for the depression, at least. Clean, attractive, well cared for; crowded with kids who for the most part looked like typical college students. I wandered among them, past the Student Union and

Ludwig's Fountain to Sproul Hall. Sproul was where the registrar's office was, on the first floor. Except for a couple of student clerks, there was nobody in it when I entered. The rush for fall registration had long since ended and things were quiet here at this time of year.

The clerk who waited on me was a young woman with a body like a colt and a face like the colt's mother: pointy ears, hair that hung down over her eyes, a long muzzle, and lots of teeth. I told her my name was William Collins and that I was a writer doing a biography about a former Cal student in the thirties, a well-known mystery writer named Harmon Crane. She had never heard of Harmon Crane—she didn't read mysteries, she said snootily; they had no redeeming literary merit; *she* read Proust, Sartre, Joyce.

Proust to Sartre to Joyce, the old double-play combination, I thought in my lowbrow way. But I didn't say it.

I said I was trying to track down information about Harmon Crane's first wife, Ellen Corneal, who had also been a student at UC in the early thirties, and would it be possible for her to let me see Ellen Corneal's records? She said no, absolutely not, it was against school policy. I argued, reasonably enough, that those records were now half a century old and that no harm could possibly be done by me seeing them at this late date. I appealed to her sense of literary history, even though we were only talking about a lowly mystery writer here. I can be persuasive sometimes, and this was one of them: I could see her weakening.

"I can't let you *see* the records," she said. She was firm about that. "Definitely not."

"How about if I ask you some questions and you tell me the answers?"

"I can't answer any questions about a person's admissions materials," she said.

"Then I won't ask any."

"Or about transcripts."

"No questions about those, either."

"Or written evaluations, personal or class-room."

"Just background data, that's all."

She relented finally, said it would take a while to look through the files, and suggested I go away and come back again in an hour. So I went out and walked around the campus, all the way past the Earth Sciences buildings to the North Gate and back again, and was standing in front of the horse-faced clerk in exactly one hour.

"You're very prompt," she said, and showed me some of her teeth. I half expected her to whinny a little to emphasize her approval of punctuality.

I asked her some questions about Ellen Corneal's family background; she kept the records at a safe distance while she consulted them and provided answers, as if she were afraid I might leap over the counter and yank them out of her hands. But what she told me wasn't very helpful. Ellen Corneal had been born in Bemidji, Minnesota; her mother had died when she was two, her father when she was eleven, and she had come to

California to live with a maiden aunt after the father's death. She had no siblings and no other relatives. The aunt had been sixty-two years old in 1932, when Ellen Corneal entered UC, and would now be one hundred and fourteen years old if she were still alive, which was a highly unlikely prospect. The Corneal woman had dropped out of school in 1933, after marrying Harmon Crane, but had returned two years later to finish out her schooling and earn her degree.

"In what?" I asked.

"I beg your pardon?"

"In what did she earn her degree? What was her major?"

"Oh. A B.A. in cartography."

"Map-making?"

"That is what cartography *is*, sir."

"Uh-huh. An unusual profession."

"I suppose you might say that. At least it was for a woman back then."

"Women have come a long way," I said, and smiled at her.

She didn't smile back. "We still have a long way to go," she said. From the ominous note in her voice, she might have been issuing a warning. I wanted to tell her that I wasn't the enemy—Kerry had once called *me* a feminist, in all sincerity, something I still considered a high compliment—but trying to explain myself to a twenty-year-old woman who read Proust and Sartre and Joyce and thought mysteries were trash was an undertaking that would have required weeks, not to mention

far more patience than I possessed. I thanked her
again instead and left Sproul Hall and then the
campus through the Bancroft gate.

But I didn't go back down Telegraph Avenue to
get to my car; I took the long way around, up
Bancroft and down Bowditch. One trip through
the sideshow was all I could stand today.

There was still nobody home on Linden Street.
So I drove back across the Bay Bridge, put my car
in the garage on O'Farrell, and went up to the
office. The door was unlocked; and when I opened
it and walked in, there was Eberhardt sitting behind his desk, scowling down at some papers
spread out in front of him. He transferred the
scowl to me as I shut the door, but he didn't say
anything. So I did the ice-breaking myself.

"Well, well," I said. "Look who's here."

"I don't want to talk about it," he said.

"Talk about what?"

"You know what. I'm not talking about it."

"All right."

"Business, that's all. Just business."

"Whatever you say, Eb."

"Kerry called, I told her the same thing."

"What did she say to that?"

"What do you think she said? She said okay."

"Good."

"Yeah. Good. You got two calls this morning."

"From?"

"Michael Kiskadon both times. He wants you
to call him."

"He say what he wanted?"

"No. But he sounded pissed." Eberhardt paused and then said, "Kerry do something to him too?"

"I thought you didn't want to talk about that."

"What?"

"What happened at Il Roccaforte."

"I don't. I told you that."

"Okay by me."

I hung up my hat and coat, poured myself a cup of coffee, and sat down at my desk with it. Eberhardt watched me without speaking as I dialed Kiskadon's number.

Kiskadon was angry, all right. He answered on the first ring, as if he'd been hovering around the phone, and as soon as I gave my name he said, "Damn it, why didn't you call me yesterday? Why didn't you tell me what's going on?"

"I'm not sure I know what you mean."

"The hell you don't know what I mean. Those bones you found up at Tomales Bay."

"How did you hear—?"

"The Marin County Sheriff's office, that's how. Sergeant DeKalb. He wanted to verify that you're working for me. *Are* you, or what?"

"Working for you? Of course I am—"

"Then why didn't you call me? How do you think I felt, hearing it from that cop?"

"Look, Mr. Kiskadon," I said with forced patience, "I didn't call you because there wasn't anything definite to report. Those bones may have nothing to do with your father."

"Maybe you believe that but I don't. They're connected with his suicide, they have to be."

I didn't say anything.

"They were a *woman's* bones," Kiskadon said.

"Did Sergeant DeKalb tell you that?"

"Yes. Something he found with the bones confirmed that."

"What something?"

"He wouldn't tell me. Nobody tells me anything." Now he sounded petulant. "I thought I could trust you," he said.

"You can. I told you, I didn't call because—"

"I want to know everything from now on," he said. "Do you understand? Everything you do, everything you find out."

I was silent again.

"Are you still there?"

"I'm still here," I said. "But I won't be much longer if you start handing me ultimatums. I don't do business that way."

Silence from him this time. Then he said, with less heat and more petulance, "I wasn't giving you an ultimatum."

"That's good. And I wasn't withholding anything from you; I don't do business that way either. When I have something concrete to report I'll notify you. Now suppose you let me get on with my work?"

". . . All right. I'm sorry, I didn't mean to blow up at you like that. It's just that . . . those bones, buried up there like that . . . I don't know what to think."

"Don't think anything," I said. "Wait for some more facts. Good-bye for now, Mr. Kiskadon; I'll be in touch."

"Yes," he said, and both the anger and the petulance were gone and that one word was cloaked in gloom.

Manic depressive, I thought as I put the receiver down. His wife was right about him; if she didn't get him some help pretty soon, somebody to fix his head, he was liable to crack up. And then what? What happens to a guy like Kiskadon when he falls over the line?

Eberhardt was still watching me. He said, "What was that all about? That stuff about bones?"

I told him. Then I asked, "Do you know a Marin Sheriff's investigator named DeKalb?"

"What's his first name?"

"Chet."

"Yeah, I know him. Why?"

"I could use an update on those bones and the other stuff from the fissure. I'm not sure he'd give it to me."

"But you think he might give it to me."

"He might. You mind calling him?"

"Shit," he said, but he reached for his phone just the same.

I got out the Yellow Pages and looked up Professional Organizations. No listing for cartographers, not that that was very surprising. So then I looked up the number for the big Rand McNally store downtown, Rand McNally being the largest map company around, and dialed it and asked to speak to somebody who could help me with a question about cartographers. A guy came on after a time, and I asked him if there was a professional organization for map-makers, and he said there was— The American Society of Cartographers—and gave me a local number to call. I also asked him if he knew a cartographer named Ellen Corneal, but he had never heard of her.

When I dialed the number the Rand McNally guy had given me, an old man with a shaky voice answered and said that yes, he was a member of the American Society of Cartographers and had been for forty-four years; he sounded ancient enough to have been a member for *sixty*-four years. I asked him if he knew a cartographer named Ellen Corneal who had graduated from Cal in 1938.

"Corneal, Corneal," he said. "Name's familiar . . . yes, but I can't quite place it. Hold on a minute, young man."

Young man, I thought, and smiled. The smile made Eberhardt, who was off the phone now and watching me again, scowl all the harder.

The old guy came back on the line. "Yes, yes," he said, "I thought I recognized the name. Ellen Corneal Brown."

"Sir?"

"Her married name. Brown. Her husband is Randolph Brown."

"Also a cartographer?"

"Well, of course. The man is quite well known."

"Yes, sir. Do you know if she's still alive?"

"Eh? Alive? Of course she is. At least, she paid her dues this year."

"Can you tell me where she lives?"

"No, no, can't do that. Privileged information."

"But she does reside in the Bay Area?"

"I'm sorry, young man."

"Would you at least give me a number where I can reach her?"

"Why? What do you want with her?"

I told him I was a writer doing a free-lance article on map-making, emphasis on women cartographers. That satisfied him; he gave me the number. No area code, which made it local. And from the first three numbers, it sounded like a Peninsula location—San Bruno, Millbrae, maybe Burlingame.

Eberhardt said when I hung up, "DeKalb's out somewhere and won't be back until after one. I'll call him back."

"Thanks, Eb."

"Goddamn flunky, that's all I am around here. Take messages, call up people, type reports. Might as well be your frigging secretary."

"You'd look lousy in a dress," I said.

"Funny," he said.

"Who wants a secretary with hairy legs?"

"Hilarious," he said. "See how I'm laughing?"

I dialed Ellen Corneal Brown's number. A woman answered, elderly but not anywhere near as shaky as the society representative, and admitted to being Ellen Corneal Brown. I told her how

I'd gotten her number and asked if she was the Ellen Corneal who had graduated from UC in 1938. She said she was. I asked if I might stop by and interview her as part of a project involving her past history—not lying to her but letting her make the assumption that it was her past history in the field of cartography that I was interested in. She wasn't the overly suspicious type, at least not without sufficient cause. She said yes, she supposed she could let me have a few minutes this afternoon, would two o'clock be all right? Two o'clock would be fine, I said, and she gave me an address on Red Ridge Road in the Millbrae hills, and that was all there was to it. It happens that way sometimes. Days when things fall into place without much effort and hardly any snags.

But not very often.

I finished my coffee and got on my feet. "I think I'll go get some lunch," I said to Eberhardt. "You want to join me?"

"No. I'm not hungry."

"Late breakfast?"

"I'm just not hungry. Why don't you go eat with Kerry?"

"She's got a business lunch today."

"Big agency client, huh?"

"Reasonably big."

"Well, I hope she doesn't get drunk and decide to dump a bowl of spaghetti over *his* head."

I didn't respond to that.

"That was a goddamn lousy thing she did the other night, you know that?" he said.

"You change your mind, Eb?"

"About what?"

"Talking out what happened at Il Roccaforte?"

"No. You heard me tell you I don't want to talk about it."

"Then why do you *keep* talking about it?"

"*I'm* not talking about it, *you're* talking about it. What the hell's the matter with you, anyway?"

I sighed. Eb, I said, sometimes I think you and Wanda deserve each other. But I said it to myself, not to him. I put my coat and hat on and opened the door.

Behind me Eberhardt muttered, "Tells her to shut her fat mouth and then dumps a goddamn bowl of spaghetti over her head, Jesus Christ!"

I went out and shut the door quietly behind me.

## FOURTEEN

Red Ridge Road was a short, winding street shaded by old trees a dozen miles south of San Francisco and a half-mile or so downhill from Highway 280. It hadn't been built on a ridge and if any of the earth in the vicinity had ever been red, there was no longer any indication of it. Score another point for our sly old friends, the developers. A lot of the houses up there had broad, distant views of the Bay; others were half-hidden in copses of trees; still others sat at odd angles, on not much land and without much privacy, like squeezed-in afterthoughts. The house where Ellen Corneal Brown lived was one of the last group—a smallish split-level with a redwood-shake roof and an attached garage, primarily distinguished from its neighbors by a phalanx of camellia bushes that were now in bright red and pink blossom.

I parked at the curb in front, ran the camellia gauntlet, and rang the bell. The woman who opened the door was in her seventies, on the hefty side and trying to conceal it inside a loose-fitting dress. White hair worn short and carefully arranged, as if she had just come from the beauty parlor. Sharp, steady eyes and a nose that came up to an oblique point at the tip.

I said, "Mrs. Brown?"

"Yes. You're the gentleman who called?"

"Yes, ma'am."

She kept me standing there another five seconds or so, while she looked me over. I looked her over too, but not in the same way. I was trying to imagine what she'd looked like fifty years ago, when she and Harmon Crane had gotten married, and not having any luck. She was one of those elderly people who look as if they were born old, as if they'd sprung from the womb white-haired and age-wrinkled like leprechauns or gnomes. I couldn't even decide if she'd been attractive, back in the days of her youth. She wasn't attractive now, nor was she unattractive. She was just elderly.

I must have passed muster myself because she said, "Come in, please," and allowed me a small cordial smile. "We'll talk in the parlor."

Age hadn't slowed her up much; she got around briskly and without any aids. The room she showed me into was a living room; "parlor" was an affectation. But it wasn't an ordinary living room. If I hadn't known her profession, and that of her husband, one look would have enabled me to figure it out.

The room was full of maps. Framed and unframed on the walls, one hanging suspended from the ceiling on thin gold chains, three in the form of globes set into antique wooden frames. Old maps and new maps. Topographic maps, geological maps, hydrographic and aviation charts. Strange maps I couldn't even begin to guess the purpose of, one of them marked with the words *azimuthal projection*, which for all I knew charted the geographical distribution of bronchial patients.

Mrs. Brown was watching me expectantly, waiting for a reaction, so I said, "Very impressive collection you have here."

She nodded: that was what she wanted to hear. "My husband's, mostly, acquired before we were married, although I have contributed a few items myself. Some are extremely rare, you know."

"I'm sure they are."

"That gnomonic projection of the Indian Ocean," she said, pointing, "dates back to the 1700s. The hachures are still quite vivid, don't you think?"

Hachures. It sounded like a sneeze. I nodded wisely and kept my mouth shut.

"Sit down, won't you," Mrs. Brown said. "I have coffe or tea, if you'd care for a hot drink."

"Nothing, thanks."

I waited until she lowered her broad beam onto a quilted blue-and-white sofa and then lowered mine onto a matching chair nearby. Mrs. Brown said, "Well then. You're interested in my cartography work, I believe you said."

"Well . . ."

"My major contribution," she said proudly, a

little boastfully, "was in the area of conic projections. I developed a variant using the Lambert conformal conic projection in conjunction with the polyconic projection, so that—"

"Uh, Mrs. Brown, excuse me but I don't understand a word you're saying."

She blinked at me. "Don't understand?"

"No, ma'am. I don't know the first thing about maps."

"But on the telephone . . . you said . . ."

"I said that I was interested in talking to you about your past history. I didn't mean your professional history; I meant your personal history. I'm sorry if you got the wrong impression," I lied. "I didn't mean to deceive you."

She sat looking bewildered for a few seconds. Then her eyes got flinty and her jaw got tight and I got a glimpse of another side of Ellen Corneal Brown, a less genteel and pleasant side that hadn't been softened much by the advent of old age.

"Who are you?" she said.

"A private detective. From San Francisco."

"My God. What do you want with me?"

"The answers to a few questions, that's all."

"What questions?"

"About your first husband, Harmon Crane."

The eyes got even flintier; if she hadn't been curious, she would have told me to get the hell out of her house. But she was curious. She said, "Mr. Crane has been dead for more than thirty years."

"Yes, ma'am, I know. I'm trying to find out why he committed suicide."

"Do you expect me to believe that? After all this time?"

"It's the truth."

"Who is your client?"

"His son, Michael Kiskadon."

"Son? Mr. Crane had no children."

"But he did. His second wife bore him a son after they were divorced and kept it a secret from him. He died without ever knowing he was a father."

She thought that over. "Why would the son wait so many years to have Mr. Crane's suicide investigated? Why would he want to in the first place?"

I explained it all to her. She struggled with it at first, but when I offered to give her Kiskadon's address and telephone number, plus a few other references, she came around to a grudging acceptance. I watched another struggle start up then, between her curiosity and a reluctance to talk about either Harmon Crane or her relationship with him. Maybe she had something to hide and maybe it was just that she preferred not to disinter the past. In any case she was what the lawyers call a hostile witness. If I didn't handle her just right she would keep whatever she knew locked away inside her, under guard, and nobody would ever get it out.

I asked her, "Mrs. Brown, do you have any idea why Crane shot himself?"

"No," she said, tight-lipped.

"None at all? Not even a guess?"

"No."

"Did you have any inkling at the time that he was thinking of taking his own life?"

"Of course not."

"But you did see him not long before his suicide?"

She hesitated. Then, warily, "What makes you think that? We had been divorced for fourteen years in 1949."

"He mentioned to a friend in September or October of that year that you'd been to see him."

"What friend?"

"A writer named Russell Dancer."

"I don't know that name. Perhaps he has a faulty memory."

"Does that mean you *didn't* visit Crane at that time?"

Another hesitation. "I don't remember," she said stiffly.

"Were you living in San Francisco in 1949?"

"No."

"In the Bay Area?"

". . . in Berkeley."

"Working as a cartographer?"

"Yes. I was with *National Geographic* then."

"Married to your present husband?"

"No. Randolph and I were married in 1956."

"You lived alone in Berkeley, then?"

"I did."

"You must have been making a good salary."

"It was . . . adequate. I don't see what—"

"Then you weren't poor at the time," I said. "You didn't need a large sum of money for any reason. Say two thousand dollars."

Her lips thinned out again, until they were like a horizontal line drawn across the lower half of her face. "Did this Dancer person tell you I tried to get money from Mr. Crane?"

"Did you, Mrs. Brown?"

"I won't answer that."

"Did Crane give you two thousand dollars the month before his death?"

No response. She sat there with her hands twisted together in her lap, glaring at me.

"Why did he give you that much money, Mrs. Brown?"

No response.

"Was it a loan?"

No response.

"All right," I said, "we won't talk about the money. Just tell me this: Did you visit Crane at his cabin at Tomales Bay?"

She took that one stoically, but her eyes said she knew what I was talking about. "I don't know what you're talking about," she said.

"Surely you must have known about his little retreat."

"No. How would I know?"

"It was common knowledge he went up there alone to write."

No response.

"*Did* you visit him there, Mrs. Brown?"

She got up on her feet, a little awkwardly because of her bulk and age, and gestured toward the entrance hall. "Get out of my house," she said. "This minute, or I'll call the police."

I stayed where I was. "Why? What are you afraid of?"

I'm not afraid," she said. "You and I have nothing more to say to each other. And my husband is due home from the country club any time; I don't want you here when he arrives."

"No? Why not?"

"You'll upset him. He has a heart condition."

"Maybe I ought to talk to him just the same."

"You wouldn't dare."

She was right: I wouldn't, not if he had a heart condition. But I said, "He might be more cooperative than you've been," and I felt like a heel for badgering an old lady this way, even an unlikable old lady like Ellen Corneal Brown. But playing the heel is part of the job sometimes. Nobody ever said detective work was a gentleman's game, not even the coke-sniffing master of 221-B Baker Street himself.

"Randolph knows nothing about that part of my life," Mrs. Brown said. She was standing next to one of the antique globes; she reached down and gave it an aggravated spin. "And I don't want him to. You leave him alone, you hear me? You leave both of us alone."

"Gladly. All you have to do is tell me the truth. Did you see Harmon Crane during the two months prior to his death?"

"All *right*, yes, I saw him."

"Where?"

"In San Francisco, at a tavern we frequented while we were married—a former speakeasy on the Embarcadero. I . . . well, we bumped into each other there one afternoon." That last sentence was a lie: she didn't look at me as she said it.

"Where else did you see him? At Tomales Bay?"

". . . Yes, once."

"Did he invite you up there?"

"No. I . . . knew he'd be there and I decided to drive up."

"For what reason?"

No response.

Money, I thought. And she just wasn't going to talk about money. I asked her, "Did anything happen on that visit? Anything unusual?"

"Unusual," she said, and her mouth quirked into an unpleasant little sneer. "He had a woman with him."

"His wife, you mean? Amanda?"

"Hardly. *Another* woman."

"Do you know who she was?"

"No." The sneer again. "He didn't introduce us."

"Maybe she was just a casual visitor. . . ."

"They were in bed together when I arrived," Mrs. Brown said. "I wouldn't call that casual, would you?"

"No," I said, "I wouldn't."

"My Lord, the look on Mr. Crane's face when I walked in!" There was a malicious glint in her eyes now; you could tell she was relishing the memory. "I'll never forget it. It was priceless."

"What happened after that?"

"Nothing happened. Mr. Crane took me aside and begged me not to tell anyone about his sordid little affair."

"Is that the word he used, 'affair'?"

"I don't remember what he called it. That was what it *was*."

"Did he offer any explanation?"

"No. The explanation is obvious, isn't it?"

"Maybe. Did you agree not to tell anyone?"

"Reluctantly."

"Did you keep your promise?"

"Of course I kept it."

"Do you remember the day this happened? The date?"

"No, not exactly."

"The month?"

"October, I think. Several weeks before his suicide."

"Before or after the big earthquake?"

". . . Before. A day or two before."

"Did you see or talk to Crane again after that day?"

Hesitation. "I don't remember," she said.

The money again, I thought. "What about the woman? Did you see or talk to *her* again?"

"I *never* spoke to her, not a word. Or saw her again."

"Can you recall what she looked like? I assume you saw her up close that day."

"I saw *all* of her up close, the little tart," Mrs. Brown said. She laughed with malicious humor.

"Red hair, white skin with freckles all over . . . hardly any bosom. I can't imagine what Mr. Crane saw in her."

I could say the same about you, lady, I thought. "How old was she, would you say?"

"Under forty."

"Had you ever seen her before that day?"

"No."

"So you don't know where she lived."

"I have no idea. Nor do I care." She glanced at a map-faced clock on the mantel above the fireplace and then gave the globe another aggravated spin. "I've said enough, I'm not going to answer any more of your questions. Please go away."

Her jaw had a stubborn set now; I wasn't going to get anything else out of her. I said, "All right, I won't bother you any longer," and got up and went to the entrance hall. She followed me to the door, stood holding it as I stepped out onto the porch.

Turning, I said, "Thanks for your time, Mrs. Br—"

"Go to hell," she said and slammed the door in my face.

On my way back to the city I put together what I had so far. It wasn't much, really, and what there was of it was open to more than one interpretation. But plenty of solid inferences could be drawn from it just the same.

Harmon Crane was married to a frigid woman. He met the redhead somewhere, San Francisco,

Tomales Bay, wherever, and they became lovers. Dancer had told me he didn't think Crane was seeing another woman, but Dancer was a drunk and you can't always trust a drunk's memory or perceptions. I was inclined to believe Mrs. Brown's story of walking in on her ex-husband and the redhead; there had been too much nasty pleasure in her voice for it to have been a fabrication.

All right. Mrs. Brown had been pestering Crane for money, a loan for some purpose or other; Crane kept refusing her. On that score I believed Dancer. But then Ellen Corneal had walked in on Crane and the redhead, and all of a sudden she had something on him, a little leverage to pry loose that "loan" she'd been after—the $2,000 he'd withdrawn from his savings account on November 6, 1949, some ten days after his return from Tomales Bay. No wonder Mrs. Brown hadn't wanted to talk about the money angle. Technically she was guilty of blackmail and she knew it.

So far, so good. But now there were the gaps, missing facts, that still had to be filled in. Assuming it was the red-haired woman's bones Emil Corda and I had found yesterday—and that wasn't a safe assumption yet—what had happened at the cabin the day of, or the day after, the earthquake? A fight of some kind between Crane and the redhead? An accidental death? A premeditated murder? And who was she in the first place? And why had Crane apparently covered up her death by burying her body in the fissure?

If you accepted Crane's culpability, the rest of

it seemed cut and dried. He came back from Tomales, he began brooding and drinking heavily—a natural enough reaction, considering he was a sensitive and basically decent man. Then Ellen Corneal blackmailed him for the $2,000: more fuel for his depression and guilt. He finally reached a point on December 10 where it all became intolerable, and he put that .22 of his to his temple and blew himself away.

Simple. The suicide motive explained at last.

Then why didn't I believe it?

Damn it, why did it seem *wrong* somehow?

# ▸ FIFTEEN ◂

When I got back to the office Eberhardt was gone again and there was another typed note on my desk. This one read:

2:45 P.M.

I talked to DeKalb. Looks like those bones you found are a woman's. Lab found woman's wedding ring, one-carat diamond in gold setting, on a finger bone. Victim was a small adult, probably between 25 and 50, but that's all they can determine so far. Skull may have been crushed prior to burial of body but they're not sure enough to make it official. Unofficially DeKalb thinks it might be homicide connected to your case. He expects to be in touch.

Items buried with bones as follows: four keys on metal ring, cigarette case (no monogram), woman's compact, gold brooch with two small safires (sp?), remains of metal rat-tail comb, remains of fountain pen, two metal buckles. DeKalb figures all this stuff contents of victim's purse.

You had one call, same pesty woman who called before. Said you'd know who she was and she'd call again. Women.

I sat down and looked out the window at the eddies of fog that obscured the city. Yeah, I thought, women. I didn't want to talk to Mrs. Kiskadon again and I hoped she wouldn't call back while I was here; it would only be more of the same I'd gotten from her up in the park.

I quit thinking about her and thought instead about the woman's wedding ring, one-carat diamond in a gold setting. Harmon Crane's redhaired lover had been married, it seemed. To someone he knew? To a stranger? No way of telling yet. And either way, that kind of affair happens all too often; it didn't have to mean anything significant, to have a direct bearing on the woman's death.

I pulled the phone over and dialed Stephen Porter's number. But it was late afternoon and he just didn't seem to be available at this time of day: no answer. On impulse I looked up Yank-'Em-Out Yankowski's home number and called that. The housekeeper answered. I identified myself, she said just a minute and went away; when she came back, after a good *three* minutes, she said Mr. Yankowski wasn't home and hung up on me. Uhhuh, I thought. I had figured the old son of a bitch for a grudge-holder and that was what he was.

The phone and I stared at each other for a time. I was debating whether or not I ought to call DeKalb and tell him about the red-haired woman. But there didn't seem to be much point in it just yet. I still had no idea who the woman might have been; for that matter I couldn't even be certain that it was the redhead's bones we'd found yesterday. Some *other* woman's, maybe. Hell, Crane might have had a steady stream of women up there at Tomales Bay, Dancer's opinion notwithstanding. Better to keep on digging on my own. I had more incentive than DeKalb did anyway: I was getting paid for this specific job, and I was a lot more interested in what had happened in late October of 1949 than he was.

I stared out the window some more. Would Amanda Crane have any idea who the red-haired woman had been? Not likely. From all indications she had worshipped her husband; if she'd had any inkling that he was having an affair or affairs, particularly in view of the fact that her frigidity was the probable cause, she was the type of woman who would have put on blinders and refused to admit the truth even to herself. And her mental state being what it was now, it would be cruel to subject her to that kind of questioning. Not that I could even get to see her again, what with that niece of hers on guard. . . .

The niece, I thought. Would *she* know anything about Harmon Crane's extracurricular activities? She couldn't be more than fifty, which made her a teenager when Crane had died; but teenagers are just as perceptive as adults sometimes—and sometimes even nosier—and there was also the possibility that she had picked up knowledge later on, from Mrs. Crane or from someone else.

What was the niece's name again? It took me a few seconds to remember that it was Dubek, Marilyn Dubek. Short-term memory loss—another indicator of creeping old age. I got the number from Information and dialed it, the idea being to determine whether or not she was home yet. If she'd answered I would have said, "Sorry, wrong number," and hung up and then driven over to Berkeley for the third time in two days. But she didn't answer. Nobody answered.

Temporary impasse.

I decided it was just as well. After four now—almost quitting time. And rush-hour traffic would be turning the bridge approaches into parking lots at this very minute. Who needed to breathe exhaust fumes for an hour or more? Who needed to put up with idiot drivers? Who needed to go to Berkeley to talk about a dead redhead when a live redhead would soon be available in Diamond Heights? Who needed the company of Petunia Pig when the company of Kerry Wade could be had instead?

I closed up half an hour early and hied myself straight to Diamond Heights.

Kerry and I went to a movie down at Ghirardelli Square. It was a mystery movie—"a nightmarish thriller in the grand tradition of Alfred Hitchcock," according to the ads. It was a film to give you nightmares, all right. And both it and its damned ads were a lie.

Filmmakers these days seem to equate suspense with gore: you're supposed to sit there damp-palmed and full of anticipation for the next gusher of blood, the next beheading, the next Technicolor disembowelment. Hitchcock knew different; every *film noir* director in the forties and fifties knew different. Character and atmosphere and mood are the true elements of suspense, cinematic or literary; it's what you *don't* see, what you're forced to imagine, that keeps you poised on the edge of your seat. Not blood, for Christ's sake. Not exposed entrails and rolling heads. Not human depravity of the worst sort.

Seven minutes into this piece of crap, the first bloody slashing took place. One minute later, while it was still going on, we got up and walked out. I've seen too much blood and carnage in my life as it is—*real* blood, *real* carnage. I don't need to be reminded of all the torn flesh, all the violated humanity, all the shattered hopes and futile dreams, all the goddamn waste. And I don't need my guts tied into knots by phony bullshit special effects that make a mockery of violent death and a mockery of its victims.

I said all of this to Kerry after we were outside the theater. I was pretty steamed up and when I get angry I tend to rant a little. Usually she just lets me rant without saying much, Kerry being of the opinion that if somebody is going to throw a tantrum, he ought to do it and be done with it. Very rational, my lady, which can be annoying as hell sometimes. This time, however, she did some ranting of her own; she doesn't like splatter movies any more than I do, especially the ones that employ name actors and hide behind the guise of "thrillers in the grand tradition of Alfred Hitchcock."

We went over to my place, ranting all the way, and had a couple of drinks to get rid of the bad taste, and then ate leftover roast and watched *I Wake Up Screaming* on the tube. *That*, by God, was a suspenseful film. Even Victor Mature had turned in a halfway decent performance for a change.

I asked Kerry to stay the night again—we wouldn't be seeing each other tomorrow night because she'd made other plans—but she declined. She had to be up and at the office early in the morning, she said. Besides, she said, we had been making love altogether too often lately. All that exertion was bad for my heart, she said, an old fellow like me.

Her cockeyed humor again. But I was not amused.

After she left, the old fellow doddered off to bed and reread the first three chapters of *Axe of Mercy*. It had been written during World War II, and it was all about fifth columnists, the black market in rubber goods and gas-rationing coupons, a fat farm called the Spread Shed, and the "Mercy Fund for War Widows" that was anything but. Most of the characters were zany, including the fifth columnists and black-marketeers, and there were all sorts of humorous scenes, descriptions, and dialogue. The last time I'd read it, a few years back, it had struck me as hilarious farce. This time I

was no more amused than I had been at the
splatter movie or at Kerry's levity.

Somehow Harmon Crane just wasn't funny anymore.

Five minutes after I arrived at the office on
Friday morning, an attorney I knew named Dick
Marsten rang up with a job offer: a female witness
in a criminal case of his had disappeared and he
wanted me to track her down. I would have liked
to lay it off on Eberhardt, but he wasn't in yet—as
usual—and Marsten had to be in court at eleven.
So I said all right, I'd come to his office right away
and pick up the details. Never turn down a paying
job, especially not when the only other one you've
got is as iffy as the Harmon Crane investigation.

I spent forty-five minutes with Marsten. Then I
returned to the office and made some calls to start
the skip-trace working. Eberhardt still hadn't
come in; he'd either gone directly out on the job—
he had a skip-trace of his own that he'd been
gnawing at since last week—or he'd taken another
day off to further mollify the Footwear Queen. If
it was the latter we were going to have a talk, Eb
and I. Whether he got offended again or not.

By the time I called Stephen Porter, it was
almost noon. He was in and as willing to help as
ever; the only thing was, he didn't have anything
to tell me. He couldn't remember any redheaded
woman with milk-white skin and freckles who
had been acquainted with the Cranes; in fact he
seemed surprised and a little shocked that Crane

had been having an affair with anyone. As far as he'd been aware, Crane had been devoted to Amanda. I didn't say anything to him about her frigidity; it wasn't the kind of knowledge that ought to be casually repeated.

I walked over to a chain restaurant on Van Ness, ate a soggy tuna-salad sandwich and drank some iced tea that tasted as if it had been made with dishwater, and walked back again. Still no Eberhardt. I called Marilyn Dubek's number. No answer. I debated calling Yankowski's home again and decided it would be a waste of time. I looked up the numbers of the novelist and the former confession writer who had known Crane, and called them, and that *was* a waste of time; neither man remembered a freckled redhead in connection with Harmon Crane.

If I had a number for Russ Dancer, I thought, I'd try picking his brain again. But I didn't have a number for him. Or did I? I dialed San Mateo County Information and asked for the number of Mama Luz's Pink Flamingo Tavern. Dancer was there, all right; but a fat lot of good that did me. He was already "about half shit-faced," as he put it, and if he'd ever met the mysterious redhead he couldn't dredge up the memory from the alcoholic bog it was mired in.

I tried Marilyn Dubek again. Busy signal this time; I took that as an encouraging sign, puttered around for ten minutes setting up a file for the Marsten skip-trace, and then redialed her number. Four rings and La Dubek's voice said, "Hello?

Marie, is that you?" I said, "Wrong number," and hung up and went to get my hat and coat. Petunia Pig was somebody I would have to talk to in person if I was going to get anything from her other than short shrift.

The sun was shining in Berkeley this afternoon, which was more than you could say for San Francisco. Not that it was any warmer over there; a strong cold wind was blowing. The wind had tugged leaves and twigs off the trees lining Linden Street and carpeted the pavement with them; more leaves covered the Dubek lawn, littered the porch stairs. As soon as the wind stopped blowing, I thought, she would be out here with a broom—or maybe her vacuum cleaner—to tidy up. She was just that type.

She answered promptly when I leaned on the doorbell. Her dyed black hair was up in curlers, her fat lips looked as if they had been stained with blueberry juice, and she was wearing a housedress that was as colorful and puckish as a page from the Sunday funnies. In one hand she carried a saucepan full of stringbeans, holding it tight-fisted like a weapon. She was quite a sight. If there had ever been a Porky in her life he had probably run off screaming years ago, in self-defense.

She glared at me, said, "Oh, it's you again," and got ready to shut the door in my face. "You can't see my aunt. She's not seeing anybody—"

"I didn't come to see Mrs. Crane," I said quickly, "I came to see you."

"Me? What for?"

"To ask you some questions."

"About Harmon Crane, I suppose. Well, I'm not answering any questions about him, not for you or any other fan."

"I'm not a fan."

"Writer, then."

"I'm not a writer."

"Well? Then what are you?"

"A private detective."

If that surprised her she didn't show it. Suspicion made her little pig eyes glitter. "Prove it," she said.

I proved it with the photostat of my license. "Now can we talk, Miss Dubek?"

"It's Mrs. Dubek, if you don't mind. Talk about what?"

"About Harmon Crane."

"Listen," she said, "what is this? Who hired you to come around here bothering us?"

"Michael Kiskadon."

"Oh, so that's it. Claiming to be Harmon's son. I don't believe it for a minute. Not a minute, you hear me?"

"I hear you, Miss Dubek."

"It's *Missus* Dubek."

I said, "Do you have any idea why Harmon Crane shot himself?"

"What?" she said. Then she said, "I'm not going to answer that. I don't have to answer your questions, why should I?" And she started to close the door again.

"If you don't answer my questions," I said, "you might have to answer the same ones from the police."

"What?"

"The police, Miss Dubek."

"Missus, missus, how many times do I have to—Police? Why should the police want to ask me questions?"

"You and Mrs. Crane both."

"That's ridiculous, I never heard of such a thing. Why, for heaven's sake?"

"Because of some bones that were found the other day at Tomales Bay. Human bones, buried at the site of the cabin Harmon Crane rented up there. A woman's bones."

She gawped at me slack-jawed. Behind her, somewhere in the house, Amanda Crane's voice called, "Marilyn? Do we have company, dear?" The Dubek blinked, glanced over her shoulder, said in a tolerable bellow, "No, Auntie, it's all right, you go back and rest," and glared at me again. "Now see what you've done," she said, using a snarl this time, and then crowded past me onto the porch and shut the door behind her.

"I'm sorry, Miss Dubek, but I—"

She made an exasperated sound through her teeth. "You're doing that on purpose," she said, "calling me *Miss* Dubek like that, trying to get me all flustered. But it won't work, you hear me? It won't work!"

"Yes, ma'am."

"Now what's this about bones? A woman's bones, you said?"

"That's right. Buried in an old earthquake fissure at Tomales Bay. Probably right after one of the bigger quakes—the one in 1949, for instance."

"You don't think *Harmon* buried those bones? My God!"

"It wasn't bones that were buried. It was the body of a woman."

"That's crazy. Harmon? Harmon and some woman?"

"You don't believe that's possible?"

"Of course not. Harmon wasn't a philanderer like that lowlife *I* married; he and Auntie were devoted to each other." She scowled and waggled the saucepan at me. "What woman are you talking about? Whose bones?"

"The police aren't sure yet. But she was probably a redhead, the kind with milk-white skin and freckles. Would you know if the Cranes knew anyone who fits that description?"

"Redhead, you say? Milk-white skin?"

"And freckles. Lots of freckles."

"How do you know all of that, anyway? What she looked like? If it was just bones that were found—"

"The police have ways," I said cryptically. "About that redhead, Miss Dubek . . ."

"You stop that now. I won't tell you again, it's missus—missus, missus, missus!"

"About that redhead, Mrs. Dubek."

Another scowl, but it was in concentration this

time. Pretty soon she said, "I remember I went up to Tomales Bay with Auntie one summer to see Harmon, 1948 or 1949, I was just a girl at the time. We had lunch with some other people; I think one of the women was a redhead . . . yes, I'm sure she was. Red hair and white skin and freckles."

"Do you remember her name?"

"Some Italian name. Her *last* name, I mean. I thought that was funny because she looked Irish—all that red hair, Irish, not Italian. And her first name was . . . let's see . . . Kate, that's it. Kate."

I said, "The last name wouldn't have been Bertolucci, would it?"

"Well, it might have been," she said. "Bertolucci. Mmm, yes, Kate Bertolucci. Her husband was the man who rented Harmon the cabin."

· **SIXTEEN** ·

My watch read a quarter of four when I drove
away from the Dubek house. I could have let a
second talk with Angelo Bertolucci slide until
tomorrow, or even until Monday; I could have
driven back to San Francisco and relaxed with a
cold bottle of Miller Lite in my living room.
Instead I turned north on the Eastshore Freeway
and headed for the Richmond-San Rafael Bridge,
the quickest route from Berkeley to Marin
County and eventually to Tomales. Bird dog on
the scent.

Traffic wasn't bad until I got onto the bridge.
Then it began to snarl and it stayed snarled all the
way through San Rafael and halfway to Novato.
Rush hour, they called it, which was a laugh—the
painful kind, like a fart in church. Nobody was
rushing this afternoon; nobody ever rushed on the
freeways after four P.M. on Friday, good old TGIF. I
quit muttering and cursing after a while and resigned myself to doing what I'd avoided doing last
night: smelling exhaust fumes, watching out for

idiot drivers, and otherwise dealing with the Great American Traffic Jam.

While I crawled along I brooded about the Bertoluccis, Angelo and Kate. It seemed probable that she was the woman Harmon Crane had been having his affair with, the woman Ellen Corneal had caught him in bed with and used for blackmail leverage; and it also seemed probable that those were her bones we'd found at the old cabin site. But identifying her raised plenty of new questions. Had Bertolucci known about the affair? And if he had, had he done anything about it? How had he reacted to his wife's disappearance? How had he explained it to his friends and neighbors?

Bertolucci had the answers to those questions. And maybe he also had the answers to two others, the two big ones: Why had his wife died? Who was responsible? I kept thinking what a queer old duck he was; and I kept remembering the way he'd looked the other day, standing out there in his vegetable patch with his shotgun in one hand and the dead and bloody crow in the other. . . .

At Hamilton Field the traffic began to move more or less normally, and once I got past Novato it thinned out enough so that I could maintain a steady sixty. I quit the freeway in Petaluma, picked up and followed the same two-lane county road I'd taken to Tomales on Wednesday. Dusk had settled when I got there; it was a few minutes before six. The fog was in, thick and restless, pressing down close to the ground so that it filled the hollows and dips and obscured the hilltops.

Building and street lights shone pale and indistinct, like daubs of yellow in a hologram seen through gray gauze.

The general store was still open; I turned off Shoreline Highway and stopped in front of it. The same dark-haired girl was behind the counter. I waited until she finished waiting on the only customer in the place and then said to her, "Hi. Remember me?"

"Oh sure," she said. "You're the man who was asking about Mr. Bertolucci the other day."

"Right. I wonder if you could answer a few more questions for me."

"Well . . . I guess so, if I can."

"Mr. Bertolucci used to be married, didn't he?"

"A long time ago, I think. Way before I was born."

"Was his wife's name Kate?"

"Kate. I *think* that was it."

"Do you know what happened to her?"

"Gee, no. She ran off with another man or something. My mother could tell you. Do you want to talk to her?"

"Where would I find her?"

"She's here, back in the storeroom. I'll get her for you."

She left the counter and disappeared into the rear of the store. Trusting people up here in the country; I could have made off with the entire cash register, not to mention its contents. Too long in the city, that was my trouble. Too many dealings with criminal types. If I lived in a place like Tomales, such thoughts would probably never even enter my head.

The girl came back with an older, graying version of herself, dressed in a leather apron over a man's shirt and a pair of Levi's. The older woman said her name was Martha Kramer and I gave her my name but not the fact that I was a detective; I told her I was a genealogical researcher trying to track down information on Angelo Bertolucci's wife, Kate, for a client in San Francisco.

"Oh, I see," she said, and nodded.

"I went to see Mr. Bertolucci on Wednesday afternoon, after I spoke to your daughter. He wasn't very cooperative, I'm afraid. He seemed . . . well, kind of odd."

"Odd is the word for it," Mrs. Kramer agreed.

"Just as I was leaving he went out into his yard and shot a crow. With a twelve-gauge shotgun."

A faint wry smile. "He does that sometimes. It used to frighten his neighbors but no one pays much attention anymore."

"He must have lived alone for a long time," I said.

"Ever since Mrs. Bertolucci left him. That must have been . . . oh, more than thirty years ago."

"October 1949? That's as far as I've been able to trace her."

"I believe it was 1949, yes."

"You say she left him. Divorced him, you mean?"

"No. Ran off."

"With another man?"

"Evidently."

"She and Mr. Bertolucci didn't get along, then."

"Not very well. Fought all the time."

"Over anything in particular?"

"His general cussedness, my mother used to say."

"Did the fights ever become physical?"

"A time or two. He was free with his fists."

"A violent man?"

"Well, you saw what he does to crows."

"Would you have any idea who Mrs. Bertolucci ran off with?"

"Lord, no. I was only a child then."

"So her affair wasn't common knowledge."

"No. But people weren't surprised, the way he treated her."

"It *was* common knowledge, though, that she'd run off?"

"He admitted it himself, more than once."

"Did he seem upset by the fact?"

"I suppose he was. Who wouldn't be?"

"And he never remarried?"

"No. Never set foot out of Tomales since, that I know of."

I took out my notebook and made some squiggles in it, mostly for show. "What can you tell me about Mrs. Bertolucci?"

"Well, let's see," Mrs. Kramer said. "Her maiden name was Dunlap; she was Irish . . . but you must already know that."

"Mmm."

"I think Mr. Bertolucci met her through her

father: He ran a plumbing supply company in Santa Rosa . . . no, he was a plumbing contractor, that's right. Used to hunt out here before all the land was posted, and Mr. Bertolucci made some of his trophies. He died a year or so before Mrs. Bertolucci disappeared."

"Did she have other relatives in Santa Rosa?"

"Not that I know of. You haven't been able to find any?"

"Not so far. Did she have any close friends here in Tomales, someone I might talk to?"

"Well . . . her best friend was Bernice Toland, but Bernice died several years back. Kate wrote her a note before she left town, said she was going away with a man; that was the first Bernice knew about it, apparently."

"Bernice never heard from her again?"

"No, never."

"Is there anybody else I might see?"

"A couple of others, I suppose, but I don't think they can tell you much more than I have."

I took their names and addresses, thanked Mrs. Kramer and her daughter, and went out to my car. For a time I sat there watching the fog swirl across the deserted highway, mulling over what I had just learned. It all seemed to fit. And what seemed to fit, too, was the way Angelo Bertolucci had dealt with his wife's disappearance—the way a man would if he had something to hide, if he'd had something to do with the disappearing.

Bertolucci was the one I wanted to talk to now; the two casual acquaintances of his wife's could wait. I started the car and swung out onto Dillon Beach Road and drove up toward Hill Street. The fog was so thick my headlight beams seemed to break off against the wall of it, smearing yellow across the gray but not penetrating it. I had to drive at a virtual crawl; I couldn't see more than twenty yards ahead.

The street sign came up out of the mist—Hill Street—and then the joining of its unpaved surface with the road I was on. Out of habit I put on the turn signal just before I started the right-hand swing.

There was a rush of thrumming sound in the fog ahead, and all at once a car came hurtling out of Hill Street, just a dark shape, no lights, like some sort of phantom materializing. I let out a yell, jerked the wheel hard right, came down on the brake pedal; the rear end broke loose and for a second or two I lost control, skidding on the rutted gravelly surface. The other driver had swerved too, which prevented a head-on collision, but as it was his car scraped along my left rear fender and booted my clunker around until it was slanted sideways across the road. The bump put an end to the skid, at least, and let me get the thing stopped. Meanwhile the other car bounced off, careened out onto Dillon Beach Road, and was almost immediately swallowed up by the gray mist. It had all happened so fast that I couldn't identify the make or model or even its color.

I shouted, "You stupid goddamn son of a bitch *bastard!*" at the top of my lungs, which wasn't very smart: coming on top of my fright, it might have given me a coronary. As it was, all I got was a raw throat and no satisfaction. I sat there for a minute or so, until I calmed down. Sat in silence, with nothing moving around me except the fog. The nearest house, the one with the Confederate flag for a window curtain, showed no light; the driver of the other car, drunk or sober, crazy or just plain witless, probably lived there. Christ!

The engine had stalled; I started it again and got the car straightened out and drove it up to Bertolucci's front gate. The palms of my hands and my armpits were damp, and when I got out the fog turned the dampness clammy and cold. Shivering, I went to the rear fender and shined my flashlight on it to check the damage. Foot-long scrape and a dent the size of my fist; the paint along the scrape was black.

I tossed the flashlight onto the front seat, muttering to myself, and then gave my attention to Bertolucci's house. Dim light illuminated its front and side windows, blurred by the fog. If he'd heard the collision he hadn't been curious enough to come out to investigate. I pushed through the gate and made my way through the tangle of weeds and mist-damp lilac bushes to the porch. The same sign still hung from the door: *Ring Bell and Come In.* I followed instructions, just as I had on Wednesday.

Bertolucci's display room was empty except for the poised animals and birds staring blankly with their glass eyes. The musty, gamy smell seemed even stronger tonight, overlain with the moist brackish odor of the fog. It was cold in there too; the old wood-stove in one corner was unlit and there weren't any furnace vents or registers that I could see.

"Mr. Bertolucci?"

One of the old house's joints creaked. Or maybe it was a mouse or something larger scurrying around inside the walls. Otherwise, silence.

I walked past the stuffed raccoon sitting up on its hind paws, the owl about to take flight with its rabbit dinner, the two chicken hawks mounted combatively on pedestals. The sound in the wall came again; the stillness that followed it had an empty quality, the kind you feel in abandoned buildings.

"Mr. Bertolucci?"

The faint echo of my voice, nothing else.

The door at the rear, behind the rodents on display in the glass cases, stood partially ajar; more pale lamplight came from the other side. I moved through an opening between the cases and shoved the door all the way open.

Bertolucci's workroom. An organized clutter: big worktable in the middle; labeled containers on a shelf underneath that held clay; plaster of paris; varnish, something called tow; tools hanging from wall racks; battered chest of drawers with each drawer labeled in a spidery hand, one of them with the word *Eyes*; a chopping block; a carborundum wheel; an electric saw; a box overflowing with cotton batting; spools of thread and twine;

tins of wax, paint, gasoline, formaldehyde, and wood alcohol; a tub of what looked to be corn meal. Dusty stacks of wooden shields and panels and mounts of various sizes, teetering in one corner; a jumble of old pieces of wire strewn in another. All this and more, shadowed and fusty in the pale light from a ceiling globe.

But no Bertolucci.

I called his name again, got the same faint echo and the same silence, and went at an angle to another door on my right. This one gave onto the kitchen, sink piled high with crusty dishes, ants crawling in a trail of spilled sugar on the floor. No Bertolucci here either. Two more doors opened off the kitchen, one to the rear of the house and one toward the front. I decided to try the rear one first, and started toward it, and that was when I first smelled the faint lingering stench of spent gunpowder.

The muscles across my shoulders bunched up; my stomach jumped, knotted, brought up the taste of bile. No, I thought, ah Christ, not again, not another one. But I went ahead anyway, pushed open the door and eased through it.

Narrow areaway, opening onto a laundry porch. And Bertolucci lying back there, blood all over him, blood on the floor and splashed on one wall—real blood, not the fake stuff they use in those damned death-mocking splatter movies. Torn and blackened and gaping hole where his chest had once been, and that was real too, and so was his twelve-gauge shotgun on the floor to one

side. Point blank range: the powder blackening
said that. And buckshot, not birdshot.

The back door was wide open; fog reached in
like searching fingers, skeletal and gray and grave-
cold. That was why I hadn't been able to smell
the burnt gunpowder until I got to the kitchen:
the wind had blown most of the odor away, even
though the weapon couldn't have been fired more
than a few minutes ago. The blood was still fresh,
glistening wet red in the spill of light from the
kitchen.

Driver of that black car, I thought. Has to be.
Not a crazy kid, not a Friday night drunk—a
murderer fleeing the scene of a just-committed
homicide. And if I'd come straight here instead of
stopping at the general store, maybe it wouldn't
have been committed at all. . . .

That's crap, I thought, you know better than
that. Then I thought: If I stand here any longer I'll
puke. I backed up and let the door wobble shut,
blocking out the carnage in the areaway. But it
was still there behind my eyes, all that blood, all
that ruined flesh, as I stumbled back through the
house to find a phone and call the sheriff's department.

# ► SEVENTEEN ◄

It was after nine before the authorities, in the person of Sergeant Chet DeKalb, allowed me to leave Tomales. DeKalb had come out even though he was off duty, because I had asked for him specifically. He wasn't pleased at having been yanked away from dinner with his family—he lived in Terra Linda and it was a long drive from there to Tomales—but he didn't take it out on me. He was polite; and when he saw the way Bertolucci's murder shaped up he even permitted a spark of interest to show through his stoicism.

We did our talking in the display room, with those stuffed things looking on. Lab men, photographers, uniformed deputies, the county coroner paraded in and out, performing the grim aftermath ritual of violent death. Outside, knots of local residents shivered in the fog, as indistinct when you had glimpses of them as half-formed wraiths. The revolving red light on the county ambulance made one of the windows alternately light up with a crimson glow and then go dark, like the winking of a bloody eye.

I told DeKalb everything I knew about Bertolucci, everything I had suspected about him and
his connection with those bones. "But now I don't
know," I said. "What happened here tonight . . . it
confuses the hell out of things."

"Not necessarily," DeKalb said. "There doesn't
have to be a correlation between your investigation and Bertolucci's death."

"Doesn't have to be, no."

"But you think there is."

"I don't know what to think right now."

"Could have been a prowler," DeKalb said. "Bertolucci caught him, tried to scare him off with
the shotgun; they struggled, the gun went off,
bang the old man's dead."

"Yeah," I said.

"Or somebody local had a grudge against him.
You said nobody seemed to like him much."

"Why *now*, though? The same week a thirty-
five-year-old can of worms opened up."

"Coincidences happen."

"Sure. I've had a few happen to me over the
years. But this time . . . I don't know, it doesn't
feel right that way."

"Hunches," DeKalb said. "You can't always
trust 'em."

"Granted. Hell, I don't see how the murder can
be tied up with Harmon Crane and the missing
wife, either."

"Anybody you can think of who might have had
a motive?"

"That's just it, I can't think of a single person or a single motive—not after all these years."

"You tell anybody your suspicions about Bertolucci and his wife?"

"No. I only found out about her this afternoon, and I came straight here afterward."

"Who told you about the wife?"

"Woman in Berkeley—Marilyn Dubek, the niece of Crane's widow. But she's fat, fifty, and a housefrau; the idea of her following me here and blowing Bertolucci away is ridiculous."

"What about the widow?"

"No way. Late sixties and mentally incompetent ever since her husband's suicide."

"Well, maybe the Dubek woman told somebody else what she told you after you left."

"Maybe. But I got here as fast as anybody could in rush-hour traffic, and I was in the general store no more than fifteen minutes. Whoever killed Bertolucci pretty much had to have arrived at the same time I did and probably a while earlier. Don't you think?"

"Seems that way," he agreed.

"I don't suppose any of the neighbors saw the car?"

DeKalb shook his head. "Nobody home at two of the houses. Old woman who lives in the other place up the way was cooking her supper; besides that, she's half-blind."

I said, "You know, if this was the perpetrator's first visit here, he might have had to stop over in the business section to ask directions."

"Already thought of that. Officers are checking it now. Let's get back to your investigation. Did you tell anybody about your first meeting with Bertolucci?"

"Just my client."

"Michael Kiskadon," DeKalb said, nodding. "I don't suppose you'd consider *him* a candidate?"

I hesitated, remembering what I'd thought yesterday morning after talking to Kiskadon on the phone—that if his wife didn't get him some psychiatric help pretty soon, he was liable to come unwrapped. And then what? I'd wondered. What happens to a guy like Kiskadon when he starts to unravel? Well, murder was one thing that happens to head cases; the sheer terrifying number of lunatics running around committing atrocities these days was proof of that. But something had to trigger a homicidal act, and I had told Kiskadon nothing about Angelo Bertolucci that could have induced a murderous rage. Besides, there was Kiskadon's physical condition: he was weak, he could barely get around unaided, he seldom left the house even for short periods. I could no more envision him driving all the way up to Tomales to confront Bertolucci than I could Marilyn Dubek.

I said these things to DeKalb and he concurred. But he felt that a talk with Kiskadon was indicated just the same. So did I, even though I did not relish the prospect; and I thought that for Kiskadon's sake, it would be better if I got to him first.

Before DeKalb let me leave, he took down the names and addresses of all the other people I had

interviewed this past week, including Russ
Dancer. Methodical and thorough, that was Chet
DeKalb—qualities possessed by all good cops,
public and private. He also sent one of the lab
men out to take scrapings of the black paint from
the banged-up fender of my car. And when I drove
away a few minutes later, past the morbid wraiths
huddled together in the mist, the lab guy and one
of the deputies were using portable crime-scene
floodlights to comb the area near the Dillon Beach
Road intersection, looking for anything that
might have come off the black car during the
collision.

The fog stayed thick and rolling, retarding my
speed, until I neared Petaluma; then it lifted into
a high overcast and I was able to make better time.
It was twenty of eleven when I came across the
Golden Gate Bridge, and eleven on the nose when
I walked into my flat. I was tired and I felt crawly
and I wanted a shower and some sleep. My stomach was giving me hell too; so even though I had
no appetite, and before I did anything else, I ate
some mortadella and a wedge of gorgonzola and a
carton of pineapple cottage cheese. Which was a
bad idea, as it turned out. The stuff congealed in
my stomach for some reason and gave me the
twin devilments of heartburn and gas.

I lay in bed belching and farting and trying to
sleep. But I couldn't get rid of the persistent image
of Bertolucci's buckshot-savaged corpse, of all that
glistening blood. And I couldn't stop thinking
about the *why* of his death, either. If it was con-

nected with what happened in 1949, and my gut instincts still said that it was, the reason for the killing escaped me completely.

Motive, motive, what was the damned motive?

I was up at seven-ten in the morning, gritty-eyed and headachy and depressed. It took a long shower, followed by three cups of strong coffee, to clear away the remnants of the nightmares that had plagued my sleep. It was always that way after I stumbled on violent death: the bad dreams, the day-after depression. Some cops had become inured to the residue of violence; I never had, which was one of the reasons I had quit the force twenty-five years ago to open my own agency. No corpses to deal with then, I'd thought; just the pain and tears of the living. Well, I'd been wrong—Christ, how wrong I'd been. I had seen more death these past twenty-five years than I ever would if I had stayed on the cops.

I called Kerry's number at eight-thirty. No answer. That stirred me up a little, until I remembered that it was Saturday: she went jogging on Saturday mornings, sometimes in Golden Gate Park, sometimes around Lake Merced, sometimes down on the Marina Green. She wasn't one of those jogging fanatics; she didn't run every day, she didn't run fifty miles a week, she just ran on Saturdays for exercise. I forgave her for it, now that she had quit trying to coerce *me* into running with her. Everybody is entitled to one small lunacy.

So I called Eberhardt's house, and he wasn't home either. *That* nettled me. Over at Wanda's again, probably; spending too damn much time with her since the Il Roccaforte fiasco, soothing her ruffled feathers. Or more likely stroking her unfeathered chest. Neglecting his work, mooning around like a lovesick jerk—he was beginning to annoy the hell out of me, and the next time I saw him I was going to tell him so. I considered calling him at Wanda's and decided I didn't want to talk to her. Nor him very badly, for that matter. Let him read about Bertolucci's death in the papers.

As early as it was, I went ahead and dialed Kiskadon's number. I figured he would probably be up by now, and I wanted to reach him before DeKalb did. He was up, all right—he answered right away—and he sounded neither happy nor unhappy to hear from me. But he didn't know about Bertolucci yet or he would have said something when I asked him if I could stop by. He wanted to know if I had news; I said yes but it would be better if we discussed it in person; he told me to come over any time. There was a bitter, hopeless note in his voice that I didn't like.

It was foggy on Golden Gate Heights; you could barely see the tops of the trees over in the park. Nobody was out and around. The whole area had a gray, abandoned look, like a neighborhood in a plague city. Some mood I was in when that sort of thought crossed my mind.

Lynn Kiskadon answered the door. Pale-featured

except for dark circles under her eyes, and bulgy again in another pair of too-tight Calvin Klein jeans. Before I could say anything, she stepped out on the porch, pulled the door against its latch, and held it there with one hand.

She said, "He's waiting in the den. He thinks you've got bad news—I can tell by the way he looks."

"I'm afraid I have."

"Oh God, I knew it," she said, "I knew it." The words were like a lament, soft and moaning and edged with self-pity. "What have you found out?"

"I'd rather say it just once, Mrs. Kiskadon."

"He won't want me in the room with the two of you."

"Why not?"

"We had another fight. Wednesday night, after you and I talked in the park. He hasn't said five words to me since."

I didn't say anything.

"I tried to call you on Thursday and again yesterday. I thought . . . I don't know what I thought. I don't know who else to turn to."

"What was the fight about?"

"He won't see a psychiatrist, he won't even talk to his own doctor. He just won't face the truth about himself."

"He sounded depressed on the phone," I said.

"Worse than I've ever seen him. He just sits in his den reading his father's books and stories. Won't eat, won't talk, just sits there until all hours. Do you *have* to tell him this news of yours?"

"I don't have a choice."

"It's really so bad?"

"Not to you or me. But it will be to him."

"Then don't tell him! God knows what he might do."

"Mrs. Kiskadon, if you're afraid of that gun of his, why don't you get it out of his desk and hide it somewhere?"

"It's in a locked drawer and he has the only key. And he's in the den all the time."

"I've still got to tell him," I said. "If I don't, the Marin County Sheriff's Department will."

"Sheriff's Department? My God, what—"

"We'd better go inside, Mrs. Kiskadon."

She made a little whiny noise, but she let me reach around her and push open the door and prod her gently inside. It was quiet in the house—too quiet to suit me right now. We went through the living room and along the short hall to the door to Kiskadon's den. I knocked and said his name, and from the inside he said, "It's open, come ahead," and we went in.

He was sitting in the recliner chair, his cane laid across his lap, a cold pipe in one corner of his mouth. The table at his elbow was stacked with pulps, issues of *Collier's* and *American Magazine* and *The Saturday Evening Post*, three of the Johnny Axe novels. He didn't look any different than he had the last time I'd been here—except for his eyes. There was no animation in them;

they were as dark and lightless as burned-out bulbs. And the whites were flecked and streaked with blood.

He said, "You'll excuse me if I don't get up. My leg's bothering me today."

I moved toward him by a couple of steps, and Lynn Kiskadon shut the door and stood back against it. Kiskadon looked at her, the kind of look that told her silently and bitterly to get out. She said, "I'm staying, Michael. I have a right to hear this too."

He didn't answer her. As far as he was concerned, she *had* gone out. He said to me, with the bitterness in his voice, "Glad tidings, I trust?"

"I'm sorry, no."

"I didn't think so. Well? I'm ready."

I told him. The evident affair between Harmon Crane and Kate Bertolucci, my suspicions, Angelo Bertolucci's murder—not softening any of it but not going into unnecessary detail either. Once, when I first mentioned the murder, Lynn Kiskadon made the little whiny noise again behind me. Otherwise the only sound in the room was my own voice. Kiskadon didn't speak or move or display any reaction to what I said; his face was as blank as his eyes.

When I finished there were maybe ten seconds of silence. Then he said, "So my father was an adulterer and a murderer. Well, well." No bitterness in his tone now. No emotion at all. The flat, genderless voice of a programmed machine.

"We don't know that he killed anyone, Mr. Kiskadon."

"Don't we? It seems plain enough to me."

"Not to me," I said. "Bertolucci could just as easily have been the one responsible for his wife's death. Maybe even somebody else."

"Just the same, my father had to be involved, didn't he? If he wasn't involved, he wouldn't have begun drinking so heavily afterward, he wouldn't have become so depressed. He wouldn't have shot himself, now would he?"

"We don't have all the facts yet—"

"Enough to suit me."

"There's still the murder last night," I said.

"I don't care about that."

"You'd better care about it, Mr. Kiskadon. I think Bertolucci was killed because of what happened in 1949."

"Does that make my father any less guilty?"

"I don't know. It might."

"Bullshit," he said.

"You don't seem to understand. This isn't an archeological expedition anymore, it isn't a simple search for the motive in your father's suicide. It's a homicide case now."

"I don't give a damn," he said.

"Is that what you're going to say to Sergeant DeKalb when he shows up?"

"To hell with Sergeant DeKalb. If he wants to arrest me for any reason, let him. I don't care. That's what *you* don't seem to understand. I don't care who killed Bertolucci, I don't care who killed his slut of a wife or why, I don't care about any of it anymore."

"Why not? Just because your father wasn't the kind of man you thought he was?"

No answer. Kiskadon wasn't looking at me either, now. He reached for the canister of tobacco on the table and methodically began to load the bowl of his pipe.

I glanced around at Lynn Kiskadon. Her expression was pleading, helpless; her eyes said, *You see? You see?*

I saw, all right. But there wasn't anything I could do about it, not for him and not for her. What could I do? I was no head doctor; I didn't know the first thing about dealing with the kinds of neuroses running around inside Kiskadon's skull. I was fortunate if I could deal with the ones inside my own.

Kiskadon struck a kitchen match and lit his pipe. When he had it drawing he said, still without looking at me, "I appreciate all you've done, but I won't need your services any longer. Send me a bill for the balance of what I owe you. Or I can write you a check if you'd prefer it that way."

Nothing to say to that except, "Have it your way, Mr. Kiskadon. I'll send you a bill." Nothing to do then except to turn and walk out of there, avoiding Mrs. Kiskadon's eyes. And nothing to do after that except to feel twice as shitty and twice as frustrated on the drive back home.

# ► EIGHTEEN ◄

Ten minutes after I came into my flat, just as I was about to call Kerry, the telephone rang. I picked up the receiver and said hello, and there was a wheezing intake of breath followed by a series of fitful coughs. So I knew it was Stephen Porter even before he identified himself.

"That box of Harmon Crane's papers I told you about," he said, panting a little. "I finally found it. It was in the basement, just as I thought, but hidden at the bottom of Adam's old steamer trunk."

"Anything among the papers that might help me?"

"Well, I really can't say. Most of them are manuscript carbons. There are some letters written to Harmon, and some by him, but they seem mostly to be business-related. Of course—" He coughed again. "Of course, I haven't read everything. Perhaps you'll be able to find something useful."

"Perhaps. When can I have a look at them?"

"Right away, if you like. I'd drop the box off to you, but I have a student coming at noon. . . ."

"No, no, I'll come by your studio. Half an hour okay?"

"Yes, fine. I'll be"—more coughing—"I'll be here."

I postponed the call to Kerry and started immediately for North Beach. The weather was better over there and the tourists and Saturday slummers were out in full force; there was no way I was going to find legal street parking. And the nearest garage to Porter's place was blocks away. So I parked in a bus zone down the street from his building, the hell with it.

Porter was wearing the same green smock and the same red bow tie, or at least identical twins to the ones he'd had on the last time I was here: both were spotted with dried clay. He had a cigarette burning in one hand and what breath he had left made burbling noises in his nose and throat.

The box was on one of the clay-smeared worktables, cardboard and largish; the papers jammed into it looked to be mostly yellow foolscap. I asked Porter if he wanted me to sort through them here, and he said, "No, you can take the box with you," and then lapsed into a coughing fit so severe it bent him double and turned his face an apoplectic beet red. I wanted to do something for him but there wasn't anything to do. I just stood there, feeling helpless, until he got his breath back.

"One of my bad days," he said. "Damned emphysema."

Damned cigarettes, I thought.

I carried the box to the studio door. Porter went

with me, firing up another Camel on the way. Walking dead man, I thought then. And tried not to let him see the pity I felt when I said good-bye.

Manuscript carbons. Handwritten notes. Typed fragments and unfinished stories. Letters from Crane's New York agent and from the editors of various book and magazine publishers. Carbons of letters from Crane to those same individuals. A few personal letters addressed to Crane. Carbons of his responses and some other personal correspondence. Most of his papers, it seemed, from 1942 until the time of his death.

Sitting at the kitchen table, thinking that Harmon Crane had been something of a pack rat, I finished sorting out the sheets of stationery and yellow foolscap and then began methodically to wade through them. The manuscript carbons first: two of the Johnny Axe novels, *Axe for Trouble* and *Don't Axe Me;* and more than thirty short stories and novelettes, most of them featuring Johnny Axe, all of them marked SOLD and bearing both a date and the name of either a pulp or a slick magazine. I riffled through some of the manuscripts from 1949. Plenty to interest a collector or a scholar; nothing to interest a detective. I put the carbons back into the box and gave my attention to the notes and fragments.

Most of the handwritten notes—none of which were dated—seemed to be ideas for stories: "Carny owner shot, geek arrested by cops, Axe hired as new geek—funny or too bizarre?" The

typed sheets were nearly all one and two pages in
length: story openings, descriptions of places and
people, clever bits of dialogue, brief plot synopses.
There were also two longer fragments. The first
was headed *Kick Axe!*, ran to fourteen pages, and
appeared to be an early draft of the opening chapter of *Axe and Pains*. I read through it, looking for
Bertolucci's name, but it wasn't there.

The other segment bore a pulpish title—"You
Can't Run Away from Death"—and was a little
over eight pages long. Unfinished pulp story, I
thought. But it wasn't. Halfway through the first
page I realized it was something much more than
that.

Numb with shock, Rick Durbin stared at
the body on the cabin floor. Carla. It was
Carla! Somebody had come here while he was
in the village buying groceries. Somebody had
beaten her to death with a chunk of stovewood.

Borelli, he thought. It had to be her husband, Borelli.

Durbin fell to his knees beside her. He
wanted to cry but he had no tears. He'd loved
her. Or had he? He didn't know. He didn't
know anything right now except that she was
dead. Murdered. Lying here so still, blood
shining in her red hair, where only an hour
ago she had been so warm and vibrant and
alive.

*What was he going to do?*

What Durbin did, on page 2, was to pick up the body, carry it outside and away from the isolated cabin on a body of water called Anchor Bay, and bury it. In an earthquake fissure: there had been a "terrifying" earthquake the day before. He did that instead of notifying the authorities because he was afraid they would suspect him of the crime. He had no proof the husband, Borelli, had murdered Carla. And he was the cabin's tenant; he was staying there alone. And Carla was another man's wife; *his* wife was back home in San Francisco. Even if he could make the sheriff believe his story, there was the scandal to consider: Durbin was a writer, he had a film deal pending in Hollywood for one of his books, the notoriety would ruin his career.

Durbin went back to the cabin and cleaned the bloodstains off the floor. Then he gathered up Carla's purse and other belongings, put them into the fissure with her body, and used dirt and grass and oyster shells to conceal his handiwork. No one would ever know, he thought; no one had suspected his affair with Carla—except Borelli—because they had been very careful to keep it a secret. There was nothing to connect Carla or her disappearance to him. With her buried, he thought, he was completely safe.

When the job was done he packed his own belongings and drove straight home to San Francisco. But he couldn't forget Carla or what he'd done. Her dead face haunted his dreams, saying over and over, "You told me you loved me. How can you do this to someone you loved?" He couldn't sleep, couldn't work. He thought time and again of returning to Anchor Bay, making a clean breast to the authorities, showing them where he had buried her; but he couldn't find the courage—it was too late, they would never believe him now that so much time had elapsed. He began to drink too much in a futile effort to drown his guilt and to ward off a growing paranoia.

Every time the telephone or doorbell rang, Durbin was terrified that it would be the police. Or, almost as bad, that it would be Borelli. Borelli was a violent man, a dangerous man. And he wasn't stupid. He knew something had been done with Carla's body. He knew who and why. He might not be satisfied to let it go at that. He might decide to eliminate the one man who knew the truth, who could put him in the gas chamber for Carla's murder. What if he comes here? What if he tries to kill me too? What if he
  What if

That was where it ended. To Stephen Porter, to me before I began to realize what had happened at Tomales Bay in October of 1949, these pages would seem to be the beginning of a pulp story, unsalable and abandoned because it was too emotional and too immoral for its time; but what it really was was a pathetic attempt by Crane to purge his demons by fictionalizing the truth—a confession that was never intended to be read, that his pack-rat tendencies had kept him from destroying after he was no longer able to continue it. Positive proof of why he had taken his own life later on, all the dark, bleak, ugly motives: guilt, fear, self-loathing, paranoia. And maybe he *had* loved Kate Bertolucci, at least a little; maybe that was part of it too. He not only hadn't had the guts to try to see her murderer punished, he had tucked her away in the ground as if she were nothing more than a dead animal.

No part of the confession had surprised me much, but seeing it all down in black-on-yellow, in Harmon Crane's own words, had deepened my own depression. I got up from the table and opened a can of Miller Lite and carried it into the front room. Patches of fog were still swirling over this part of the city; I stood in the bay window, watching the clash of blue and gray overhead and thinking of how Kiskadon would react if he read those pages. Well, he *wasn't* going to read them, not if I could help it. He had fired me this morning; I no longer had an obligation to share my findings with him.

My findings. What was I doing here this afternoon, anyway, rummaging through all those old papers, fueling my rotten mood by wallowing in a poor dead writer's thirty-five-year-old weakness and torment? My job was done, for Christ's sake. I had been hired to find out why Crane killed himself, and I had found out, and I had been summarily fired for my efforts. And that was that.

Well, wasn't it?

Bertolucci's murder, I thought. Somebody killed him and the reason is linked to Harmon Crane and the hell with all this thinking. The job's not done yet and you know it. Quit maundering about it.

I finished the beer and went back into the kitchen and sat down at the table again. All right. Business correspondence. Letters from his agent informing him of acceptance of novels and short stories, of subsidiary rights sales on the Johnny Axe series. Other letters from the agent suggesting slick magazine story ideas or offering market tips. Letters from editors asking for revisions on this or that project. A two-page rejection letter detailing the reasons why a pulp editor was returning a story, across the first page of which Crane had scrawled the word *Bullshit!* Carbons of Crane's responses to some of the above. Carbons of cover letters sent with manuscript submissions to his agent and to various editors. Other business letters discussing financial matters with his agent, or making a specific point in rebuttal to an editorial request for revision; the latter were often phrased satirically, to take the sting out of the words: "Johnny Axe would *never* shoot an unarmed man, Mr. E., no matter that the unarmed man in this case is a 7-foot-tall Hindu snake charmer bent on remolding the shape of Johnny's spine. I have it on good authority that Mr. A. would not even shoot the *snake* unless it were packing a loaded gat."

Nothing for me there; I went on to the personal letters addressed to Crane, those dated the last few months of 1949. Fan mail, most of them, including a note on baby blue stationery from a woman in Michigan who said she had had "a wickedly erotic dream about dear Johnny Axe" and wondered if Mr. Crane ever passed through East Lansing on his way to and from New York because she'd *love* to meet him. Nothing from Kate Bertolucci. Nothing from Angelo Bertolucci. A scribbled note from Russ Dancer, suggesting a possible collaborative story idea; Crane had written at the bottom: "Come on Russ—trite!" A fannish note from Stephen Porter, telling Crane how much he'd enjoyed *Axe of Mercy*. Nothing from anyone else whose name I was familiar with.

Which left me with the carbons of personal letters Crane himself had written. The bulk of these were responses to fan letters, including a polite but unencouraging note to the lady in East Lansing. Letters to Russ Dancer and a couple of other writers, most of which were both humorous and scatological in tone; none of these was dated later than September of 1949. Only a few bore a post–October 15 date, and among those was a personal note dated December 7, Pearl Harbor Day:

*Dear L:*
   *This is a difficult letter to write. Doubly so because I can't think straight these days (yes,*

*I know the booze only makes it worse). But there's no one else I can turn to.*

*You know how I feel about Mandy. She's more important to me than anything else. If anything happens to me I want you to see to it she's cared for, financially and every other way. Can I count on you to do that?*

*The fact is, I can't go on much longer. I can't sleep, I can't eat, I can't work. Sometimes I think I'm close to losing my mind. There is too much festering inside me that I can't talk about, to you or to anyone else. No one must ever know the truth, least of all Mandy. It would hurt her too much.*

*Life terrifies me more than death, yet I've been too much of a coward to put an end to it. At least I have been up to now. Soon I may find the strength. Or perhaps circumstances will take it out of my hands. In any case I will be better off dead, free of all this pain. And Mandy will be better off without me, even though she will never understand why.*

*As Johnny might say, I axe no mercy and I seek no help. There is no mercy or help for me. I know what I am. I ask only your word that you will take care of Mandy.*

That was all. If he'd had anything else to say, it had gone into a postscript on the original.

I read the carbon again, then a third time. Further proof that Crane had been contemplating suicide for some time before December 10; that

his mind had deteriorated to the point where
death was the only answer. A little rambling toward the end: his mental state combined with the
alcohol. Otherwise, coherent enough. Nothing
unintelligible about it, nothing off-key.

Yet it struck an odd note for me, and I couldn't
figure out why.

Mandy was Amanda, of course. But who was L?
why was he or she the only one Crane felt he
could turn to about his wife? I knew of no one
close to Crane whose first or last name began
with the letter L. A nickname?

Maybe Porter would know. I went into the bedroom and rang up his studio and got him on the
line. And he said, "L? No, I can't think of anyone
at all. Certainly none of Harmon's intimates had
a name beginning with that letter."

Back into the kitchen to reread the carbon. That
same odd note . . . but why? Why?

The answer continued to elude me, even after
three more readings. Put it aside for now, I
thought, come back to it later. I paper-clipped it
to Crane's fictionalized confession and left those
sheets on the table. The rest of the stuff I put back
into the cardboard box. Then I got another beer
out of the refrigerator and went to call Kerry.

I needed some cheering up—bad.

She came over and cheered me up. A little while
later I thought about rereading the carbon another
time, but I didn't do it; I didn't want to get

depressed all over again. Instead I reached for
Kerry and suggested she cheer me up some more.

"Sex maniac," she said.

"Damn right," I said.

I cheered her up, too, this time.

At nine-thirty that night the telephone rang.
Kerry and I were back in bed, watching an intellec-
tual film—*Godzilla vs. Mothra*—on the tube. I
caught up the receiver and said hello, and Wanda
the Footwear Queen said, "You know who this
is?" in a voice so slurred I could barely understand
the words. Drunk as a barfly—the kind of drunk
that teeters on the line between weepy and nasty.

"Uh-huh," I said.

"Juss want you know I hate your guts. Hers too,
lil miss two fried eggs. Both your guts."

"Listen, why don't you go sleep it off—"

"Whyn't *you* go fuck yourself, huh?" she said,
and I sighed and hung up on her.

"Who was that?" Kerry asked.

"The voice of unreason," I said.

And I thought: Poor Eberhardt. Poor, blind, stupid Eberhardt.

# ▸ NINETEEN ◂

Sunday.

Kerry and I went downtown to the St. Francis Hotel for an early brunch, something we do occasionally. Afterward she suggested a drive down the coast and I said okay; the fog and high overcast had blown inland during the night, making the day clear and bright, if still windy. But I wasn't in much of a mood for that kind of Sunday outing. Not depressed so much today as restless—what a Texan I had known in the Army called a "daunciness"; I couldn't seem to relax, I couldn't seem to keep my mind off Harmon Crane and Michael Kiskadon and that damned letter carbon addressed to somebody with the initial L.

As perceptive as she is, Kerry read my mood and understood it. We were in Pacifica, following Highway One along the edge of the ocean, when she said, "Why don't we go back?"

"What?"

"Back home. You're not enjoying yourself and neither am I. You can drop me at my place if you'd rather be alone."

233

"Uh-uh. We'll go back, but I don't want to be alone. I'll only brood."

"You're doing that now."

"I'll do it worse if you're not around."

It was noon when we got back to the city. I drove to Pacific Heights—doing it automatically, without consulting Kerry. But she didn't seem to mind. Inside my flat, she went to make us some fresh coffee and I sat down with the box of Harmon Crane's papers. I reread the letter carbon. I reread the fictionalized confession. I reread the carbon one more time.

I was still bothered. And I still didn't know why.

Kerry had brought me some coffee and was sitting on the couch, reading one of my pulps. I said to her, "Let's play some gin rummy."

She looked up. "Are you sure that's what you want to do?"

"Sure I'm sure. Why?"

"You get grumpy when you lose at gin."

"Who says I'm going to lose?"

"You always lose when you're in a mood like this. You don't concentrate and you misplay your cards."

"Is that so? Get the cards."

"I'm telling you, you'll lose."

"Get the cards. I'm not going to lose."

She got the cards, and we played five hands and I lost every one because I couldn't concentrate and misplayed my cards. I *hate* it when she's right. I lost the sixth hand, too: she caught me with close seventy points—goddamn face cards, I never had learned not to hoard face cards.

"You're a hundred and thirty-seven points down already," she said. "You want to quit?"

"Shut up and deal," I said grumpily.

And the telephone rang.

"Now who the hell is that?"

"Why don't you answer it and find out?"

"Oh, you're a riot, Alice," I said, which was a Jackie Gleason line from the old "Honeymooners" TV show. But she didn't get it. She said, "Who's Alice?" The telephone kept on ringing; I said, "One of these days, Alice, bang, zoom, straight to the moon," and got up and went into the bedroom to answer it.

A woman's voice made an odd chattering sound: "Muh-muh-muh," like an engine that kept turning over but wouldn't catch. But it wasn't funny; there was a familiar whining note of despair in the voice.

"Mrs. Kiskadon? What's the matter?"

She made the sound again, as if there were a liquidy blockage in her throat and she couldn't push the words past it. I told her to calm down, take a couple of deep breaths. I heard her do that; then she made a different noise, a kind of strangled gulping, that broke the blockage and let the words come spilling out.

"It's Michael . . . you've got to help me, please, I don't know what to do!"

"What about Michael?"

"He said . . . he said he was going to kill himself. . . ."

I could feel the tension come into me, like air filling and expanding a balloon. "When was this?"

"A little while ago. He locked himself in his den last night after that Marin policeman left, he wouldn't come out, he sat in there all night doing God knows what. But this afternoon . . . he came out this afternoon and he had that gun in his hand, he was just carrying it in his hand, and he said he . . ."

"Easy. Did you call his doctor?"

"No, I didn't think . . . I was too upset. . . ."

"Have you called anyone else?"

"No. Just you . . . you were the only person I could think of."

"All right. Is your husband in his den now?"

"I don't know," she said, "I'm not home."

"Not home? Where are you?"

"I couldn't stay there, I just . . . I couldn't, I had to get *out* of there. . . ."

"Where are you?" I asked her again.

"A service station. On Van Ness."

"How long have you been away from your house?"

"I don't know, not long. . . ."

"Listen to me. What did your husband say before you left? Tell me his exact words."

"He said . . . I don't *remember* his exact words, it was something about shooting himself the way his father did, like father like son, it was crazy talk. . . ."

"Did he *sound* crazy? Incoherent?"

"No. He was calm, that awful calm."

"Did he say anything else?"

"No, no, nothing."

"What did he do?"

"Went back into the den and locked the door."

"And then you left?"

"Yes. I told you, I couldn't stay there. . . ."

"How soon did you leave?"

"Right away. A minute or two."

"So it hasn't been more than fifteen or twenty minutes since he made his threat. He's probably all right; there's no reason to panic. You go back home and try to reason with him. Meanwhile, I'll call his doctor for you—"

"No," she said, "I can't go back there alone. Not alone. If you come . . . I'll meet you there. . . ."

"There's nothing I can do—"

"Please," she said, "I'll go home now, I'll wait for you."

"Mrs. Kiskadon, I think you—"

But there was a clicking sound and she was gone.

I put the handset back into its cradle. And left it there: I couldn't call Kiskadon's doctor because I didn't know who he was; she hadn't given me time to ask his name.

When I turned around Kerry was standing in the bedroom doorway. She said, "What was that all about?"

"Kiskadon threatened to kill himself a while

ago. His wife is pretty upset; she wants me to go over there."

"Do you think he meant it?"

"I hope not."

"But he might have."

"Yeah," I said, "he might have."

"Then what are you waiting for? Go, for God's sake."

I went.

The green Ford Escort was parked in the driveway when I got to Twelfth Avenue and Lynn Kiskadon was sitting stiffly behind the wheel. She didn't move as I pulled to the curb in front, or when I got out and went around behind the Ford and up along her side. She didn't seem to know I was there until I tapped lightly on the window; then she jerked, like somebody coming out of a daze, and her head snapped around. Behind the glass her face had a frozen look, pale and haggard, the eyes staring with the same fixed emptiness as the stuffed rodents in Angelo Bertolucci's display cases.

I reached down and opened the door. She said, "I didn't think you were coming," in a voice that was too calm, too controlled. She was one breath this side of a scream and two breaths short of hysteria.

"Did you check on your husband, Mrs. Kiskadon?"

"No. I've been sitting here waiting."

"You should have gone in—"

"I can't go in there," she said.

"You have to."

"No. I can't go *in* there, don't you understand?"

"All right."

"You go. I'll wait here."

"You'll have to give me the key."

She pulled the one out of the ignition and handed me the leather case it was attached to. "The big silver one," she said. "You have to wiggle it to get it into the lock."

I left her, went around the Ford and over onto the porch. I had just put the house key into the latch when I heard the car door slam. I didn't turn; I finished unlocking the door and pushed it open and walked inside.

Silence, except for the distant hum of an appliance that was probably the refrigerator. I went into the living room by a couple of paces, half-turning so that I could look back at the doorway. Lynn Kiskadon appeared there, hesitated, then entered and shut the door behind her.

"I couldn't wait out there," she said. "I wanted to but I couldn't. It's cold in the car."

I didn't say anything. Instead I went through into the hallway and along it to the closed door to Kiskadon's den. There wasn't anything to hear when I put my ear up close to the panel and listened. I knocked, called Kiskadon's name, and then identified myself.

No answer from inside.

Lynn Kiskadon was standing behind me, close enough so that I could hear the irregular rhythm of her breathing. There was a knot in my stomach and another one in my throat; the palms of my hands felt greasy. I wiped the right one on my pantleg, reached out and turned the doorknob. Locked.

I bent to examine the lock. It was the push-button kind that allows you to secure the door from either side. I straightened and looked at Mrs. Kiskadon; her skin seemed even paler now, splotched in places so that it resembled the color of buttermilk. "He might not be in there," I said. "He might be somewhere else in the house. Or outside."

"No," she said. "He's in there."

"I'll look around anyway. You wait here."

"Yes. All right."

It took me three minutes to search the place and determine that Michael Kiskadon wasn't anywhere else on the premises or in the yard out back. The knots in my stomach and throat were bigger, tighter, when I came back into the hallway. Lynn Kiskadon hadn't moved. She was standing there staring at the door as if it were the gateway to hell.

I said, "No other way inside except this door?"

"No."

"What about the window?"

"You'd have to use a ladder from the yard."

"Do you have a ladder?"

"Yes, but it's not high enough. We always hire somebody to do the windows, you see. There's a

man who comes around, a handyman . . . he has a
very high ladder."

"Mrs. Kiskadon, the only way I can get in there
is to break down the door. Do you want me to do
that?"

"Yes."

"You're sure?"

"Yes. Go ahead, do it. Break it down."

I caught hold of the knob. And a thought came
to me: This is the way it was thirty-five years ago,
the night Harmon Crane died. I shook it away.
One sharp bump of my shoulder against the panel
told me it was a tight lock and that I wasn't going
to get in by using that method. I stepped back,
used the wall behind me for leverage, and drove
the sole of my shoe into the wood just above the
latch. That did it. There was a splintering sound
as the bolt tore loose from the jamb-plate, and the
door wobbled inward.

*This is the way it was that night thirty-five
years ago. . . .*

I stayed in the doorway, trying to shield Mrs.
Kiskadon with my body. But she pushed at me
from behind, hit me with her fist, came past me.
When she saw what I saw at the opposite end she
made a thin, keening noise. I caught hold of her,
but she fought loose and did a stumbling about-
face and tried to run away into the hall. She didn't
get any farther than the doorway before both her
voice and her legs gave out. She fell sideways into
the jamb, hard enough so that her head made an
audible smacking noise against the wood.

She was on her knees when I got to her, shaking her head and moaning. But she wasn't hurt and she wasn't hysterical; just disoriented. I picked her up without resistance and carried her into the living room and put her down on the couch. She stayed there, not looking at me, not looking at anything in the room. I waited a few seconds anyway, just to make sure, before I went back into the den.

Kiskadon lay slumped over the desk top, left arm outflung, right arm hanging down toward the floor; his right temple was a mess of blood and torn and blackened flesh. Looking at him, I didn't feel any physical reaction—nothing at all this time except for the pity, always that same terrible feeling of pity. Second gunshot corpse in three days, and this one not nearly as bad as Bertolucci's had been. Maybe that was it. An overload that had temporarily short-circuited me inside.

Harmon Crane's way out, I thought. Just like that night in 1949.

A phone sat undisturbed on the desk, but I didn't want to use that one if there was another in the house. I started away—and something on the floor to one side and slightly behind the desk caught my attention. It was a brown leather handbag, overturned so that some of its contents had spilled out. I moved closer and leaned over to look at the items: comb, compact, lipstick, wallet. But no keys. From that position I could also see the weapon; it wasn't in Kiskadon's hand, it was all the way under the chair on the left side—a Smith

& Wesson snub-nosed .38, the kind known as a belly gun.

The sick feeling started then: short-circuit back the other way. But it was a different kind of sickness, as much a product of the actions of the living as of the presence of the dead. I clamped my teeth together and swallowed to keep it down.

Suicide, I thought again. Like father, like son. Only now I didn't believe it.

# ► TWENTY ◄

As if things weren't bad enough, Leo McFate was in charge of the Homicide team that responded to my call.

McFate and I didn't get along. We had had run-ins a time or two in the past, but not for the usual reasons that an abrasiveness develops between cops and private detectives. The thing was, McFate didn't think of himself as a cop; he thought of himself as a *temporary* cop on his merry way to Sacramento and a job with the attorney general's office. He had ambitions, yes he did. He dressed in tailored suits and fancy ties, he read all the right books, he spoke with precise grammar, diction, and enunciation, he went to all the important social functions, and he sucked up to politicians, newspaper columnists, and flakes off the upper crust. He also considered himself a devilish ladies' man, with special attention to those women from eighteen to eighty who had money, social status, and the Right Connections. He didn't like me because he thought I was beneath him. I didn't like him because I knew he was an asshole.

He came breezing in with another inspector, one I didn't know named Dwiggins, gave me a flinty-eyed look, and demanded to know where the deceased was. That was the way he talked; sometimes it was very comical to listen to him, but this wasn't one of them. I took him to the den and showed him the deceased. "Please wait in the kitchen," he said, as if that was where I belonged. And when I didn't trot off fast enough to suit him he said, "Well? Do what I told you."

I wished Eberhardt were here; Eberhardt knew how to get under McFate's skin and deflate him. I hadn't figured out the knack yet. All I could think of was to tell him to take a handful of ground glass and pound it up his tailpipe. Instead I turned without saying anything and went into the kitchen. Antagonizing cops is a stupid thing for anyone to do, and that goes double if you happen to be a private investigator.

McFate kept me waiting fifteen minutes, most of which time I spent prowling the kitchen like a cat in a cage. Once I thought of going in to check on Mrs. Kiskadon, but I didn't do it; I did not want to see her until after I had talked to McFate, and not even then if I could avoid it. She was in the bedroom, or had been just before McFate's arrival. She had got up off the couch while I was telephoning and walked in there and laid down on the bed with the door open. The one time I'd looked in on her she had been lying on her back, stiff-bodied, eyes closed, hands stretched out tight against her sides, like an embalmed corpse that had been arranged for viewing.

I felt keyed up, twitchy. Lynn Kiskadon and her dead husband were on my mind, but other things were rumbling around in there too. Things that I was beginning to understand and things that didn't seem to want to jell yet. None of them was very pleasant, but then murder never is.

When McFate finally came in I didn't give him a chance to be supercilious. I said, "There are some things you ought to know," and proceeded to explain about Kiskadon and Harmon Crane and the rest of it. Then I told him what I suspected about Kiskadon's death. He'd have figured it out himself eventually—it was pretty obvious, really, once you had all the facts—but I didn't feel like waiting around for his wheels to start turning on their own initiative.

McFate looked at me the way an entomologist would look at a not very interesting bug. I looked right back at him, which was something I never enjoy doing. The son of a bitch is handsome on top of everything else: dark hair gray at the temples, precisely trimmed mustache, a cleft in his chin as big as a woman's navel. No wonder the ladies loved him—those of nondiscriminating taste, anyway. Hell, no wonder the *politicians* loved him.

He said, "You think it's a one-eight-seven? Why?"

One-eight-seven is police slang; Section 187 of

the California Penal Code pertains to willful homicide. "I didn't say that," I said.

"If his wife killed him, it's a one-eight-seven."

"I know that. But I didn't say I think she killed him. I said I think she's covering up. She knew he was dead long before we found him."

"I repeat: Why?"

"Three reasons. First, her actions today, the things she said to me on the phone and after I got here—they don't ring true. She said she didn't call her husband's doctor because she was too upset. She didn't call the police either. And she didn't try to get a friend or a neighbor to help her. Instead she left the house, drove down to Van Ness, and called me. Why? Because she wanted someone who knew how suicidal he'd been to find the body; she didn't want to admit that he was dead *before* she left here."

"Hardly conclusive," McFate said.

I said, "Then there's the gun."

"What about the gun?"

"It's under Kiskadon's chair. You saw that. If he shot himself, how did it get all the way under there?"

"It fell out of his hand and bounced on the carpet," McFate said. "If you remember, his right arm is hanging down near the floor."

"Leo," I said, and watched him wince. He hates for me to call him Leo; he would prefer that I call him Mr. McFate, or maybe just sir. "Leo, the gun is lying all the way under the chair, over on the *left* side. Even if it fell out of his hand, it's not likely that it could bounce more than a foot on a shag carpet."

He scrowled at me. "I suppose you deduce from that that Mrs. Kiskadon threw the weapon under the chair."

"She had something to do with it being there, yes. I can't say whether or not she threw it under the chair, or whether or not she actually shot him. But she was in the room when he died."

"And just how do you deduce *that?*"

"Her handbag, Leo. On the floor behind the desk with half its contents spilled out."

"I saw it," he said stiffly. "I assumed she dropped it when the two of you found the deceased."

"Uh-uh. She didn't have that bag or any other when I got here. Not in her car, not in her hand when she followed me in. She told me her husband had come out of the den earlier, waving the gun around, and then went back in there and locked the door; she didn't say *she'd* been in there, and she would have unless she had something to hide. And if she wasn't in the den, what was the purse doing in there? And why is it upended on the floor unless there was a struggle or something that led to the shooting?"

McFate didn't say anything. But he was thinking about it now. You didn't have to beat him over the head with logic—not too hard, anyhow.

"The car keys must have been in her coat pocket," I said. "Either that, or she scooped them up off the floor before she ran out. I guess you noticed that the door has a push-button lock. Kiskadon probably pushed the button when he went in there for the last time; all she did was shut the door on her way out, maybe without even realizing it. All she was interested in was getting away from here."

McFate said grudgingly, "If you're right, then she must have murdered him."

"Not necessarily. It could have been an accident—a struggle over the gun. Why don't you ask her?"

"I don't need you to tell me my job."

"God forfend I should ever try."

"Wait here," he said, and stalked out.

I waited, but not for long. I was even twitchier now and the kitchen seemed too small and too much of a reminder of the life the Kiskadons had shared before today, when what they shared became death. People were moving around out in the hall; I opened the door and looked out. The assistant coroner had arrived and Dwiggins was ushering him into the den. I came out of the kitchen and wandered down there, being careful not to get in anybody's way.

At an angle I could see part of the room, but not the part where the body lay. One of the lab men was down on his knees, poking among the splinters of wood that my forced entry had torn from the jamb. I watched him—and the thought came to me again that this was the way it had been thirty-five years ago, on the night Harmon Crane died. Man is shot in a locked office, door gets busted in, the cops come and poke around and clean up the remains. Some things don't change in thirty-five years; some things never change.

And who says lightning doesn't strike twice? It had struck twice in this case, one father and one son all those years apart, one suicide and one manslaughter. . . .

Twice, I thought.

Or *was* it one of each? Kiskadon's death had looked like a suicide but wasn't. Why not the same with Harmon Crane? Even with that locked door, the door that the police back then had said couldn't have been gimmicked—wasn't it possible Crane had been murdered after all?

*Twice*, I thought. Twice!

And I had it. At first, just the simple misdirection gimmick that had fooled the police and everyone else in 1949. But once I had that much, I began to see the rest of it, too: the distortions and subterfuge and misconceptions that had befuddled me, the full circumstances of Crane's death, the significance of that letter carbon, the probable reason Angelo Bertolucci had died and the name of the person who had murdered him. All of it exposed at last, dark and ugly, like those mildewing bones out on the rim of Tomales Bay.

I considered telling it to McFate, but that would have been like telling it to the wall. Besides, it wasn't his case; it was only peripherally related to Kiskadon's death. DeKalb was the man I wanted to tell it to. But not yet, not until I got some personal satisfaction first.

Before long McFate reappeared. I was still in the hallway, still twitchy because I wanted to be on my way. He showed me his scowl and said, "I thought I told you to wait in the kitchen."

"I had to go to the toilet. What did Mrs. Kiskadon say?"

". . . You were right," he said in reluctant tones. He was looking, now, at the top button on my jacket. "She admitted it."

"I thought she might. She isn't a very good liar."

"No, she isn't."

"She didn't murder him, did she?"

"An accident, she claims."

"It probably was," I said. "She's not the type to commit premeditated homicide."

McFate said with heavy sarcasm, "Thank you for your expert opinion."

"You're welcome. How did it happen?"

"Her husband spent the night in his den, just as she told you. She tried to talk him out this morning but he wouldn't come, not until about noon."

"And he was waving the gun around when he finally showed."

"Yes. He threatened to shoot himself and she told him to go ahead, she couldn't stand it any longer. Fed up, as she put it. He reentered the den and she followed him. She'd been about to go for a drive, just to get away for a while, which is why she was carrying her handbag."

"Uh-huh."

"Kiskadon sat at his desk. She tried to reason with him, but he wouldn't listen; he put the weapon to his temple and held it there with his finger on the trigger, saying he intended to fire."

"Uh-huh," I said again. "At which point she panicked and tried to take it away from him. They struggled, she dropped her handbag, and the gun went off."

"So she alleges."

"How did the gun get under his chair?"

"It fell on the desk after the discharge," McFate said. "She must have swept it off onto the floor; she doesn't remember that part of it very clearly."

I nodded. "Poor Kiskadon. If she'd left him alone, he probably wouldn't have gone through with it. Suicides don't make a production number out of what they're going to do, usually; they just do it."

"Really? You're an accredited psychologist as well as an expert in criminal behavior, I suppose."

"If you say so, Leo."

The scowl again. "I don't like you, you know that?"

"That's too bad. I think *you're* the cat's nuts."

"Are you trying to insult me?"

"Me? Heavens no. How's Mrs. Kiskadon?"

"Weepy," McFate said, and grimaced. He didn't like women to be weepy; he liked them to be a) cooperative, b) generous, and c) naked. "Dwiggins is calling a matron and her doctor."

"Are you going to book her?"

"Certainly."

"You could go a little easy on her. She's no saint, but she has had a rough time of it."

"You're trying to tell me my job again. I don't like that."

"Sorry. Is it all right if I leave now?"

"You'll have to sign a statement."

"I can do that later, down at the Hall."

"What's your hurry? You seem impatient."

"There's somebody I have to see."

"Oh? And who would that be?"

"A lady friend. You can understand that, can't you?"

"The redhead I met once? What's her name?"

"Kerry Wade. Yes."

"Attractive woman. I can't imagine what she sees in you."

"Neither can I. Look, Leo, can I leave or not?"

"Leave. I'm tired of looking at you." His superciliousness was back; he had resumed control of things. "Give my regards to Ms. Wade."

"I'll do that," I said. "She thinks you're the cat's nuts, too."

But it wasn't Kerry I was planning to see. It was Thomas J. Yankowski, the retired shyster, the prize son of a bitch.

Yank-'Em-Out Yankowski—murderer.

# ▸ TWENTY-ONE ◂

There was nobody home at Yankowski's house except for the snarling brute that guarded the place. It came flying at the sound of the bell, just as it had the first time I'd been here, and slammed into the door and then stood there growling its fool head off. I went back up the stairs and over to the street-level garage door and peered through the mail slot. Dark-shadowed emptiness looked back at me from within.

But if I could help it I wasn't going to go away from here empty-handed. I set out to canvass the neighbors, and I would have tried every house in this section of St. Francis Wood if it had been necessary. But it wasn't. The second one I went to, diagonally across the street from Yankowski's, produced just the kind of occupant I was looking for: a fat woman in her fifties, with hennaed hair and rouged cheeks, who minded other people's business along with her own and who didn't mind talking about it.

"Well, no, I *don't* know where Mr. Yankowski went today. Not *exactly*, that is." She was also the type who speaks in italics; emphasis was very important to her, so you'd be sure to take her meaning. "But he *might* be out at Fort Funston."

"Oh?"

"Yes. I happen to know he goes there on weekends. He likes to watch those young people with their gliders. *Hang* gliders, they call them. That's a very dangerous sport, don't you think? Hang gliding?"

"Yes, ma'am."

"He likes to walk along the cliffs too, Mr. Yankowski does. He's quite spry for a man of his years. I wish my *husband* were half so energetic—"

"Excuse me, ma'am. Can you tell me what kind of car Mr. Yankowski drives?"

"Car? Why, it's a Cadillac. Yes, *definitely* a Cadillac."

"Black, isn't it?"

"Oh yes. Black as a nigger's bottom," she said, and gave me a perfectly guileless smile.

I went away from her without another word.

Fort Funston is at the far southwestern edge of the city, off Skyline Boulevard above and beyond Lake Merced—a fifteen-minute drive from St. Francis Wood. Thre isn't much there except for the launching and landing area for hang-glider enthusiasts and close to a mile of footpaths along the cliffs overlooking the sea. One of the more scenic but undervisited sections of the Golden Gate National Recreation Area.

It was after five when I rolled in there, less than an hour before sunset, and only a scattering of cars was still parked in the big lot. The only people I saw were a trio of muscular young guys furling a glider and tying it to a rack across the top of an old Mustang. I spotted the black Cadillac immediately, parked over by the restrooms—the only one in the lot. I pulled alongside it and got out and looked at the license plate. One of the personalized ones: MR TJY. Yankowski's, all right. I went around to examine the driver's side.

Unscratched, undented. And gleaming with what had to be new paint. The whole damn *car* had been repainted.

He was a shrewd bastard, Mr. TJY. He'd had bodywork done on the Caddy right away, followed by the brand-new paint job, and I should have known that was what he'd do. Hide anything that might be incriminating and hide it quick. And no ordinary body shop—the type that keeps records and cooperates with the police—to do the work, either. He'd been a shyster for too many years not to pick up the name of somebody who would do repair work, sanding, and painting on the QT, for the right price.

And there, goddamn it, went the only solid piece of evidence linking Yankowski to the murder of Angelo Bertolucci.

I moved away from the Caddy, over to the main asphalt path that led out onto the cliffs. Sunset Trail, they called it, and it was an apt name: the sunset starting on the horizon now, in deep golds streaked with red, was quite a sight from up here. Just as impressive, from farther along, was the view you had of Ocean Beach all the way to the Cliff House in the hazy distance. Not so impressive, lying closer in, were the offshore dredgers and the long finger of the pipeline pier that were part of an endless city sewage project.

Irregular sandy paths branched off the main path, meandering through dark red and brown and green iceplant to the rim of the cliffs. A few people were out there, one of them with an easel set up, painting the sunset; none of them was old enough to be Yankowski. I stayed on Sunset Trail. I have a thing about heights, and the dropoff over there was sheer and at least two hundred feet to the strip of beach below.

Benches were strung out at intervals along the trail, and on one of them a fifth of a mile from the parking lot I found Yankowski. He was sitting there alone, nobody else within a hundred yards, watching the quicksilver shimmer of the dying sun on the water. The wind was strong and turning cold and I wasn't dressed warmly enough; goosebumps had spread up my arms and across my shoulders. But old Yank-'Em-Out was bundled up in a heavy mackinaw and gloves and a Scottish cap, and he looked as relaxed and comfortable as he had the day I'd talk to him in his own backyard.

He didn't pay any attention to me until I stopped in front of him, blocking his view, and said, "Hello Yankowski."

His frown was full of displeasure. "You again. I thought I told you I didn't want anything more to do with you."

"Yes? Well, you're going to have plenty more to do with me, Counselor. Starting right now."

"I am not," he said, and he got up and pushed past me and started back along Sunset Trail. At first I thought he was going to stay on it, which would have made bracing him easier for me; instead he veered off onto one of the sandy paths toward the cliff edge. I hesitated—I just don't like heights—but I went after him anyway, skirting scrub bushes and passing over tiny dunes like faceless heads with iceplant for hair.

Yankowski stopped a few feet from the edge, where the ground rose a little and then fell away sharply into an eroded declivity. I stopped too, but a couple of steps farther back and at an angle to him. Still, I was close enough to the edge so that I could look down part of the cliff face, see the surf licking at the beach far away at the bottom. The gooseflesh rippled on my arms and shoulders, a sensation that had nothing to do with the wind or the cold.

"Yankowski."

He turned. "Damn you, go away. Leave me alone."

"No, You're going to talk to me."

"Why should I?"

"Because I know you killed Angelo Bertolucci," I said. "And I know why."

He had a good poker face, from all his years in

court, but he couldn't keep his body from stiffening. His gloved hands hooked into fists—and then relaxed. He watched me silently out of dark, cold eyes that had no fear in them, only wariness and an animal cunning.

I said, "Well? Do we talk?"

"You talk," he said. "I'll listen."

"Sure, why not. I've got the whole thing figured out, starting with Harmon Crane. I'll tell you the way I think it was; you tell me if I'm right."

He pursed his lips and said nothing. Past him, the fiery rim of the sun was just fusing with the ocean; the swath it laid across the water was turning from silver to gold.

I said, "All right. Crane liked to get away from the city from time to time, to be alone for a week or two; he worked better that way. He liked the isolation of Tomales Bay and he rented a cabin up there from Angelo Bertolucci. Bertolucci didn't like Crane much, but he liked Crane's money. What Crane liked was Bertolucci's wife, Kate.

"I don't know how long he and Kate Bertolucci had been seeing each other, when or how it started. Doesn't matter. Doesn't matter either that they both had reasons for turning to each other, or what those reasons were. What's important is that they had an affair, and that Bertolucci found out about it.

"Bertolucci went to the cabin one day in late October of 1949, probably with the idea of catching his wife and Crane together. But she was there alone; Crane had gone to buy groceries. There was an argument; Bertolucci lost his head and clubbed her to death with a piece of stovewood. Then panic set in and he ran.

"Crane came back and found the body and *he* panicked. Instead of notifying the county sheriff, he cleaned up the blood and buried Kate's body in a fissure opened by an earthquake the day before. After which he packed up and beat it back to San Francisco. But the whole ugly business was too much for his conscience. Guilt began to eat at him. And paranoia: he was afraid Bertolucci might decide to come after *him* too. He started hitting the bottle; he didn't have the guts to do anything else, including confront Bertolucci.

"Six weeks or so went by and nothing happened except that Crane's mental condition kept getting worse. He thought about killing himself but he didn't have the guts for that either, not quite. He almost wished Bertolucci would come and do it for him."

I paused. "How am I doing so far, Yankowski?"

He stayed silent, unmoving. His eyes were small and black under the bill of his cap—little poison-drops of hate.

"So then came the night of December tenth," I said, "and Crane's death. But it wasn't suicide, the way everybody thought—the way I thought myself until this morning. That locked office was what threw all of us. The police had ruled out any gimmick work with the door and windows; it had to be suicide. Only it wasn't, it was murder."

Yankowski said, "And I suppose you think I murdered him."

"No. I think Bertolucci murdered him, just as Crane was afraid he might. And I think you covered it up for Bertolucci by making it look like a suicide."

"Now why would I do that?"

"Because you were in love with Amanda Crane and you didn't want Crane's affair and the rest of it to come out; you knew she was the fragile type and you were afraid of what the scandal might do to her. But you miscalculated, Yankowski. You did it all for nothing. Her mind wasn't even strong enough to withstand a suicide; she cracked up and never recovered. And you, the big Prince Charming, you abandoned her. You weren't about to saddle yourself with half a woman who needed constant care—not a fast-rising young shyster like you."

He said between his teeth, "You son of a bitch."

"Me? That's a laugh, coming from one as nasty as you."

His hands fisted again. He seemed to lean forward a little, shifting his weight. The hate in his eyes was as cold and black as death.

"Go ahead," I said, "try it. But *you'll* be the one who goes over the edge, not me. I've got forty pounds and fifteen years on you."

The tension stayed in him a couple of seconds longer; he glanced away from me, down the sandy cut to the cliff wall and the beach far below. Then he relaxed, not slowly but all at once. He liked living, Yank-'Em-Out did, and he wanted to hang on to the time he had left. I watched him regroup. You could almost see the internal shifting of gears, almost hear the click and whir of the shrewd little computer inside his head.

Pretty soon he said, "You think you know what happened at Crane's house that night? Go ahead, tell me."

I relaxed a little too, but I stayed wary. And I kept my feet spread and planted on the firmer footing of the iceplant. I said, "To begin with, Crane didn't telephone you and ask you to come to his house; it was the other way around. You went to see him at *your* initiative."

"Did I? Why?"

"Because he sent you a letter asking you to take care of Amanda if anything happened to him; he either knew or suspected how you felt about her. The letter mentioned suicide, too—he must have worked himself up to the point where he figured he could finally do it—and also hinted that he had a deep dark secret he couldn't tell anyone, least of all his wife. You're not the type to let a challenge like that go by. You went to his place to try to pry it out of him."

"How do you know about this alleged letter?"

"Crane kept a carbon of it. I found it among some papers of his."

"You claim it was addressed to me? That it has my name on it?"

I didn't lie to him; if his memory was good enough, he knew better. I didn't say anything. But

I was certain that the letter *had* been addressed to him; once the rest of it came clear, so had the meaning of the "Dear L" salutation. "L" wasn't the first letter of somebody's name. It was the first letter of Yankowski's profession. Dear L: Dear Lawyer.

Yankowski said, "It makes no difference either way. If such a letter exists, I submit it contains nothing incriminating to me and I deny ever receiving it."

"We'll see what the law has to say about that."

"The law," he said. Contempt bracketed the words. "Don't talk about the law to *me*, detective. The law is a tool, to be used and manipulated by those who understand it."

"What a sweet bastard you are."

We watched each other—the two old pit bulls, one of us with the stain of blood on his muzzle. The wind gusted, swirling particles of sand that stung my cheek. Out to sea, the bottom quarter of the sun had slid below the horizon. The surface in front of it looked as if it were on fire, the dredgers close to shore as if they were burned-out hulks that the flames had consumed before moving on.

"You want to hear the rest of it?" I said at length. "Just to prove to you I know what I'm talking about?"

"Go ahead. Talk. I'm listening."

"Bertolucci also picked the night of December tenth to pay a visit to Crane. Maybe he'd been watching the house; that would explain how he knew Crane was alone. He might have gone there with the intention of murdering Crane; he might only have wanted to talk to him, find out what he'd done with Kate's body. Still, he had to've taken the *potential* for another murder along with him. I figure that's one of the reasons he waited so long. He was scared and confused and no mental giant besides; it took time to nerve himself up.

"So Bertolucci went into the house. Probably walked right in; I was told Crane never locked the front door. He found Crane in his office, drunk as usual, trying to work up the last bit of nerve he needed to shoot himself; that twenty-two of his must have been out in plain sight. As drunk as Crane was, as much as he wanted to die, maybe he invited Bertolucci to shoot him, get it over with. Or maybe it was Bertolucci's idea when he saw the twenty-two. In any case Bertolucci had gotten away with his wife's murder up to then and he wanted to keep on getting away with it. So he used that twenty-two—put it up against the side of Crane's head and pulled the trigger.

"Enter Thomas J. Yankowski, servant of the people. Bertolucci might have shot you too; I wish to Christ he had. But it must have taken all his nerve to do the job on Crane. You got him calmed down, you got the full story out of him, you got him to trust you. Easy pickings for a glib young shyster. You told him you'd help him, gave him some kind of song and dance, then sent him on his way. And when he was gone you rigged the murder to look like suicide."

"Fascinating," he said. "How did I accomplish that?"

"Oh, you were smart. You didn't try anything fancy; you came up with a method so simple and clever everybody overlooked it. Until now. Until Michael Kiskadon got himself shot and killed in his den earlier today, under circumstances similar to what happened to his father. You didn't know about that, did you? Kiskadon's death?"

Yankowski was silent again.

"The first thing you did when you were alone with Crane's body that night was to type out the suicide note on his machine. But you wanted the phrasing to be just right—Crane's style, Crane's words, not yours. You'd brought along his letter to you and you realized that if you excerpted parts of it, it would make a perfect suicide note. So that's what you did: lifted sentences and partial sentences right out of the letter, changing nothing but the tenses here and there.

"I saw the text of the suicide note in the old newspaper accounts, early in the week. When I read the letter carbon something about it struck me as odd, but I couldn't put my finger on it until this morning, after I found Kiskadon. Then it came to me how similar the letter was to the suicide note, phrases like 'life terrifies me more than death.' Crane was in no shape that night to plagiarize himself, either consciously or unconsciously—not exact wording in the exact order he'd used in his letter to you. Somebody else *had* to have typed the suicide note. And that somebody had to be you."

"Why did it have to be me?"

"Because there's only one way the cover-up gimmick could have been worked, and the only man who could have worked it is the one who broke into the office later on, in the presence of Amanda Crane. You, Yankowski. Couldn't have been Adam Porter; his brother told me Adam was frail and frail men don't go busting in doors, not when there's a healthy young buck like you around. *You* broke into Crane's office that night. And not once—twice.

"That's the explanation in one word: twice. After you typed the suicide note you went out into the hall, shut the door behind you, locked it with the key, and broke it in so that there'd be evidence of forced entry. Then you put the key in the lock on the *inside* and shut the door again. No one could tell from the hallway that it had been forced.

"You left the house then, making sure you weren't seen, and waited around outside somewhere until Porter and Amanda returned home from dinner. At which point you pretended to have just arrived. When the three of you went upstairs to Crane's office, you grabbed the doorknob and pretended it was locked. 'We'd better break in,' you said. You threw your weight against the door, holding tight to the knob to provide some noise and resistance, and then let go and the door popped open. Porter and Amanda were too upset to notice anything amiss; and besides, there was plenty of evidence that there *had* been a forced entry. You also had Porter to verify to the police that the door was forced in his presence and that the key was in the lock on the inside."

Yankowski still didn't have anything to say. He looked away from me again, out to where a freighter, like a two-dimensional silhouette, seemed about to be engulfed by the shimmery fire on the horizon. The wind was even colder now. Distantly a foghorn sounded, spreading the news that fogbanks were lying out there somewhere and might soon be blowing in.

I said, "For thirty-five years you got away with it, you and Bertolucci. Ancient history, half-forgotten, and the two of you probably long out of touch. But then Kiskadon showed up. And I showed up. You weren't worried at first; you didn't figure I could dig deep enough after all that time to get at the truth. But my bet is you hunted up Bertolucci just the same, first to determine if he was still alive and then to warn him about me.

"My visit to Bertolucci on Wednesday didn't seem to unnerve him much; but when I found his wife's bones that same day—he read about it in the papers or heard about it somehow on Thursday—he got nervous and called you. You went up there to see him. With the intention of killing him to keep him quiet? No, probably not. But something happened when you got to his house, an argument of some kind: he was a crazy old coot and you're a mean bugger when you lose your temper. He probably waved that shotgun at you, and you took it away from him and let fly with both barrels.

"You didn't find out until later that it was my car you ran into when you were tearing out of there. If you needed any more reason to have the damage to your car fixed, that was it. Nice repair work, too; nice new paint job. But the authorities will find out who did the work for you."

"I doubt that," Yankowski said.

"Even if they don't, there'll be something else to tie you to Bertolucci and the murder."

"I also doubt that," he said, "since everything you've said is an outrageous tall tale." He seemed to have relaxed completely, to have regained his arrogant manner. The hate was still in his eyes, but it was shaded now by a thin veil of amusement. He took out one of his fat green cigars, turned his back to the wind, and managed to get the cigar fired with a gold butane lighter. When he faced me again he said, "You don't have a shred of proof to back up any of your allegations and you know it. You can't prove that I conspired with Angelo Bertolucci to cover up a murder in 1949. A letter addressed to me that happens to resemble Harmon Crane's suicide note is hardly evidence of any wrongdoing on my part. The police were satisfied that Crane's death was suicide; you have no legal grounds for reopening the case after all these years. You have no proof that I ever even met this man Bertolucci. You have no eyewitnesses who can identify me as being in or near his home on the night of his death. You have no physical evidence of any kind against me. You have noth-

ing, in short, except a great deal of fanciful speculation. Fiction, not fact."

"That isn't going to stop me from taking it to
the authorities," I said.

"Do as you like. But I warn you, detective. I'd
like nothing better than to instigate a lawsuit
against you for harassment and defamation of
character."

"And I warn *you*, Yankowski, you won't get
away with it this time. Not this time."

He smiled at me mirthlessly around his cigar.
"Won't I?" he said, and turned his back—a gesture
of contempt and dismissal—and walked a short
distance away. Stood there smoking and looking
out to sea, with his back still turned.

Frustration was sharp in me; he was right and I
knew it, and I hated him, too, in that moment, as
much as I have ever hated any man for his corrup-
tion. The hatred brought on an irrational impulse
to go over and give him a push, one little push
that would send him hurtling to his death. Immediately I swung around and went the other way,
back through the sand and iceplant to Sunset Trail
and along it to the parking lot.

I could never have done it, of course—pushed
him off that cliff, killed him in cold blood. It
would have made me just like him, it would have
turned my soul to slime. No, I could never have
done it.

But on the long drive home, thinking about him
standing up there so smug and sure, so goddamn
*safe*, I almost wished I had.

# · TWENTY-TWO ·

I did not call Sergeant DeKalb that night, although I considered it. What I had to say to him, the full story of Yankowski's guilt, was better dealt with in person. It could wait until the morning.

On Monday, before I drove up to San Rafael to see him, I stopped by the office to find out if there had been any weekend calls. And damned if Eberhardt wasn't already there, even though it was only ten past nine—making coffee and cussing the hot plate because it was taking too long to get hot.

"Surprise," I said as I shut the door. "The prodigal has returned."

"What the hell does that mean?"

"You haven't been around the past few days."

"Yeah, well, I took a long weekend. So what?"

"So nothing. But a lot of things have been happening."

"So I read in the papers. You can't keep your ass out of homicide cases, can you? One of these days somebody's going to shoot it off for you."

"Or part of it. Then I can be as half-assed as you."

"Is that supposed to be funny?"

"No, I guess not."

"I don't feel very comical today," he said.

"Neither do I."

"Then don't try to be funny." He smacked the hot plate with the heel of his hand. "Frigging thing takes forever to get hot," he said.

"Any calls on the machine? Or didn't you check it?"

"I checked it. No calls."

"Figures." Leaving my coat on, I went over and cocked a hip against my desk. "Where'd you go for the weekend?" I asked him.

"Up to the Delta."

"Fishing?"

"Yeah."

"Wanda go with you?"

Pause. Then he said, "No."

"I kind of figured she didn't."

"Yeah? Why?"

"She called me up Saturday night."

"What for?"

"To tell me she hated my guts. Kerry's too."

"Drunk?"

"Sounded that way. Eb, listen . . ."

"Shut up," he said. He put his back to me and went to his desk and sat down. Out came one of his pipes and his tobacco pouch; he began loading up, getting flakes of the smelly black shag he used all over his blotter.

Neither of us said anything for a while; we just sat there, Eberhardt thumbing tobacco into his pipe as if he were crushing ants, me listening to the coffee water start to boil on the hot plate.

He said finally, "What else she say on the phone?"

"She told me to go fuck myself."

"Yeah," he said. "Anything else?"

"No. I hung up on her."

"Nothing about us, then. Her and me."

"No. What about the two of you?"

"We broke it off," he said.

"Broke it off? You mean your engagement?"

"The whole thing. It's finished between us. Kaput."

That threw me a little; it was the kind of surprise that usually comes only on birthdays and Christmas. I said, "When did this happen?"

"Tuesday night. Big goddamn battle. I haven't seen her since and I won't either."

"What was the battle about?"

"What do you think?" he said. "She kept bad-mouthing you and Kerry. Drinking vodka like it was water and ranting like a crazy woman. Kept saying she was gonna get back at the two of you. Do something drastic, she said. Talk to one of her ex-husbands, get him to throw a scare into Kerry some night—shit like that."

"She'd better not go through with it."

"She won't. It was just crazy talk."

I said diplomatically, "Well, I guess she had a right to be upset."

"Upset, sure, but not out for blood. Not crazy. No damn right to act that way at all."

He defended us, I thought, Kerry and me. *That's* what the big blowup was all about.

"Made me look at her different," he said, "made me think maybe she wasn't the woman I figured she was. Made me compare her to Kerry, you want to know the truth." He looked away from me abruptly, out into the airshaft behind his desk. "Ahh," he said, "the hell with it. She's a bitch, that's all. I always did have a knack for picking bitches."

"Eb . . ."

"Look at Dana. First-class bitch."

Dana was his ex-wife and not nearly as bad as he tried to paint her. Maybe Wanda wasn't either— but I wouldn't have wanted to bet on it.

"Eb, why didn't you tell me this on Wednesday or Thursday?"

"Didn't feel like talking about it," he said. "I needed to get away for a few days, get her out of my system."

"And? She out of it now?"

"Not completely. But she will be. All I got to do is keep thinking about what she called me."

"What did she call you?"

"Never mind." He lit his pipe and puffed up enough smoke to make the office look and smell like a grass fire.

"Come on, Eb, what did she call you?"

"I said never mind. I don't want to talk about her anymore, all right?"

I let it drop. But a while later, as I was getting ready to leave for San Rafael, Eberhardt said out of the gray of his pipe smoke, "Tits aren't everything, for Christ's sake."

"What?"

"Tits. They're not everything."

"Uh, no, they're not."

"Man is attracted by more than that in a woman. Man looks for somebody he can be comfortable with, somebody he can *talk* to. You know what I mean?"

"Sure I do."

"She said I was a piss-poor excuse for a man because all I cared about were her tits. Said I was a baby—a tit wallower. How the hell do you like that?"

"The nerve of the woman," I said, straightfaced.

I managed to make it out of the door and over to the stairs before I burst out laughing.

Kerry laughed, too, when I told her about it that night. In fact, she thought "tit wallower" was the funniest expression she'd heard in *months*. She kept repeating it and then sailing off into whoops and snorts.

When she calmed down I said, "So now you're vindicated, lady."

"Vindicated?"

"The Great Spaghetti Assault. It was a damned stupid thing to do, but it got all the right results."

"Mmm," she said. Her eyes were bright with

reminiscence; she really did hate Wanda a lot. "And I'd do it again, too, if I got drunk enough."

"I'll bet you would."

"For Eberhardt's sake."

"Right."

"God, what a relief she's out of his life. The idea of having to attend their wedding gave me nightmares. She probably would have worn white, too."

"Probably."

"And Eberhardt would have been in a tuxedo. He'd have looked like a big bird, I'll bet. A black-winged, white-breasted tit wallower," she said and off she went into more whoops and snorts.

I sighed and picked up her empty wineglass and went into the kitchen to refill it. We were in her apartment tonight, because the weather was still good and the view from her living room window is slightly spectacular on clear nights. When I came back she had herself under control again. "I'll be good," she said when I handed her the wine.

"Uh-huh."

"No, I will. I'll be serious. You're in a serious mood tonight, aren't you?"

"More or less."

"Michael Kiskadon?"

"Yeah. He's been on my mind all day."

"Have you heard anything more about his wife?"

"Some. I talked to Jack Logan at the Hall; she's still in custody, still holding up all right."

"Is the D.A. going to prosecute her?"

"Probably not. She didn't murder her husband; all she did was try to cover up her part in the accident. Any competent lawyer could get her off without half trying."

"Lawyers," Kerry said, and made a face.

"Yeah."

"Yankowski—what about him? *He's* not going to get off, is he?"

"That's the way it looks," I said. "DeKalb went to see him today, after we talked, and he didn't get any further than I did. The law can't touch him for what he did in 1949. And there's just no proof that he killed Bertolucci. Unless DeKalb can find out who did the repair work and paint job on his Cadillac, there's nothing at all to tie him and Bertolucci together."

Kerry seemed to have grown as sobersided as I felt. She scowled into her wineglass. "It's not right," she said. "He's a cold-blooded murderer. He *can't* get away with it."

"Can't he? A lot of things aren't right in the world these days, babe. Who says there has to be justice?"

"I'd like to believe there is."

"So would I," I said. "But I'm afraid there isn't."

# ◂ EPILOGUE ▸

Well, maybe there is. Sometimes.

Eight days later, at 6:20 in the evening, Thomas J. Yankowski suffered a fatal heart attack while watching the news on TV. He didn't die immediately; he died forty minutes later, in an ambulance on the way to Mission Emergency Hospital. He had a history of heart trouble—he'd had a mild attack a few years ago, as Eberhardt had mentioned to me—but I like to think the seizure was the direct result of the stress and strain of having committed one crime too many. I also like to think he was coherent during the last forty minutes of his life, that he believed the attack was punishment for his sins and perhaps he faced an even greater punishment to come.

Not that any of that matters, of course. What matters is the simple fact that he was dead, just as Kate Bertolucci and Harmon Crane and Angelo Bertolucci and Michael Kiskadon were dead; and now the pathetic little drama they had enacted was all over. Ashes to ashes, dust to dust. A few insignificant bones scattered and lost in the graveyard of time.

It makes you wonder. Sometimes there is jus-

tice, yes. But does *that* matter, either, in the larger
scheme of things—whatever that scheme may be?

Maybe it does.

Like love, like compassion and caring and
friendship—maybe it does.

*Turn this book over*
*for more mystery*
*and adventure with*

THE "NAMELESS DETECTIVE"

This one is for the memory of *Black Mask, Blue Book, Golden Fleece, Green Ghost Detective, Red Star Mystery,* and all the other magazines of the colorful pulp era.

# LABYRINTH

◆

THE VANISHED

## ○ **ONE** ○

The dead girl lay in a twisted sprawl, like something broken and carelessly discarded, among the reeds and bushes that grew along the edge of Lake Merced.

I could see her from where I stood alone on the embankment thirty feet above, and I could watch the movements of the half-dozen Homicide cops and forensic people who were down there with her. One of the cops was Eberhardt. He knew I was waiting up here, but he had not paid any attention to me since my arrival a couple of minutes ago; he wasn't ready yet to tell me why I had been summoned out of a sound sleep at seven A.M. to the place where a young girl had died.

It was a cold gray Wednesday morning in November, and the wind blowing in across Skyline carried the heavy smells of salt and rain. Pockets of mist clung to the reeds and trees and underbrush around the lake shore, giving the concrete pedestrian causeway at the south end an oddly insubstantial look, like an optical illusion. The

whole area seemed desolate at this hour, but that was illusion too: Lake Merced sits in the southwestern corner of San Francisco, not far from the ocean, and is surrounded by public and private golf courses, upper- and middle-class residential areas, San Francisco State College, and the Fleishhacker Zoo.

It had been awhile since my last trip out here. But when I was on the cops a number of years ago I had come to the lake at least once a month, sometimes with Eberhardt, because the police pistol range was nearby to the west. Another inspector had had a small sailboat in those days, moored over at the Harding Boat House, and if the weather was good the three of us would take it out on Saturdays or Sundays. Lake Merced is bigger than you would expect an in-city body of water to be, and because of its location, removed from the tourist areas downtown and along the Bay, it's a recreation area pretty much reserved for the natives.

Behind me I heard another vehicle come wheeling in off Lake Merced Boulevard. I turned, saw that it was a city ambulance, and watched it maneuver to a stop among the blue-and-whites and unmarked police sedans—and my car—that were strewn across the wide dirt parking area opposite Brotherhood Way. Two attendants in white uniforms got out and opened up the rear doors. While they were doing that, a coroner's car swung in and joined the pack; the guy who

stepped out of it, carrying a medical bag, came over and stopped beside me.

"Where is it?" he said, as if he were asking about a tree stump or a piece of machinery. He seemed to think I was one of the Homicide inspectors. "Down there?"

"Yeah," I said. "Down there."

"Sorry I'm late." But he did not sound sorry; he only sounded aggrieved. "Goddamn car wouldn't start."

I had nothing to say to that. He shrugged, pulled a face, gave me a short nod, and began to make his way down to where the dead girl was.

I looked away again. The knots of people along the bicycle paths that flanked the parking area—college kids from S.F. State, residents of the lakeview townhouses down the way, reporters and TV-remote crews—seemed to be getting larger; cars crawled along Lake Merced Boulevard, filled with eager gawking faces. Ghouls, all of them. There were half a dozen uniformed patrolmen working crowd control in the area, but the cops knew and I knew that the crowds would not be dispersed until after the body was taken away.

The cold bite of the wind was making my eyes water. I rubbed at them with the back of one hand, reburied the hand in my topcoat pocket, and bunched the material tight around me. Filaments of black, like veins, had started to form in the overcast sky; we were going to have rain pretty soon. I considered waiting inside my car, where I

could use the heater to chase some of the morning chill—but before I could make up my mind to do that, Eberhardt's voice called my name from below.

I stepped back to the edge of the embankment and saw him peering up at me, beckoning. "Okay," he said, "you can come on down."

So I let out a breath and picked my way along the slope, using the vegetation there to keep my balance on the wet grass. When I got to where Eberhardt was, he turned without saying anything and led me to the girl's body.

"Take a look," he said then, "tell me if you recognize her."

She was lying on her stomach, but her head was canted around so that most of her face was visible toward the lake. There was one hole on the left side of her forehead, black-edged and caked with dried blood, and a second just below the collarbone. Shot twice, with what was probably a small caliber weapon judging from the size of the entry wounds and because there did not seem to be any exit wounds. She had been young, maybe still in her teens, and she had been attractive; you could tell that even with her features blanked and frozen in death. Long dark hair, pug nose, sprinkling of freckles across her cheekbones. Wearing a suede coat, tennis shoes, jeans, and one of those football-type jerseys, red and white, with the number forty-nine on it.

I had never seen her before.

My stomach coiled up as I looked at her. After a couple of seconds I swung around and stood staring out over the wind-wrinkled surface of the lake. I had seen death before—too much death, too many bodies torn and ravaged by violence—but each time was like the first: a hollow feeling under the breastbone, the taste of bile, a sense of sadness and awe. I had never learned to inure myself to it, never become jaded or detached enough, the way some cops did, to treat it as an abstract.

But this time I felt something else, too—a kind of dull empty rage. A young girl like that, robbed of life before she had much of a chance to live it. Why? Where was the sense in such a brutal act? No matter what she might have done to someone, no matter what she might have been, she could not have deserved to die this way.

Beside me Eberhardt said, "Well?" His voice was sharp and gruff, and I knew him well enough after thirty years to understand that the girl's death had touched him too.

I shook my head. "I don't know her, Eb."

"You sure?"

"I'm sure."

"All right. We'll talk up top. I'm finished here."

He asked the assistant coroner if he could release the body, got an affirmative nod, and the two of us climbed back up to the parking area. I watched him gesture to the ambulance attendants and then take out one of his flame-blackened briar

pipes and clamp it between his teeth. He was my age, fifty-two, and an odd contrast of sharp angles and smooth blunt planes: square forehead, sharp nose and chin, thick and blocky upper body, long legs and angular hands. His usual expression was one of sourness and cynicism—a false reflection of what he was like inside—but now his face had a dark, brooding cast. I wondered if he were thinking about his niece, the one who was not much older than the dead girl by the lake.

When the ambulance attendants came past us with the stretcher and disappeared below, Eberhardt said to me, "Her name was Christine Webster. Mean anything to you?"

"No."

"We found her purse in one of those bushes on the slope," he said. "Address on her driver's license is Edgewood Avenue, up by the U.C. Med Center. She was twenty years old and a student at S.F. State; student I.D. card in her wallet, along with the license."

"None of that rings any bells," I said.

"You working on anything connected with the college?"

"No. I'm not working on anything at all right now."

"You know anybody up around the Med Center?"

"I don't think so, no. Look, Eb—"

"Not much else in her purse. Except one thing."

"What thing?"

"One of your business cards," he said.

"So that's it."

"That's it. Kind of funny for a girl that young to be carrying around a private eye's business card, don't you think?"

"I think. Christ."

"But you're positive you never saw or heard from her?"

"I'd remember if I had."

"What about phone calls or letters from unidentified women. Anything like that recently?"

"No. I'm sorry, no."

"You hand out many of those cards?"

"A fair amount, sure," I said. "Insurance companies, lawyers, bail bondsmen, skip-trace clients, friends, casual acquaintances—hell, I must have distributed a thousand or more over the past few years."

There were sounds on the slope behind us, and we both turned to look as the ambulance attendants struggled up with the stretcher. When they got to the top and started past us, a ripple of movement and sound passed through the watchers along Lake Merced Boulevard. You could almost see them all leaning forward for a better look, even though the shell of Christine Webster was just a small shapeless mound beneath the sheet and restraining straps.

Eberhardt said, "Bastards."

"Yeah."

He got a little box of wooden matches out of his

pocket, hunched over to shield his hands from the wind, and used four of the matches to get his pipe lighted. "Okay," he said then. "She picked up your card somehow, and maybe she was planning to contact you, but for whatever reason she never did. The point is, is there a connection between that and her death?"

I had been wondering the same thing. The idea of it bothered me; I had not known the girl existed until this morning, when she no longer did exist, and yet the fact that she'd had my business card was a thread linking her life and mine. If there was a connection, and if she *had* come to me about her problem, could I have done anything to prevent her murder? But that kind of thinking never got you anywhere. I had allowed myself to indulge in it in the past and I had promised myself, for a number of reasons, that I was not going to do it anymore.

For the sake of argument I said, "It could be she had the card as a gag. You know, the way kids do—flash it on her friends, make up some kind of story to go with it."

"Maybe."

I stared over at where the attendants were loading her body into the ambulance. "Could it have been robbery?" I asked. "Or attempted rape?"

"It wasn't robbery," Eberhardt said. "There're thirty-three dollars in her wallet and a gold engagement ring on one of her fingers. And it doesn't

figure to be rape; she wasn't molested or otherwise abused."

"Street shooting?"

"Possible but not likely. She lived way the hell
up on Edgewood, and with Thanksgiving coming
up there won't be any night classes at the college
for the next couple of weeks. Seems doubtful
she'd have been wandering around here alone at
night. Coroner's rough estimate as to time of
death is between nine P.M. and midnight."

"She could have been killed somewhere else," I
said. "Or picked up somewhere else and forced
into a car and brought here."

"Uh-uh. See that old blue Mustang down at the
end there? Belongs to Christine Webster. Lab boys
have been over it already; no bloodstains or anything else that figures to be important. The way it
looks, she either drove here to meet someone or
came willingly with the person who shot her."

"Anything in the area that might point to the
killer?"

"Nothing. She was shot at close range with a
small caliber handgun—.25 or .32, probably. Then
she either fell down the slope or was rolled down
it after she was dead. College kid out jogging at
six-thirty spotted the body and called us. That's
all we know for sure so far."

The ambulance started up and eased out onto
the street. The rubberneckers all turned to watch
it fade out of sight toward the campus. End of

show. They began to drift away singly and in small groups.

Eberhardt said, "So that's that for now. You can take off, *paisan*. I'll let you know if we turn up anything definite."

"Do that, huh? A thing like this . . ."

"Yeah, I know," he said. "Go on, get out of here. I'll be in touch."

I went over to my car and managed to get inside and away from there without being hassled by the media types that were still hanging around. The sky had grown darker; droplets of rain began to spatter against the windshield. I could still feel the chill of the wind and I turned the heater up as high as it would go.

Twenty years old, I thought, and somebody shot her dead. My business card in her purse and somebody shot her dead.

I stayed cold all the way downtown.

# ∘ TWO ∘

It was after nine when I reached the Tenderloin
and parked my car in the Taylor and Eddy lot, not
far from where I have my office. I thought about
going into a nearby greasy spoon for some breakfast, but I had no appetite; the image of the dead
girl was still sharp in my mind. Instead I locked
the car and hustled straight up the hill on Taylor.

The rain kept on coming down, alternating between a drizzle and a fine mist, and the wind was
gusty enough to slap the coattails around my legs.
At this hour and in this weather the streets were
pretty much empty. The dark wet sky made them
and the old buildings look dingier and more un-
appealing than usual. Even the faint pervading
smell of garbage seemed stronger.

The Tenderloin used to be, and on the surface
still was, a section of lunchrooms and seedy bars
and secondhand bookstores; of low-rent apartment buildings and cheap hotels inhabited by
transients, senior citizens with small pensions,
nonviolent drifters, and the Runyonesque street

characters that were as much an institution in
San Francisco as they once were in New York. It
used to have character, the way Broadway-Times
Square did in the old days, and you could walk its
streets in relative safety. But in the past couple of
decades it had changed—had lost all of its flavor
and taken on instead a kind of desperate sleazi-
ness. The transients and senior citizens were still
there, but the street characters had been replaced
by drug addicts and drug pushers, small-time
thugs, fancy-dressed pimps and hard-eyed whores.
You walked on Eddy or Mason or Turk or lower
Taylor these days, and you saw porno bookstores
and movie houses spread out like garish weeds;
you saw men and women openly buying and selling smack, coke, any other kind of drug you can
name; you saw spaced-out kids, drunks sleeping
it off in doorways, elderly people with frightened
eyes watchful for purse-snatchers and muggers
because the Tenderloin has the highest crime rate
in the city.

I asked myself again why I didn't, for Christ's
sake, move my office to a better neighborhood.
Business had not been all that good recently, and
maybe part of the reason was my location. Who
wants to put his trust in a private investigator
with an office on the fringe of the Tenderloin?

Moving made good sense—but the problem was,
I couldn't really afford to move. The rent in my
building was reasonable enough, even though the
landlord was making noises about kicking it up

again; the price of an office in a more respectable
area was beyond my means. Besides which, I had
occupied this one ever since I left the cops and
went out on my own fourteen years ago; I liked it
there, I felt comfortable there.

So I was not going to move and that was that.
Just keep on toughing it out, I told myself. Hell,
you've had plenty of practice at toughing things
out, right? Particularly in the past year and a half.

When I entered my building and started across
to the elevator I noticed the white of an envelope
showing inside my mailbox. There were envelopes
inside all the other boxes, too. Uh-oh, I thought,
because it was too early for the mail; and there
was only one other person with access to the
boxes. I opened mine up and took out the envelope: my name hand-written on the front, the
building owner's name and address rubber-
stamped in the upper left-hand corner. Greetings
from your friendly landlord.

I said something under my breath, stuffed the
envelope into my coat pocket, and took the elevator up to the third floor. My office was cold; and
it still seemed to retain the faint smell of stale
cigarettes. I had not smoked a cigarette in seven-
teen months, ever since finding out about the
lesion on my left lung, but I had averaged two
packs a day before that. Maybe the walls and
furnishings had permanently absorbed the smoke
odor. But probably it was just a ghost smell—a
similar kind of thing to the imagined sensations

an amputee feels once he has lost an arm or a leg. When you live with something for most or all of your life you never quite adjust to the fact that it's gone.

The first thing I did was to check my answering machine. Up until the beginning of this year, I had subscribed to a regular service; but then inflation had forced them to raise their rates, and that in turn had forced me to go out and buy the machine. It was something I should have done years ago, maybe, except that I had an old-fashioned outlook on the conventions of the private detecting business—I supposed because I identified strongly with the fictional eyes and cops in the pulp magazines I had read and collected for more than thirty years. I had always wanted to emulate the Spades and Marlowes and Race Williamses, and if that was childish and self-deluding, as a woman named Erika Coates had once claimed, then so be it. It was my life and the only person I had to justify my feelings to was myself.

I did not expect to find anything on the machine: I list my home number on my cards and in the phone book in case anybody decides on the weekend that he needs a private investigator, reasonable rates, strict confidence at all times. But I had had at least one call because the little window on one corner had a round white spot in it. I worked the controls and listened to my voice play back the message I had recorded. Then a woman's businesslike voice said, "Yes, this is Mrs. Laura

Nichols. Would you please call me as soon as possible?" She gave a number, repeated it—and that was all.

I wrote the name and number down on the pad. Then I went over and fiddled with the steam radiator until the pipes began banging and thumping. Took my coffeepot into the alcove, emptied out the dregs of last Friday's coffee, filled it with fresh water from the sink tap in there, and put it on the hotplate to heat. Morning ritual.

Sitting at the desk, I opened the letter from my landlord. It said what I expected: my rent was being raised thirty dollars a month, effective December 1. No explanation, no apology. Nice. Some time ago the California voters had passed the Jarvis-Gann tax-reform initiative, Proposition 13, which gave property owners a 60 percent tax cut per annum; and ever since the governor had made a lot of noise about owners passing on some of that savings to renters. Result: a thirty-dollar increase on an office in the goddamn Tenderloin.

I threw the letter into the wastebasket. The thing with Christine Webster and my business card had already made it a lousy Monday; this was just the icing. Well, maybe Mrs. Laura Nichols, whoever she was, had something positive to offer. Like a job. I had not worked at anything in five days and I needed both the activity and the money.

So I pulled the phone over, dialed the number I

had written down. While I waited I sat looking at the poster blow-up of a 1932 *Black Mask* cover that I had tacked up on one wall. It was not exactly appropriate for a business office, but I liked it and that was what counted. Eberhardt, on one of his infrequent visits here, had said that it made the place look like something out of an old Bogart movie. Me and Bogie and Sam Spade—

The same businesslike female voice said hello in my ear. I asked, "Mrs. Nichols?" and she said yes and I identified myself.

"Oh, yes—good. Thank you for calling."

"How can I help you, Mrs. Nichols?"

"Are you free to accept a confidential job? It would be on a full-time basis for at least two weeks."

"Yes, ma'am. Depending on what it involves, of course."

"It's a rather delicate family matter, concerning my brother. I'd prefer not to discuss the details on the phone, but it isn't anything unseemly. We can discuss it at my home, if you don't mind driving out. I'm sure it will be worth your time."

"When would you like me to come?"

"As soon as possible," she said. "The address is 2519 Twenty-Fifth Avenue North. In Sea Cliff."

I raised an eyebrow. Sea Cliff is a synonym for money in San Francisco; you don't live there unless your yearly income is around six figures. "I can be there within the hour," I said.

"Fine. I'll expect you."

She rang off, and I cradled the handset, gazing

again at the *Black Mask* poster. Full-time job for at least two weeks, working for a lady in Sea Cliff? It was the kind of thing that always happened to the pulp private eyes, but that happened to me about as often as a woman who said "yes" on the first date. So there figured to be a catch in it somewhere that I was not going to like. The last time I had worked for a rich client—one of the few times in my career—I had wound up in the hospital with a knife wound in my belly. I still had the scars, one you could see and one you couldn't.

But then, why expect the worst? Maybe it was all going to be fine; maybe for a change I was going to get a break. I stood up and poured myself a quick cup of coffee. Then I locked the office and went down and out to pick up my car.

# ° THREE °

Twenty-five nineteen Twenty-Fifth Avenue North turned out to be a massive beige stucco house separated from its neighbors by a lot of bright green lawn. Its architecture was so old-California Spanish that it looked as if it belonged in Los Angeles instead of San Francisco: red-tile roof, decorative wrought-iron balconies framing all of the windows, front portico with a black-beam archway, wall patterns here and there done in four colors of mosaic tile. There were even mosaic tile inlays in the series of terraced steps that led up from the street.

I parked in front and climbed the steps. The rain had stopped, but the morning was still damp and dismal-gray with overcast; the wind here was blustery, knife-edged. Behind and on both sides of the house you could see the broad choppy sweep of the ocean and the entrance to the Bay, and through the low clouds the towers of the Golden Gate Bridge, the brown hills of Marin, the cliffs at Land's End. The view would be spectacular on a

clear day, which was what made the Sea Cliff area prime real estate; even now it was pretty impressive.

A big brass knocker shaped like a lion's head sat in the center of the front door, but I found a doorbell button and used that instead. Chimes sounded faintly inside, faded to silence. Another ten seconds went by before a peephole above the knocker opened and an amber-colored eye peered out at me. A woman's voice, different from the one on the phone, said "Yes?" in the tone people use on door-to-door salesmen.

I gave my name and added that Mrs. Nichols was expecting me.

Pause. "You're that private detective."

"Yes, that's right."

Another pause. Then the voice said, "Just a moment," and there was the scraping of a lock, the door opened, and I was looking at a tall slender woman in her early twenties. She had fine, pale-blonde hair cut short in the style we used to call shag and a pale sensitive face dominated by high cheekbones. The amber eyes were wide and striking. She wore one of those long button-down skirts that are supposed to be popular now, a white blouse and a little black knit vest.

"Come in, please."

I went in. She shut the door, locked it again, waited for me to give her my coat, and then hung it away in a closet—all without smiling, speaking, or even looking at me. We went down a dark hall

and through another of those Spanish archways
into a living room. The floors were tiled and
carpetless; my heels clicked so loudly that it
made me a little self-conscious, the kind of feeling
you get when you walk through a church or
maybe a museum.

The young woman gestured to a large bulky
sofa. "I'll tell my mother you're here," she said.

"Thank you."

She went away through the arch. I sat on the
sofa with my hat on my knees and looked at the
room. The Spanish effect seemed overdone, as if
the people who lived here were trying too hard to
create an atmosphere of old-world gentility. The
antique furniture included a refectory table, a
pigeonhole desk, several big chairs with flat wood
arms and bare wood backs; a massive rococo chan-
delier hung from the ceiling. On the far side a set
of narrow glass doors gave access to a patio that
had a mosaic tile floor and a lot of bushes and
plants growing out of brown urns. It was all dark
and ponderous, a little depressing. There was not
much color anywhere; even the old paintings on
the walls were somber-hued. About the only modern things in the room were a stereo unit and a
typewriter on the desk, and they seemed out of
place.

I sat there for about two minutes. There was no
sound anywhere, not even the ticking of a clock.
Then I heard steps on the hall tiles, and got on
my feet as a large handsome woman in her late

forties or early fifties appeared at the arch. She came through it like a stockholder entering a board room: poised, purposeful, self-assured. A tailored green pants suit set off carefully coiffed blonde hair and the same amber eyes as her daughter, just a little darker under long curling lashes. There was a diamond as big as a grape on the ring finger of her left hand.

No smile from her either. She said, "I'm Laura Nichols," and offered me her hand, then shook mine in the same businesslike way. Her eyes went over me in frank appraisal, but there was nothing in them or on her face to tell what sort of impression she was getting. She asked me to sit down, and when I did she went over and arranged herself in one of the heavy wooden chairs.

"Would you care for coffee? Tea?"

"Thanks, no."

She nodded as if she approved of my answer. "Then I'll get directly to the point," she said. Her enunciation was careful and precise; I had the feeling that everything she did would be with care and precision. "I've asked you here because of my brother, Martin Talbot. He's had a very unfortunate experience, you see."

"Oh?"

"Yes. Two nights ago, while he was driving back from a Los Angeles business trip, he fell asleep at the wheel of his car near South San Francisco. The car veered into another lane, struck another car, and caused it to spin into an overpass abut-

ment. Martin wasn't hurt, miraculously enough, but one of the two people in the other car was killed."

A very unfortunate experience, she'd said. That was some way of putting it.

Mrs. Nichols went on. "The driver of the second car, a man named Victor Carding, also escaped serious injury; it was his wife who died. Later, in the hospital, my brother insisted on seeing Carding and spoke to him alone for a minute or two. During that time the man called Martin a murderer, threatened his life, and then tried to attack him. Two interns came in and restrained him just in time."

"You're afraid Carding might try to carry out his threat—is that it?"

"Yes. He's due to be released from the hospital today."

"Have you talked to the police?"

"Of course. As soon as Martin told me."

"And?"

"They seem to feel there's nothing to worry about. When they spoke to Carding he told them he couldn't remember threatening Martin or trying to attack him. He claims not to hold my brother responsible for what happened."

"Well, that's probably the case," I said. "People do and say things in shock and grief that they don't really mean."

"Perhaps. But we can't be certain of that. Carding is a construction worker, a common laborer;

there's no telling what a man like that is capable of."

*Common laborer*, I thought. Why do people like her always use the word "common" as if there was some social stigma attached to being a blue collar worker? Christ, we're *all* laborers of one kind or another.

I said, "What does your brother think?"

"That Carding would be justified if he chose to seek revenge."

"I'm not sure I follow that, Mrs. Nichols."

"You would have to know my brother to fully understand," she said. "He's an unusual man."

"In what way?"

"In many ways. Our father was a banker, quite well-to-do, and when he passed on he left Martin and me a substantial sum of money. Martin refused to accept his share of the estate; it was his belief that he had no right to the inheritance because he hadn't earned the money himself. He worked his way through college, received a degree in electrical engineering, and proceeded to follow his own path in life. He has been moderately successful, I'll admit—"

She broke off because her daughter, silent as a wraith, had appeared in the archway. Mrs. Nichols gave her a somewhat annoyed glance and said, "What is it, Karen?"

"Do you mind if I come in?"

"I'm discussing a business matter, dear."

"Yes—with a private detective. About Uncle

Martin. I've a right to know what you're planning, why you want a detective."

Mrs. Nichols pursed her lips and looked at me. The look said that children really could be difficult at times, couldn't they? I kept my expression stoic and attentive; I had no opinion on the subject of children. And none I cared to show about a mother who appeared to think of her twenty-odd-year-old daughter as a child.

"Oh, all right," she said to Karen. "Come in, if you must. You won't leave me alone, I suppose, until you do find out."

The girl came inside and sat on one of the chairs at the refectory table—with her knees clasped together and her posture erect and her hands folded in her lap. I wondered if there were still such things as finishing schools. If so, Karen had no doubt been sent to one—whether she wanted to attend or not.

All of Mrs. Nichols' attention settled on me again. She said, "As I was about to say, my brother is also the most moral man I have ever known. He lives by the strictest code of behavior imaginable; what is right is right, what is wrong is wrong, and there are absolutely no gray areas or extenuating circumstances. I'm sure that's why he's still a bachelor at forty-four; he simply never found a woman who measured up to his standards."

I said, "He feels guilt over the accident, then?"

"That is an understatement. He has barely slept since it happened, eaten almost nothing, and

hasn't gone back to his job or even left his house except for short walks around the neighborhood. He considers himself to be just what Carding called him: a murderer. His 'negligence'—his word, not mine—caused the death of another human being. He even expressed the desire to stand trial for manslaughter; thank God that isn't legally possible. The point is, if Victor Carding attempted to harm him, I doubt Martin would try to prevent it. He is altogether on Carding's side on the matter, if you see what I mean."

"Yes," I said, "I see what you mean."

"In view of that, it's my duty to have him protected. That's why I called you."

I frowned at her. "You want me to act as his bodyguard?"

"Essentially, yes."

"Why would he consent, feeling as he does?"

"He wouldn't, if he knew about it."

"*If* he knew about it?"

"Martin lives across the street from Stern Grove; you can see his house from inside the park, front and back. What I want you to do is watch the house for any sign of Carding and also to follow Martin whenever he goes out walking. He's a compulsive walker, you see; and of course he refuses to ever drive a car again."

I knew there'd be a catch, I thought. Damn, I knew it.

I shifted on my chair. I had been offered a lot of different jobs over the years, not a few of them of

the screwball variety, but this was something new out of left field. Bodyguard-from-a-distance. Christ. People get the damnedest ideas into their heads.

Karen apparently had a similar reaction. She said, "I don't think that's a very good idea, mother."

"Don't you, now?"

"No. Victor Carding isn't going to come after Uncle Martin; I don't believe that. But even if he did, what could this man do about it?"

"I'm afraid your daughter's right, Mrs. Nichols," I said. "Carding could just ring the doorbell and attack your brother when he answers; there wouldn't be time enough for me to stop him. Or he could let Carding inside, of his own free will. In that case I couldn't just break in—not without a hundred-percent certainty that an attempted murder was about to take place. I'm a private investigator, not a police officer. I don't have any more rights than you or any other private citizen."

"Don't you suppose I'm aware of all that?" Mrs. Nichols said. Her voice was cool, almost patronizing, as if she felt now that she was dealing with a pair of "children" instead of just one. "But there *might* be something you could do. You *might* be able to prevent another tragedy. If no one watches over Martin, then no one can prevent anything from happening in an emergency."

She more or less had a point. But I said, "You'd

want me to keep this watch on your brother for at least two weeks?"

"Yes. If nothing were to happen in that time, I would feel satisfied that Carding's threat was meaningless."

"Would you want a full twenty-four-hour vigil?"

"Certainly."

"That's a three-man job," I said. "I'd have to hire two other operatives and pay them full salary."

Karen said, "You know what he's saying, don't you, mother? It would cost a small fortune—"

"I know what it will cost." There was frost in the lady's voice now; she did not like to be argued with. "The expense is of little importance. Your uncle's safety is all that matters."

"I still don't think it's a good idea—"

"I don't care *what* you think, young woman. And I'll thank you to be quiet from now on or else leave the room."

Karen glanced at me, looked back at her mother, and then lowered her eyes to her folded hands. I thought I saw her lips form words, thought I recognized what they were; but it was difficult to be sure with her head bowed and the lighting in there. If I was right, though, the words explained a good deal about her side of this mother-daughter relationship.

What she seemed to say was, "Stubborn old bitch."

Mrs. Nichols asked me, "Do you have any more questions or observations?"

"No, I don't think so."

"Well, then? Will you accept the job?"

I thought it over. It was screwball, all right. Judging from what she had told me about Martin Talbot, he needed the services of a psychiatrist a lot more than those of a private detective. But if the surveillance did last at least two weeks, the kind of money involved would pay my groceries, the rent on my flat, and the just-raised rent on my office for the next few months. You can turn down a prospective client when there's a question of ethics; but when you're dealing with sensitivities, and when you have to worry about making ends meet, it's no damned contest at all.

"Yes, ma'am," I said. "I'll accept the job."

# ° FOUR °

Martin Talbot's house was located on the corner of Twenty-first Avenue and Wawona, directly across from the north-side entrance to Stern Grove—a fourteen-block-long park and recreation area on the west side of the city, a mile or so from San Francisco State College and Lake Merced. It was a modest stucco affair, boxy-looking, painted white with a red tile roof, that stood shoulder-to-shoulder with its immediate neighbors. In front were a tiny patch of trimmed lawn, a brick staircase, a built-in garage under what would probably be the living room windows. Behind the house was a tiny fenced yard; you would be able to see the side gate and at least part of the rear porch from within the park.

It was after two o'clock when I got there. I parked my car on Wawona, facing east, and entered the park through the gate in its cyclone border fence. The rain had not started up again, but it was in the air and in the bite of the wind. Nobody else was out and around that I could see;

the rolling lawns, the kid-sized soccer field, the short driving range for golfers to practice their chip shots, the sunken putting green, all looked deserted.

There were no benches to sit on, but in this weather it would not have mattered if there had been; it was too damned cold to sit out in the open. I wandered around for a time on the wet grass, to refamiliarize myself with the landscape and to see how far I could go east and west and still have a clear view of Talbot's house. Cars drifted by now and then and there was a steady whisper-and-rumble of traffic over on Nineteenth Avenue; otherwise it was a pretty quiet area. You could even hear water dripping off the eucalyptus and other trees that lined the north rim of Stern Grove's deep, wide central grotto.

When my nose and ears began to burn I went back out to sit in the car. What I wanted more than anything right then was some hot coffee. I wished I had thought to buy a thermos and fill it from the pot in my office; I had driven there after leaving Sea Cliff, to make some calls and check my answering machine, and there were stores in the vicinity where I could have got a thermos. I made a mental note to do that tomorrow, before I came back out here.

I started the engine, put the heater on full blast until I was warm again. Then I opened up a 1943 issue of *Black Mask*. But trying to read on a surveillance is not much of an idea; you can't

concentrate because you have to keep glancing up after every paragraph or two in order to stay alert. At the end of fifteen minutes I gave it up—and just sat there.

Nothing happened over at the Talbot house. Nothing happened anywhere, except that a woman with a poodle on a leash came walking down Wawona behind me, crossed the street in front of my car, and entered the park. She gave me a curious glance as she passed, the kind that meant she was wondering what I was doing there.

I sighed a little. Curious neighbors, like as not, were going to present a problem eventually; you *could* run a two-week, round-the-clock stakeout in a residential area without arousing suspicion, but the odds were against it. Both Bert Thomas and Milo Petrie—a pair of retired cops who worked part-time as guards and field operatives— had mentioned the fact to me when I called them from my office. They had been willing to take the other two eight-hour shifts, but neither of them figured the job to last the full two weeks. Which made three of us. Sooner or later one of the neighbors was liable to get suspicious enough and worried enough to make a police complaint, and that would be the end of it. Not because the police would hassle us, although they might if there was pressure applied; there was nothing illegal in a surveillance conducted by licensed private investigators. But because word would get around the neighborhood, and if we tried to keep on watching

the Talbot house, the whole thing would turn into a circus full of rumor-mongering and gawking citizens. And that wouldn't do anybody any good, least of all Martin Talbot.

A crazy damned job. But I was committed to it now, for as long as it lasted. I shook my head and wondered why I never got the kind of cases the pulp private eyes did. No slinky blondes with bedroom eyes and horny dispositions. No stolen jewels or missing heiresses. No danger and intrigue among the decadent rich. Well, maybe I ought to consider myself fortunate. If I never got laid by my lady clients, I also never got hit on the head or had shoot-outs with hired gunmen in dark alleys. Better a nice safe dull stakeout like this than a knife wound in the belly. Or being trapped in a mine cave-in in the Mother Lode, which was another thing that had happened to me on a past case.

Over in the park, next to where her poodle was squatting and soiling the grass, the woman stood peering in my direction again. So I got out of the car and hoisted the hood and pretended to fiddle around with the engine. That made her lose interest in me; when she came out a couple of minutes later she passed by without a glance. And she did not look back as she followed the poodle along the far sidewalk.

I waited until she turned out of sight on Twenty-third Avenue; then I closed the hood and got back into the front seat. And sat there again, trying not

to look at my watch every minute or two. It was only a little past three-thirty; four and a half hours to go on my abbreviated shift. We had settled on a regular timetable beginning at eight tonight—Bert Thomas would be on from then until four A.M., Milo Petrie from four until noon, and me from noon until eight P.M. Which gave me the best of the three shifts, but they didn't mind and the prerogatives were mine.

My mind fidgeted from one thought to another, the way minds do when you're just sitting somewhere and not doing anything with your hands. One of the things it kept coming back to was the murder of Christine Webster. I had called Eberhardt while I was in the office, but he had no further information to give me. The city coroner had not finished his post-mortem examination at that time, and the Homicide inspectors assigned to the case—Klein and Logan—had only just begun interviewing the dead girl's friends and relatives.

Why did Christine have my business card when they found her? That and other questions kept on nagging at me. What kind of trouble had she been in that would make her consider seeing a private detective? Did the trouble have anything to do with her murder? If she'd had the card for any length of time, why hadn't she called me or come to talk to me?

Twenty years old. Dead. Murdered.

Why? Who and why?

I had a vivid mental image of her lying among the reeds and bushes, all bloody and twisted, and the anger cut at me again and made me feel restless. But there was nothing I could do about her—a dead girl I had never known. Nothing I could do about anything at the moment. Just sit and wait, sit and wait—

Martin Talbot appeared on the small front porch of his house.

I sat up straighter, watching him as he started down the brick staircase. I knew for sure it was Talbot because Laura Nichols had given me his description earlier, along with one of Victor Carding that she had pried out of her brother. Large, fair-skinned man with fanshell ears and close-cropped, wheat-colored hair. Wearing a tweed overcoat today, no hat or muffler. He turned toward me at the sidewalk and crossed the street ten yards ahead of my car, moving with a mechanical stride, head held stiff and motionless, like an automaton activated by remote control. Even at that distance, I could see that his expression was almost masklike, without animation.

He went through the gate into the park. I waited another ten seconds and then left the car to follow after him. He was a compulsive walker, Mrs. Nichols had said; so he was probably not going anywhere in particular. But the restlessness was still inside me and I was glad to be out and moving around with at least some sense of purpose, to help pass the time.

Talbot led me across the grass to the rim of the grotto, onto a path through the trees, down the steep wooded slope on a series of switchbacked trails. When he reached the grotto he turned to the west, went past and through shaded picnic areas, a wide green with a stage on the south side where concerts were held on summer Sundays, the deserted parking lot that fronted a rustic club building, another green, and finally to the lagoon at the far end.

He stopped on a strip of graveled beach, stood looking out at a handful of ducks floating on the gray water. Rushes and tule grass grew along the near shore; they made me think again of the place at Lake Merced where Christine Webster had been found. The absence of people and the dark sky gave the area a kind of depressingly secluded atmosphere, even though the backsides of several houses on Wawona and Crestlake Drive lined the north and south embankments above. The wind made wet whispery sounds in the pine and eucalyptus branches, built little waves that lapped over the gravel at Talbot's feet.

There were more picnic benches near the lagoon, beneath a shelter-roof attached to a set of restrooms; I started over there just to keep from waiting at a standstill. As I neared the restrooms Talbot turned from the lagoon and plodded up in the same direction, at an angle to the nearest of the benches. But he did not look at me, or even seem to know I was there. He sat on the bench,

stiff-postured, as motionless as a block of wood, and stared out at the lagoon again.

I hesitated, debating with myself. There was something about him, a vague impression I could not quite define, that made me want to take a closer look at him. The last thing you want to do on a surveillance is to approach the subject, make him aware of you—but this was not an ordinary surveillance and Talbot was not an ordinary subject. He seemed to have little awareness of externals: a man lost deep inside himself, suffering in his own private hell. If I spoke to him, chances were he would not remember me five seconds afterward.

All right, then. I moved away from the restrooms and circled around to approach him from the front, moving at a casual pace. He did not seem to see me even when I blocked off his view of the lake. I stopped two feet from where he was sitting. His face was narrow and bonily irregular, I saw then, with deep creases like erosion marks in the cheeks and forehead. The whites of his eyes gave the impression of bleeding: his sister had been right about him not sleeping much since the accident. But there was something else in those eyes, in the fixed vacant stare of the pupils— something that made the hair on my neck bristle.

"Excuse me," I said. "Would you have the time?"

It took him three or four seconds to respond; then he blinked slightly and focused on me. "I'm

sorry. What did you say?" Polite voice, but as empty as the bloodshot eyes.

"I was just wondering what time it was."

"I'm afraid I don't know. I'm not wearing a watch."

"Thanks anyway." I paused. "Cold out here, isn't it."

"Yes. Cold."

I wanted to talk to him some more but there was nothing else to say. I just nodded and pivoted away, and immediately his gaze fixated on the lagoon again; he had not moved any part of his body except his head during the brief exchange between us.

Back beside the restrooms, I leaned against the wall with my hands shoved deep into the pockets of my coat. The wind seemed colder now. Whether or not Talbot was in danger from Victor Carding, I thought, that look in his eyes said he was in greater danger from himself. Much greater danger.

It was the look of a man who wants to die.

Talbot left the lagoon a little past five, made a perimeter loop of the park on Crestlake Drive and Nineteenth Avenue, and went back into his house. It was dark by then; he put all the lights on one by one, as if he could not bear to face the night hours unless he was surrounded by light. Chasing shadows—literally. But there were no lights to chase the shadows and the darkness that seemed to be inside him.

The minutes between six and eight o'clock dragged away. I stayed in the car the whole time, fidgeting, putting the heater on now and then to keep warm. Once I saw Talbot's silhouette at a window on the Wawona Street side; but it was gone seconds later. He did not come outside again.

Bert Thomas showed up at eight sharp to relieve me. I spent a little time talking to him, letting him know my feelings about Talbot. Then I took myself away from there and drove straight home to my flat.

I had to park three blocks away, which was par for the course; garages are at a premium in Pacific Heights because most of the buildings are older apartment complexes or converted private homes like the one I live in. A ripe smell greeted me when I let myself into the flat; I had forgotten to take out the garbage again. But then, I had never been much of a housekeeper and I was used to ripe smells, dirty dishes, dustballs under the furniture, and soiled laundry and other items scattered around the floors. About the only thing I made an effort to keep neat was my collection of pulps—over six thousand of them now, on standing bookshelves along the living room walls.

In the kitchen I got a beer from the refrigerator. Drank some of it on my way into the bedroom, where I keep the telephone. The bed, as we used to say when I was a kid, looked like it belonged in a whorehouse after a raid; I pushed aside a wad of blankets, sat down on the bare mattress. And

lifted the phone receiver and dialed the Nichols'
number.

Mrs. Nichols answered. I told her who was calling, and she said immediately, "Is everything all
right with Martin? Why aren't you at his house?"

"I've got a man there," I said. "And no, I'm
afraid everything isn't all right."

"What? Do you mean Victor Carding—?"

"No, there's been no sign of Carding. It's your
brother's mental state I'm worried about, Mrs.
Nichols."

"His mental state?"

"I think he might be suicidal," I said.

She made a sound that might have indicated
surprise, incredulity, or a combination of both.
"That's ridiculous," she said. "Martin? Good God,
I told you he was fanatically moral; he'd be the
last person in this world to commit suicide. Whatever gave you such an idea?"

"I had a close look at him today. He strikes me
as a pretty sick man."

"Nonsense. He'll snap out of it sooner or later.
It's just a matter of time."

"I'm not so sure of that, ma'am."

"Well I am."

"Have you tried to get him to see a doctor?"

"I suggested it, yes. For something to help him
sleep."

"But he refused?"

"Yes. He has an aversion to drugs."

"Couldn't you talk him into it. Or bring a doctor around to examine him?"

Pause. "My brother is *not* mentally ill," she said in a cold, flat voice. "And I won't have someone like you telling me he is."

Someone like me, I thought. Just another common laborer, and what the hell did common laborers know about anything? I took a swallow of beer to drown the sharp words that were on my tongue; there was nothing to be gained in telling her off.

"Are you still there?"

"Yes. I'm still here."

"You were hired to do a specific job," she said. "I assume you wish to continue doing it. Is that correct?"

I had already asked myself the same question. If I backed off the case she would only hire someone else—assuming she could find someone else to take it on, as unorthodox as it was. Maybe there wasn't much Bert and Milo and I could do to protect Martin Talbot from himself or from someone else, but at least we could try; at least three people who understood the situation would be keeping a steady watch on him.

And I needed the money. I *needed* that money, damn it.

"Yes," I said.

"Then I'll thank you not to bother me again with your opinions. You're to call only if you have something to report about Victor Carding. And

you're to send me a detailed written report at the beginning of next week. Is that understood?"

"Understood."

"Fine. Good-night, then."

"Good night, Mrs. Nichols."

I made the kind of gesture Italians always use to convey disgust and banged down the receiver. Some lady, Laura Nichols. Some nice sister. No mental illness in *her* family, by God. No brother of *hers* could have come unhinged enough to take his own life. Poor Martin was just a little eccentric, that was all. He'd snap out of it eventually; it was only a matter of time.

Poor Martin, all right.

Poor bastard.

# ◦ FIVE ◦

On Thursday morning I spent a couple of hours in my office, going through the mail and catching up on some paperwork. There were no messages on my answering machine and I had no calls while I was there. No one had rung me up at home either, so I assumed that nothing much had happened at Talbot's during the night. Nothing, at least, that Bert or Milo knew about.

I called the Hall of Justice at ten o'clock to check in again with Eberhardt. But he was out on a field investigation, the cop I talked to said, and was not expected back until early afternoon. The cop was not at liberty to say if there were any new developments on the Christine Webster homicide. At eleven-thirty I tried again, just in case; Eb still had not returned. I would just have to wait until tonight, when my shift on Talbot was finished, and then call him at home for an update.

I locked the office, picked up my car, and headed over Twin Peaks to Stern Grove. The weather was better today: still cold and windy,

but the overcast had lifted and patches of blue sky were visible between shifting cloud masses. It would make surveillance a little easier because I could spend more time moving around in the park and less time sitting like a lump in the car.

Milo Petrie was waiting for me, standing just inside the park gate, when I came down Wawona off Nineteenth. I made a U-turn alongside the Talbot house, parked where I had yesterday, facing east, and went over to join him.

"How'd it go, Milo?"

"Quiet," he said. He was a lean, hawk-nosed guy in his sixties, bundled up in a heavy car coat, a longshoreman's cap, and a pair of gloves. Like Bert Thomas, he was a retired patrolman out of the Ingleside station. "And goddamn cold, too. I haven't been on an early-morning stakeout in twenty years; almost froze my balls off."

"Anything happen on Bert's shift?"

"He said no. Subject stayed inside and didn't have any visitors. Lights were on all night, like maybe he didn't go to bed."

"Talbot come out this morning?"

"Yep. A little after eight. He walked all the way down Nineteenth to the Stonestown shopping center. Gave me a chance for some exercise, anyway."

"What did he do in Stonestown?"

"Nothing much," Milo said. "Wandered around, sat in the mall for awhile. No contact with any-

body. He led me straight back here about thirty minutes ago."

I nodded. "Okay. No need for you to hang around; you look like you could use some coffee and hot food."

"And a stiff shot of brandy." He hesitated, glancing over at the house. "This Talbot's in a pretty bad way, you know? Funny look in his eyes—like he's half-dead inside."

"Yeah, I know."

"I've seen that look before," Milo said. "Jumper on the Golden Gate Bridge had it back in '68; I tried to talk him out of going over but he jumped anyway. You ask me, Talbot's a potential Dutch."

"I've been thinking the same thing. But his sister doesn't believe it, and she's the only one who could have him committed for observation."

"If I was her, I'd be a hell of a lot more worried about him knocking himself off than anyone else trying to do it for him."

"Me too," I said. "But the way things are, I don't see anything we can do except play it her way. And hope for the best."

Milo shook his head. "People," he said.

When he was gone I went through the gate into the park. There were a few more people around today: a couple of kids throwing a football back and forth, a man walking an Irish setter on a leash, an elderly couple carrying a small silver-flocked Christmas tree that they had probably bought at the lot over on Nineteenth and Sloat. I stood on

the park road and watched the kids. The one nearest me missed a catch and the ball rolled to a stop about twenty feet away; when he picked it up I called out for him to peg it to me—just being friendly, trying to pass the time. He threw it back to the other kid instead, grinned at me, and gave me the finger.

Christmas trees before Thanksgiving. Citizens letting their dogs crap all over a public recreation area. Young kids giving the finger to adults old enough to be their grandfather. And a twenty-year-old girl lying in the morgue with two bullets in her body. And an honest man, a moral man, tearing himself apart with guilt. And a stubborn, narrow-minded woman who would rather believe in an unlikely threat than in the real danger of mental illness.

People, Milo had said.

Yeah. People.

I walked over to the driving range. Came back to the gate. Walked up the park road again. Watched the kids again, staring at the one who had given me the finger until it made him nervous enough to stop playing catch and head down into the grotto with his friend. The cold was beginning to bother me, as it had yesterday, and I was also a little hungry; I had eaten nothing for breakfast except some cereal. Before leaving my flat, though, I had made some sandwiches, and I had bought a thermos near my office and filled it with

coffee. Time for lunch, I thought. I turned back for the gate—

Just in time to see the taxi come gliding along Twenty-first Avenue and pull up in front of the Talbot house.

The driver blew his horn a couple of times. Immediately the front door opened and Martin Talbot appeared, wearing the same tweed overcoat of yesterday. There seemed to be purpose in his stride as he came down the stairs and crossed to enter the cab.

I was running by then, out through the gate and around the front of my car. The taxi pulled away, left on Wawona, as I fumbled the door open and slid inside. If the driver had caught the light at Nineteenth, I might have lost them; midday traffic was pretty heavy along there, clogging all three southbound lanes. But the signal was red, and it stayed red long enough for me to swing out and close to within half a block.

Talbot's sudden departure by cab was surprising. From what Laura Nichols had told me, he had not gone anywhere since the accident except for those periodic walks around the neighborhood. So why this trip? And why the seeming purpose in his stride?

The taxi swerved over into the left-turn lane at Nineteenth and Sloat; I managed to do the same. And to make the light with them. They cut over onto Junipero Serra, turned left again at Ocean Avenue, and followed Ocean to the City College.

Over the hill to Geneva, then, and straight out
past the San Mateo Country line and the Cow
Palace.

An uneasiness had begun to grow in me, and it
kept on growing when the driver swung right on
Bayshore Boulevard and headed up the long sweeping hill beyond. I was pretty sure I knew where
Talbot was going, now. And I was right: on the
other side of the hill the cab made another right-
hand turn and entered Brisbane on Old Country
Road.

My hands were tight around the wheel as I
turned in after them. Brisbane was a small town
of maybe four thousand people, nestled in the
curves and cuts along the eastern slopes of the San
Bruno Mountains overlooking the Bay. It had
some similarities in appearance and population
mix to Sausalito, although it was more of a bedroom community than an artistic one. A place
where all sorts of different types lived, from paint-
ers and sculptors to business executives to blue
collar workers.

It was also the place, Mrs. Nichols had told me,
where Victor Carding lived.

Why would Talbot be on his way to see Carding?
Three possible answers, as far as I could tell.
One—he wanted to talk it out with the man, ask
forgiveness, seek some sort of relief for his guilt.
Two—he was after punishment instead of relief,
either verbal or physical. Three—the initiative

was Carding's, not Talbot's, and Talbot was responding to a telephone summons.

The first or the second seemed the most probable. The only reason Carding could have for requesting a meeting was that he intended to carry out his threat; but if you're going to kill a man you don't invite him to your house to do it. The first answer was the best of the lot, though it could still mean trouble; the second was volatile as hell. Dicey situation any way you looked at it.

But the big question was, what was I going to do about it?

I followed the cab up San Bruno Avenue, hanging back a full two blocks. At Glen Parkway it turned right, hooked through the center of town, and then began to climb upward on the network of narrow twisting roads that crisscrossed the slope. Most of the houses up there either clung to the steep hillside below the roads, with carports and entrances at road level, or sat on little knolls or inside man-made cutouts. They ran the spectrum of architectural types and building materials: country cabin, plain frame, box, old Spanish, false Southern Colonial, ultramodern hexagonal and octagonal; brick, redwood, pine, stucco, old gray stone, whitewashed block. The only things they all had in common were balconies and wide picture windows, to take advantage of a panoramic view of the Bay, parts of San Francisco, the East and South Bay cities.

I lost sight of the taxi half a dozen times as we

climbed the rutted, switchbacked roads, almost lost it completely once at a three-way intersection. But I was still behind them when they turned onto Queen's Lane, near the highest perimeter of the village. The road looped around and through an undeveloped section—vertical hillside on the left, slope on the right wooded with scrub oak and bay and horse chestnut trees—and the taxi disappeared again for eight or ten seconds. When I neared the center of the loop, where a dirt-faced turnaround had been cut out of the bluff wall, I had them back in sight. And they were just pulling up beyond a gravel driveway seventy-five yards downrange.

I braked, veered over onto the turnaround. Half a minute later Talbot got out of the cab and stood next to a rural-type mailbox, looking up the driveway; from where I was, I could not see the house there. At length he headed up the drive, walking stiff-backed but with that same sense of purpose, and disappeared from sight. The cab stayed where it was, parked on the verge; Talbot had evidently told the driver to wait.

Okay, I thought, here we go. Play it one step at a time. I set the emergency brake, got out, and went down the road at a fast trot. The wind slapped at my face; it was strong up here, pungent with the spicy scent of bay leaves. Overhead the sun seemed to be trying to break through the clouds, creating a bright metallic glare that made me squint.

The house came into view when I was thirty yards from the driveway. It was set on a piece of level ground above the road, its backside close to a notch machine-carved out of the hill—a pretty attractive place for someone Mrs. Nichols had referred to as a "common laborer." Smallish, square-shaped, made out of brick and brick-colored wood. Wide, roofed porch across the front, decorated with planterboxes full of ferns. Half-hidden on the far side was what looked to be a two-car garage; the driveway bent around in that direction.

Talbot was up on the porch, just standing there before the door, waiting.

I slowed to a walk, watching him. Just as I reached the mailbox, he pivoted abruptly and came down off the steps. Nobody home, I thought—but the sense of relief I felt was premature. Talbot stopped after a couple of paces, turned, and stared over toward the garage. A few seconds later he started toward it. And vanished again around the side of the house.

Maybe Carding was at work or had gone somewhere else; but maybe, too, he was out in the garage and had not heard or had chosen to ignore the doorbell. Give Talbot half a minute, I told myself. If he doesn't show by then, better get up there.

Behind me I heard a car door slam. Then a voice yelled, "Hey! You there!"

I turned. It was the cabbie, a youngish guy,

heavy-set, wearing a poplin windbreaker and a pugnacious expression. "You talking to me?"

"That's right, buddy. You been following me?"

Ah Christ, I thought, this is all I need.

"Thought I spotted a tail when we started up here," the cabbie said. "What the hell you been following me for?"

"Nobody's following you," I said. I looked up at the house again. Still no sign of Talbot.

"I figure different," the cabbie said belligerently. He came away from the taxi, stopped twenty feet from me, and put his hands on his hips. "I don't stand for shit like that."

The thirty seconds were up. I could feel my chest beginning to tighten; sweat formed cold and sticky under my arms. Something going on in that garage. Talbot would have come out by now if there wasn't.

"You hear what I said, fatso?"

Fatso. I gave him a go-to-hell look and started up the drive, hurrying. The cabbie came after me; I could hear his shoes crunching on the gravel. Wind currents swayed the scrub oak and the brownish grass on the hillside above, made faint whispering murmurs in the afternoon stillness. But nothing moved and nothing made a sound anywhere around the house or the garage.

"Turn around, goddamn it!" the cabbie yelled behind me. "Come on, you son of a bitch!"

That was enough; I could not afford to let it go any further. I whirled on him, glaring. "I'm here

on police business, smart guy," I lied in a hard
tight voice. "You understand? Police business. You
want to make trouble, fine, I'll have your ass
thrown in jail for obstruction of justice."

He pulled up short and blinked at me. Most of
the belligerence faded out of his expression; he
began to look uncertain and a little worried.

"Now go on, get back to your cab," I said. "And
don't say anything about me to your fare when he
comes back. *Capici?*"

"Hey," he said, "hey, I'm sorry, man, I didn't
know you were a cop—"

"Move it!"

I put my back to him, the hell with him, and
trotted the rest of the way up onto the flat. The
drive made a wide loop there, around and alongside the house; I cut off it at a sharp angle, onto
hard-packed earth. When I neared the porch corner, the whole of the garage materialized ahead of
me. One of its double doors was standing part-way
open and I could see that there were lights on
inside; but that was all I could see. Still no sign
of—

And that was when the gun went off.

The flat cracking sound was unmistakable; I
had heard the report of a handgun too many times
in my life. I broke into a lumbering run. There
was no second shot—no other sounds of any kind
from inside the garage. Instinct warned me against
barging in there, but I did it anyway: I caught the
edge of the closed door half and swung myself
around it, through the opening by two steps.

I was braced to find a dead man lying on the floor, and that was what I found. But what surprised me, what made me stare wide-eyed, was that it was not Martin Talbot.

The dead man had to be Victor Carding.

He lay sprawled on his side near a long cluttered workbench, both legs bent up toward his chest as if he had tried to assume a fetal position before he died; there was blood all over the front of his blue workshirt. Three feet away, between Carding and a partly open rear window, Talbot stood looking down at the body. His arms were flat against his sides, and in his right hand was a snub-nosed revolver.

The light in there came from a drop-cord arrangement suspended from one of the ceiling rafters; the cord and its grilled bulb cage swayed a little, so that there was an eerie shifting movement of light and shadow across Talbot's face. He looked ghastly: twisted-up expression of sickness and torment, eyes popped and unblinking, mouth slacked open like an idiot's.

The hollow queasy feeling was in my stomach again. And there was a rancid taste in my throat; you can never tell what a man with a gun in his hand will do. But he did not even seem to know I was there. His gaze was half-focused, vacant, and the gun stayed pointed at the floor, loose in his grasp.

I took a couple of cautious steps toward him. He did not move. Three more paces, each one

slow and measured, brought me up close on his right. Still no movement. And no resistance when I reached down, closed my hand around the revolver, and eased it out of his cold fingers.

I let out the breath I had been holding and backed off. The gun was a Smith and Wesson .38 caliber; the stubby muzzle was still warm. I dropped it into my coat pocket and sidled around so that the dead man was between Talbot and me. Then I knelt to take a closer look at the body.

No doubt that it was Victor Carding. He matched the description Laura Nichols had given me: thin, gaunt, sallow-faced. He had been shot once in the chest; the blood was coagulating around the wound. There were no other marks on him that I could see, and nothing on the floor near him except a couple of sealed envelopes—PG&E bill, letter from a bank—that might have been jarred out of a pocket when he fell.

When I straightened up Talbot blinked and focused on me for the first time. He said, "I killed him," in a hoarse empty voice—the kind of voice, if you've ever heard it, that can raise the hairs on your scalp.

"Easy, Mr. Talbot."

"He shouted at me, called me a murderer. Because I killed his wife, you see. Murderer, he said. Murderer, murderer."

I went over to him again and took his arm. I wanted him out of there; I wanted out of there

myself. The mingled smells of oil and dust, cord-
ite and death, were making me a little nauseous.

"I just . . . I couldn't stand it," Talbot said. "I
lost control of myself. The gun . . . it was on the
workbench. I picked it up, just to make him stop,
but he lunged at me and it went off. I killed him.
He was right, I *am* a murderer. . . ."

Gently I prodded him toward the door. He came
along without protest, moving like a sleepwalker.
Outside, in the wind and the leaden daylight, I
took several deep breaths to clear the death-smell
out of my nostrils. Both the cabbie and the hack
were gone; he had probably heard the shot and
decided he wanted no part of what was going on
here. Nobody else seemed to have heard it; the
nearest neighbor was across the road and fifty
yards down.

I took Talbot around the front of the house, up
onto the porch. The door was unlocked. Inside, I
sat him down in a chair and then hunted up the
telephone.

"I murdered him," Talbot said again, as I picked
up the receiver. "I murdered him."

No you didn't, I thought. No way.

Talbot had *not* killed Victor Carding.

myself. The trapped smells of oil and dust and
oc the death were making me sit in the distance.

"I ... I ..." I couldn't make it," Talbot said "I
don't know ...how ... he  ... ... was pa
windsinges ... he could ... of to make him wy
but it at my and it went off." K said that

he was rake with a practice.

Gently I pried him toward the couch. He came
along without protest, moving like a sleepwalker.
Outside in the wind and the feeder, the was

# ○ SIX ○

It took the local cops exactly fourteen minutes
to get there. But it was a long fourteen minutes.
Talbot kept staring off into space, dry-washing his
hands and muttering over and over the same
things he had said in the garage. Watching him
and listening to him gave me a creepy, nervous
feeling. He was right on the edge of a breakdown—
and that was something I was not equipped to
handle.

When I finished with my call to the police, I
dialed the Nichols' home in Sea Cliff; I figured
Laura Nichols ought to know about this as soon
as possible. But there was no answer. I put down
the receiver and prowled around the living room
with Talbot's voice grating in my ears. On the
mantelpiece was a framed color photograph of
Carding, a plain gray-haired woman, and a kid in
his twenties wearing a Fu Manchu mustache. The
Carding family—and two of them dead in less
than a week. I shook my head and took a turn
through the rest of the house, not touching any-

thing. The place was cluttered and dusty, and in the kitchen were a couple of empty bourbon bottles and the smell of spilled whiskey. Aside from that, the condition of each of the rooms seemed ordinary enough.

The distant wail of sirens, when they finally came, was a relief. I went out on the porch to wait and breathe more of the fresh air. The sirens grew louder and closer, and pretty soon a pair of Brisbane police cars came speeding along Queen's Lane, swung up the drive, and plowed to a halt. Three uniformed cops piled out, one of them wearing sergeant's stripes on the sleeve of his jacket. The sergeant's name was Osterman, it turned out, and he was in charge.

I showed him the photostat of my investigator's license, told him about Talbot being inside, answered preliminary questions, and handed over the gun. Osterman told me to wait there; then, before I could explain why I knew Talbot had not shot Victor Carding, he and one of the other cops headed for the garage. The third cop went inside the house to talk to Talbot.

There was a kind of *deja vu* in the next thirty minutes; I had been through it all too often before—the last time just two days ago, at the scene of Christine Webster's murder. More Brisbane police units had arrived and were controlling the inevitable bunch of ghouls that had gathered down on the road. A dark brown Cadillac with MD plates showed up: the doctor I had asked

them to send when I called. Then a county ambulance, probably from South San Francisco. Then another car with MD plates, this one containing a harried-looking guy who I assumed was acting coroner for this bailiwick. Then a TV-remote truck that was not permitted up the drive because there was no room; the area in front of the house looked like a parking lot as it was. And while all of this was going on, Osterman went into the house, came back out after ten minutes looking even grimmer than before, and returned to the garage. Neither he nor anyone else said a word to me.

Finally, while I paced back and forth waiting for Osterman to get around to me again, a light-green Ford sedan joined the string of other cars down on Queen's Lane. A fat man in a rumpled suit got out of it, spoke to one of the cops down there, and was allowed to proceed up the drive on foot. The way he moved, in a waddling gait like a latter-day Oliver Hardy, made me stop pacing and stand looking at him as he approached.

Well, what do you know, I thought. Donleavy.

He recognized me at about the same time, raised an eyebrow and then one hand in greeting. I went forward to meet him.

"How are you, Donleavy?"

"Not too bad," he said. We shook hands. "Been what—seven, eight years?"

"About that." I had met him, way back then, during the course of an ugly kidnapping and mur-

der case in Hillsborough—the one on which I had got the knife wound in the belly.

He said, "So what're you doing here? Mixed up with murder again, are you?"

"I'm afraid so. How about you? Aren't you still with the DA's office?"

"Nope. County CID the past four years. Brisbane police don't have the facilities to handle a homicide investigation, so they ask us to come in whenever they get one. I was over in San Bruno on a routine matter; that's why I got sent. Lucky me."

"Lucky you."

"Where's the body?"

"In the garage. The coroner's with it now."

"Any suspects?"

"Yes and no," I said. "There's a man inside the house named Martin Talbot; I found him with the dead man. He had what was probably the death weapon in his hand—a .38 caliber revolver—and he confessed to me that he'd done the shooting. But he didn't do it. I doubt if anybody did; I think it might be suicide."

Donleavy studied me. He looked older, grayer, maybe a little fatter, and his eyes seemed even more sleepy than I remembered them. The impression he gave was one of softness and mildness—but that was an illusion. He was shrewd and dedicated, and he could be pretty tough when he had to be.

"You know this Talbot, do you?" he asked.

"I know some things about him. I'm working for his sister."

"Why would he confess to a murder he didn't commit?"

"It's a long story," I said. "You want it now or after you've seen the body and talked to Talbot?"

"Make it after." He clapped me on the arm and waddled off toward the garage.

Another five minutes went away. Then Donleavy returned alone and entered the house. The coroner put in an appearance not long after that, to tell the ambulance attendants that they could have the body. Osterman was with them when they brought it out from the garage; he stood near me, not saying anything, while the attendants loaded the stretcher.

Just as the ambulance started down the drive, the house door opened and everybody inside came out. The local doctor and one of the uniformed cops had Talbot between them, hanging onto his arms; he still moved like a sleepwalker. They put him into the doctor's Cadillac and wasted no time taking him away in the wake of the ambulance.

Donleavy was still up on the front porch; he gestured to me to join him. I did that, with Osterman behind me, and the three of us filed into the living room.

I asked Donleavy, "Did you talk to Talbot?"

"A little. Doctor wanted to get him to the hospital for observation; he's in a pretty bad way."

"He confess to you?"

"Yep, he did."

"To me, too," Osterman said. "It's an open-and-shut case."

"No," I said, "it isn't. He didn't kill Carding."

"What?"

Donleavy said, "Go ahead, you can lay it out now."

"Let me give you the background first." And I told them about the accident in which Carding's wife had been killed. About Talbot's obsessive guilt. About what Laura Nichols had hired me to do. About following Talbot here this afternoon.

"He doesn't sound like a probable murderer, I'll admit that," Donleavy said when I was done. "But he claims he picked up the gun in self-defense, more or less, and it went off by accident. It could have happened that way."

I shook my head. "There are at least three good reasons why it couldn't."

"Which are?"

"One is the time factor," I said. "I was down at the foot of the drive when he disappeared toward the garage. It was thirty seconds before I started up after him, and another two minutes or so until I heard the shot. Say three minutes, maximum. Talbot would have had to walk to the garage, enter, confront Carding, listen to enough verbal abuse to make him pick up the gun, and then shoot Carding when he lunged forward—all in three minutes or less. If that isn't impossible, it's the next thing to it."

"You sure about the amount of time?"

"Positive."

"What's the second reason?"

"Talbot claims Carding shouted at him, shouted accusations. But I didn't hear any shouting; I didn't hear anything at all from the garage until the gun went off. A yelling voice would have carried almost as far as the shot, quiet as it is around here. And I heard the shot loud and clear."

Osterman was frowning. "Maybe Carding didn't shout after all; maybe he spoke in a normal voice and Talbot, mixed up as he is, remembered him as yelling."

"Then why would Talbot have picked up the gun in such a hurry? If somebody's talking to you in a normal or slightly raised voice, even making accusations, you wouldn't have much cause to fear for your safety. Or to grab a weapon just to shut him up."

Donleavy said, "Let's hear the third reason."

"That's the clincher. I took a close look at Carding's body less than five minutes after the shot: the blood around the wound was coagulating. He'd been dead at least fifteen minutes by then, maybe longer."

"You could be wrong about that," Osterman said. "You're not a forensic expert."

"No, but I've seen a lot of blood in my life. Believe me, I can tell the difference between fresh and coagulating."

Donleavy ruminated for a time. Then he said,

"Your theory is that Carding killed himself, right?"

"Right. Probably because he was despondent over the death of his wife."

"Gun suicides don't usually shoot themselves in the chest, you know."

"I know. But it happens once in a while—often enough to take it out of the implausible category."

Osterman said, "It doesn't make any sense to me. Why the hell would Talbot shoot off the gun if Carding was already dead? Why would he want to make it look like he'd committed murder?"

"Because he believes he *did* commit murder," I said. "And not just one murder—two. Carding's wife in the accident and now Carding as a result of it."

"Elaborate on that," Donleavy said.

"Look at it this way. Talbot's a man so full of guilt that he can't live with himself; he wants to be punished for what he did—wants to die but doesn't quite have the courage or the strength to take his own life. So he decides to confront Carding, either because he hopes to provoke himself into a suicidal state or because he hopes to provoke Carding into carrying out the threat against his life.

"But when he gets here he finds Carding dead in the garage of a self-inflicted gunshot wound. For Talbot it's a pretty terrible irony: He's the one who wants to be dead, to kill himself, but it's

turned out the other way around. He's got a double load of guilt to deal with now and he can't handle it; he really starts to unravel.

"Then he hears the cab driver hassling me out on the drive and realizes somebody's about to find him there with the body. In his mind he's already killed Carding; why not just go ahead and make it look like murder? That way he can be arrested and prosecuted; he won't be dead, but at least he'll be punished.

"He picks up the gun, either from the floor or from Carding's hand, and fires a shot into the roof or one of the walls. And when I come in he blurts out his confession. Simple as that in the factual sense; damned complex in the psychological sense. But I'll bet that's the way it happened."

Osterman was unconvinced. "It still sounds screwy to me," he said.

"Maybe not," Donleavy said. He hooked his fingers around his coat lapels and rocked back and forth; when he did that he looked more than ever like Oliver Hardy. The resemblance was uncanny sometimes, even without the little toothbrush mustache, and it made me wonder if at least some of the mannerisms were calculated—an act to keep the people he dealt with off guard. "I've done some reading in criminal psychology; you should see a few of those case histories."

"Well—if you say so."

"Besides which, there're two empty chambers

in the gun and just a single wound in Carding's body. And Talbot only fired one shot."

"Carding could have kept one chamber empty," Osterman said. "Or he could have fired a round days or weeks ago."

"Yeah, I know. Still, you'd better have your men comb the garage for a bullet hole and a .38 slug."

"Whatever you say."

Osterman gave me a curt nod, as if he were annoyed with me for making waves in what he still considered an open-and-shut case and went on out. When he was gone, Donleavy asked me, "What's Laura Nichols' address and telephone number?"

I told him and he wrote the information down in a spiral notebook. "I called her just after I reported the death," I said. "She wasn't home."

"I'll try her again pretty soon," he said. "You got a card for yourself? Home and office numbers?"

"Sure." I handed him one from my wallet.

He said, "I guess that's it for now; you might as well go on home. I'll call you later today or tomorrow."

"Fine."

We shook hands, and I went out and down the wind-swept drive to Queen's Lane. There were still half a dozen citizens hanging around the area; one of them, a kid in his late teens, cut over near me as I turned up toward where I'd left my car.

"What happened up there, mister? Was it a suicide?"

"Yeah. Suicide."

"The old boozehound knocked himself off, huh?" the kid said. "Wow." And he grinned at me. People.

It was dusk by the time I got back into downtown San Francisco. I went straight to my office and checked the answering machine. No messages. Then I sat down to make some calls.

There was still no answer at the Nichols' home; either Laura Nichols was still out somewhere or she had returned and Donleavy had got in touch with her, and she'd left again to see her brother. I rang up Bert Thomas and Milo Petrie, told each of them the stakeout was finished and what had happened in Brisbane. My last call was to the Hall of Justice, and this time Eberhardt was in. But—

"I'm busy right now," he said. He sounded snippy, the way he does when he's being overworked. "You planning to be home tonight?"

"I was, yeah."

"I'll drop by later, sometime after seven."

I had nothing more to do in the office after that; I locked up again and drove home to my flat. From there I gave the Nichols number another try, with the same nonresults.

I got a beer out of the refrigerator, put a frozen eggplant parmagiana in the oven, and sat down to look at the house mail. The only thing of interest

was a sales list from a pulp dealer in Ohio. The guy's prices were kind of high, even for the over-inflated pulp market, but he had three issues of *Thrilling Detective*, one of *Mammoth Mystery*, and one of *FBI Detective* that I needed and that I thought I could afford. I wrote him a letter and a check—and wondered as I did so just how much I had spent this year on pulps. Too much, probably; that was one of the reasons why I was always short of money. But then, outside of my work, collecting pulps was the only real passion I had in life. What good was money if not to use to indulge your passions?

The telephone rang while I was eating my supper. A reporter from the *Chronicle* wanting to know if I had any statement to make concerning the murder of Victor Carding. I said no, politely, and hung up. When I had finished supper and was putting the dirty dishes into the sink with the other dirty dishes the phone rang a second time. Another reporter, this one from one of the TV stations. I told him the party he was looking for had been called to Los Angeles on business and would not be back for a week. Who was I? An associate named Phil Marlowe, I said, and then hung up on him too. Media people bring out the worst in me—I suppose because their business is disseminating sensationalistic crime news and mine relies on avoiding too much lurid publicity. The public eye versus the private eye.

I tried once more to call Laura Nichols. Nobody

picked up this time, either. So I plunked myself down in the living room with a 1936 issue of *Popular Detective*, to read and wait for Eberhardt.

The phone rang again at seven fifteen. Another damned reporter? I went into the bedroom and caught up the receiver and said hello with my finger on the cut-off button.

But it wasn't a reporter. "This is Donleavy," his soft sleepy voice said in my ear. "I've got some news for you."

I took my finger off the button. "Good news, I hope."

"Not from your point of view. I talked to Talbot again; so did a couple of psychologists. He still maintains he's guilty and nobody can shake him. We've got no choice except to charge him with suspicion of homicide."

"What? Christ, I explained why he couldn't have done it."

"Sure you did. But you *could* be wrong about the time element and the silence in the garage before the shot. And about the blood coagulation, too; coroner wasn't able to pinpoint the exact time of death. I'm not saying you are wrong, understand. Just that the rest of the evidence indicates you might be."

"What evidence? Look, didn't Osterman's men find a second bullet in the garage?"

"No," Donleavy said, "they didn't."

"But it's got to be there. Otherwise the whole thing doesn't make sense."

"It makes sense the way Talbot tells it."

"No, it doesn't. There's just no way he could have killed Carding. The man committed suicide."

Donleavy made an audible sighing sound. "You're a hundred percent wrong about that, my friend," he said. "Lab boys tested the victim's hands for nitrate traces and his clothing for powder marks; there weren't any. He hadn't fired a gun and he wasn't shot at point blank range: it couldn't possibly be suicide. Victor Carding *was* murdered."

# ◦ SEVEN ◦

When Donleavy rang off I went into the kitchen, got out another bottle of beer, and sat brooding with it at the table. I had been so positive I was right about the day's events in Brisbane— and I still thought so, damn it, at least where Martin Talbot's actions and motivations were concerned. No way could I have been mistaken about the time element *and* the silence before the shot *and* the coagulating blood; I had been sharply conscious of time, I had been listening for sounds of any kind, I knew well enough when blood was coagulating and when it was fresh. So it added up the same way as before: Talbot had found Carding dead, picked up the gun, and fired a harmless shot—because he believed, just as I had believed, that Carding committed suicide, and because of a double-dose of guilt and a desire for punishment.

But then where the hell was the second bullet?

It had to be in the garage; why hadn't Osterman's men found it?

The real surprise, though, was the fact that Carding was not a suicide but a murder victim. A man whose wife has just died in an automobile accident seems an unlikely candidate for homicide; you would think that old enemies, for instance, would consider the tragic loss of a loved one retribution enough. It could have been one of those random thrill killings—but that kind of psychopathic personality usually ties up his victims or slays them execution-style, and in addition almost never leaves his weapon behind. It could have been a burglar whom Carding surprised in the act—but as messy as the house was, it had not been searched for valuables; and burglars, like psychotics, seldom leave weapons behind. Anyway, what would a burglar be doing in the garage in the first place? It could have been a drinking companion of Carding's, and the shooting a result of a drunken argument—but the body had not smelled of alcohol when I examined it, nor were there any whiskey bottles that I could remember seeing in the garage. So again, why would Carding have been shot there instead of inside the house?

Speculation was not going to get me anywhere, I decided. There were just too many things I did not know. About Victor Carding: What kind of man had he been? What kind of life had he led, who were his friends and his enemies? And also about the gun: Did it belong to Carding? If not,

was it registered to anyone else? Or traceable in any other way?

Maybe the answers to one or more of those questions would point up the truth. Or maybe Donleavy and Osterman would get lucky and find a neighbor who had seen the killer leave and could identify him. Talbot and the cabbie and I would have seen him ourselves if we had arrived just a short time earlier; Carding could not have been dead more than a few minutes when I found him.

Well, in any case Donleavy was a first-rate cop and it was a good bet that he would get to the bottom of things sooner or later. Which was enough for me—but what about Laura Nichols? How was she taking it? Assuming she knew by now; I had neglected to ask Donleavy, in the wake of his revelations, if he had got in touch with her.

I stood and returned to the bedroom and re-dialed the Nichols number. This time, on the fourth ring, there was an answering click; Karen Nichols' voice said a moment later, "Yes? Hello?"

"Is your mother there, Karen?" I asked when I had identified myself.

"No. She left hours ago."

"Do you know what happened today?"

"Yes. Some friends and I were at Civic Center all afternoon; I just found out a few minutes ago. Mother left me a note to call her at the hospital. God, it's just terrible. I still can't believe it."

"Your uncle didn't kill Victor Carding," I said.

"I know that. He couldn't hurt anyone. But the

police think he did, in spite of what mother says
you told them. They have him under arrest at the
hospital."

"They'll change their minds when they've had
a chance to investigate further."

"Are you really sure of that?"

"Pretty sure. Did your mother say when she'll
be home? I'd like to talk to her."

"No, she didn't. But she wants to talk to you,
too. She said to give you a message if you called:
You're to see her tomorrow morning as early as
possible."

"At your home?"

"Yes."

"Did she tell you why, specifically?"

"Mother never tells me why she does anything,"
Karen said, and there was undisguised bitterness
in her voice. "Never. She just goes ahead and does
it."

I let a couple of seconds pass before I said, "I'll
come by around nine, then."

"All right."

"And try not to worry. Your uncle's receiving
the medical care he needs; things'll work out okay
in the long run."

"Will they? I hope you're right."

We said goodbye and I put the receiver back into
its cradle. I hoped I was right too—and I also
hoped that Mrs. Nichols did not want to see me
tomorrow morning so she could tell me face to
face what a lousy detective she thought I was. She

was not the most understanding and compassionate of women; the way she treated and alienated her daughter was proof of that. So she was probably capable of blaming me for not keeping her brother—and the family name—out of this mess; and of stopping payment on the retainer check she'd given me. Which would make a difficult situation even more difficult.

But then, maybe she had something else on her mind. Unpredictable was another adjective you could use to describe her.

In the living room I sat down again with the issue of *Popular Detective* and tried to read. No good; I was too restless now to concentrate on the exploits of pulp detectives. I put the magazine aside and wondered when Eberhardt was going to show up.

Two seconds later, in the crazy coincidental way things happen sometimes, the downstairs door buzzer went off. I crossed to the speaker unit mounted beside the door, pushed the Talk button, and asked who it was. Sure enough, Eberhardt's voice said, "It's me, hot shot. Buzz me in."

I buzzed him in. And then opened the door and waited for him to come clomping up the stairs and along the hall. When he reached me he nodded and grunted something unintelligible. Moved past me to stand looking around at my sloppy housekeeping, his head wagging in a mildly disgusted way, as I shut the door.

"You ever clean up this pigsty?"

"Only when I'm entertaining a lady."

"Not getting much, then, are you?"

"Not getting much," I agreed. "Sit down. You want some coffee? A beer?"

"Make it a beer."

I went to the kitchen, got a couple of bottles of Schlitz out of the refrigerator. When I came back Eberhardt had cleared some of the crap off the sofa and was sitting with his legs splayed out in front of him. He looked tired, irritable, and even more sour-faced than usual.

He said as I handed him a beer, "Seems you had a pretty busy day for yourself."

"You heard about what happened in Brisbane?"

"I heard about it, all right. Makes two murders in two days you're mixed up in."

"Eb, I'm not mixed up in the Christine Webster shooting."

"No, huh?" he said mildly.

"No," I sat down. "Any leads yet on who killed her?"

"Nothing definite. We haven't been able to trace her movements past seven P.M. on Tuesday. Her roommate, Lainey Madden, had a date that night; and just before she left at seven, Christine told her she was planning to spend a quiet evening at home."

"How about a lead on why she had my card in her purse?"

"That we've got," Eberhardt said.

"You do? What is it?"

"She'd been getting anonymous letters and telephone calls," he said. "The threatening kind. Lainey Madden says she was considering going to a private detective about them."

"Were they death threats?"

"Not in so many words. Veiled stuff."

"How long had she been getting them?"

"About two weeks."

"She have any idea who was responsible? Or why?"

"Not according to the Madden girl. Neither of them could imagine why anyone would have it in for Christine."

"Could it be a sex thing?"

"Maybe yes, maybe no." Eberhardt took some of his beer. "Christine kept the letters and the roommate turned them over to us; nothing sexual or obscene in any of them. Or in any of the calls either, apparently. There *is* a sex angle, though. Which you already know about if you read today's papers."

"I didn't read them; I guess I should have. What is it?"

"She was pregnant," he said.

"Ah—Jesus."

"Yeah. Four months along."

"You get a line on the father?"

"Damned good line. She was engaged to a kid she met at S.F. State last semester. Only man in her life the past six months, Lainey Madden says."

"What did the kid have to say when you talked to him?"

"We didn't talk to him. He's disappeared."

"Disappeared?"

"Missing since last Sunday night. From up at Bodega Bay."

Bodega Bay was on the coast about sixty-five miles north of San Francisco. I asked, "What was he doing up there?"

"Working in the commercial fishing business," Eberhardt said. "He decided to skip school this semester, the way we heard it, because he was running low on money. Nobody's seen or heard from him since around nine P.M. on Sunday."

"Well, I guess that makes him your number one suspect."

"Sure. But it's not as simple as it might look. Not by a damn sight, it isn't."

"You mean because of the threats? Maybe the kid made them himself."

"Maybe. Thing is, there're complications now— a whole new can of worms."

"What can of worms?"

"One you seem to be smack in the middle of."

"Me?"

"You. And the missing kid."

"Eb, what the hell are you getting at?"

"The kid's name is Jerry Carding," Eberhardt said sourly. "He's Victor Carding's son."

## ◦ **EIGHT** ◦

I sat there and gawked at him. All I could think of to say was, "Jesus Christ."

"Uh-huh," he said.

"When did you find this out?"

"Yesterday afternoon. Didn't mean much then, where you're concerned; I didn't know you were working on a case that involved Victor Carding. Logan and Klein went to Brisbane to talk to Carding last night. That's how we learned the kid is missing; Carding's been trying to locate him ever since the accident, to tell him about his mother's death. He didn't have any idea where Jerry might have disappeared to, he said. Told the inspectors his son was in love with Christine, couldn't possibly have killed her—the usual stuff you expect to hear from a father. And that was it, until we heard about his murder late this afternoon and how you were involved in that too."

I stood up and took a couple of turns around the room; I was still trying to get my thoughts sorted

out. Eberhardt drank beer and watched me expressionlessly.

After a time he said, "I talked to your friend Donleavy before I came over here; he filled me in. He also told me the nitrate test on Carding's hands proved negative, and that there weren't any powder marks on his clothing. So it couldn't have been suicide the way you thought."

"I know. He called me with the same news."

"How sure are you this Martin Talbot is innocent?"

"Positive. I'd swear to it in court."

"It'd make things simpler if you were wrong."

"I suppose so." I lowered myself into the chair again. "First Christine Webster, then Victor Carding. And Jerry Carding is missing. You think he could have been a target too?"

"You mean murdered like the others? Some nut with a grudge wasting not only what's left of the Carding family but also the kid's girlfriend? Come on."

"Hell, crazier things have happened," I said. "It could be a psycho deal."

"I doubt it. Not that kind."

"So maybe not. But there's another kind I can think of."

"I'll bet I know what it is. The kid himself is a psycho; he went berserk and murdered both his girl and his old man. Right?"

"Right. That would pretty much explain everything, including his disappearance."

"Sure it would," Eberhardt said. "It's the best theory we've got so far. But it's also got too many holes and loose ends to suit me."

"Such as?"

"The kid's character profile, for one thing. Friendly, serious-minded, well-adjusted; wants to be a journalist. No quirks, no apparent hangups. Pacifist on political and ideological issues. Everybody Logan and Klein talked to said he's got strong feelings against violence of any kind."

"People aren't always what they seem to be, Eb. Things can happen inside them—pressures, compulsions, psychological shifts."

"You think I don't know that? But there are usually indications, small attitude changes of one kind or another. And according to the people who know him, Jerry Carding's the same kid he always was."

"Then why did he vanish all of a sudden?"

"Yeah—why? I sent a man up to Bodega Bay today, but he hasn't been able to dig up any answers so far." Eberhardt got out a pipe and a pouch of tobacco, began loading one from the other. "Anyhow," he said then, "another thing is the time element. The kid dropped out of sight on Sunday, Christine was killed on Tuesday, and Victor Carding was murdered today. If somebody goes berserk, it doesn't take him two days to commit his first homicide and two more days to commit his second."

He was right, of course. But for the sake of

argument I said, "So maybe he didn't go berserk. Maybe he just went insane—the cunning kind of psychosis. He plans his murders, carries them out at two-day intervals."

"Nuts," Eberhardt said. "And that's not a pun. Cunning lunatics don't go after friends and members of their own families; they pick random victims. They also operate in a set pattern, the same kind of MO in each case. There's no pattern here. Take the weapons, for instance."

"Weapons? Plural?"

"Plural. Webster and Carding weren't shot with the same gun. The girl was killed with a .32 caliber weapon—and there was no sign of it near her body. Carding was killed with the .38 you found in Talbot's hand. Like I said: no pattern, but plenty of holes and loose ends."

"You figure two different murderers, then?"

"Not necessarily. But it looks that way."

I did a little brooding. "Has Donleavy been able to trace the .38?"

"No. It doesn't seem to be registered anywhere. Probably an outlaw weapon."

"But it would have belonged to Victor Carding."

"It could have."

"And so could the missing .32."

"I suppose so."

"Was Carding upset about Christine's death?"

"Klein said he was, yeah."

"What did he have to say about his son's relationship with her?"

"Not much. Why?"

"Did he seem to approve of it?"

"Yes. What are you leading up to?"

"A possible answer, maybe."

"Which is?"

"Suppose Carding hated Christine for some reason," I said. "Suppose he was responsible for those threatening calls and letters. And suppose he was the one who killed her—lured her out to Lake Merced on some sort of pretext; she knew him well enough to have gone there to meet him after dark. Then suppose Jerry found out about it, confronted his father today, lost his head and grabbed up the .38 and shot him. Revenge motive."

Eberhardt lit his pipe. "I don't like it much," he said between draws.

Neither did I, but I said, "It is possible."

"Possible, but damned unlikely. Donleavy and the Brisbane police searched the Carding property; they'd have found the .32 if it was there."

"Carding could have got rid of it after shooting the girl."

"Okay, I'll give you that point. But what's the motive? Why would a man hate his son's girlfriend enough to want her dead?"

"I don't know. Maybe he was the unbalanced one, not Jerry. Maybe his wife dying sent him around the bend."

"He'd still need a motive, crazy or not."

"Well, what kind of guy was he? What were his attitudes, prejudices, things like that?"

"We're still checking and so is Donleavy. But he seems to've been a pretty average sort. Worked as a carpenter and construction laborer, built the Brisbane house himself fifteen years ago, got along well with his neighbors. Devoted to his wife and had a good relationship with Jerry, who's an only child; Klein says he was grieving deeply over the wife's death and worried about the kid's disappearance. His only vice appears to've been booze. He'd been arrested once for drunk driving and once for public drunkenness, and he was about half-smashed last night—a borderline alcoholic." Eberhardt shrugged and wreathed himself in a cloud of pipe smoke. "There's nothing in any of that to support your theory."

"No," I said.

"It just won't wash. It doesn't explain why Jerry disappeared from Bodega Bay, or why he wouldn't have surfaced between Sunday and today. And how could he have known his old man was the one who killed Christine? Clairvoyance?"

"Okay, Eb, it was just an idea."

"You got any others you want to hash out?"

"No. I don't suppose the neighbors noticed anything today, before Talbot and I showed up?"

"Uh-uh. Donleavy and the Brisbane cops drew a blank."

I finished my beer, thought about getting another one, and decided against it; my stomach already felt bloated and gaseous. For a time I watched Eberhardt pollute the room with more

acrid pipe smoke. It had a heavy smell and it made my nostrils itch. Give me cigarette smoke any day, I thought—good old cigarette smoke. Finally I stood and went over and opened one of the bay windows a little, to let in some fresh cold air.

"Still bothers you, huh?" Eberhardt said when I came back.

"What?"

"Not being able to smoke yourself."

"Sometimes. Not too much anymore."

"You're a hell of a lot better off. I wish I could quit."

"You could if you had something growing on a lung."

He made a face. "Yeah," he said.

I stifled a belch and sat down again. "You think it's possible that the two murders are unrelated?"

"Anything's possible."

"But you don't think so."

"Hell no. Jerry Carding's girlfriend and father both get shot to death within two days of each other, and the kid himself drops out of sight; there's got to be a connection somewhere." He paused and tapped the stem of his pipe against his teeth. "There's already one connection we know about," he said.

"Meaning me."

"Right. Your business card is in the girl's purse; you're working for the sister of the guy who accidentally killed Carding's wife; and you find Carding's body."

"That *is* coincidence, Eb. At least as far as I know."

"Maybe. Maybe not. First you heard of Victor Carding and the Talbot/Nichols clan was yesterday morning?"

I nodded. "After I left you at Lake Merced."

"Any special reason why the Nichols woman picked you out of all the other private eyes in the book?"

"She didn't tell me if there was."

"What did she have to say about Carding?"

"Just that he'd threatened her brother's life after the accident, and tried to attack him, and she was afraid he might come after Talbot again."

"She didn't indicate she knew Carding personally?"

"No. She called him a 'common laborer,' but that doesn't have to mean anything."

"Did she mention Jerry Carding at all?"

"No."

"Well, that corroborates what she told Klein and Logan tonight. They talked to her at the hospital where Talbot's being held. She says she never aid eyes on either of the Cardings or heard of them before the accident. Talbot claimed the same thing a little while later."

"What about Karen Nichols?"

"Who's she?"

"Mrs. Nichols' daughter. She's a few years older than Jerry and Christine, but they're still in the

same general age group. It could be she knew one or both, or at least knew of them."

"I'll have Klein talk to her tomorrow. Anybody else in the immediate family?"

"Not that I know about. I got the impression Laura Nichols is either a widow or divorced."

Eberhardt smoked in silence for a time. Then he said, "This job Mrs. Nichols hired you to do—didn't it strike you as a little screwy?"

"Sure. But she was determined, and I couldn't see any reason for turning her down."

"Let's try this on for size: She had an ulterior motive in setting up a round-the-clock surveillance on her brother."

"Like what?"

"Like she wanted to provide him with an alibi. If he was being watched at all times by a team of private detectives, he couldn't be suspected of Carding's murder. Only Talbot crossed her up by deciding to pay a call on Carding today."

"Which would make her Carding's killer?"

"Right. And the motive could be that she was more afraid of Carding carrying out his threat against Talbot than she let on; so she decided to take care of Carding before he had a chance to come after her brother."

"I don't know, Eb," I said. "I guess she could be loony enough to come up with a plot like that, but it sounds farfetched to me. TV cop show stuff."

"Yeah, you're right. I don't buy it either. It

doesn't involve a connection with Christine Webster, or explain the kid's disappearance or half a dozen other things."

We kicked it around a while longer, over another beer each, but we were both fresh out of workable theories. The problem was, there still weren't enough facts in yet—and the pieces we did have were jumbled and shaped with odd angles. It might be days or weeks before the right pattern began to emerge. If it ever emerged at all.

Eberhardt left at eleven-thirty and I went straight to bed. But my mind was too full of questions to shut down right away; I tossed around for more than an hour before I finally drifted off. The whole business was damned frustrating. I was involved and yet I was not involved. I was a link between the two murders and yet I knew little about any of the people or any of the motivations and relationships in either case. The idea of sitting passively by waiting to be told bits and pieces as they developed did not appeal to me much—and yet there was nothing else I could do.

What could I do?

# ○ NINE ○

The weather shifted again on Friday morning, the way it often does from day to day in San Francisco: A thick fog had come rolling in and turned the city into a bleak study in gray. It was particularly heavy in Sea Cliff, obliterating most of the ocean and Bay and all of the Golden Gate Bridge when I got out there a few minutes past nine. Most of the time I like the fog—it can create a certain sinister atmosphere, or the illusion of it, that appeals to my imagination. But not on this day; it seemed more depressing than anything else and made me feel as gray as everything looked.

I left my car in front of the Nichols house and plodded up the terraced steps and pushed the doorbell button. Pretty soon the peephole opened; the eye that peered out at me this time belonged to Laura Nichols. The peephole closed again and the door swung inward.

She was wearing a lavender pants suit today, but she did not look quite as poised or self-assured; the blonde hair was less carefully coiffed and there

were dark smudges under the amber eyes. When she said, "Come in, please," her voice seemed subdued, with none of the coldness or arrogance of Wednesday night. So maybe she isn't going to give me any trouble, I thought. Which would be a good thing for both of us; the way I felt I was just liable to backtalk her if she started in on me.

I entered, gave her my coat, and then followed her down the tiled hallway. The living room seemed even darker and more cheerless today because of the fog swirling on the patio beyond the glass doors. I sat on the sofa again and she sat on the same chair as before, and we looked at each other.

She said, "Thank you for coming."

"Sure. I'm sorry about your brother, Mrs. Nichols."

"Yes. So am I, God knows."

"How is he?"

"Not good." She played with the diamond ring on her finger, took a breath as if preparing herself for a difficult chore, and looked back at me. "I . . . well, I owe you an apology. It seems you were quite right about Martin's mental state."

I did not say anything.

"I should have listened to you," she said. "But it seemed so . . . I just couldn't believe . . ."

She broke off and glanced away; emotions flickered across her face. She was under a good deal of strain, it seemed—and it was not easy for a woman like her to admit to a serious mistake in judg-

ment. But at least she *was* admitting it, which was a point in her favor. And to a virtual stranger at that. I felt myself softening toward her. Not much, but a little.

I asked, "What do the doctors say?"

"That Martin has suffered a severe guilt trauma followed by suicidal depression."

"Will they be able to bring him out of it?"

"They have no opinion yet," she said. "What they're afraid of is that he's lost all will to live and may never regain it."

"Do they believe his confession?"

"They say they can't be sure. Martin keeps insisting he murdered Victor Carding; he seems to believe it even if it isn't true."

"Has he been charged yet?"

"Yes. The county policeman, Donleavy, claims they had no choice." She appealed to me with her eyes. "You told them he couldn't have done it. Why wouldn't they believe you?"

"They don't disbelieve me," I said. "But it's your brother's word against mine, and all the evidence seems to agree with his version of what happened."

"Damn the evidence!" she said with sudden vehemence. "That's all I've heard since last night—from the police, from my attorney, and now from you. Martin is *innocent*."

"Yes, ma'am. And the chances are good the police will prove that themselves, even if your brother won't retract his confession. They're not

going to stop investigating; sooner or later they'll dig up the truth."

"Will they? And if they don't?"

"I can't answer that, Mrs. Nichols," I said. "I don't think he'll be brought to trial; but if he is, my testimony might be enough to convince a jury—"

"Martin must *not* be brought to trial," she said. "I couldn't bear the ordeal, the publicity . . . no, it has to be resolved now, as soon as possible."

My feelings toward her quit softening and went the other way again. The ordeal, the publicity— yeah. She was suffering, all right, but it was as much for herself as it was for Martin Talbot. Bad enough that he was mentally ill and had been charged with homicide; what if he was put on public display in a courtroom and then convicted? What would her friends and neighbors say? How could she hold her head up?

"I want you to conduct your own investigation," she said.

That caught me off guard; I was still thinking what a cold and self-pitying woman she was. I blinked at her. "Me?"

"Yes. I have confidence in your ability and your methods. If anyone can get to the bottom of this quickly, you can."

Sure I can, I thought. I said, "I doubt that, Mrs. Nichols. There's nothing much I could do that the police aren't already doing themselves."

"The police think Martin is guilty; they won't

be trying to prove his innocence. You will be because you *know* he's innocent."

"I'm not sure they'd allow me to work on a murder case, even on a peripheral basis," I said. "They don't like private citizens getting involved."

"You won't be interfering with them, will you? Why should they prevent you from earning your living? Besides, aren't you already involved?"

I hesitated. She was right, of course, and not just about my being already involved. I had got permission in the past to make private inquiries on cases involving homicide, so long as I did not get in the way and promised to report any findings immediately. I doubted that Eberhardt would turn me down on this one; he might even feel my poking around was a good idea, considering the circumstances. And the same went for Donleavy, too.

*What could I do?* I had asked myself last night. Well, this was the answer. If I undertook an investigation it would give me a chance to help Talbot if I could—for his sake, not for Laura Nichols'—and a chance to do something about the death of Christine Webster. It would also keep me active, and keep me involved so maybe I could find out for myself why I *was* involved.

And then there was the money. . . .

"All right," I said, "I'll do what I can, Mrs. Nichols. But on two conditions."

"Yes?"

"One, that the police allow it. And two, that you're completely honest with me."

She bristled a little at that. "Do you suppose I haven't been honest with you?"

"I didn't say that. I only meant that I can't do anything at all for your brother unless I know everything you know. Is there anything you didn't tell me the other day? About him, or about the accident, or about Victor Carding?"

"Of course not. I kept nothing back."

"You'd never heard of Carding before the accident?"

"I had not."

"What about his son Jerry?"

"I didn't know he had a son until the police told me at the hospital last night."

"Christine Webster?"

"No."

"Lainey Madden?"

"No. Who is she?"

"The dead girl's roommate."

"I'm not familiar with the name."

"Was anybody else involved in the accident?"

"No. Only Martin and the Cardings."

"Did Carding make any other threats against your brother? Call him at home later, write him a letter?"

"I'm sure he didn't. Martin would have told me."

I had been watching her pretty closely; if any of her answers had been lies or evasions, I could not

tell it from her expression or from her voice. "Just one more question," I said. "How did you happen to pick me when you decided to hire a detective?"

"You were recommended to me."

"By whom?"

"My attorney, Arthur Brown. I asked him for the name of a competent investigator and he gave me yours. He said you had once done some work for another of his clients."

The name was familiar; I remembered meeting Brown once a couple of years ago, through the client she'd mentioned—a civil case involving a substantial damage suit. He was a partner in an old, established Sutter Street law firm and had, as far as I knew, an impeccable reputation.

So much for that. I got up on my feet; I was more than ready to be on my way—not just because I was anxious to go to work, but also because I wanted out of that dark cheerless house and out of Laura Nichols' company. Working for her was one thing. But the less I had to do with her otherwise, the better I would feel.

We said a few more things to each other, about my calling her right away if I had any trouble with the police, about money, about verbal and written reports. Then she showed me to the door. Neither of us bothered to say goodbye.

I drove through the fog to Geary Boulevard, stopped at a service station there, and called the Hall of Justice from their pay phone. Eberhardt was in his office—and in a foul mood, too. When

he came on the wire he said irascibly, "You going to check in ten times a day, maybe? There's nothing new; I just got off the phone with Donleavy."

"I didn't call to check in," I said. I told him about the interview with Mrs. Nichols and her proposal that I conduct a private investigation.

"I might have figured," Eberhardt said. "You don't know when to quit, do you?"

"I guess not. Is it okay if I go ahead?"

"Hell, I don't care. You know the rules."

"You mind if I talk to Lainey Madden?"

"Be my guest."

"Could you let me have the address?"

"What am I, your flunky? Look it up in the goddamn phone book. She's listed."

And he banged the receiver down in my ear.

# ∘ TEN ∘

Edgewood Avenue, off Parnassus near the University of California Medical Center, was a hillside street so steep you had to park perpendicular to the curb. I squeezed my car into a slot a third of the way up, directly in front of the address I had found in the telephone book. The building was an old Eastlake Victorian that had long ago been cut up into apartments; but its facade had undergone a recent facelift and its gables and columns and porch pediments were painted in bright colors—orange and blue, mostly—like a lot of refurbished Victorians in the city these days.

I went up past a couple of Japanese elms to the front porch. On the row of four mailboxes there I found *C. Webster—L. Madden* listed for Number Three; I pushed the intercom button above the box. There was no response at first and I thought that maybe she was not home after all; when I'd dialed her number from the pay phone I had gotten a busy signal and taken that to mean she was

in. But then the speaker unit made a staticky noise and a woman's voice said, "Yes? Who is it?"

I told her who it was and why I was there. Silence for a few seconds; then the voice asked, "You're the detective the police told me about? The one whose card Chris had?"

"Yes, that's right."

The electronic lock on the door began to buzz. I got over there and inside and climbed an old-fashioned staircase to the second floor. The door with the numeral three on it was closed; but as soon as I knocked it edged partway open on a chain. Half of a pale face appeared in the opening.

"May I see some identification?"

"Sure." I got my wallet out and held the photostat of my license up for her to look at.

When she finished examining it she closed the door long enough to take the chain off and then pulled it wide. She was a pretty girl about Christine's age, with long straight black hair and huge sad colt-brown eyes; the pale skin had a translucent quality, etched now with lines and shadows. She was wearing what may or may not have been mourning clothes: black slacks and a black pullover sweater.

"I'm sorry if I seemed suspicious," she said. "It's just that what happened to Chris has made me a little paranoid."

"I understand," I said.

She stood aside and let me come in. The living room was good-sized, furnished with inexpensive

items made of blonde wood and upholstered in bright patterns, decorated in a way that was feminine without being girlish. Impressionistic oil paintings hung on three of the walls, and there were a lot of colored glass mobiles suspended from the ceiling. On one end table was an enormous white paper rose in a pewter vase.

Lainey sat on the couch, drawing her knees up under her; I took one of the chairs. "I know this must be a difficult time for you," I said tentatively. "I won't keep you long."

"It's all right. I want to do everything I can. Are you working with the police?"

"No. For Martin Talbot's sister."

"Oh—yes. I read about Jerry's father in the papers this morning; it was a shock all over again. It's all so . . . frightening."

I had no words for that; I just nodded.

"Poor Jerry," she said. "First Chris being killed and then his father. . . ." She shivered and was silent.

"Do you know Jerry well?" I asked.

"Pretty well. I met him when Chris started going with him about six months ago."

"How did they meet?"

"A friend of Jerry's introduced them at State."

"Could you tell me the friend's name?"

"Dave Brodnax."

"How would I get in touch with him, do you know?"

"Well, I don't know where he lives, but he's still going to State. And he's on the football team."

"What about Jerry's other friends? Do you know any of them?"

"The only one I've met is Steve Farmer," Lainey said. "He used to go to State too, but he's been working in Bodega Bay for almost a year. He's the one who got Jerry his job up there."

"When did you last see Jerry?"

"Two weeks ago. He came down on the weekend to see Chris."

"Did he usually come down on weekends to see her?"

"Yes. Except for this past one."

"Why didn't he come then?"

"He told Chris he had some important work to do."

"Did he say what it was?"

"No. Just that it was something he was writing."

"Writing? You mean creatively?"

"I guess so. He wants to be a journalist; maybe it was an article or something. He did one once on salmon fishing and sold it to the *Examiner* for their Sunday magazine."

"Did he give any indication that he might be planning to leave Bodega Bay on Sunday night?"

"Chris didn't tell me if he did."

"And you don't have any idea why he disappeared or where he might have gone?"

"No, none. That's part of what makes every-

thing so confusing—Jerry disappearing like that, for no reason. . . ."

I asked, "Did Jerry know Christine was going to have a baby?"

It was five or six seconds before she answered that. Wetness glistened in her eyes, as if she were thinking of the death not only of her friend but of Christine's unborn child; she swallowed a couple of times. "Yes," she said. "Chris told both of us when Jerry was here that last time."

"While all three of you were together?"

"No, separately. But I know she told him because she said so."

"What was his reaction?"

"Well, neither of them wanted to have a baby right away. But Chris wanted it and so did Jerry. They weren't going to, you know, have an abortion."

This line of questioning was not getting me anywhere. And it was making me feel awkward and uncomfortable because of the tears it had put in Lainey's eyes. I went on to something else.

"Did you know Jerry's father?"

"No, I never met him."

"Had Christine met him?"

"Yes. A couple of times."

"Did they get along?"

"I think so. Chris said he drank a lot, but she seemed to like him anyway."

"Did Jerry ever talk about him?"

"Talk about him?"

"What kind of relationship they had, like that?"

"Not that I can remember," Lainey said. A pair of angular creases like an inverted V formed above the bridge of her nose. "Do you think there's some sort of connection between Chris' murder and Mr. Carding's? Is that why you're asking about him?"

"It's possible, yes."

"But I thought Martin Talbot killed Jerry's father. I mean, the papers said he confessed. . . ."

"He did confess," I said, "but he wasn't telling the truth. He's a sick man. But he's not a murderer."

The frown creases deepened. "You can't believe *Jerry* did it? Not just to Chris but his own father? That's crazy. He'd have to be some kind of monster and he's not, he's just not."

"I don't believe it," I said. Which was not the whole truth—I didn't disbelieve it yet, either—but it was what she wanted to hear. "Still, it's a fact that both his fiancee and his father were murdered within two days of each other. And that he's disappeared."

She shook her head in a numb way and hugged herself, as though she felt chilled.

I asked gently, "Had you ever heard of Martin Talbot before you read his name in the papers this morning?"

"No. Never."

"Do the names Laura Nichols or Karen Nichols mean anything to you?"

"Nichols? No, nothing." Another headshake. "I

just can't understand any of this. It seemed so obvious who'd killed Chris, and now . . ."

"Obvious who'd killed her?"

"Yes. She'd been getting threatening calls and letters for more than two weeks. Did you know about that?"

I nodded.

"Well, I thought it was him, the motherfucker."

The last word made me blink. I had more or less grown used to hearing women young and old use street language, the way a lot of them did these days, but the expletive was jarring and a little incongruous coming out of Lainey Madden. I wondered if she even realized she'd said it, as confused and angry and wrought up as she was.

"Maybe it was," I said. "What can you tell me about the threats?"

"Not very much. Chris couldn't imagine who was making them and neither could I. We thought it was one of those, you know, creeps who get their kicks from scaring women."

"It *was* a man who made the calls?"

"I think so. I listened in once on the bedroom extension; the voice was sort of muffled, but it sounded like a man."

"What did he say?"

"Just a lot of crazy stuff about getting Chris, making her pay for what she'd done to him. He never said what it was supposed to be that she'd done."

"The letters said the same kind of thing?"

"Pretty much. Do you want to see one of them?"

"You still have one? I understood you'd given them all to the police."

"I thought I had," she said. "But I found one I'd overlooked after they were gone. It's just like the others."

Lainey stood and disappeared through a doorway on the far side of the room. Half a minute later she came back and handed me a single sheet of inexpensive white paper business-folded into thirds.

I unfolded it. Typed in its approximate center was a sort of salutation and four short sentences; no signature of any kind. The typeface was pica and I could tell from the look of it that it belonged to a machine with a standard ribbon, rather than one of those newer carbon jobs. I could also tell that the typewriter was probably an older model: the "a" was tilted at a drunken angle and the upper curve of the "r" was chipped off at the top.

It read:

Ms. Christine Webster,

You are going to pay for what you did. One way or another, I promise you that. You bitch, I'll hurt you worse than you hurt me. I'll HURT you.

Creepy stuff, all right. The product of a sick mind. I refolded it and put it down on the coffee

table. Lainey left it where it lay; she seemed not to want to touch it any more.

I said, "How many of these were there?"

"Six. They came about every other day."

"Where were they postmarked?"

"Here in the city."

"Did Christine contact the police about them?"

"Yes. But they said there wasn't anything they could do because he hadn't tried to *do* anything to her. Well, maybe he did do something to her," she said bitterly. "And now it's too late."

"Did she tell Jerry about the threats?"

"No. He would have quit his job and come down here to be with her, and she didn't want that; he couldn't be with her twenty-four hours a day. But she was going to tell him if they kept on much longer."

"You told the police she was thinking about seeing a private detective," I said. "When did she decide that?"

"Last week."

"Was my name mentioned at all?"

"No. And I don't know where she got your business card; I didn't even know she had it until the policemen asked me about it."

"Do you have any idea why she didn't get in touch with me?"

"I guess because she hadn't made up her mind yet. I told her seeing a detective was a good idea, but she thought it would cost too much; she didn't have much money."

It wouldn't have mattered to me, I thought. I would have tried to help if she'd come to me; I take jobs for the money but I don't turn them down, not this kind, because of a lack of it. God, why didn't she come to me?

Useless thinking again. I pushed the thoughts away and asked Lainey, "You're sure Christine had no personal enemies? Old boyfriends she'd broken up with, men she'd turned down, people she might have offended in some way?"

"I'm as sure as Chris was. Do you think her killer is someone she knew?"

"Yes," I said. "Unless she'd have gone out to Lake Merced at night to meet a stranger."

"I guess she probably wouldn't have. But she *was* a pretty trusting person, you know. And a kind person, too." Lainey shook her head. "She never hurt anybody, that's the thing. Oh, she was forever trying to tell people how to run their lives—but in a nice way, just trying to help them. She never hurt anybody."

"Had anything unusual happened to her recently, before the threats started? Anything she might have done or been involved in?"

Lainey gave that some thought. "No, I'm sure there wasn't," she said at length. "A girl she knew did commit suicide a little over a month ago, but that didn't have anything to do with Chris."

Suicide again. "What girl was that?"

"Her name was Bobbie Reid. She worked in the same building Chris did downtown—Chris had a

part-time job with the Kittredge Advertising Agency—and they got to know each other."

"Were they close friends?"

"No. Chris didn't see her socially as far as I know."

"Why did Bobbie take her own life?"

"Chris said she was depressed about some sort of personal problem. One night she just swallowed a whole bottle of sleeping pills."

"Did Chris know what this personal problem was?"

"I think she did, but she didn't want to talk about it. She said Bobbie was dead and there was no use talking about the dead—" Lainey winced: Here we were talking about Christine and Christine herself was dead. "She could be kind of close-mouthed at times. Like she didn't tell me or Jerry she was pregnant until after she'd known it herself for weeks."

"Do you have any idea who Bobbie worked for?"

"No. The Kittredge Agency is in a big building in the Financial District and it must have at least a hundred offices in it."

"Is there anything else you can tell me about her?"

"That's all I know. Is it really important? I just don't see how her suicide could be connected with Chris' murder."

"Neither do I," I said. "But it's something that ought to be checked out, just in case. Did you tell the police about Bobbie Reid?"

"No, I don't think I did. It didn't occur to me then; I was pretty upset."

"I'll take care of it."

She nodded. And from outside, in the direction of the Medical Center, there was the faint shriek of a siren. Lainey cocked her head, listening to it—and shivered and hugged herself again. "Is it cold in here?" she said. "It feels cold."

"A little," I said, even though it wasn't. "I think I'd better be going. I don't have any more questions."

"All right. Will you let me know if you find out anything?"

"Of course."

"I won't be home for the weekend, though. I'm flying down to San Diego tonight. That's where Chris' parents live, you see, and the funeral is tomorrow." She wrapped her arms more tightly around herself. "I hope a lot of people come," she said. "Chris liked people."

The siren kept on wailing in the distance, like a discordant note in a dirge.

Or the scream of a young girl dying.

## ∘ ELEVEN ∘

I stopped for lunch at a cafe on Irving Street. Not because I wanted food; I had no appetite after the interview with Lainey Madden. But I had not eaten breakfast and my stomach was kicking up hunger pangs. It was already a quarter of one, and it seemed like an intelligent idea to give the digestive juices something to work on.

Over a tasteless hamburger and a cup of coffee I took my first look at what the *Chronicle* had to say about the murders. Both stories—a news report on the Carding homicide and an update on the death of Christine Webster—were on page two, the front page being given over to reports of trouble in the Middle East and a big Gay Rights march through Civic Center. There was suggestion of a possible link between the two cases and some attention was paid to Jerry Carding's mysterious disappearance from Bodega Bay; otherwise it was pretty straightforward stuff, no open speculation, just the basic facts. Martin Talbot was said to have confessed to the Carding murder, but the police

were still investigating. My name was mentioned three or four times. There was even a paragraph on my career background in which I was referred to as "something of a Sam Spade type, the last of San Francisco's lone-wolf private eyes."

When I finished forcing down my hamburger I took the paper outside and deposited it in a trash receptacle. Then the last of San Francisco's lone-wolf private eyes got into his car and drove through the cold gray fog to S.F. State College.

There was no street parking near the Nineteenth Avenue entrance, so I turned into Park Merced and left the car in front of an apartment building on Cardenas. The woodsy campus, when I finally got onto it, was crowded but relatively quiet. It had not always been that way. I remembered the television footage from back in 1968: a student strike protesting the war in Vietnam and demanding a Third World Studies department and an open admissions policy; disruption and cancellation of classes, rock-throwing incidents; and our present U.S. senator, S. I. Hayakawa—then president of S.F. State—calling in the police riot squad to bust a few heads. Sad times back then. Ugly times. And all because of a war that we should have stayed the hell out of in the first place.

Well, things change—even for the better sometimes. The kids still looked the same, though, at least to my crusty old private eye: long hair and frizzed hair and Afros, beards, the kind of clothing my generation would have called Bohemian.

Whatever happened to suits and ties and girls in
winter outfits and summer dresses? The question
made me smile mockingly at myself. Pining away
for your lost youth, huh? I thought. You Sam
Spade type, you. Come on, who cares what college
students wear as long as they're happy and getting
themselves an education? And most of these kids
looked happy enough—maybe because it was Friday and they had the weekend and Thanksgiving
vacation to look forward to, or because, for now
anyway, all was right in their world.

But then I remembered that Christine Webster
had been one of them not too long ago, and I
stopped smiling. She had no world anymore—not
this one, at least. And neither did her unborn
child.

I bypassed the Administration Building; I had
already decided that there was no point in trying
to locate Dave Brodnax through the Registrar's
Office. College administrators are chary these
days of giving out any information on students,
including class schedules, and the fact that I was
a detective would carry no weight at all. Lainey
had said Brodnax was on the football team; I
thought that maybe I would be able to get to him
through the coach or somebody else in the Physical Education department.

As it turned out, finding Brodnax was easier
than I had anticipated. The first young guy I
stopped for directions told me the football team
had just begun its daily practice in Cox Stadium;

the last game of the season was tomorrow afternoon. He explained how to get to the stadium, over on the north side of the campus, and I made my way in that direction. Halfway there, I heard voices yelling the way football players do. They led me straight to the backside of the press box and an open gate in a cyclone fence.

Cox Stadium was laid out below in a kind of grotto, surrounded by wooded slopes, with more trees and undergrowth beyond the north end zone. Picturesque. The stands were made out of concrete and had rows of wooden benches; I was on the home side. I went through the gate and down fifty or sixty steps toward the field. The players, about four dozen of them in pads and practice jerseys and maroon helmets, were spread out across the turf running plays and banging into tackling dummies and doing wind sprints. The grass was pretty chewed up and deep furrows striped it where the yardlines were. It was not getting as much care as it should, probably because of maintenance cutbacks by the college when Proposition 13 limited their tax revenue.

I left the stands and crossed the track that ovaled the field and went to the sideline benches. A dark guy in his thirties was standing there, writing something on a clipboard. He wore a maroon windbreaker and had a whistle strung around his neck; I thought that he must be one of the coaches.

He glanced up as I approached him. It was cold

down there and his cheeks had a brick-colored tinge. "Something I can do for you?"

"I'd like to see Dave Brodnax, if that's okay."

"Is it important?"

"Yes, sir, it is. Just tell him it's about Jerry Carding and Christine Webster."

The names seemed not to mean anything to him; maybe he only read the sports sections in the daily papers. But he said, "All right, I'll send him over," and moved away toward where a group of beefy-looking kids were just starting to practice the recovery of fumbles.

I watched him pick one out of the group, say something to him. The kid looked over at me, nodded at the coach, and then came trotting over. He took off his helmet just before he got to me, and I saw that he had a wild shock of reddish hair and two or three hundred freckles. He was at least four inches over six feet and would weigh in at around 240—some big kid. The knuckles on his hands looked as large as walnuts.

"Hi," he said, "I'm Dave Brodnax." His voice was surprisingly soft for someone his size, and it matched the look in his eyes: grave, troubled. "You another policeman?"

"Not exactly." I introduced myself. He knew my name from the newspapers and seemed willing enough to answer questions when I explained to him why I was investigating.

"But there's not much I can tell you," he said.

"I don't have any idea who could've killed Christine or what happened to Jerry."

"The last time you talked to Jerry was when?"

"About a month ago when he and Steve came
down from Bodega Bay for the weekend."

"Steve Farmer?"

"Right. Steve lives up there now, but his folks
are here in the city. He brought Jerry down a few
times, so he could visit them while Jerry was
seeing Chris."

"Jerry doesn't have a car?"

"No. He did have one until last spring, but he
sold it because he needed money to finish out the
semester here at State."

"How did he get to San Francisco when Farmer
didn't bring him?"

"Borrowed Steve's car or took the bus."

"Uh-huh. What was the job he had up there?"

"Deckhand on one of the commercial salmon
boats," Brodnax said. "I don't know which one."

"Did he like doing that?"

"He thought it was okay. But it was just a way
for him to make enough money so he could come
back to school. He wants to be a writer, you know.
One of those investigative reporters, like Wood-
ward and Bernstein."

"Then as far as you know, he wasn't having any
problems in Bodega Bay? Nothing that would
make him drop out of sight as suddenly as he
did?"

"Not as far as I know. I guess Steve could tell you if he was."

"Where does Farmer work?"

"At a place called The Tides. As a tally clerk and warehouseman at the fish market there."

I asked him about Jerry Carding's relationship with his father. His answers were pretty much the same as the ones Lainey Madden had given me: they'd got along fine, no major disagreements that Jerry had ever mentioned. Brodnax had met Victor Carding on a couple of occasions and professed a general liking for him, although "he was into booze kind of heavy and made some slurs about blacks once." And if he had disapproved of Christine for any reason, Brodnax did not know about it.

"I understand you introduced Jerry and Christine," I said then. "Is that right?"

"Yeah. She was in my psych class during the spring semester and I took her out a couple of times. But the vibes weren't right for anything heavy between us. She and Jerry connected right from the first; it seemed to be the real thing for both of them."

"Did you see much of her after she began going with Jerry?"

"Not too much. With Jerry a few times around campus."

"Did she ever mention anything that might have been bothering her?"

"You mean those threats she'd been getting?"

Brodnax shook his massive head. "I didn't know about them until the police told me. Chris never talked much about herself."

"Do you know the names Martin Talbot or Laura or Karen Nichols?"

"No. I didn't recognize them in the papers this morning and I still don't."

"How about Bobbie Reid?"

He frowned at that and shifted his helmet from one hand to the other. "Bobbie? What's she have to do with Chris' murder?"

"Maybe nothing, but her name came up. You knew her, then?"

"I met her a few times, yeah."

"Here at the college?"

"No. Steve Farmer used to go with her."

Now that was interesting. Christine and Bobbie knew each other, Bobbie used to date one of Jerry Carding's best friends, Bobbie commits suicide, and Christine is murdered. Another connection—but where, if anywhere, did it lead?

I asked, "How long ago was this?"

"A year or so. They were pretty involved for a while."

"Why did they break up?"

"I don't know. Steve wouldn't say anything about it afterward; I don't think it was a friendly split."

"Was he hurt? Angry?"

"Both, I guess. But he got over it."

Did he? I wondered. "Did you see Bobbie at any time after the break-up?"

"No, not once."

"Do you know any of her other friends?"

"Just Steve."

"Jerry knew her, though?"

"Sure. Same way I did, through Steve."

"Did he ever talk about her?"

"I can't remember if he did."

"Why would she take her own life? Any ideas?"

"No. But she was a spacey chick."

"How do you mean?"

"Emotional, hyped up all the time."

"Drugs?"

"No," he said, "I don't think she was into that. A little pot, maybe, but that'd be all. She was just . . . I don't know, intense, freaky. Like she couldn't get her head together. I can't explain it any better than that."

The wind blowing across the floor of the stadium was bitter cold; I could feel my ears and cheeks burning. And I had run out of questions. So I said, "Okay, Dave, thanks. I won't keep you any longer."

He nodded solemnly. "I wish there was more I could do to help," he said. "I keep thinking something's happened to Jerry too. If he's all right, why hasn't he shown up all week? Or why hasn't somebody found him?"

"Somebody will, son. Sooner or later."

He nodded again and gave me his hand: his grip

was as gentle as his voice. Then he put his helmet on and trotted onto the field, and I turned back toward the stands.

On the way there I noticed that the team's place-kicker had begun practicing field goals at the north end. He was a soccer-style kicker and pretty good, judging from the forty-yarder he put squarely between the uprights. The second kick I watched him try, from forty-five yards out, hit the crossbar, caromed straight up, hit the crossbar a second time, and fell through: good.

For some reason, my mind being what it is, that made me think of a country-and-western song that had been popular several years ago, a religious novelty item with the more or less unforgettable title of "Drop-Kick Me, Jesus, Through the Goal Posts of Life." Uh-huh. Well, some of us got drop-kicked through, all right. But some of us missed wide right or wide left, or just by inches, and some of us—like Christine Webster—got blocked at the line of scrimmage.

And then there were the ones like me. We made it through, but not without hitting the damned crossbar a few times on the way. . . .

From the college I drove downtown and stopped at the main library in Civic Center where I spent half an hour looking through month-old issues of the *Chronicle* and *Examiner*. I found nothing at all about Bobbie Reid—no news story, no obituary, not even a funeral notice. Which meant that

her death, like so many deaths in a city as large as San Francisco, had not been deemed important enough or unusual enough to warrant coverage; and that her body, like Christine Webster's, had been claimed by out-of-town relatives and her funeral held elsewhere.

There would have to be a police report on file, though, because the Homicide Detail is required by law to investigate all suicides. Eberhardt could look it up and use it to begin digging into Bobbie's background.

As for me, it seemed that a drive up to Bodega Bay was the next order of business. I had no leads to pursue here, no leads at all except for the tenuous link to Steve Farmer's involvement with Bobbie Reid; maybe I could find out something by talking to Farmer or by nosing around among the people in Bodega who knew Jerry Carding. On the way out of the library, I decided I would head up the coast first thing in the morning.

It was almost five o'clock by then. I had not been to my office all day and I had been out of touch since before eleven; it was possible that there was a message or two on my answering machine. Better check it out, I thought, and then call Eberhardt from there before he knocks off for the day.

Taylor Street was only a few blocks from the library, but it took me ten minutes to get there because of the rush-hour traffic. I coaxed the car into a narrow parking space near my building,

went inside and looked through the slot in the mailbox. Nothing. The elevator was being cranky again: it made grinding noises and shuddered a lot on the way up. But it determined not to break down and strand me between floors, as it had once for twenty minutes a couple of years ago. I got out of it in a hurry, making a mental note to use the stairs until the landlord got the thing fixed again, and moved down the hall to the office door.

And pulled up short when I got to it.

The door was cracked open about six inches.

The skin along my back prickled; I could feel my stomach muscles begin to wire up. I had locked the door last night—I was always careful about locking it when I left the office because of the kind of neighborhood this was. The building had no janitor, and the only other person with a key would be the landlord; but he was not in the habit of paying uninvited calls on his tenants.

It was quiet in the hall except for the muffled, desultory clacking of a typewriter from one of the offices at the far end. But when I edged closer to the door I could hear another sound—a low pulsing beep, the kind a phone makes when it's been off the hook for more than thirty seconds. The slit between the door and jamb let me see nothing but darkness and the faint smeary glow from the lights in the building across the street.

I stayed where I was for another ten seconds, listening to the beep from the phone. Then I put the heel of my hand against the panel, held a

breath, and gave the door a hard shove and went in across the threshold by one step, reaching out for the light switch on the inside wall.

There was nobody in the room or in the little alcove off of it; I could see that and sense the emptiness as soon as the overhead lights blazed. But what I did see made me recoil, stunned me with an impact that was almost physical.

The office had literally been torn apart.

# ◦ TWELVE ◦

Wanton, senseless destruction. All the drawers in the filing cabinets standing open and their contents strewn across the floor. The magazines from the table in the visitor's area ripped apart. The *Black Mask* poster pulled off the wall and shredded out of its frame. Everything swept off the desk, everything emptied out of the desk drawers. The typewriter still on its stand but the ribbon unwound from the spools like twenty feet of jumbled black intestine. The dregs from the coffee pot splashed on one wall; granules from the jar of instant coffee hurled around over the scattered papers. Jagged slash marks in the padded seat and back of my chair. Worms of white glue squeezed out over part of the desk and part of the client's chair. A long deep gouge in the desk top, made with a knife or maybe my letter opener. And in the alcove, all the supplies scraped off the shelves, my spare change of clothes cut into strips, and a can of cleanser sprinkled over the tangle on the floor.

I started to shake, looking at all of that. A savage, impotent rage welled up inside me; I had that ugly feeling you get when something like this happens, this kind of personal violation: a combination of pain and hatred and confusion that makes you want to smash something yourself.

The more I looked at the carnage in there, the wilder I felt. In self-defense I caught hold of the door, backed into the corridor, and shut out the sight of it. It was two or three minutes before the shaking stopped and the black haze cleared out of my head. Before I could trust myself to go talk to anybody.

The office across the hall was vacant and had been for weeks; I went back past the elevator, toward the clacking of the typewriter. A guy named Faber who ran a mail-order business had the office adjacent to mine, but there were no lights on inside and the door was locked. The fourth office, where the typewriter sounds were coming from, belonged to a CPA named Hadley. I opened the door and went in there.

Hadley was sitting at one of two desks across the room, hunt-and-pecking on a small portable. He looked up as I entered and gave me one of his smarmy grins. He was a thin bald-headed guy in his forties, with a fox-face and a wise-ass sense of humor.

"Well, if it isn't the dago private eye," he said. "How's the snooping business these days?"

"Knock it off, Hadley. I'm in no mood for bull-shit."

He took a closer look at my face, and the grin wiped away in a hurry. "Hey," he said, "what's the matter with you? You look—" He stopped there, but he did not have to say it; we both knew how I looked.

"You see anybody at my office today?"

"No. Why?"

"Hear anything down there?"

"Like what?"

"Like noise. Like a lot of damn noise."

"I didn't hear any noise. What—"

"You been here all day?"

"No. I was out from eleven until about two."

"What about Faber across the hall? He come in today?"

"I don't think so; he usually doesn't on Fridays. Listen, what the hell happened?"

"Somebody busted up my office, that's what happened."

"Busted it up? You mean vandalized it?"

"That's what I mean."

Hadley began to look worried, but not for my sake. "You know who did it?"

"If I did, I wouldn't be here talking to you. You sure you didn't see anybody or hear anything while you were around?"

"Positive. Busted up your office, huh?" He looked around his own office, as if he were visualizing the same kind of thing happening here.

"This building isn't safe any more," he said. "Raise the goddamn rent and it isn't even safe. Maybe we'd better think about moving out."

"Yeah," I said, "maybe we'd better."

I left him and went back along the hall to my door. When I opened it and bent to look at the lock I did not see any fresh scratches or signs of forced entry. But it wasn't much of a lock; a kid could have picked it with a bubblegum card. I got a tight hold on myself, stepped inside, and shut the door behind me.

The destruction was not any easier to look at, but I could face it now without feeling as though I would come unglued. I stood still for a time and asked myself why. For God's sake, why?

Tenderloin junkie looking for money to buy a fix? Maybe. One of the tenants on the second floor had had his office broken into a few months ago and his petty-cash box looted, and there had been a couple of other break-ins over the years. But never my office, never a detective's; no money here, even a junkie knew that. Besides, what pawnable items there were, like the typewriter and the answering machine, had not been carried away.

Kids, vandals? More likely. Except that there were none of the vandal's trademarks: words spray-painted on the walls, puddles of urine or piles of feces. Except that pure vandalism was one of the few crimes that did not happen much in the Tenderloin, and especially not to one office in

a building that was locked up at night and full of people during the day.

Somebody looking for something in my files? But I had no information that anyone would want, or at least none I could imagine anyone wanting; just a lot of case-report carbons, most of which were old and nearly all of which were mundane. That sort of thief, looking for something he couldn't find, might take out his frustration on the office itself—only this was not an act of frustration. It had taken time, a lot of time, to do all this damage. And that made it an act of frenzy, done by somebody with—

—a sick mind. And whoever had been threatening Christine Webster, who had maybe killed her, had a sick mind; the anonymous letter Lainey Madden had shown me confirmed that. The same person? Possible—and yet it didn't seem to make much sense. Why come after me? My involvement was minimal enough and I knew even less and posed a far smaller threat than the police. And what would destroying my office accomplish in any case?

Still. The time was right: somebody vandalizes the office while I'm in the middle of two linked murder cases. It could be one of the people I had met and talked to in the past few days. Or it could be somebody I had yet to meet and talk to; my name had been all over the papers. Jerry Carding? Steve Farmer?

Somebody.

*Why?*

The beeping from the disabled phone penetrated and sent me wading through the debris on the floor, around to the far side of the desk. The phone was lying there in two pieces, the receiver hooked over one of the chair legs. I picked it up and put it back together and set it down on the slashed chair seat. The answering machine was upside down under the window; I picked that up too and laid it on top of the typewriter.

I dialed the Hall of Justice and asked for Eberhardt. Got him half a minute later. "It's me again," I said.

"Now what? I was just on my way home."

I told him what now. There was a silence. Then he said, "Christ, can't you stay out of trouble for one day?" but he no longer sounded annoyed or irascible.

"Lecture me some other time, will you? This isn't my fault."

"Bad, huh?"

"It couldn't be much worse."

"You think it's connected with the Webster and Carding cases?"

"I don't know what to think. Maybe."

"All right. I'll be there in twenty minutes."

"Bring a couple of lab boys with you. There might be prints."

"Twenty minutes."

I hung up and fiddled with the switches on the answering machine. It seemed to be working

okay—and there was a message on it, from Donleavy. His voice said I should call him at his office in Redwood City and then proceeded to give the number.

The message told me something else, too: my office had been vandalized sometime today, during business hours. If it had happened last night Donleavy would not have been able to reach me because of the disabled phone.

I dialed his number right away; it was better to be doing something constructive than brooding at what was left of this place. And it turned out that he was also still in.

"Thought you'd want to know," he said. "I had a couple of my men make another search of the Carding garage and the grounds around it; they found the second bullet."

"Good. Where?"

"Outside the garage window, in a bush."

"So that's what happened to it. Sure, the window was part way open, now that I think about it. I should have remembered that before. You going to withdraw the charges against Talbot now?"

"Not yet. Chances are he fired the bullet through the open window, considering where it was found and a Ballistics report confirming that it came from the murder weapon; but there's no way of proving he did. Carding could have fired it himself, sometime prior to his death."

"But you do believe Talbot is innocent?"

Donleavy made a sighing sound. "What I believe

doesn't seem to hold much water around here. The DA's still planning to prosecute."

"Has Talbot's condition changed any?"

"Status quo. He's been under sedation most of the day. That's a preliminary treatment in cases of suicidal depression, the doctors tell me."

"No other developments, I guess?"

"Nope. How about with you? I talked to Laura Nichols this afternoon at the hospital; she said she'd hired you to do some investigating of your own."

"Yeah. I was going to call you about that tonight. You mind?"

"Your buddy Eberhardt doesn't mind. Why should I?"

"I told him about Bobbie Reid and her connection with Christine Webster and Jerry Carding. "Might be something in that, at least where the Webster case is concerned; I'll pass it along to Eberhardt. I don't see how it could tie in with the Carding homicide, though."

"Neither do I," Donleavy said. "Anything else?"

"My office was vandalized today. Torn apart. I'm standing here in the wreckage right now, waiting for Eberhardt."

"Rough. Any idea who did it?"

"No. But I'm not so sure it's coincidence."

"How come?"

"Nothing stolen, for one thing. What time did you leave your message on my machine?"

"About eleven. Why?"

"Whoever did it knocked the phone off the hook," I said. "So it had to have happened sometime between your call and when I got here a little after five. Which pretty much lets out street kids; they don't vandalize business offices in broad daylight."

"So you think it ties in with the two homicide cases?"

"That's what I'm afraid of."

After we rang off I looked around at the destruction again, in spite of myself. My gaze settled on the shredded *Black Mask* poster. It was no special loss; I could get another one made from the magazine cover. But it made me think of my collection of pulps. The damage here would amount to no more than a few hundred dollars—but what if the same kind of thing happened at my flat? Those six thousand pulps had to be worth more than thirty thousand dollars at the current market prices; most were irreplaceable, at least where I was concerned, and I had damned little personal property insurance. The thought of them being demolished started me shaking all over again.

I got on the horn to Dennis Litchak, a retired fire captain who lives below me, and asked him to go upstairs and check on my flat; we had exchanged keys some time ago, as a general precaution between neighbors. He was gone the better part of ten minutes and I did a lot of fidgeting while I waited. But when he came on again he

said, "Everything's okay. You didn't have any visitors."

I let out a breath. "Thanks, Dennis."

"What's up, anyhow?"

"I'll tell you about it later."

I went over to the window and stood looking down at the misty lights along Taylor Street. The pulps were still in my mind. My flat was not nearly so easy to get into as this office, but it was a long way from being impregnable; sooner or later, somebody could get inside and destroy or even steal those magazines. That was a fact and I had damned well better pay attention to it. Have another lock put on the front door and the back door. And increase my personal property insurance right away, no matter how much it cost for the premiums. And then just hope to God I did not come home someday to find what I had found here.

A couple of minutes passed. Then two cars pulled up at the curb below—Eberhardt's Dodge and an unmarked police sedan—and Eb and two other guys got out and entered the building. I returned to the desk and cocked a hip against one corner of it, where there were none of the drying worms of white glue. Pretty soon I heard the grinding of the elevator, then their steps in the hall, and the door opened and they came in.

Eberhardt took one long look at the office and said, "Jesus Christ."

"I told you it was bad."

"Looks like a psycho job," one of the other guys said. He had a field-lab case in one hand. "Somebody doesn't like you worth a damn."

"Yeah."

While the lab boys went to work, picking their way through the mess on the floor, I stepped into the hall with Eberhardt. He said then, "Hell of a thing to walk into. You okay, *paisan?*"

"More or less."

"Don't make a grudge deal out of it, huh?"

"You know me better than that, Eb. Besides, if anybody finds out who did it, it'll be you. Or Donleavy, maybe."

"If there's a connection."

"The more I think about it, the more likely it seems."

"We'll see."

"Did your man find out anything new in Bodega?"

"Nothing positive," he said. "The Carding kid left all of his belongings behind when he disappeared, but that may not mean much; none of what little stuff there is is worth anything. And if anybody up there knows where he is or why he left, they're not talking. Friend of his, Steve Farmer, did say that he'd been kind of secretive for a few days. Maybe writing an article of some kind; that's what Farmer thinks."

I remembered Lainey Madden saying that Jerry had not come down to San Francisco last weekend for that same apparent reason. I said, "Farmer

didn't have any idea what this article might be about?"

"No. There wasn't any sign of it among Jerry's effects, either."

"Well, I'm going up there tomorrow myself. Maybe I can nose up something. Okay with you?"

"Go ahead. But it'll probably be a waste of time."

"I know. One thing I can do, though, is ask Farmer about a girl named Bobbie Reid. He used to date her, and she was also a friend of Christine Webster's. She committed suicide about a month ago, because of some sort of personal problem."

Eberhardt cocked an eyebrow. "You find all that out today?"

"Yes. From Lainey Madden and Dave Brodnax."

"You can be a pretty good cop when you set your mind to it," he said without irony. "What else do you know about this Reid girl?"

I filled him in on what few other details I had learned. "The suicide report ought to tell you her next-of-kin," I said, "and maybe who some of her other friends were."

"I'll have Klein check it out."

It was another fifteen minutes before one of the lab guys put his head out and said they were finished. Eberhardt and I went back inside. Most of the file papers and folders had been gathered up into loose stacks, and the rest of the wreckage had been stirred around in a methodical sort of way; the desk and chairs and file cabinets and a few

other things had a fine dusting of fingerprint powder on them.

"We found two dominant sets of latents," one of the lab boys said, "but one set is bound to be yours. Are your prints on file with the Department?"

"Yes."

"Okay. We'll just have to hope the other set is on file too—somewhere. And that they belong to whoever laid into this place."

"How long will it take to run a check?"

"Not too long, local and state. If we have to go to the FBI," he said wryly, "it could take days."

Eberhardt said, "Call him at home later tonight or first thing in the morning, either way. I'll give you the number."

"Right."

"Anything else?"

"Not much," the other guy said. "Lock on the door wasn't jimmied; probably picked with a credit card or something. Smudges on a couple of the papers that seem to be oxblood shoe polish. No help in that, though, unless it's a rare brand that can be traced to certain dealers." He shrugged. "And that's it."

The three of them left not long afterward. When they were gone I spent some time scraping the dried glue off the desktop, putting things back into the drawers. But my heart wasn't in it. It would take me at least a day to sweep up the floors, scrub the walls and furniture, sort out the

files, get somebody to cart away the slashed chair and somebody else to bring in a new one. Next week—when some of the pain and anger had dulled and I could face the task with a sense of detachment.

I got out of there at eight-thirty. And home a little before nine. I forced myself to eat a sandwich I did not want and thought about calling Laura Nichols; but I had nothing of substance to report and no desire to talk to her in any event. I did call Dennis Litchak again, to tell him I would be away tomorrow and to ask him to check on the flat for me from time to time. He said he would.

At a quarter of ten, just as I was about to head into the shower, the phone rang. It was one of the lab guys: they had run the second set of latent prints through the state and local computers. No card match, no ID. Whoever the prints belonged to had never been fingerprinted in the state of California.

Terrific.

So I took my shower and went to bed and eventually to sleep. And had a nightmare about coming home, opening the front door, and being inundated by toppling stacks of pulp magazines, all of which had been ripped to pieces. Voices kept screaming accusations at me, saying things like, "Look what you've done to us! You're supposed to be the last of the lone-wolf private eyes; why didn't you protect your own kind?" Then the voices became eyes, thousands of eyes that glared

balefully at me while I fought to keep from drowning in a sea of shredded pulp paper.

It was absurd stuff, of course, with comic overtones. But it scared the hell out of me just the same.

# ∘ **THIRTEEN** ∘

Until the early sixties Bodega Bay had been a quiet and old-fashioned commercial fishermen's province. People from the bigger Sonoma County towns like Santa Rosa and Petaluma went there to buy fresh crabs and other seafood, or to use one of the nearby beaches, and families came up from San Francisco once in a while to take in the scenic beauty of the Sonoma coastline; otherwise the natives had the place pretty much to themselves.

But then Hitchcock filmed his suspense movie, *The Birds*, on and around the bay, at the village of Bodega close by, and at the complex of bayfront buildings called The Tides, and that resulted in a good deal of publicity and national prominence. Before long Bodega Bay became something of an "in" place to visit or even to live at, and it began to change accordingly. Along with streams of sightseers in the spring and summer months, artists of one type or another, enterprising merchants, retired couples, sport fishermen after salmon or sea bass all flocked there; land devel-

opers built a couple of fancy motels and at least
one expensive community of homes, called Bodega Bay Harbor; antique and souvenir shops
sprang up everywhere. Today, less than two decades later, it was a different place. The rugged
coastline was still the same, and most of the old
buildings and landmarks along Highway 1 were
still there, but all the charm and attractiveness
seemed to be gone. The impression you got was
one of creeping suburbia: another twenty years
and all the hills and cliffs and beaches would
probably be covered with houses, fast-food fran-
chises, shopping centers.

That was the feeling I had, anyway, when I got
up there a few minutes past noon on Saturday—
my first visit to Bodega Bay since a Sunday outing
with Erika Coates eight years ago, in the good
days before the breakup of our relationship. But
then, maybe part of the feeling was my mood, and
part of it, too, the heavy low-hanging fog that
shrouded the coast and gave everything new and
old a cheerless aspect. The mist was so thick it
was almost like rain; I had to use my windshield
wipers since passing through Valley Ford ten miles
back.

I turned off the highway into the parking lot
around which The Tides was built. There were
only three other cars in the lot and nobody out
and around that I could see; even the road was
more or less deserted. I parked in front of the

Wharf Bar and Restaurant and got out into the fog
and an icy wind.

This place, at least, did not appear to have
changed much. All the same buildings—The
Tides Motel, the small ice house, the Union 76
dock, the barber shop and souvenir shop—and all
of them still painted white with garish orange
roofs and trim. Even the weathered signs on the
front of The Tides Wharf, a long low structure
that housed the restaurant and a fresh-fish market, looked to be the same.

I went over and onto the pier that led around
and along the Wharf's backside. The bay was
an oily grayish-black color, wind-rumpled into
whitecaps; the red-and-white buoys that marked
the crossing channel and three high-masted
fishing boats, anchored downwind, rocked in the
swells. You could not see much of Bodega Head
across the bay, and the narrows that led into the
ocean at the southern end, bounded by a pair of
rock jetties, were all but obliterated. The sea air
smelled sharply of salt and dark rain: another
storm building somewhere out on the Pacific.

An archway opened off the pier into the warehouse area where fish-market employees weighed,
cleaned, and packaged catches brought in by the
commercial boats. On my right as I walked
through were round concrete tanks used to keep
shellfish fresh; the long room to my left was lined
with wooden benches and cluttered with large
carts on oversized metal wheels, small dollies,

stacks of wooden pallets, rows of storage lockers, a Toledo weighing scale, and two big refrigeration units.

At the far end a young guy dressed in a sweatshirt and Levi's was hosing down the concrete floor. As I approached he turned and then released the hand shut-off on the hose. He had intense brown eyes, a square flattish face, and a mop of light-brown hair parted in the middle and swept back over his ears. Across the front of his sweatshirt, in maroon letters, were the words *San Francisco State College.*

"Steve Farmer?" I asked him.

He gave me a somewhat wary look. "That's right."

I told him my name. "I'd like to ask you a few questions about Jerry Carding, if you don't mind."

"You're that private detective, aren't you? The one in the papers."

"Yes."

The wariness went away; his eyes took on a worried, unhappy look. He dropped the hose, ran a hand through his shaggy hair. "Well, I can't help you much. I don't know what happened to Jerry; I've already told the police that. But one thing's sure: he didn't disappear because Chris got pregnant *or* because he had anything to do with her murder. He loved her; they were planning to get married. And he's a nonviolent person. He couldn't harm another human being, not for *any* reason."

I nodded. "Everyone I've talked to says essentially the same thing."

"Don't you believe it?"

"I'd like to. When did you last talk to Jerry?"

Farmer sighed. "The day before he disappeared. Last Saturday. We had a beer together after work."

"What did you talk about?"

"Nothing much. He was in a hurry to get home."

"Home?"

"I mean the Darden house over in Bodega. That was where he was living."

"Did he say why?"

"No. Just that he had some work to do."

"The article you told the police about?"

"I think so."

"Did he ever hint as to what it might be about?"

"Never. But he seemed to think it was important."

"How long had he been working on it?"

"I don't know. He'd been kind of excited for three or four days, though."

"Excited in what way? Nervous? Eager?"

"Eager," Farmer said. "When I asked him about it he said it was a secret and I'd find out when everybody else did."

"Who're his other friends here? Anyone he might have talked to about what he was writing?"

"Just Sharon Darden, I guess. Her mother owns the house where Jerry lived; she rents out one of her rooms. But I talked to Sharon after Jerry van-

ished; she doesn't know anything more than I do."

"How close were she and Jerry?"

"If you mean were they making it together, the answer is no. I told you, Jerry was in love with Chris. He's not the kind of guy who screws around on his lady."

"I just wondered if they were good friends."

"Pretty good. If Jerry'd told her anything, she'd have mentioned it to me or the police. She wouldn't have any reason to keep it to herself."

"When did you first find out Jerry was missing?"

"Monday morning. Gus Kellenbeck called me because Jerry hadn't reported for work."

"Kellenbeck?"

"He owns the Kellenbeck Fish Company," Farmer said. "Jerry did odd jobs for him."

"Oh? I thought he worked as a deckhand."

"He did, off and on. But he couldn't make enough money doing that, so he went to work for Kellenbeck."

"This fish company is where?"

"A little ways north of here, on the highway."

"Is it open on Saturdays?"

"Yeah. Every day but Sunday."

"Which boat did Jerry work on?"

"The *Kingfisher*. Andy Greene's troller."

"And where would I find Greene?"

"Over at the marina, probably. On the other side of the bay. He lives on board the *Kingfisher*."

I asked him about Victor Carding, and got a

replay of the unenlightening answers Lainey Madden and Dave Brodnax had given me. Then Farmer paused, frowned, and asked:

"Do the police think Jerry had something to do with what happened to his old man? Is that why you're asking about him?"

"It's a possibility."

"Not to me, it isn't. I thought they arrested the guy who shot Mr. Carding; that's what the papers said."

"Martin Talbot isn't guilty," I said.

"He confessed, didn't he?"

"Yes. But he's not guilty. There are psychological reasons why somebody would confess to a crime he didn't commit."

Farmer half-turned and stared over at one of the refrigerator units. After a time he said, "How can anything like this happen?" but he seemed to be talking more to himself than to me. "Jerry's mother dead in an accident, his father murdered, Chris murdered—everybody he cared about just . . . wiped out. What if he's dead too?"

Yeah, I thought. What if he's dead too?

He faced me again. "Jerry's not a killer, he's a victim. You understand? He's a victim whether he's all right or not."

"I understand, son."

He seemed suddenly a little embarrassed, as if he felt he had displayed too much emotion in front of a stranger. "Look, I, uh, I've got work to do. Is there anything else?"

"Just a couple of things. Is Martin Talbot's name familiar to you?"

"No. I never heard of him until yesterday."

"How about Laura Nichols? Karen Nichols?"

"No."

"About Christine—did she have any enemies you might know about?"

"You mean somebody who'd make those threats the paper said she'd been getting?" He shook his head. "No. Whoever that crazy bastard is, he must be the one who killed her."

"So it would seem," I said. And then asked him the question I had been saving for last: "What can you tell me about Bobbie Reid?"

His reaction was immediate: he jerked slightly, as if I had swatted him one, and his face closed up and something flickered in his eyes that might have been pain. "What does Bobbie have to do with any of this?"

"I don't know that she has anything to do with it. But she and Chris were friends."

"The hell they were."

"You didn't know that? It's true, Steve."

"Bobbie's dead," he said stiffly. "She killed herself more than a month ago."

"So I've been told. Do you know why?"

"No." But he said the word a little too fast, it seemed to me. "Listen, I don't want to talk about Bobbie, okay?"

"You'll have to talk to somebody about her sooner or later. If not me, then the police."

"She couldn't have anything to do with what happened to Chris. How could she? No—I've got enough dead people to think about as it is."

I wanted to press him further, but it would not have done any good; his expression said that he was not going to do any more talking no matter what I said. "All right, Steve. Have it your own way. Thanks for your time."

He was no longer looking at me. He said, "Yeah," and bent to pick up the hose. I watched him walk away from me, open the nozzle, and begin to wash the floor again. But this time he did it in hard, jerky sweeps, with the stream of water thinned down to a jet.

I went out and down the corridor between the fish market and the restaurant. My hands and feet were cold; I decided on a cup of coffee before I made any more stops.

Inside the restaurant I sat near the windows overlooking the bay and did some brooding while I waited for one of the waitresses to serve me. Steve Farmer seemed like a decent enough kid, and his concern for Jerry Carding had struck me as genuine. But I was pretty sure he had lied about not knowing or at least suspecting the motive for Bobbie Reid's suicide. Why? Deep personal feelings that had nothing to do with murder? Or for reasons that did have something to do with murder?

I wondered if Farmer had lied about anything else, or held back information of some kind. I

wondered if the relationships between the young people in this business were what they seemed to be. Add all those questions to the dozen or so others that had accumulated, shuffle them together with the known facts, and what did you get?

Nothing.

So far, not a damned thing.

There was not much to the village of Bodega—just a grocery store, a post office, a tavern, a garage-and-filling station, a few more antique stores than I remembered, and an old country church. I had neglected to ask Steve Farmer how to get to the Darden house, so I stopped in at the grocery to ask directions. The woman there said the Darden place was up on the hill above the village, lots of ice plants out front, can't miss it.

When I drove up past the church I discovered that it *wasn't* a church, not any more; it was a galleria dispensing local artwork. Sign of the times. And of what had happened to the Bodega Bay area. The old values, the old traditions, did not seem to mean much any more. At least not to those who worshipped at the shrine of the Almighty Buck.

The road curled around behind the galleria and wound upward along the face of the hill. From there on a clear day you would have a fine view toward the ocean; now, all you could make out

through the screen of fog were vague surrealistic outlines, like backgrounds in a dream.

The Darden house turned out to be a rambling two-story structure at least as old as I was. The ice plants in the fenced-in yard gave the place a good deal of color: vermillion and lavender and pink, all glistening wetly in the mist. I parked in front, climbed out, and went through the gate and up a crushed shell path to the porch.

Just as I reached it, a slender attractive woman in her mid-forties came around one corner on a branch of the shell path. She wore a scarf over short graying hair, a pair of man's dungarees, and a heavy plaid lumberman's jacket; in her right hand were several sprigs of rosemary. She smiled when she saw me—a nice smile, friendly, infectious.

"Hello there," she said. "Something I can do for you?"

I returned the smile. "Mrs. Darden?"

"Yes?"

Her expression sobered when I showed her the photostat of my license and told her why I was there; a troubled sadness came into her hazel eyes. It was the kind of sadness you see in people who have faced tragedy and known sorrow in their own lives. She had lost someone close to her once, I thought. Her husband, maybe. Farmer had implied that she and her daughter were the only two Dardens who lived here; and she was still wearing her wedding ring.

"It's terrible," she said, "what's happened to Jerry's family and fiance. Just awful."

"Yes, ma'am."

"I just hope that . . . well, that no harm has come to Jerry too." She sighed and shook her head. "His disappearance is a complete mystery to us. To my daughter Sharon and me, I mean."

"Would your daughter be home now?"

"No, I'm afraid not. She's gone to Santa Rosa for the day with her young man." Mrs. Darden paused. "Come inside, won't you? It's much too cold to talk here."

She led me into the house and then into a parlor appointed with forties-style furniture and an odd combination of feminine and masculine objects: hand-painted glass paperweights and a rack of well-used pipes; porcelain figurines and an old cavalry sword hanging above the fireplace mantel; oval cameo portraits in delicate frames and an oil painting of a square-rigged clipper ship. I declined her invitation of something to drink, waited until she had shed her coat and the sprigs of rosemary and seated herself in a padded Boston rocker, and put myself down on the couch.

I asked, "When did you last see Jerry, Mrs. Darden?"

"The night he disappeared. Around nine o'clock."

"What was his mood?"

"Oh, he seemed very excited—very intense.

He'd been in his room all day, working; he didn't even join us for meals."

"He was writing something, is that right?"

"Yes," she said. "He'd borrowed Sharon's typewriter a few days before and I could hear it clacking away during the evenings and all day Sunday. I asked him what he was writing, and so did Sharon, but he wouldn't tell us. He was just like a little boy with a secret."

"When he left the house, was it on foot?"

"Yes."

"Alone?"

"Oh yes."

"Did he say where he was going?"

"To the post office, he told Sharon. He had two envelopes with him."

"What sort of envelopes?"

"Large manila ones."

"Both stamped and addressed?"

"Only one, I believe. Seems to me the other was blank."

"Did you or Sharon notice the name on the addressed one?"

"No, we didn't."

"I understand the police found nothing helpful among Jerry's belongings," I said. "No carbon of what he'd been writing, no discarded papers of anything like that."

"Nothing at all, no."

"Did they take his things away with them?"

"They didn't seem to feel that was necessary.

I've left everything in Jerry's room, just as it was. We're still hoping he'll come back."

"Would it be all right if I looked through them?"

"Surely. I was just going to suggest that you do."

She took me upstairs, into a spacious room at the rear of the house. Jerry Carding had added no personal touches to the furnishings, except for a stack of books on the writing desk set between the room's two windows, and a framed photograph of Christine Webster on the nightstand. The photo gave me a cold hollow feeling: I had only known her in death.

The rest of Jerry's belongings did not amount to much, as Eberhardt had said. Enough clothing to fit into the suitcase in the closet, all of it casual, mod-styled, and inexpensive. A pair of sneakers and a pair of old fisherman's boots. A cheap pocket calculator. A packet of wheatstraw cigarette papers, the kind kids use nowadays to roll marijuana joints. So maybe he smokes a little grass, I thought. So what?

So nothing.

I looked at the books on the writing desk. Dictionary, thesaurus, college journalism text, a couple of novels, and the rest a selection of popular accounts of investigative reporting. There was nothing hidden between the pages of any of them; the cops would have found it if there had been.

The typewriter was an old Smith-Corona manual that had seen a lot of wear. Beside it were several sheets of white dime-store paper. On a

hunch I took one of the sheets, rolled it into the platen, and typed out the words "Jerry Carding" with one forefinger. But the "a" key was not tilted and the "r" key was not chipped; the threatening letters to Christine Webster had not been written on this machine.

I lifted the typewriter and looked at the rubber pad underneath. All that was there besides some dust was a small corner torn off a piece of thin paper. But not typing or book paper; the corner was glossy and colored brown with a line of black. I picked it up and took a closer look. Off a label of some kind, I thought. Or maybe a decal. The back of the glossy side was gummed.

I held it out to Mrs. Darden on the tip of my finger. "Can you guess what this might have come from?"

She peered at it. "I'm afraid not, no."

It may or may not have had any significance; I decided I ought to keep it just in case and put it into my shirt pocket.

We went downstairs again. In the foyer I said, "Would you mind if I came back and spoke to your daughter?"

"Of course not," Mrs. Darden said. "But I'm afraid Sharon won't be back from Santa Rosa until late this evening."

I had already given some thought to spending the night in Bodega Bay; it seemed like a reasonable idea, assuming I did not turn up anything conclusive in the next couple of hours. I said, "I

think I'll probably stay over until tomorrow. I could drop by again in the morning."

"That would be fine. You could come around ten-thirty, we'll be home from church by then."

"Thanks, Mrs. Darden."

"Not at all," she said gravely. "Sharon and I both want to do everything we can to help."

The Kellenbeck Fish Company was a long narrow red-roofed building set at a perpendicular angle to the shore, so that most of it extended out into the bay on thick wooden pilings. A salt-grayed sign hanging below the eaves in front stated its name and said that Gus Kellenbeck was owner and proprietor. There were a couple of ancient, corroded hoists off to one side of a gravel parking area; wedged in between them was a dusty green Cadillac. One other vehicle, a well-traveled Ford pick-up, sat with its nose at an angle to the highway.

I took my car in alongside the pick-up, got out, and went to a shedlike enclosure built onto the front of the main structure. The door there was locked. So I walked around to the side, where a narrow catwalk followed the building's length. The catwalk took me onto a dock about fifty yards square, with a pier in somewhat ramshackle condition attached to it. The pier jutted another fifty or sixty yards into the bay; a lone salmon troller was tied up at the end of it, bobbing in the choppy water.

A middle-aged guy was doing something with a seine net near a row of iron crab pots. I crossed to him and asked where I might find Gus Kellenbeck.

"His office," the guy said laconically. "Inside."

I went into the building through a pair of open hangar-type doors made out of corrugated iron. The warehouse was cluttered with much the same type of equipment and storage facilities as inside The Tides Wharf, except that there was more of it. A bank of machinery, with a crisscross of conveyor belts fronting it, took up a portion of the wall at the upper end. On my left was a cubicle that would be the office; a single grime-streaked window was set beside a closed door. I could not see inside it from the entrance.

The wooden floor was wet and slippery with fish scales; I picked my way across it to the cubicle. When I knocked on the door a hoarse voice said, "What is it?"

I opened the door and looked in. A short bearish guy sat behind a desk cluttered with papers and junk, an open ledger book in front of him and a pencil tucked over his right ear. There was also a bottle of Canadian whiskey on the desk, along with a glass half-full of liquor. The guy glanced at me, glanced at the bottle, scowled, and put his hands flat on the ledger book. He did not look too happy to have a stranger find him drinking on the job, even if he did own the place.

"Mr. Kellenbeck?"

"Yeah?"

"Okay if I come in? I'd like to talk to you."

"What about?"

"Jerry Carding."

That made him scowl again. But he waved an admitting hand at me, closed the ledger, and got up on his feet. He was thick-featured and olive-complexioned, with blue-black hair that was a snarl of ringlets; his nose had been broken at least once, and improperly set, and it seemed to list at a forty-five degree angle toward the left side of his face. His eyes, sea-green flecked with yellow, were heavy-lidded and bloodshot.

I went in and shut the door behind me. Kellenbeck watched me come over in front of the desk; he still did not look happy. He said, "You a policeman?"

"No. Private investigator."

When I gave him my name he said, "Oh, yeah," and then scowled a third time. "How come you're here? I thought the cops were handling the kid's disappearance."

"They are. But I'm working for Martin Talbot's sister. With police sanction."

"Police sanction, huh? All right, sit down."

I took the only other chair in the office, Kellenbeck plunked himself down again in his swivel chair, pinched the bridge of his nose as if he had a headache, and looked at the bottle again. A moment later he caught it up by its bare neck and put it away inside one of the desk drawers.

"So what do you want to know?" he said.

"Well, do you have any idea where Jerry might have gone?"

"Assuming he didn't do any killings, you mean?"

"Assuming that."

He shrugged. "Where do kids go these days? They spend a little time someplace, pretty soon they move on like—what do you call them?"

"Nomads?"

"Yeah. Like nomads."

"Except that Jerry didn't take any of his belongings with him," I said.

"No? I didn't know that."

"Did you see him last Sunday, Mr. Kellenbeck?"

"No. Saturday was the last time, when he knocked off for the day."

"Did he say anything to you then? Give you any indication he might be planning to go away?"

"Not a word," Kellenbeck said. He took a short greenish cigar from a humidor on his desk and began to unwrap it. "I was kind of surprised when he didn't show up on Monday morning, because he'd never missed a day before and always came in right on time. So I called up the Dardens, where he was living, and that friend of his, Steve something, works down at The Tides. Trying to get in touch with him, you know? But he'd just taken off without telling nobody where he was going."

"May I ask when you pay your employees?"

"Middle of the week. Wednesdays."

"Did Jerry ask you for his wages on Saturday?"

"No, why?"

"Well, he had three days pay coming," I said. "Seems a little odd that he didn't ask for it if he was planning to leave Bodega Bay the following night. He's not a wealthy kid; he'd need money wherever he was going."

Kellenbeck scowled one more time. "I never thought of that," he said. He lit his cigar with a wooden kitchen match. "Maybe he wasn't planning to leave on Saturday. Maybe he only got it into his head the next day."

"Maybe. But what would make him decide to go that suddenly, without waiting to collect his salary?"

"You got me. I can't figure it."

"Did he mention anything to you about an article he was writing?"

"Article? You mean like the one he did on salmon fishing?"

"Something he was working on before he disappeared."

"What would that be?"

"I don't know. That's what I'm trying to find out."

"First I heard of it," Kellenbeck said. "He never said a word to me about writing anything."

"Do you know if he had trouble with anyone around here?"

"What kind of trouble?"

"A fight or an argument of some kind. Like that."

"If he did, I never heard about it. He got along with everybody, far as I know. An easygoing kid."

I asked a few more questions and learned nothing from Kellenbeck's answers that I did not already know. When I got up to leave he stood, too, and put out his hand; I took it. He said, "Anything else I can do, you let me know."

"I'll do that," I said, and left him chewing on his cigar and eyeing the glass of whiskey that was still on his desk.

The wind cut at me in icy gusts when I came out onto the dock. Overhead, low-flying tendrils of mist sailed inland at a pretty good clip, but out over the ocean the fog had lifted somewhat and you could see the black-rimmed clouds above it. The day had turned darker, colder; the bay was frothed with whitecaps now, and the smell of salt and ozone had sharpened. It would not be long before the storm blew in and the rains came.

And where is he? I thought. What happened last Sunday night?

What happened to Jerry Carding?

## ○ **FIFTEEN** ○

The road that curled around the northern lip of the bay was relatively new and in good condition; but it was also slick with mist, and the tires on my car were starting to bald a little. I drove at a circumspect twenty-five, squinting through the arcs made by my clattering windshield wipers.

Erika and I had taken this road, I remembered, on that long-ago Sunday outing. It followed the bay's edge toward the jetty and then hooked back up to the top of Bodega Head. From up there you could watch the surf hammering at the jagged rocks below; and you could see the excavation scars where the government had begun work on a proposed nuclear power plant twenty years ago. A public hue and cry had kept them from going through with their plans: this was earthquake country and nobody wanted to be sitting in the shadow of a nuclear reactor if a big quake hit. We had talked about that, Erika and I, standing up there on the Head, holding hands like a couple of young lovers. And later we had gone back to The

Tides to eat crab cioppino before driving home to San Francisco. And that night, after we had finished making love, Erika had said jokingly, "You know something, old bear? You make the earth shake pretty good yourself."

Bittersweet memories . . .

The marina for both commercial and pleasure craft was located in the northwest corner of the harbor, opposite several scattered cottages and homes built along the lower slopes of Bodega Head. It was fairly small and laid out like a squared-off letter W—three long board floats with slips flanking each of them, separated by narrow channels but connected on the shoreward end by a walkway. Less than a dozen boats were moored there now, most of them commercial trollers.

I eased my car onto the shoulder near somebody's driveway, crossed the road, and stepped onto the ramp that led out to the slips. The wind was strong enough here to numb my cheeks and make my eyes water; above the sound of it you could hear the boats rubbing and banging against the floats. They all seemed deserted at first, but when I reached the ramp's end I noticed movement on one off to my right, in a slip two-thirds of the way along the nearest float. I peered over there. The lettering on the stern read *Kingfisher*, and below that, *Bodega Bay.*

I climbed down a short metal ladder onto the swaying float and made my way carefully along the boards. A stocky well-muscled guy dressed in

denim trousers and a thin sweatshirt, no coat, was kneeling on deck; long copper-colored hair fanned out in the wind behind him like a horse's mane at full gallop. He had the engine housing up, and there was an open tool box and an assortment of wrenches and things laid out on a strip of canvas beside him. I had a glimpse of the engine—a GMC 6-71 diesel—but I could not see what he was doing to it.

I stepped up close to the stern gunwale. "Ahoy!" I shouted over the wind. "Ahoy there!"

He came around quickly, a box wrench he had been using upraised in one hand. There were smudges of grease and oil over the front of his sweatshirt, on his hands and arms as well. He owned one of those dark brooding faces, with an aggressive jaw and deep-sunk eyes under heavy brows, that some women seem to find attractive; but now it was pinched-up with annoyance. The cold had turned his lips the color of raw liver; I wondered what he was trying to prove by not wearing a coat of some kind.

He said, "What the hell do you want?"

"Are you Andy Greene?"

"Who wants to know?"

I told him. "Can I come aboard?"

"What for?"

"I'd like to talk to you—"

"I haven't got time to talk now."

"It won't take long."

"I'm busy, friend."

"It's important. I'm here about—"

"Some other time," he said. "Blow away, friend."

Pleasant bastard, aren't you? I thought. I said, "Look, *friend*, all I want is a few minutes of your time—a few answers to some questions about Jerry Carding. Then you can get back to whatever you're doing and I'll be on my way."

Some of the aggressiveness went out of his expression, but not all of it. He got onto his feet, balancing himself on the pitching deck with his feet spread. "The private eye from Frisco, right?" he said.

"That's right."

The deep-sunk eyes studied me; they did not seem very impressed by what they saw. "So what's your interest in the kid?"

"Professional interest. He's part of a case I'm working on."

"What case?"

"You've heard about it. The murders of Jerry's fiance and father."

"They got the guy who killed his old man," Greene said.

"Did they? I'm not so sure."

"Yeah? You think the kid did it?"

"No," I said. "Can I come aboard or not? I don't like shouting this way."

"Waste of time for both of us," he said. "I can't help you, friend. I already told the cops all I know."

"Which is what?"

"Which is nothing. Last time I saw the kid was two weeks ago, when he went out fishing with me. He didn't say a word about going away and I don't have any idea where he went. Okay? Now I got work to do."

He turned away from me and knelt again in front of the Jimmy diesel. I stayed where I was for ten or fifteen seconds, watching him. Irritation was sharp in me—but there was nothing I could do. The boat was his property; if he did not want me aboard, or to do any more talking to me, those were his privileges.

"Maybe I'll see you again, Greene," I said, just to find out if he had anything else to say. But I could have saved my breath. He bent forward, inside the engine compartment, and the only answer I got was the faint clank of the box wrench against metal.

Most of the gray daylight was gone by the time I got back to The Tides; it was almost four-thirty. Shadows covered the rolling hills to the east, and the scattered lights up there had a wet glistening look through the fog. Cold rainy night coming up—and there was nothing for me to do now except wait it out and hope that tomorrow turned out to be a more productive day.

In the trunk of my car I keep a small overnight bag for unplanned layovers such as this one. I got it out, carried it into the motel office to register,

and then took it up to the room I was given. The cold seemed to have seeped into my bones; my feet felt as if I had been walking barefoot in six inches of snow. So I took a quick shower and afterward made a cup of instant coffee with one of those hot-water dispensers motels put in for guests these days. Then I propped myself up on the bed to do some thinking.

Jerry Carding. He was a central figure, all right. And I was becoming convinced that if I could find him, or discover what had happened to him, I could begin to piece together an explanation for everything.

Go over the facts again, I thought. What did I know and what could I surmise from that knowledge? Well, I knew that he had disappeared sometime after nine o'clock last Sunday night, after leaving the Darden house with a couple of manila envelopes presumably containing an article he'd written. Had he mailed the stamped and addressed envelope? No way of knowing yet. If he had, to whom? Newspaper, maybe, or a news magazine: Jerry had seemed to think the article was important, which meant its subject matter had to be of some news value. But then why hadn't the article surfaced by now, been turned over to the police? Blank. Why had Jerry taken the unaddressed envelope with him? Planning to show it to somebody, possibly—but that seemed inconsistent with the cloak of secrecy he had wrapped around this project of his. Unless—

Blackmail?

No, I didn't like that. From all I had found out about Jerry Carding, a blackmail scheme would be foreign to his nature; what he seemed to care most of all about was establishing a career for himself as an investigative reporter. And if blackmail was what he'd been up to, why take the trouble to write the article at all? Whatever he'd found out, the knowledge alone, would have been enough.

Try it another way, then. Suppose he *had* uncovered something not only newsworthy but damaging to somebody; and suppose this somebody, call him X, found out in turn that Jerry was writing his article and was afraid of public exposure. X could have waylaid him at the post office, before the stamped envelope could be mailed. That would explain Jerry's sudden disappearance—why he failed to ask Kellenbeck for his salary, why he left all his belongings behind—and it would provide a grim probable answer to the question of whether or not he was still alive.

Better theory, that one, but not much better. How could X have known Jerry was on his way to the post office? From watching the Darden house? Farfetched. And if X knew about the article, why wait until Jerry had finished it before going after him? And how could X have found out in the first place, with Jerry being as close-mouthed as he was?

Questions.

And more questions: How could a discovery in Bodega Bay, or an article written about it, tie up with a shooting in San Francisco two days later and a shooting in Brisbane two days after that? Where did the Talbot/Nichols family fit in? Where did Bobbie Reid fit in? What was the significance of the threatening letters and telephone calls to Christine Webster? Why had my office been vandalized? Did the torn corner from the label or decal I had found in Jerry's room mean anything? Did Andy Greene's surly reticence mean anything?

It was like trying to make your way through a labyrinth: you kept moving around, taking this path and that, and all you seemed to find were new and more confusing twists and turns. Unless you figured out the right turns before too much time had passed, or blundered into them, you could become hopelessly lost.

And right now I felt about as lost as you could get.

Hunger pangs drove me out of there at six, down to the Wharf Bar and Restaurant. Where I ate a Crab Louie, drank two bottles of Schlitz, and brooded out at the dark waters of the bay. No rain yet, but the fog had dissipated somewhat and the sky was thick with swollen clouds; the wind made angry moaning sounds and rattled the window glass from time to time. The weather and the nonproductive brooding combined to make me feel frustrated and a little depressed.

I went back to my room and put in a long distance call to Eberhardt's home in San Francisco to see if he had any news. No answer. Out somewhere with his wife for dinner, probably. I tried Dennis Litchak's number; he was in, as he almost always was, and he assured me that everything was fine with my flat. I told him I would be spending the night in Bodega Bay. He told me not to worry, he'd keep on checking until I got home. So much for that.

The first drops of rain began to splatter against the window.

I debated calling Laura Nichols, decided what the hell, she *was* paying my wages, and had the motel operator dial her number. It was Karen Nichols who answered. I told her who was calling and asked if her mother was home.

"Yes," she said, "but our lawyer's here and they're having a conference. I suppose I can interrupt them if you want to talk to her."

"That's not necessary. I'm just checking in."

"Where are you? You sound far away."

"In Bodega Bay. Trying to get a line on Jerry Carding."

"Oh. Then you're still investigating?"

"Still at it, yes. But I haven't found out much so far."

"How long will you be there?"

"Until tomorrow sometime. Let me give you the number here, just in case." I did that, and then

said, "While I've got you on the phone I'd like to ask you a couple of things."

"What things?"

"Do you or your mother know anyone in Bodega Bay?"

"No."

"Is the name Bobbie Reid familiar to you?"

"Who?"

"Bobbie Reid. R-e-i-d."

"No. Who's she?"

"Someone whose name came up. How about Steve Farmer?"

"No."

"Dave Brodnax?"

"No."

"Lainey Madden?"

"No."

So much for that, too.

I could not think of anyone else to call except Donleavy, and I had already wasted enough long-distance money as it was. So I turned on the TV set and sat staring at it. Opiate of the masses—but not for me, not tonight. I got up again after ten minutes and shut it off.

Sheets of rain now, buffeting the window.

Mournful whistle-and-howl of the wind.

Saturday night, I thought. Not a good night for a man to be alone, especially not in a storm and place where he has no friends. A night for company, for good conversation, for a warm fire. For a woman. How long since I had last gotten laid? Too

damned long. Crusty old bachelor with a beer belly, sloppy habits, and a collection of pulp magazines. No wonder I wasn't getting laid; who would want to climb into the sack with somebody like that? Getting old, too. The last of San Francisco's lone-wolf private eyes . . .

Nuts. San Francisco's only private eye who sits around motel rooms feeling sorry for himself.

I went to the window, stood looking out for awhile and watching rain drool down the glass. Too early to go to bed . . . did I feel like reading? No, but it was better than thinking myself into a blue funk. I took out one of the pulps tucked into the overnight case with the rest of my stuff—a 1940 issue of *Detective Fiction Weekly*—and lay down under the covers with it.

One of the featured novelettes was called "Finger of Doom" and I started to read that first. But I must have been a lot more tired than I'd thought; halfway through the story my eyelids began to feel heavy, my attention wavered and dulled. And I dozed, woke up, tried to read some more, and promptly dropped off for good.

Which had to be one of the few times anybody ever fell asleep reading a story by Cornell Woolrich. . . .

# ° SIXTEEN °

I was up at eight o'clock on Sunday morning and in a better frame of mind: ten hours' sleep and a new day. Most of the storm seemed to have blown inland during the night; the rain had slackened to an intermittent drizzle. The overcast was still thick and at a low ceiling, but it did not seem quite as oppressive as it had yesterday afternoon and evening.

When I finished shaving I went out to hunt up breakfast and a Sunday newspaper. No luck. The Wharf Bar and Restaurant was not open this early, nor was anything else in the immediate vicinity. I bought a copy of Saturday's Santa Rosa *Press-Democrat* from a coin-operated machine in Bodega, took it back to the motel, settled for another cup of free instant coffee, and enlightened myself with day-old news.

At ten I gathered my things together and checked out. It was ten-thirty on the nose when I pulled up in front of the Darden house. If nothing else, I was at least punctual.

Mrs. Darden answered my knock and admitted me. She was wearing a tweed suit today, with a blue scarf at the throat, and her graying hair had been neatly brushed for church. Handsome woman, all right. The smile she let me have was warm, as if I were an old friend come to pay a social call.

We went into the parlor, where a girl about eighteen was standing near the fireplace. You could see right away that she was Mrs. Darden's daughter: same short hair, hers being a tawny brown, same attractive features, same hazel eyes, same infectious smile. Besides age, the major differences between them were height and chest development; Sharon was about four inches taller and two bra sizes smaller, which gave her a somewhat willowly look. She was dressed in an ankle-length wool skirt and a bulky knitted sweater.

Her mother introduced us and then excused herself and left the room. Sharon and I sat down. She said, "Mom told me about your talk yesterday. I can't tell you much more about Jerry than she did, I'm afraid."

"This article of Jerry's—he never gave you any clue as to what it was about?"

"No. The only thing he ever said was that it was something which would establish his career as a journalist."

"He seemed positive about that?"

"Oh yes, very positive."

"Can you think of any sort of unusual occur-

rence in this area recently?" I asked. "Anything that might inspire him?"

"No, there's just nothing. Not much ever happens in Bodega." She said that last sentence not as if she were unhappy about the fact, but as if she were rather proud of it.

Mrs. Darden came back in carrying a tray laden with a porcelain coffee service and a plate of homemade breakfast pastries. She put the tray down on the coffee table, poured a cup for me, and urged that I help myself to the pastries. I did that, not so much to be polite as because I was pretty hungry. And within five seconds, despite using a cake plate and a napkin, I managed to get powdered sugar all over my pants and on the carpet as well. The slob strikes again.

"Oh please, it's all right," Mrs. Darden said when I apologized. There was an almost wistful note in her voice, as though she had once been used to having things spilled on the carpet and was recalling other times it had happened. Maybe her husband had been messy, too; that would explain it.

I put the pastry down for the time being, before I dropped it and the plate too, and sipped some coffee. Then I said to Sharon, "You talked to Jerry before he left last Sunday night?"

"Yes. Only for a minute."

"What did he say?"

"Just that he was going to the post office. I asked him if he had finished his article, if that was what

was in the envelopes he had, and he said yes. The only other thing he said was to leave the key out for him."

"Key?"

"To the front door."

"It's our policy not to give out keys to boarders," Mrs. Darden said. "But we do put one under a flower pot on the porch whenever no one is home, or if we know a boarder is going to come in after we're in bed."

I thought that over. "Then you always lock the front door when you retire?"

"Yes."

"What time do you usually go to bed on Sundays?"

"Around eleven."

"And it was after nine when Jerry left?"

"Yes," Sharon said. "Just after."

"About how long would it take him to walk from here to the post office and back again?"

"Well—thirty mintues or so."

"Which indicates he was headed somewhere else besides the post office," I said. "Otherwise he would have expected to be back by ten, when you were both still up, and he wouldn't have asked for the key to be left out. Is there any sort of taxi service in the village?"

"No. None."

"Bus service on Sunday night?"

"No."

"So Jerry either planned to walk to where he

was going or he was being met by someone." I did some more ruminating. "He was excited, intense, when he left here?"

Sharon nodded.

"Yet he'd just finished writing his article," I said, "and was about to put at least one copy in the mail. And he'd spent all day at the typewriter. He should have been relieved, exhausted—but not still excited. It had to be whatever he was going to do after leaving the post office, or whoever he was going to see, that made him that way."

"But it could still have something to do with the subject of his article, couldn't it?" Mrs. Darden asked. "Even though he'd finished it?"

"Yes. It probably did. How many places in the village are open on Sunday night?"

"Just the tavern. Everything else closes by six."

Sharon said, "Doesn't Mr. Ingles stay open until ten, mom?"

"You're right, I believe he does."

"Mr. Ingles?" I said.

"He owns the Sonoma Cafe. It's on the road just outside the village. You may have noticed it as you drove in."

I hadn't noticed it, but I nodded anyway. And then tackled the pastry again, this time without embarrassing myself, and drank the rest of my coffee. Immediately Mrs. Darden refilled the cup.

I asked, "Do you know where Steve Farmer lives?"

"Across the bay," Sharon said. "On Salmon Creek Road, above the marina."

That was a long walk from Bodega—more than five miles. But if it was Farmer that Jerry had been going to see, for whatever reason, Farmer could have met him here at the post office. Or anybody else could. Or he could have hitchhiked somewhere.

"Do Steve and Jerry get along well?"

"Sure. They're pretty close."

"Did either of them ever speak about a girl named Bobbie Reid?"

"No-o. Is that somebody they know in San Francisco?"

"It's somebody they knew," I said, "and who knew Christine Webster." I did not see any reason to go into detail. "What can you tell me about Gus Kellenbeck?"

"We don't know him very well," Mrs. Darden said. "He only moved here about four years ago, when he bought out what used to be Bay Fishery; and he seldom comes into Bodega. I do know that he's a good businessman. The past couple of years haven't been a boom for anyone in the fishing business—mostly because of poor salmon runs. But he's managed to keep the plant operating at a profit. Or so the talk is. He pays the fishermen top dollar for their catches."

"One of those fishermen being Andy Greene?"

"Yes."

"What's your opinion of Greene?"

"Not very high," Sharon said. "He has a nasty mouth."

"And a nasty disposition," Mrs. Darden added.

"Has he ever been in trouble of any kind?"

"Not that we know about."

"Did Jerry get along with him?"

"I believe so. He never said anything against the man."

"And he also got along with Kellenbeck?"

"Yes. He seemed to."

I tendered a few more questions, without learning anything else of interest and then finished my second cup of coffee and rose to go. In the foyer both Sharon and her mother wished me luck, and I thanked them for their help, and Mrs. Darden let me out. She seemed almost disappointed to see me leave; her parting smile struck me as even warmer than her welcoming smile. Maybe I reminded her of her husband in more ways than one. Maybe she found me attractive and desirable and wished she could get to know me better.

Maybe I was an idiot.

Too much libido, that was my problem these days, brought about by too long a period of celibacy. What I ought to do pretty quick, even if I had to pay for it, was get my ashes hauled—as we used to say in the good old days. Otherwise I was going to start salivating every time a woman looked at me with anything except revulsion.

I drove down into the village and parked near the tavern. It was not far from the post office;

somebody going in or out could have seen Jerry Carding last Sunday night. Longshot, but it might pay off.

It didn't. The tavern had just opened for business and the bartender on duty only worked until six on Sundays; he did give me the name and address of the night barman, but when I hunted up the place and talked to the guy a few minutes later, he had nothing to tell me. He knew about Jerry's disappearance—it was evidently a major topic of conversation in the Bodega Bay area—but did not know the kid by sight. Last Sunday had been a slow night, he said. Just a few regulars, all of whom had come in early and stayed until around eleven or so. He could not remember anyone arriving or leaving between nine and nine-thirty.

So all right. If Jerry had met someone at the post office and been driven away in a car, I was out of luck; I could not go around knocking on every door within a five-mile radius on the off-chance that someone had been passing by at an opportune moment. Which left me with Mr. Ingles at the Sonoma Cafe. And an even longer longshot: Jerry would have had to leave the village on foot in order to be seen passing the cafe, and Ingles would have had to look out at just the right time in order to see him.

The Sonoma Cafe turned out to be a standard roadside diner—small frame building set back some distance from the highway, facade un-

adorned by anything except a sign bearing its name. It was open but not doing any business; the lunch counter and a row of brown vinyl booths were deserted. The only person in there was a guy in his sixties, fussing over a pot of something on the stove that had the aroma of fish stew.

He kept on fussing until I sat down at the counter: then he turned and came over to me. He was wearing a white shirt, a bow-tie, and an apron, and he had a shrewd bright-eyed look about him. On his scalp were tufts of hair as thin and fine and colorless as dandelion fluff.

"Afternoon," he said.

"Afternoon. That stew smells good."

"You bet. Like a bowl?"

"Sure." Mrs. Darden's pastry had not done much for my hunger.

He ladled some into a bowl, put the bowl and a couple of packets of crackers on a plate. When he set the food in front of me I said, "Would your name be Ingles?"

"It would. How'd you know?"

"Mrs. Darden mentioned that you owned this place." I went on to tell him who I was and what I was doing in Bodega.

He looked more than a little interested: the village-gossip type, I thought. He leaned on the counter and studied me with his shrewd eyes. "Read about you in the papers," he said. "Private eye, eh? Never met a private eye before. Don't look nothing like Jim Garner, do you?"

"Jim Garner?"

" 'The Rockford Files.' Mean you don't watch that show on TV?"

"No."

"Ought to. Got lots of action, lots of cars getting smashed up."

"Uh-huh." I tasted the stew. A little salty but otherwise not bad. "Do you know Jerry Carding, Mr. Ingles?"

"Sure do. Used to eat in here once in a while. Damned funny the way he disappeared; damned funny. Got the whole town buzzing."

"I was hoping you might have seen him last Sunday night. Say between nine and ten?"

"Nosir," he said immediately. "I'd of remembered it if I had. How come you're asking me? Police didn't come around when they was here." He sounded disappointed that they hadn't.

"This is one of the few places open on Sunday nights," I said. "And there's a chance he left the village on foot. Is it possible one of your customers saw him?"

"One of my customers? Well now." Ingles scratched his scalp and seemed to do some memory cudgeling. "Zach Judson, maybe."

"Oh?"

"Zach stopped in for a cup of coffee around nine, as I recall. On his way home from some lodge doings in Tomales. Stayed about a half hour. Could be he saw the boy; ain't talked to him since."

"Does Judson live in Bodega?"

"Nope. Jenner."

Jenner was a tiny place about fifteen miles up the coast. I said, "Could you give me his telephone number?"

"Nosir."

"Pardon?"

"I said nosir, I won't give you his number."

"Why not?"

"Because he don't have a telephone," Ingles said, and cackled at his own humor. "Old Zach's deaf as a post in one ear and half-deaf in the other. Wouldn't hear a phone ringing if he was sitting on it."

"You *can* give me his address, can't you?"

"Sure. Cost you a buck, though." He winked at me. "Service charge."

A buck. And a thirty-mile round trip to Jenner that would probably turn out to be a waste of time; for all I knew Judson could be in Tomales again for more lodge doings, and it was doubtful that he had seen Jerry Carding anyway. But what else did I have to do? Hunt up Steve Farmer and try to pump him again about Bobbie Reid? That was about it—and it struck me as a last resort, the thing to do before tossing in the towel and heading home to San Francisco.

I sighed and got my wallet out and put a dollar bill on the counter. Ingles made it disappear in two seconds flat, as if he was afraid I might change my mind. Then he grinned at me and said,

"Zach's is the last house on the west side of the highway, just before you get into Jenner. Big old gingerbready place, looks like it'd fall down if a good wind come along."

"Thanks." I finished my stew, gave him some more money for that, and slid a dime tip under the plate when he wasn't looking. The stew had not been all that good and neither had he.

As I started out he called after me. "Tune in 'The Rockford Files' one of these nights. That Jim Garner's a real good detective."

Me too, I thought wryly. Even if I don't have my own TV show.

I headed the car north on Highway 1. The winding two-lane road had little traffic for a Sunday afternoon, but the fog had come back again, heavy and wet, and it made the pavement slick and visibility poor; it was forty-five minutes before I crossed the bridge spanning the Russian River and approached Jenner.

The hamlet—what there was of it—was located at the mouth of the river, where it widened out and joined the ocean. To the west, between the road and the water, were a lot of tide flats and a few houses. The last house south of Jenner matched Ingles' description: a ramshackle twenties-style structure that seemed to list inland, as if the constant wind off the sea had been too much for it. A lone cypress tree grew in the muddy front yard, wind-bent and leaning companionably in the same direction; parked near it was a 1940s

vintage Chevy pick-up. Lights glowed behind chintz curtains in one front window.

I took my car into the yard and put it next to the pick-up. When I got out a fat lazy-looking dog came around from behind the house, barked once in an indifferent way, and then waddled off again. I climbed sagging steps onto the front porch and rapped on the door.

Nobody answered. Ingles had said Zach Judson was all but deaf, I remembered; I tried again, using my fist this time, pounding hard enough to rattle the wood in its frame. That got results. The door creaked open pretty soon and a guy about seventy peered out at me through wire-framed spectacles. He had a gnarly face, a mop of unkempt white hair, and one of those big old-fashioned plastic hearing aids hooked over one ear.

He said, "Yep?" in a tone that wondered if I was going to try to sell him something.

"Mr. Judson?"

"Yep?"

I told him my name. "I'm a detective, and I—"

"You say detective?"

"Yes, sir. Investigating the disappearance of Jerry Carding."

"Who?"

"Jerry Carding."

"Never heard of any Jerry Carling."

"Carding, Mr. Judson. Jerry *Carding*."

"Never heard of any Jerry Carding."

"The story's been in all the papers and on TV—"

"Don't read the papers. Don't own a TV."

"He vanished from Bodega last Sunday night, between nine and ten o'clock," I said. "A young fellow about twenty, dark hair, Fu Manchu mustache. I understand you were in Bodega around that time and I thought you might have seen him."

"Yep," Judson said.

"Sir?"

"Yep. Did see him."

Well now. "Where was this, Mr. Judson?"

"On the highway. Near Ingles' cafe."

"Was he alone?"

"Yep. Hitchhiking."

"He thumbed you, then?"

"Yep."

"But you didn't stop for him?"

"*Did* stop for him. Used to hitch rides myself, back when. Decent young fella. Polite, good manners. Missing, you say?"

"Yes." There was a tenseness inside me now; this was the kind of break I had been looking for. "You took him where, Mr. Judson?"

"What?"

"Where did you take him?"

"Not far. Just up the road a ways."

"How far up the road?"

"To the Kellenbeck Fish Company," he said.

## ○ SEVENTEEN ○

I did some hard thinking on the way back to Bodega Bay.

Jerry Carding had hitchhiked to the Kellenbeck Fish Company last Sunday night. All right. Zach Judson had not seen him approach the plant, but it was a safe assumption that it had been Jerry's destination; there was nothing else in the vicinity, no other businesses or private homes. Meeting someone there? Could be. But then why not meet in Bodega instead? As it was, Jerry had had to walk partway and hitch a ride the rest of the way.

The other possibility was that he had gone to the fish company to look for something, either inside the building or somewhere around it. Something connected with the article he'd written; that seemed likely. Ten o'clock on a Sunday night—a nocturnal prowl. It was the kind of thing an adventurous kid, a kid who wanted to be an investigative reporter, might do.

But what had happened then? Had Jerry completed his search, with or without finding what

he'd come after, and later hitchhiked away from Bodega Bay? Or had somebody found him there and been responsible for his disappearance?

And the big question—why? What was there about the Kellenbeck Fish Company that would inspire a "career-making" article and a secret late-evening visit? Yes, and why go there *after* he had finished the article?

I focused my thoughts on Gus Kellenbeck. According to Mrs. Darden, the past couple of years had not been a boon for anyone in the fishing business; yet Kellenbeck had managed to keep his plant operating at a profit. It was possible that he was mixed up in some sort of illegal enterprise, such as price-fixing or substituting and selling one kind of processed fish for another. But that sort of thing had little news value; it happened all the time, in one form or another. Even a novice like Jerry would have known that.

What *else* could it be?

What else . . .

There was an itching sensation at the back of my mind, the kind I seem always to have when there's something caught and trying to struggle out of my subconscious. Something significant I had seen or heard. It gave me a vague feeling of excitement, as if I were poised on the edge of breakthrough knowledge: remember what it was, take that one right turn, and I would be on my way into all the other right turns that led out of the labyrinth.

Only it would not come, not yet; the harder I tried to get hold of it, the tighter it seemed to wedge back. Let it alone, then. It would pop through sooner or later, the way nagging bits of information you can't quite remember—names, dates, titles of books or movies—come popping through once you stop thinking about them.

It was four-thirty and just starting to get dark when I neared the Kellenbeck Fish Company. On impulse I swung the car onto the deserted gravel area in front. The building had a dark abandoned look in the fog and the late-afternoon gloom; closed on Sundays, I thought, nobody here. But I got out anyway and went around onto the rear dock.

The corrugated iron doors were closed and pad-locked; I could see that without going over there. Instead I wandered to the foot of the rickety pier. There was nothing on it, no boats tied up at its end. Beyond, the gray water was scummed with mist. And on the opposite shore, Bodega Head was just a lumpish outline dotted here and there with ghostly lights from the houses above the marina.

I turned to look at the building again. The itching sensation came back, but with the same nonresults. Maybe if I had another talk with Kellenbeck, I thought; maybe that would help me remember. At the least I could see how he reacted when I mentioned Jerry Carding's visit here last Sunday evening.

So I returned to the car and drove to The Tides

and hunted up a public telephone. There was a listing for Kellenbeck in the Sonoma County directory with an address in Carmet-by-the-Sea. Carmet was an older development of homes a few miles back to the north, right on the ocean: I had passed by it twice on the trip to and from Jenner.

I got there inside of twenty minutes, but it was another ten before I located Kellenbeck's place; the homes were well spread out along the east side of the highway and the fog made it difficult to read the street signs. The house turned out to be a big knotty-pine A-frame with a lot of glass facing out toward the Pacific. Even for Carmet, where homes would not come cheap because of the view, it looked to be worth a pretty good chunk of money. Kellenbeck was doing well for himself, all right—maybe too well for the owner of a minor fish-processing plant. You did not buy or build a house like this with just a small-businessman's profits.

The trip here seemed to be a wasted effort, though. All the windows were dark, and so were those in the adjacent garage. Just to be sure I went up onto the porch and rang the bell. No answer.

A pair of mist-smeared headlights poked toward me as I was coming back to the car. Kellenbeck? But it wasn't; the headlights belonged to a low-slung sports job, not the Cadillac I had seen yesterday at the fish company, and it drifted on by.

I got into the car and sat there and tried to decide what to do next. Take another room for the

night at The Tides Motel and then brace Kellenbeck tomorrow—that seemed like the best idea.
The other alternative, hanging around here and
hoping that he *did* show up before long, had no
appeal. For all I knew he was out somewhere for
the evening, visiting friends or indulging his fond-
ness for liquor; and I had no idea where to go
looking for him—

The itching again.

Then, all at once, I remembered.

It came out of my subconscious clear and
sharp—something I had seen, something odd—
and right on its heels was another fragment. I put
on the dome light, took out the torn corner I had
found in Jerry Carding's room at the Darden
house, and looked at it. Then I began to construct
a mental blueprint, testing it with some of the
questions I had asked myself and other people the
past few days. And I remembered something else
then, one more fragment. And sketched in a few
more connecting lines.

And there it was.

Not a complete blueprint; it didn't explain all
the twists and turns, did not show me all the way
to the end. But the things it did show made sense:
What it was Jerry had found out, the subject of his
article. Why he might have gone to the fish company last Sunday night. Why he had disappeared.

Why his father had been murdered in Brisbane
on Thursday.

Yet I had no proof of any of it. It was speculation,

personal observation—just like my account of what had happened when Martin Talbot discovered Victor Carding's body. Eberhardt and Donleavy would want to check it out if I took it to them cold, and so would the Federal authorities; but no search warrants could be obtained without some sort of evidential cause, and if Kellenbeck was alerted there might not *be* any evidence left to find. He could take steps to cover himself, bluff through even a Federal investigation, get off scotfree.

I *had* to have proof, damn it. Something solid to back up my theories. And I knew where I might be able to find it. . . .

No, I thought then. Uh-uh. You don't break laws, remember? Or go skulking around in the night like the pulp private eyes. You want to get your license revoked?

You want a murderer to maybe go unpunished? Call up Eberhardt. Lay it in his lap.

Not without proof. You could *try* to get it; go there, see how things look. At least make the effort.

I spent another couple of minutes arguing with myself. But it was no contest: I started the car and went away to skulk in the night.

The Kellenbeck Fish Company was still dark and so wrapped in fog now that it had a two-dimensional look, like a shape cut from heavy black paper. I drove on past it by a hundred yards,

parked off the road alongside a jumble of shoreline rocks. From under the dash I unclipped the flashlight I keep there and dropped it into my coat pocket. Blurred yellow headlight beams brightened the road behind me; I waited until the car hissed past and disappeared into the mist before I got out and hurried back toward the building.

The night had an eerie muffled stillness, marred only by the ringing of fog bells out on the channel buoys and the faint lapping of the bay water against the pilings; the crunch of my footfalls seemed unnaturally loud as I crossed the gravel parking area. When I got to the shedlike enclosure I paused in the shadows to test the door there. Locked—and so secure in its frame that it did not rattle when I tugged on the knob. If I was going to get in at all, it would have to be at the rear.

I crossed to the catwalk. It was pitch-black along there; I stayed in close to the building wall, feeling my way along it until I came out onto the dock. The writhing fog created vague spectral shadows among the stacks of crab pots, brushed my face with a spidery wetness. Visibility was not more than two hundred yards. Even the lights on Bodega Head were swaddled, hidden inside the fogbanks.

The padlock on the corrugated doors was an old Yale with a heavy base and a thick steel loop. You would need a hacksaw and an hour's work to cut through it, and I was not about to try such shenanigans anyway. I felt nervous enough as it was. Cold sweat had formed under my arms, the palms

of my hands were damp, sticky. Maybe the pulp detectives were good at this sort of thing; maybe Jim Garner was on "The Rockford Files." Not me.

I moved to the far side of the doors. In the wall there, near where the crab pots were, was a window made opaque by an accumulation of grime. When I stepped up close to it I could see it was the kind with two sashes, one overlapping the other vertically. I put the heel of my hand against the frame of the lower piece and shoved upward. Latched at the middle but not at the bottom. And a loose latch at that because it rose a quarter of an inch before binding with a creaky sound. It could probably be forced without too much trouble.

Which brought me to the moment of reckoning. The only way I was going to get inside was through this window; so I either forced it or gave the whole idea up. All I was guilty of so far was trespassing. But if I forced the window it was felony breaking-and-entering—a crime that would cost me my license and maybe put me in prison if anybody found out about it.

*If* anybody found out, I thought. Who was going to find out? If I discovered what I expected to, I could tell Eberhardt I came by it in a legal fashion. A little white lie. And Kellenbeck's arrest and conviction for murder would go a long way toward appeasing my conscience.

I wiped moisture off my face, hunched my shoulders against the wind blowing in across the water, and laid both hands on the sash frame. Bent

my knees and heaved upward. The lock creaked again; the window pane rattled. I dipped lower, locked my elbows, heaved a second time. A third. A fourth—

There was a loud groaning noise, then a sudden snapping, and the sash wobbled upward.

The noise made me jerk my head around and look furtively around the empty dock. A seagull screeched somewhere in the fog—a cry that sounded almost mocking. I took a couple of deep breaths; my heart was pounding as if I had just run the quarter-mile. Then I eased the sash up as far as it would go, swung my leg over the sill. And ducked under and up into blackness heavy with the odors of fish and brine.

With my back to the window, I got the flashlight out, shielded the lens with my hand, and switched it on. Shellfish tanks, a massive refrigeration unit that gave off palpable waves of cold. Beyond, where Kellenbeck's office was, the bank of machinery and conveyor belts formed a mass of shadowy outlines.

I shuffled away from the window and around the nearest of the tanks, holding the flash pointed downward at thigh level. The light glistened over the fish scales speckling the floor, picked out a stack of crates just in time to keep me from plowing into them. My mouth was dry; I worked saliva through it as I stepped off to the left, lifted the flash and unshielded it long enough to make a single horizontal sweep. Open floor past the

crates, except for the machinery and four big weighing scales set side by side like a row of deactivated robots. In the gloom ahead there was a dullish reflection of the beam: the window in the office cubicle.

Following the light, I made my way over there. The closer I got to it, the more hushed the warehouse became; I could no longer hear even the muffled ringing of the fog bells. The scraping of my shoes on the slick floor was the only sound.

The door to the office was closed. Locked? No; it opened silently when I rotated the knob. I stepped inside, leaving the door open, and let the light flicker over Kellenbeck's desk. Same clutter of papers and junk that I had seen yesterday. Except for one thing. And I found that right away, in the bottom desk drawer where I had watched Kellenbeck put it.

The bottle of Canadian whiskey.

The evidence.

I hauled it out by its cap so I would not smear any clear fingerprints on the glass. Shined the flash on it. The label carried the name of a popular brand and was brown with a black-lined square around the edges—the same colors, the same pattern, that was on the torn corner from Jerry Carding's room. Which was part of what I had remembered earlier. The first thing, the one that had been itching at the back of my mind, was the way Kellenbeck had kept looking at the bottle while I was talking to him, the way he had caught it up

so quickly by its bare neck and put it away inside the drawer. I had already seen him drinking from it during business hours; why hide it unless there was something about it he did not want me to notice. Something I *had* noticed, but without realizing it at the time.

The bare neck: it had no tax stamp.

And the label would be counterfeit.

Bootleg liquor.

That was where Kellenbeck's profits were coming from and that was what Jerry Carding had found out: Kellenbeck was an illicit-whiskey distributor.

Most people think of bootlegging as something that went out with Prohibition; but the fact is, it's still a multimillion dollar business in the United States. And not just in the South. It goes on along the West Coast too, just as it used to in the days of the Volstead Act when ships outfitted as distilleries—big stills in their holds, bottling equipment, labels for a dozen different kinds of Canadian whiskey—were brought down from Canada and anchored twenty-five miles offshore. Nowadays the stuff was probably made at some isolated spot across the border and carried down the coast by freighter or large fishing boat. But it would still be handled in pretty much the same way: picked up by small craft, stored somewhere nearby until it could be trucked out to customers throughout the state.

Kellenbeck's big mistake was committing mur-

der to keep his activities a secret; his little mistake was drinking his own hooch instead of the genuine stuff. Maybe he liked it because it packed a heftier wallop. Yeah, well, it was going to help wallop him right into San Quentin.

I made a hurried check through the rest of the desk and through the papers on top of it. Everything seemed to pertain to the fish company operations, as did everything in the single file cabinet. But I did find two more bottles of bootleg tucked away inside a small storage closet. On impulse I took one of them and wedged it out of sight behind the file cabinet. Just in case the bottle missing from his desk made Kellenbeck suspicious and he decided to get rid of the rest of it. In a sense I was tampering with evidence, but that was a technicality and the hell with it; I was in pretty deep as it was. And it would insure that the Justice Department investigators found something incriminating when they showed up with search warrants.

Time for me to get out of here, I thought. Past time: I had been in the building for half an hour—I was more nervous than ever now, and sweating like the proverbial pig. I caught up the desk bottle, swept the flash over the office once more: everything looked as I had found it. Then I went out, closed the door behind me, shielded the flash beam again and trailed it back across the warehouse.

When I reached the window the cold air from

the refrigeration unit and the icy wind blowing in from outside made me shiver. I hunched my shoulders, switched off the flash. Out on the dock fog swirled around the crab pots, giving them an insubstantial, surreal look in the darkness. Quickly I lifted one leg over the sill, straddled it, and started to swing out.

Movement behind the nearest of the crab pots.

A board creaked.

*Somebody there—*

Blinding white light errupted out of the mist, pinned me, made me recoil and crack the back of my head against the window sash.

"Stay where you are, asshole," a harsh voice said behind the glare. "I've got a gun; I'll blow you away if you move."

But it was not Gus Kellenbeck.

The voice belonged to Andy Greene.

EIGHTEEN

## ○ EIGHTEEN ○

I stayed frozen, half in and half out of the window, the damned bottle in my right hand and hanging out where Greene could see it. Fear climbed up into my throat and lodged there like a glob of bitter mucus. The light burned against my eyes; I squeezed the lids down to slits.

"All right," he said. "Let go the bottle."

"Listen, Greene—"

"Now, goddamn it!"

I released the bottle, heard it clatter on the dock and roll back in against the wall. At the same time I turned my head a little so I was no longer looking directly into the glare. Tendrils of fog curled through the beam, capered at its edges like will-o'-the-wisps. And gave Greene, behind it, a dark ectoplasmic look, as if he were something only half-materialized. The wet touch of the mist against my face made my skin crawl.

"Back inside," Greene said. "Nice and slow. Then turn around and walk away from the window."

The muscles in my arms and legs were cramped with tension; the joints did not seem to want to bend, so that when I forced myself back off the sill it was in awkward, mannequin-stiff movements. The jet of light dipped lower, came forward through the opening. I pivoted away from it, blinking, licking at the gun-metal taste in my mouth. And then began to pace toward the shellfish tanks.

Behind me Greene made scraping sounds as he climbed through the window. The skin on my back was still crawling; it was bad enough to face a man with a gun, even when you couldn't see him, but to have him behind you in the dark was twice as unnerving.

When I reached the first of the tanks, ten paces away, Greene's voice said, "That's far enough." I stopped, made a careful three-quarters turn back toward him. He was moving laterally to his left, along the inner wall; the flash beam stayed centered on me, flickering a little with his movements. Then he came to a standstill, and seconds later there were a series of faint clicks. The darkness shrank into random pockets of shadow as high-wattage bulbs strung along the rafters winked on.

I did some more blinking. Greene shut off a big four-cell flashlight, jammed it into the pocket of a blue pea jacket; then he motioned me over toward the locked entrance doors, where there was nothing for me to get my hands on, and halved the distance between us when I got there. His face

was expressionless. But the deep-sunk eyes looked as cold and flat and deadly as the Browning 9 mm automatic in his right hand.

Looking at him, I felt swirls of black rage under the fear. Rage at him, at Kellenbeck, at what had been done to Jerry Carding and his father. And rage at myself for coming here like a damned fool, breaking the law, getting caught up this way. Stupid. *Stupid.*

We stood watching each other for eight or ten seconds. Then I said, "What happens now, Greene?" My voice had sounded cracked when I started to speak at the window, but these words came out in the same hard monotone he had been using.

"What do you think happens?"

"You call up Kellenbeck. He calls up the county police and has me arrested for breaking-and-entering."

Greene showed me his teeth. "You'd like that, wouldn't you," he said.

"Why should I like it?"

"Go ahead, play dumb if you want. But you don't bluff your way out of this."

"Neither do you," I said. "Not any more."

"What the hell does that mean?"

"It means I'm not the only one who's onto you."

"Bullshit. Cops knew anything, *they'd* be here, not you."

"They'll be here before long. Count on it."

"Not tonight. Not while you're still around—"

There was a sudden banging sound in the front part of the building, where the tacked-on shed was. Greene tensed. I half-turned, looking up toward a closed door adjacent to the bank of machinery—but the glimmer of hope inside me died in the next second when the door opened and Gus Kellenbeck came shambling through.

"Andy? I saw the lights, I—" He quit talking and pulled up short, gaping at me and at the gun in Greene's hand. His eyes had a glassy look and there was a slackness to his mouth; he seemed to sway a little. "Jesus, Andy," he said in a different voice. "Jesus."

I moved sideways a couple of steps, carefully, so I could see both of them without swiveling my head back and forth. The Browning moved with me.

When Greene looked at Kellenbeck again his upper lip flattened in against his teeth. "You goddamn drunk," he said, and that told me all I needed to know about how things stood between the two of them. Maybe the bootlegging had been Kellenbeck's scam in the beginning, and he had brought Greene in for the use of his boat; but whether or not that was it, Greene was the one running the show now.

"I only had a few," Kellenbeck said. "I lost track of the time." He slid a hand across gray-stubbled cheeks, across his slacked mouth. "What's *he* doing here, Andy? Why'd you bring him here?"

"I didn't bring him here. I saw him snooping

around your house and decided to follow him, see
what he was up to. Good thing I did. He came
straight here, busted in, and searched your office;
I nailed him on the way out."

Damned *fool*, I thought again. It must have been
Greene in that low-slung sports job in Carmet.
And him again in the car that passed after I parked
down the highway; I had been too intent on getting into the building, on playing the souped-up
detective, to notice it was the same car both
times.

"He knows, then," Kellenbeck said. He sounded
sick and frightened.

"Sure he knows. What's the matter with you?"

"How did he find out?"

"How do you think? You and that fucking
hooch. I told you not to keep any of it around."

Kellenbeck moved forward a couple of steps. A
belch came out of him; he wiped his mouth again.
"Andy," he said, "Andy . . . "

"Shut up."

"Let him say it, Greene," I said. The rage was
stronger, blacker, inside me now—and that was
good because it smothered the fear. Blood made a
surflike pounding in my temples.

"You shut up too."

I looked at Kellenbeck. "He's planning to kill
me, all right. Is that what you want? Another
murder on your conscience?"

"Andy, for Christ's sake . . ."

"Killing me won't get you off the hook," I said.

"What do you think will happen if I disappear like Jerry Carding—two disappearances within a week? The cops will be all over this place. And they'll find out, Kellenbeck, just like I did—"

"One more word," Greene said, "I'll blow you away right now."

He meant it; I could hear it in his voice and see it in his eyes when I faced him. I locked my teeth together, made myself stand still. Made myself not think about dying, because if I did the rage and the thin edge of panic would prod me into doing something crazy, like trying to jump him for the gun.

"He's right, Andy," Kellenbeck said. His face had a collapsing look, as if all the muscles had loosened at once. "You know he is."

"The hell he's right. We can cover this one too."

"How?"

"Get rid of any more hooch you've got stashed, stay out of touch with the people up north. Let the cops come around; there won't be anything for them to find."

"But suppose he's told somebody something?"

"He hasn't told anybody anything. He's just a smart-guy private dick, that's all. Working on his own."

"I don't know, Andy. Another killing . . . I don't know if I can handle it, face the cops again, all those questions. . . ."

"Sure you can, Gus. You'll be fine, baby."

There was something in the way Greene said

that, something in his voice that jarred an insight into my mind. Kellenbeck was a drunk and he was coming apart; it was a good bet he would let something slip to the police, maybe even blurt out a confession, when the pressure got too heavy. And Greene knew that as well as I did.

He was planning to kill Kellenbeck too.

I wanted to say something to Kellenbeck, try to turn him against Greene. But I knew if I did that, Greene would use the gun on me without hesitation. He was in total command: there was nothing I could do and nothing Kellenbeck could do.

Not yet, I told myself. Not *yet*.

Kellenbeck belched again, sickly. "Okay," he said. "I guess we got no choice. But Jesus, let's get it over with."

"Your car right out front?"

"Yeah."

"You sober enough to drive?"

"Yeah."

"Head out, then. Get the car started."

Kellenbeck nodded, put his back to us, and went into the shed with uneven jerky strides. When the outer door banged a few seconds later Greene said to me, "Your turn. Move."

I moved. The joints in my legs still felt stiff and there was a tight prickling sensation in my groin. I had an impulse to grab hold of the door on my way through, try to slam it shut between us; but it was standing too wide, and Greene had crowded up close behind me. The shed was full of boxes,

tools, machine parts—none of them within reaching distance. I opened the outer door, kept my hand on the knob for a second. Greene jabbed me with the automatic. And I let go, struggling with my control, and went out into the cold darkness.

Fog crawled over the highway, obscured all but a three-hundred-yard strip of it. No headlights showed anywhere in the mist. Kellenbeck's Cadillac was slewed in near one of the hoists a few feet away; the engine was running and the lights were on. Greene told me to get into the back seat, slide over against the far door—and waited until I did that before he got in with me, holding the Browning in close to his body so there was no chance of me making a lunge for it.

"Okay," he said to Kellenbeck. "You know where."

Nothing from Kellenbeck. His breathing was rapid and irregular; I could smell the sour whiskey fumes even from where I was. The shape he was in, I thought he might kick the accelerator hard enough to buck the car and throw Greene off-balance. I braced my feet and body, tensing. But Greene anticipated that too; he issued a sharp warning to take it easy, drive slow. And Kellenbeck, obeying, crawled the damned car out of the lot and onto the highway, northbound.

I sat with my hands fisted on my knees, watching Greene in the faint glow of the dashlights. He was sitting half-turned toward me and he still had the gun pulled in against his chest. I thought:

God, if I could get my hands on him I'd tear him in half. I thought: I'm being taken for a ride, private eye being taken for a goddamn ride just like in the pulps. I thought: Is this how Jerry Carding felt—twenty-year-old kid, scared, shaking, on his way to die?

Wild thoughts. Breeding more wild impulses. The rage and the fear boiling inside me now like gases coming to an explosion point. I had to do something to keep the lid on my control; if I didn't, if I gave in to the impulses—

I said, "Where are we going? Your boat, Greene, is that it? A little trip out into the ocean?" Talking was the answer. Making words to keep from making myself dead. "Sure. The deep-six. Take me out a mile or two, shoot me or knock me out, weight my body, and I'm gone without a trace. Just like Jerry Carding."

Greene had nothing to say.

"Let's see if I can put it together," I said. "How did Jerry find out about the bootlegging? Overheard the two of you talking, maybe when you didn't know he was around. Sure, that makes sense. So he does a little investigating, gets hold of a bottle of hooch or the label off of one. But instead of going to the police right away he decides to write an article first; that way, when the story breaks, he can have it published immediately. He'll not only be a full-fledged hero, he'll be an overnight sensation as a journalist.

"He finishes the article on Sunday night, takes

the original and his only carbon down to the post office. But he doesn't mail both of them. Just the carbon, to somebody for safekeeping; the original he keeps with him. Then he heads straight for the—"

"Shut up," Kellenbeck said. "Andy, tell him to shut the hell up. I don't want to listen to this."

Greene said, "Let him talk. The hell with it."

"Then Jerry heads straight for the fish company," I said. "Why? Because he's found out Sunday is the night you take the boat out to pick up a load of whiskey—not every Sunday but once or twice a month, say—and he's also found out you leave from the warehouse when you do go, sometime after ten o'clock. If you're heading out that night he'll call in the Coast Guard and have them waiting when you get back; and he'll also have the original of his article ready to turn over to one of the San Francisco papers. If you're not going out, he'll carry the article back to his room and wait another week or however long it takes until you do.

"When he gets to the fish company he hides somewhere to watch and wait. And the two of you show up. Then something happens—maybe he makes a noise, maybe he's not hidden as well as he thinks—and you grab him. You find the article, you read it, you know he's onto you. It's the kid's death warrant."

We had reached the north rim of the bay. Ahead, through the windshield and through swirls of fog,

I could see the turn-off for the road that looped around to Bodega Head.

"But first you've got to know if there are any other copies of that article. You force him to tell you about the carbon, who he mailed it to, and it turns out to be his father down in Brisbane. You can't get the carbon out of the post office; you've got to wait until it's delivered. So the next day you go down to Brisbane and watch Victor Carding's mailbox until the mail is delivered and then check for the carbon.

"Only it doesn't show up on Monday, or on Tuesday or Wednesday either; the mail service being what it is, the envelope isn't delivered until Thursday. But Carding gets to the box before you can, maybe because he's looking for some word from his son. He picks up the mail—the article and a couple of bills—and opens Jerry's envelope right away and starts to read. That leaves you no choice. You brace him with the .38 you were carrying then, take him into the garage, and shoot him. Then you put the gun in his hand—make it look like suicide, keep the police from doing too much digging."

Kellenbeck had made the turn and we were starting around toward the marina. I could just make out the ghost shapes of masts and hulls through gaps in the fog screen.

"But even if Martin Talbot hadn't arrived a few minutes later to screw things up, it wouldn't have worked. No nitrate traces on Carding's hands or

powder marks on his clothes: he couldn't have shot himself. The police would still have known it was murder.

"You see how it is, Greene? It's the little things people like you always overlook, the little things that trip you up. It'll be some other little thing, or a combination of them, that finally puts your ass in the gas chamber."

That got a small noise out of Kellenbeck. Greene said, "Smart guy. You like to listen to yourself trying to be smart? Go on, talk some more. Talk all you want while you still can."

But I was through talking. And through teetering on the brink of panic. The wildness was gone; I had talked myself calm, gotten a lock again on emotions and impulses. Intellect was going to get me out of this if anything was. If I panicked, there was no way out: I was a dead man for sure.

We had drawn abreast of the marina now. Vague shimmers of light marked the location of houses along the Head, but there were no lights among the boats—just pale night bulbs scattered above the ramp and the floating walkways. The road, as it had been all the way over from the main highway, was a wet empty stripe in the darkness.

Kellenbeck eased the Cadillac onto the shoulder opposite the ramp. Greene got out first, waited for Kellenbeck, and then motioned me across the seat. There was more wind here and it stung my cheeks with icy wetness; the air was painfully cold in my lungs. I glanced down the road, up at

the outlines of the nearest house, over at the boat slips. Nothing stirred anywhere. No help anywhere.

We went across the road and up onto the ramp, Kellenbeck in front of me and Greene behind me by six paces. Sounds drifted out of the fog; the creak of caulked joints and rigging, the thud of a hull against a board float, the buoy bells. I kept moving my head in quadrants, looking for something, anything, to give me an opening, a chance for escape. Fog, wind, empty boats, black water—nothing.

At the end of the ramp Kellenbeck went down the short metal ladder without turning; I heard the thump he made as he dropped off onto the nearest float. When I got to the ladder I turned to face Greene. But he had halted too, and there were still six or seven feet between us—too far for me to even think about making a play for the gun. He waited until I descended the ladder before he approached it, and then it was at an angle so that I had no way of lunging up at him between the handrails. There was nothing I could do except leave the ladder and sidestep along the swaying float. Watch him come down only when I got far enough away to suit him.

Kellenbeck was already on board the *Kingfisher*, standing with his back to the wheelhouse. The water was choppy enough to rock the troller; he had his feet spread wide and one hand up at his mouth, as if the motion had combined with the

alcohol in his system to make him nauseous. I
came up abaft, hesitated again. Greene slowed and
made an impatient slicing gesture with the gun.
Kellenbeck reacted as though it was meant for
him too: He turned as I climbed over the gunwale
and groped his way inside the wheelhouse.

I backed over there, adjusting my balance to the
deck roll. Greene swung aboard. Binnacle lights
went on inside, one of them a chart lamp that cut
away most of the blackness. The wheelhouse, I
saw as I stepped through the entrance way, was
about ten feet square and empty except for operating equipment and a pair of wooden storage
lockers; the bulkheads were all bare. On the port
side was a narrow companionway that would lead
below decks to Greene's sleeping quarters.

I moved to the starboard bulkhead and put my
back to it. Kellenbeck was next to the wheel; the
glow from the lights gave his face a surreal cast.
Greene stood framed in the entrance way, his left
shoulder braced at its edge, the gun cocked toward
me at his right hip.

"What the hell're you waiting for?" he said to
Kellenbeck. "Start the engine. You know where
the keys are."

Kellenbeck's throat seemed to be working spas-
modically. "I don't feel so good, Andy. You got
any liquor on board?"

"No."

"You sure? Christ, I need a drink bad."

"I said no. I want you sober; it'll be tricky

enough following the channel in this fog. Now get to it."

In shaky movements Kellenbeck fumbled under the binnacle, came up with a set of keys, and spent fifteen seconds fitting one into the ignition and firing the diesel. The powerful engine made a guttural throbbing noise, like the magnified purr of a cat, and I could feel the vibrations beneath my feet.

Greene stepped inside and one pace to his right, toward me. "Cast off the lines, Gus."

I watched Kellenbeck walk around behind him and disappear astern. My nerves were beginning to jangle again; the panic simmered just below the surface of my thoughts. Time was running out. Once we were out into the bay, my chances would be twice as slim as they were now—and once we passed breakwater at the Bodega Head jetty, into open sea, they would be all but nonexistent. Now was the time to make my move, while I was alone here with Greene. Except that I had no move to make. Maybe I would have to jump him sooner or later, but I could not bring myself to do it yet. It was the last thing to do, the last move, because in close quarters like these I knew it would probably be the last move I would ever make.

Two or three long minutes passed before Kellenbeck came back. One hand was hovering at his mouth again; he looked even sicker than before. When he took the wheel Greene backed over to

the entrance way, braced himself the way he had earlier.

Kellenbeck put on the running lights, the windshield wipers, an outside spotlight that sliced a thin diffused beam into the mist. He worked the throttle and we began to creep forward out of the slip, into the narrow marina channel. Wind-swells increased the roll-and-sway of the boat; I put my hands flat against the bulkhead and widened my stance. At the wheel Kellenbeck began to make a series of liquidy gagging sounds that were audible even above the diesel pulse.

Through the windshield, fog churned and appeared to hurl itself in gray streaks against the glass. I could see patches of black water but nothing else: It seemed we were out of the marina now and into the bay.

Kellenbeck was still gagging.

The boat rolled left, pitched right, rolled left.

And Kellenbeck let go of the wheel, lurched around, said, "Andy, Jesus, take over, I got to puke." And clamped both hands to his mouth and came staggering toward the entrance way.

Right between Greene and me.

My reaction was instinctive and immediate, without thought of any kind. I lunged off the bulkhead and into Kellenbeck, caught hold of his jacket to keep him in front of me—Greene yelled something, Kellenbeck gagged again and vomited through his hands—and propelled him into Greene and all three of us sandwichlike out onto

the deck. The gun fired, cracking, but Greene's arm had been thrown out to the side; the bullet hummed off into the night. He went down with Kellenbeck sprawled half on top of him, still yelling, kicking viciously to free himself. I stayed on my feet—but momentum and the deckroll flung me off-balance against the starboard gunwale.

Greene got his arm free, swung the gun around. I threw myself overboard.

The gun cracked again just as I cleared the gunwale. I felt a hard slapping along the edge of my right shoe; the leg jerked in reflex and the knee bent up against my chest, and that made my body, already twisted into an awkward position, curl around instead of flattening out as I fell. I hit the water on my neck and right shoulder with enough impact to flip me over, slice me backward through the surface.

It was like dropping naked into a snowdrift. The subfreezing temperature constricted my lungs, deflated them in a convulsive exhalation. Brackish water streamed into my mouth before I could snap it closed again. I fought to get my legs down and under me, body turned into a horizontal plane. But by the time I managed that the pressure in my chest was acute and painful; I had to have air—and I had to orient myself—before I could start to swim.

I stopped thrashing arms and legs, let the water's buoyancy bob me up like a cork. When my

head broke surface I opened my mouth wide and filled my lungs in gasping breaths. Salt stung my eyes, laid a film across them; at first I could not see anything except smeary blackness. Then the movement of the water shuttled me half-around, and on my left I could make out a blurred shimmer of red and green: the *Kingfisher*'s running lights. I blinked half a dozen times until the lights steadied into focus. The boat was a dark shape that seemed to be floating spectrally in fog, maybe twenty yards away and still angled away from the marina. No movement on the deck astern—which had to mean that Greene was up and inside the wheelhouse, about to swing the troller around.

I struggled, kicking again, to face the opposite direction. More shapes loomed up through the mist: boats rocking in the marina slips. How far away? Seventy-five yards? A hundred?

Trapped air had billowed my overcoat around me; I ripped at the buttons and wrenched out of it. And at the same time scraped off my waterlogged shoes. Behind me I could hear the guttural throb of the diesel climb in volume. I twisted my head to look back there.

The boat was thirty yards away now and just starting into a tight left-hand turn.

I scissored up and into a rapid crawl. The direction of the wind and what current there was were in my favor; I did not have to fight through the swells. But the water was freezing cold: Before long my arms and legs began to numb, to feel

heavy, and I was forced to shorten and slow my stroke. Each breath burned as if I were inhaling slivers of dry ice.

*Don't think about the cold. Swim!*

Stroke.

Stroke.

Head up: The marina was maybe thirty or forty yards distant now. I could see the dull fuzzy glow of the nightlights, the end of the center float, the entrances to the two channels on either side.

Stroke.

Stroke.

Stroke—

Off to my left a beam of light sprayed out over the water; the throb of the diesel seemed to build to a roaring. I rolled onto my side, dragged my head around again.

The troller was fifteen yards behind me, coming at about quarter-throttle but at an angle to the west. The hand-operated spotlight probed around in an arc, glistening off streamers of fog. Greene had not seen me yet—but it would only be a matter of seconds until he did.

I sucked in as much air as I could hold and took myself under, just as the beam swung closer and the bow veered toward me.

When I had kicked straight down for maybe ten feet I swam in a blind forward breaststroke. In my mind I counted off ten seconds, fifteen. The amount of salt in the water kept trying to buoy me up; my arms felt as if there were lead sinkers

tied to them and a cramp was starting to form in the calf of my left leg.

Twenty seconds.

And the troller passed above me—not directly overhead but close enough so that I could hear the water-muffled whine of the diesel, feel the turbulence created by the screws.

I made myself count off another five seconds. Then I clawed upward, broke surface just as the pressure mounted to an intolerable level in my chest; my lungs heaved, the intake of air sent out shoots of pain. The *Kingfisher*'s wake pitched me around like a piece of flotsam, the salt film and rivulets of water obscured my vision. I shook my head, breathing in pants and gulps. Had to shake it twice more before I could see where the boat was: between me and the marina, twenty yards away and running diagonally to my left.

I kicked out and swam half a dozen uneven strokes. Struggled clear of the wake with my head and my eyes fixed on the troller. It turned perpendicular to the marina and then began to veer around hard right; the spotlight sliced a down-slanted arc through the blackness, swinging toward me. I dragged in air and tensed for another dive.

But then the bow straightened, and I saw that the boat was going to bypass me this time by a good fifteen yards. The light jerked back the other way. Greene had no idea where I was; he was hunting blind in the fog. I stopped swimming and

treaded water, so that only my head bobbed above the surface. I was afraid of giving my position away with splashes and churned-up foam.

The *Kingfisher* drew abreast—and growled past without changing trajectory.

I lowered my head, flailed out again. The cramp in my calf was worse now: hot wire of pain jabbing all the way up to the hip.

Stroke.

Stroke.

Leg stiffening up.

Stroke.

Agony.

Stroke.

How much farther? Head up. More of the center float visible, boat moored in the right-hand slip rearing up black but distinct, left-hand slip empty. Twenty yards, maybe less.

Stroke.

Leg on fire.

Stroke.

The diesel sound—I could no longer hear it except as a low rumble. Greene, the boat, where were they now?

Drifting in the swells forty or fifty yards distant. Throttle shut off, just drifting.

Movement on deck near the starboard gunwale; a mass of heavy shadows, distorted by the fog. Then they seemed to separate, amoebalike. I thought I saw a blackish lump drop down over the side, thought I heard a splash.

Kellenbeck? Dead, dumped overboard?

*Swim!*

Flex the leg, suck in air, crawl forward. Pain. Numbness. Heart hammering in a wild cadence. Not enough air; gasps and whimpers coming out of my throat.

Stroke.

Stroke.

Less than ten yards.

Stroke.

Engine sound climbing again.

Leg locked up, useless, can't swim anymore—

—dog-paddle then, dog-paddle—

—almost there, *get* there—

—and the edge of the float came up in front of me and I hauled one leaden arm out of the water and fumbled at the slick wood, felt the sharp rib of a barnacle cut into my palm. Got a grip on the upper rim of the float and hung on, pulling myself in against it.

Behind me the throb of the diesel grew louder.

I managed to get both forearms onto the float, tried to heave myself up out of the water. But I had no strength left; my whole body trembled with exhaustion and the pain in my leg was hellish. Clinging there, I twisted to look back over my shoulder.

The spotlight and the *Kingfisher*'s bow were pointed straight toward the marina channel a few yards to my left.

Get away from here, I thought, get into the other channel.

Fingers clawing at the boards, I pulled myself toward the right-hand corner of the float. The troller was nearing the channel; Greene throttled down and I saw the black hull buck in the swells, the bow drift left until he corrected. The light flicked toward me—

I heaved around to the channel side just before it swept over the float. Pulled my hands down and shoved the palms against the barnacled underside to hold my head low in the water, beneath the float's upper edge. Above and beyond me, the light illuminated the rigging and wheelhouse of the boat moored in the near slip. And then cut away as the *Kingfisher* passed into the channel.

Some of the desperation faded; my mind was sluggish, but I had control of it. Control of my breathing too. I pushed up, dragged forward to the inner corner. Heard the troller's engines whine into reverse. Heading into his slip, I thought. But then what? Did Greene think I was still somewhere out in the bay? That I had drowned? That I had made it in here? He might just leave the boat and make for Kellenbeck's Cadillac—but it was more likely he would take that flashlight of his and prowl the floats, searching for me.

Stay where I was, hide under the float if he came this way, wait him out? No good. The numbness was spreading and I was beginning to feel almost warm; I knew what that meant well

enough. The frigid water had robbed me of body heat: Another few minutes and I would no longer be able to feel or do anything, I would lose consciousness, I would freeze and then drown. I *had* to get out of the water, even if it mean exposing myself. And I had to do it in the next minute or so, before Greene finished docking the *Kingfisher*.

I anchored both forearms on the float again, squirmed upward. But my shoulder and back muscles, and the lower half of my body, were so weak it was like trying to boost up a two-hundred-pound slab of meat; I managed to get my breastbone over the edge and that was all. I hung there, kicking with my good leg, straining frantically to keep from sliding backward.

The engine sound decreased to an idling rumble: Greene had maneuvered into his slip.

I threw my right arm out, clutched at the float's inner edge to hold myself in position—and my chilled fingers brushed over a rusted iron ring imbedded there, part of a rope tied through it. Cleat. And the bow line on the boat above me. I caught hold of the rope and tugged on it. The boat made a creaking noise, rocked forward; the line slackened enough for me to get it looped once around my wrist. Then I put my left hand down flat on the boards, heaved up, pulled back on the rope at the same time. Flopped my body from side to side. Heaved, pulled, flopped until my chest, stomach, abdomen cleared the edge—

—and I was out of the water and dragging myself forward, knees scraping over the rough wood.

Across the opposite channel the *Kingfisher*'s spotlight and running lights winked out. The diesel shut down. Silence settled around me, broken only by the fog bells and the wheezing plaint of my breathing.

Thin gusts of wind stung my face, cut through the numbness and took away the false feeling of warmth; I began to shake with chills as I lifted back into a kneeling position. When I got my right foot planted and a two-handed grip on the bow line I hoisted and levered myself upright. Almost fell when I tried to put weight on the cramped leg; it buckled and pitched me sideways against the boat. I let go of the rope, grabbed onto the gunwale to steady myself.

The wheelhouse blocked off my view of Greene's slip. Blocked off his view, too. Nothing stirred in any other direction except tracers and puffs of fog. I swung myself on board, good leg first, and hobbled to the port wheelhouse bulkhead. Eased along it and around to the aft side.

Unlike Greene's, this wheelhouse had a door; it was shut, but when I depressed the latch it popped open. Into the heavy blackness inside. Shut the door again. Down on all fours so I would not bang into anything and make a carrying noise. Then I crawled over to the helm and lifted up to peer through the mist-streaked windshield.

The pale nightlights let me see part of the float

where Greene's slip was. And he was there, moving away from the ramp toward the bay end. Going to look for me, all right. Near the end he stopped and raised his arm: A shaft of light stabbed out from that big flash of his, swept back and forth in a restless arc over the water. Pretty soon he turned onto the right-angled outer arm, shone the beam across the channel toward where I was. I ducked down, stayed down until the hazy glow disappeared from the glass.

When I raised up again he was hurrying back toward the ramp. I might have lost sight of him in the fog except that he still had the flash switched on; I could see it flicking out between the moored boats—and I could follow it all the way past the ramp and around onto the connecting walkway.

Coming out here, too.

I crawled back along the bulkhead, feeling with my hands. Storage locker aft, near the door—but it was padlocked. I groped above it. Touched cold metal that my fingers told me was a wood-handled steel hook, attached to the bulkhead with clips. Gaff, for hooking and holding heavy fish. Weapon. I took it down, crept back under the wheel. Knelt there gripping it across my chest.

The sodden clothing clung like a wrapping of ice; tremors racked me and I had to lock my teeth together to keep them from chattering. The cramp had loosened a little, but the leg still ached. All of me ached: muscles, joints, bones. My face was still with saltcake; the rest of my skin had a

puckered feel, cold and hot at the same time, as if with fever.

Pneumonia, I thought.

Flickers of light shone beyond the windshield, went on past. Muffled slap of Greene's shoes on the float outside. Could he tell I had come out of the water there, climbed on board this boat? No. Float was already wet, sloshed over, and the deck was wet too from the dripping mist. He might decide to check out each of the moored boats, but that wasn't likely; take too much time, and he could not be sure of what had happened to me. For all he knew I had made it to shore and was already on my way to summon the cops. He just could not afford to hang around much longer.

Another ten seconds passed.

Come on, you son of a bitch. Move out, start running.

Ten more seconds.

Light in the glass again, centered there for an instant. Then it moved off. Footfalls, fading.

Darkness except for the nightlights.

Silence.

I let out a breath through my nostrils. But stayed where I was for a time, listening. Still no sounds from outside. Raised up again, leaned close to the windshield. Emptiness across the way, no movement of any kind. Faint movement of light far down to the right, though, reflected off the fog—Greene over on the float?

Half a minute. Forty seconds.

And the beam reappeared, hazed and steady, on the walkway at the shore end. Moved along there and around onto the west-side float, dancing out again between the boats. Stopped at the *Kingfisher*, traced a path up across the deck, splashed over the wheelhouse. Probed inside. Vanished.

More waiting, face pressed close to the glass. One minute. Two. Three. The light poked back out, retraced across the deck and down onto the float. Shut off again in front of the ramp. Four beats. Black silhouette: Greene climbing up the metal ladder, something large and squarish in his right hand. Suitcase?

Then he was gone, swallowed by the mist and the darkness.

I used the gaff as a fulcrum to push myself onto my feet. Left foot took my weight now, but I would have to favor the right just in case. I leaned against the binnacle, staring out. More waiting, to make sure he didn't decide to come back.

Emptiness.

Okay, enough. Enough. Back along the bulkhead to the door, out on deck. Over the gunwale, still hanging onto the gaff, and down the float to the connecting walkway.

Stillness.

Around to the ramp. Up the ladder in cautious movements, to peer down the ramp at the highway.

Deserted highway: Kellenbeck's Cadillac was gone.

Onto the ramp, along the ramp. Stumbling a little now; legs wobbly, threatening to give out. The wind welding clothing to skin, making me shake like a man with palsy.

Drop the gaff, cross the road. Packed-dirt driveway there, leading up to where houselights glowed behind the screen of fog. Up the driveway. Stumbling again, falling, getting up. House taking shape—gray hexagonal thing with a wrap around porch and switchback stairs leading up. Climb the stairs, lean panting beside the door. Knock on the door. Somebody coming, somebody opening up—

And it was over.

God—it was over.

# ∘ TWENTY ∘

The next few hours were a time I lived through with a kind of schizoid detachment: part of me seemed to retreat, to become a disinterested observer, while the other part continued to operate more or less normally. Temporary reactional dysfunction, the psychologists call it, induced by a period of intense physical and emotional stress. And the hell with them and their fancy labels.

The people who lived in the house were the Muhlheims, a couple of artists in their forties. They were helpful and solicitous types and the first thing they tried to do was to get me out of my wet clothes; but all I could think about was using the phone. Muhlheim wrapped a blanket around me while I called the county police in Santa Rosa. I used Eberhardt's and Donleavy's names to get through to a lieutenant named Fitzpatrick and laid out the story for him in clipped sentences, some of which I had to repeat because of the way my teeth kept clacking together; the only thing I omitted was mention of the private

eye as a horse's ass: my breaking into the Kellenbeck Fish Company. Fitzpatrick asked a couple of
terse questions, and my answers and the urgency
in my voice seemed to convince him I was telling
a straight story. He instructed me to stay where I
was, said he would take care of contacting other
police agencies.

When I hung up I let Muhlheim show me to the
bathroom. He and his wife had listened to my end
of the conversation with plenty of interest, but to
his credit he did not try to question me. He gave
me some dry clothes—we were about the same
size—and left me alone to strip and take a five-
minute, steaming-hot shower. Which only just
dulled the edge of my chill, but which at least
stopped the shaking.

Mrs. Muhlheim had a pot of hot tea and another
blanket waiting when I came out. Plus some salve
for the barnacle cuts on my hands. Ten more
minutes passed, most of it in silence; the tea
warmed me a little more. Then there was a sharp
rapping on the front door. And things began to
happen.

Two highway patrolmen. Questions. A guy from
the Coast Guard station at Doran Park. A pair of
county Sheriff's deputies. More questions. Another highway patrolman. A telephone call to
Santa Rosa made by one of the deputies. And after
that they took me out of there, bundled in an old
overcoat offered up by Muhlheim, and down to
the Highway Patrol substation south of Bodega.

Fitzpatrick, a youngish guy with an authoritarian manner, arrived from Santa Rosa. More questions. Report from the Coast Guard: They had fished Kellenbeck's body out of the bay near the marina, shot once through the heart. A doctor showed up, summoned by somebody along the line, and spent a little time examining me. No fever, he said, no other signs of incipient pneumonia. He gave me some pills to swallow, told me to see my physician if I developed any serious symptoms, and went away.

Eberhardt called from his home—Fitzpatrick had notified the Hall of Justice and they in turn had contacted Eb—and I was allowed to talk to him. In concerned tones he asked how I was. I said I was fine, wonderful, that son of a bitch Greene had come within minutes of killing me dead. Then I told the story all over again, for the fifth or sixth time. I'll get back to you in the morning, he said. Yeah, I said.

Greene was still at large. But there was an All-Points Bulletin out on him, Fitzpatrick told me—it was only a matter of time. The head of the Alcohol and Firearms Unit office in San Francisco called. I got to talk to him, too, and answer some more questions, and listen to him tell me he would send agents up in the morning to interrogate me "when you're feeling better."

I was so tired by this time, from all the talk and the pills and the physical and mental strain, that I had trouble holding my head up. I asked Fitzpat-

rick if I could please, for Christ's sake, be taken
somewhere so I could get some sleep. Yes, he
supposed I had been through enough for one night.
Damned right, I thought. Put you up at The Tides
Motel, somebody said, that okay? Just dandy.

Out of there finally and into a car, Fitzpatrick
driving. Where was my car? he asked. Up by the
Kellenbeck Fish Company. Keys? Lost in the bay,
they were in my overcoat pocket, but there's another set in a little magnetic box behind the rear
bumper. He'd have somebody pick it up and bring
it to the motel.

Motel. Check-in. Room. They went away, saying
they would talk to me again in the morning. Bed.
Sleep. Dreams of ice and water, guns and darkness, dead faces floating at the bottom of the sea.

Long, bad night . . .

A knocking on the door woke me. I sat up a
little groggily and it took me a few seconds to
orient myself, remember where I was. Gray light
in the room, filtering in through half-closed
drapes over the window. I squinted at my watch.
It was a good old waterproof Timex and still ticking away, undamaged by the salt water last night;
the hands read eight-twenty-five.

I swung my feet out, sat on the edge of the bed.
The knocking came again. I called, "Just a minute," and then stood up in a tentative way, testing
my legs. Stiff, with a faint weakness in the joints.
Same feeling in my arms. My head was stuffy and

there was congestion in my lungs, the kind I used to have before I gave up cigarettes. Otherwise I seemed to be in reasonably good shape for what I had been through.

I put on Muhlheim's clothes and went over and opened the door. Fitzpatrick. He asked me how I was, but not as if it mattered a great deal to him, and handed me my car keys.

"Greene?" I said.

He shook his head. "Not yet. But we'll get him, don't worry."

"I'm not worried. Just eager."

"Sure. Federal agents are here; they said they'd be over to see you later this morning. So don't go anywhere for awhile."

"How about after I see them? Can I leave for home then?"

"You can as far as I'm concerned," Fitzpatrick said. "But stop by the substation before you go; there's a statement waiting for you to sign."

After he left I went into the bathroom and looked at myself in the mirror. Beard stubble, puffy eyes, mottled skin, hair sticking up every which way like a fright wig: face to scare little children with. I turned out of there, put on Muhlheim's overcoat, left the room, and hunted up my car. Reversed the procedure, carrying my overnight case, and then went to work on the beard stubble with a razor.

While I shaved I did some heavy thinking for the first time since early last night. Not about

Greene and what had happened in the bay; that brush with death, and my own foolishness that had led to it, was something I did not want to relive. What I did think about was the bootlegging and the murders of Jerry Carding and his father. And about all the questions that were still unanswered, the one major question that was still unanswered.

Who had murdered Christine Webster?

The mental work got me nowhere. And yet, if I kept going over things enough times, maybe there was something I knew and could remember—like the little things I had known and remembered about Kellenbeck and the Cardings. Maybe . . .

The telephone rang just as I finished toweling off. I went into the other room, picked up the receiver. And listened to Eberhard't voice say, "It's me. How you feeling this morning?"

"Fair. Better than I ought to."

"No after effects?"

"None I want to talk about."

"Yeah," he said. "Guy in the Highway Patrol office up there told me where you were. According to him, no word on Greene yet."

"I know. Fitzpatrick came by a few minutes ago."

"You wouldn't be planning to stick around up there until he's caught?"

"Hell no. I'll be home as soon as they're done with me."

"When'll that be?"

"Sometime this afternoon, I guess. I've got to go sign a statement. And see a couple of Federal agents before that."

"Me too," he said. "I just got off the phone with one of the Alcohol and Firearms boys."

"Have you talked to Donleavy?"

"Little while ago."

"Is he dropping the charges against Martin Talbot?"

"That's what he says. But the Carding murder is still officially open until Greene turns up. Or some kind of incriminating evidence does." He paused. "The Christine Webster case is still open too, damn it."

"Greene didn't kill her, Eb," I said.

"So you managed to tell me last night. You're probably right—but I'd like it better if you weren't."

"I would too. But there's just no motive for him to've shot the girl. Jerry Carding only had two copies of his article the night he was killed; there wasn't a third he could have mailed to Christine."

"Greene might have been afraid he'd told her something," Eberhardt said, "and went after her for that reason."

"It doesn't add up. Why would Greene be more worried about Christine than, say, Steve Farmer or Sharon Darden—people right here at Bodega Bay? And if he had wanted to kill her, why wait until Tuesday night to do it? And why shoot her with a

.32 instead of the .38 he used on Carding or the Browning automatic he tried to use on me?"

Eberhardt sighed. "I can't argue with any of that," he said. "All right, Greene didn't kill Christine. But then who did? And why? Where's the connection?"

"Maybe there isn't one. Not a direct one, anyway."

"Coincidence?"

"That's what I'm thinking."

"I don't like coincidences worth a damn."

"Neither do I, usually. But they do happen, Eb. They even happen in bunches sometimes."

"Bunches?"

"I'm starting to wonder," I said, "if maybe there aren't a lot of coincidences in these two cases."

"Meaning what? You got another theory?"

"No. Just a feeling so far. Did you dig up anything on Bobbie Reid, by the way?"

"Not much. She was the private type: no close friends, kept pretty much to herself. Her parents live in Red Bluff and they're the ones who claimed the body; neither of them had much contact with Bobbie in the past year, said they didn't know why she committed suicide. Didn't seem too broken up about it, either. Nice folks."

"What about the people where she worked?"

"Same thing. She was a legal secretary in a law office downtown; none of her coworkers knew her very well. Her boss, Arthur Brown, says he'd been thinking about firing her just before her death—

late for work on a regular basis, withdrawn, moody, fouled up an important brief. . . ." Pause. "Hold on a second, will you?" He covered the mouthpiece but I could hear muffled voices in the background. A few seconds later he came back on. "I've got to go; the Alcohol and Firearms people are here. Call me when you get back to the city."

"I may call you sooner than that," I said.

"What?"

"Maybe inside an hour."

"What the hell are you talking about?"

"I'm not sure yet. I'll get back to you when I am."

I rang off and went over and stood looking out through the bayside window. More fog today, swirling heavily over the ruffled surface of the bay. Like the thoughts swirling over the surface of my mind. Facts, memory scraps, additions and subtractions—all swirling and then beginning to coalesce into the missing part of the blueprint.

For the first time, then, I could see the complete design of the labyrinth. And it only had three connecting sides. The open end, the missing side, was nothing but coincidence—multiple coincidence.

Our stubborn refusal to accept that, particularly on this kind of *Grand Guignol* basis, was what had been hanging us up all along. Part of everything had begun with accidental occurrence and some of the complications had been built on it: a car driven by Martin Talbot crashing into one

driven by Victor Carding; Christine Webster having my business card and Laura Nichols deciding she needed a private detective; Talbot and me arriving at the Carding house just after Carding's murder; all the suicides real and attempted and bogus; interrelationships among the people involved; even things like Greene showing up at Kellenbeck's house just in time to spot me last night. Three parts connective tissue to one part coincidence.

I thought I knew now who had killed Christine and I had a hunch as to why. But I needed the answer to one more question before I could be sure. Just one more question.

I put on Muhlheim's coat again, went out and down across the parking lot. The cold wind made my eyes water and started my nose running; my chest still felt badly congested. If I was smart I would make an appointment tomorrow with Doctor White. The shape my lungs were in, pneumonia was a threat I could not afford to overlook.

Inside The Tides Wharf I walked around into the warehouse area behind the fish market. Deserted. I came back out to the counter where a balding guy in a white apron was fileting salmon and asked him if Steve Farmer had reported for work today. The guy said yes, he was in the restaurant on his break.

So I crossed over there and stepped inside. Farmer was sitting at one of the tables near the windows; he was alone and seemed to be brooding

into a cup of coffee. When I went to him and said, "Hello, Steve," he looked up at me with pained and listless eyes.

"Oh," he said, "it's you."

I sat down. "I guess you know about Jerry."

"I heard this morning. It's all people are talking about."

"I'm sorry it had to turn out this way."

"Sure." He stared into the cup. "Jerry too," he said. "All of them—just like I was afraid it would be."

Yeah, I thought, all of them. But I said, "I need the answer to a question, Steve. You're the only person who can give it to me."

"What question?"

"Why did Bobbie Reid commit suicide?"

His face started to close up again, the way it had before, but this time it did not quite make it—as if Jerry Carding's death had taken the edge off his feelings about everything else. He rested an elbow on the table, cocked the hand against his forehead like a visor. "Why do you have to keep bugging me about Bobbie? It's all finished now, for God's sake. Her suicide doesn't have anything to do with the murders."

"Yes it does. It's got everything to do with Christine Webster's murder."

He gave me an anguished look from under the visored hand. "But I thought Andy Greene and Gus Kellenbeck—?"

"No. They killed Jerry and his father, yes. But

not Christine." I paused and then asked him again, in a gentler tone: "Why did Bobbie commit suicide?"

"I don't know, not for sure. She had hang-ups. . . ."

"What hangups? Steve, why did you break up with her?"

"I didn't. She broke up with me; she . . . found somebody else. . . ."

"Who?"

"I don't know. Somebody *else*, that's all."

"Another man?"

His shoulders sagged; he dropped both forearms to the table edge and slumped over them with his head bent. "No," he said, "not another man. She was making it with a woman. I loved her and she turned gay on me, she turned into a lesbian. . . ."

Bingo.

## ° **TWENTY-ONE** °

I called Eberhardt back ten minutes later and laid it all out for him: who I believed had shot Christine Webster and why. He said it sounded reasonable but he would need proof, not speculation and hearsay, before he could make an arrest; but he agreed with me that he would not have too much trouble finding it. With luck he could have the whole ugly business wrapped up by the end of the day.

The Justice Department investigators showed up not long afterward, and I spent two hours making another statement and answering an endless string of questions. When they were finally done with me I had a headache and an achy feeling in my joints; but I also had their permission to go back to San Francisco. Twelve minutes after they left I was on my way to the Highway Patrol substation. And twenty minutes after that I was on my way home—sniffling and hacking up phlegm with the heater on full blast.

It was a few minutes past three when I crossed

the Golden Gate Bridge. The fog there was as thick as it had been up the coast; you could not see the bridge towers or much of Alcatraz or Angel Island, and the hills and buildings of the city had a gray distorted look. But that was all right. I liked the fog more than ever now, because without it I would not have survived last night's ordeal with Greene.

I drove down Lombard, straight up Laguna. Predictably, the closest parking space to my building turned out to be two blocks away. My joints ached even more now and I had developed a scratchy throat; the two-block walk in the cold did me no good at all.

I gathered up my mail and let myself in. When I got up to my door I felt a twinge of apprehension, remembering what I had found at my office on Friday. But both locks were secure and nothing had been disturbed inside: the pulps were still on their shelves, the bachelor's mess on the furniture and floor was just as I had left it.

Brew up some tea, I thought, take another cold pill, and get into bed. So I threw Muhlheim's coat on the couch—I would have to remember to get the coat and the rest of his clothing cleaned and shipped back to him pretty soon—and headed toward the kitchen.

On the way I shuffled through the mail. And one of the envelopes made me stop in the doorway. It was plain-white and business-sized, with

no return address. And the "r" in my name was chipped, the "a" in the street address tilted.

Christ. I tore it open, pulled out a single sheet of white paper, and unfolded it. My name was typed there, too, and below it three lines:

> You'd better leave me alone. If you don't, I'll do something to YOU next time, not just your office. I mean that. Leave me ALONE.

I held up the envelope and looked at the post-mark. Mailed Saturday night. Sure, that figured. She must have written it right after my call—

Somebody knocked on the door.

Frowning, I turned to look over there. Dennis Litchak, probably, because the downstairs door buzzer had not sounded; he must have seen or heard me enter and come up to talk. Well, I was in no mood or condition for company right now. I went to the door, thinking that I would get rid of old Dennis in five seconds flat, and opened up.

Karen Nichols stood in the hallway outside.

"I've been waiting for you all day," she said. "Waiting and waiting for you. I thought you'd never come home."

In her right hand was a .32 caliber revolver.

The muscles in my stomach and groin contracted; I could feel heat come into my cheeks and a shaking start up inside. This was the second time in eighteen hours that a gun had been

pointed at me, that I had tasted sudden fear and come up against sudden death. It had been bad enough with Greene, but this was worse because I was sick and exhausted and because it meant coping all over again, trying to beat the odds twice in a row.

I still had hold of the door and I considered throwing it shut, diving out of the way. But I would have had to step back to do that, to get the door in front of my body, and my reflexes were shaky and not to be trusted. She had already moved forward to the threshold, too, and her finger was tight against the trigger. Too risky. Stay calm, I told myself, find another way. Don't do anything to make her shoot.

"Back up and let me in," she said. "Somebody might come."

I let go of the door, retreated in slow careful steps. She came inside and pushed the door almost shut behind her with her free hand. Her face was so pale that I could see the fine tracery of veins beneath the skin, but there was nothing in her expression or in the wide amber eyes to indicate how unbalanced she was. She looked normal, in full control of herself, and that scared me even more than if she'd been wild-eyed and gibbering. She could errupt into violence at any second, on the slightest provocation—the way she must have when she destroyed my office.

She said, "You got my letter," and I realized I

still had it and the envelope and the rest of the mail in my left hand.

"Yes. I got it."

"I shouldn't have sent it. I shouldn't have sent any of the letters to that Webster bitch either. They didn't do any good. Nothing does any good. Except this." She raised the gun slightly and looked at it as if it were a new-found friend, an ally. "This is the only way."

"You don't want to shoot me, Karen," I said.

"Yes I do. I have to. You won't leave me alone. I thought if I went to your office last week and talked to you . . . but you weren't there, and I thought if I went in and did things to it, it would hurt you enough to make you go away. But you didn't, you just kept on and on. When you asked me about Bobbie on Saturday night I knew what I had to do. I knew this was the only way. I waited for you all afternoon and all evening. And all day today. Why didn't you come home?"

Without moving my head much I looked left, right—but I was standing in the middle of the carpet and there was nothing in a five-foot radius that I could use to disarm her. The nearest piece of furniture was the couch, three paces to my right. And nothing on it except the overcoat, a pulp magazine, a couple of throw pillows.

"Karen, listen to me—"

"No. I don't want to listen. I just want to do what I have to before it's too late."

Throw pillows. *Throw* pillow?

"It's already too late," I said. "The police know the truth."

Her forehead puckered; she bit her lip. "I don't believe you."

Long odds. Even if I could get over to the couch, pick up one of the pillows, it would take a perfect toss to hit the gun before she fired, throw her off-balance long enough for me to rush her. But what other choice did I have? It seemed to be either that or try to jump her cold.

I said, "It's true, Karen. The police have been out to your house today, they've matched the typing on the letters with the typewriter in your living room; they know you wrote them to Christine."

"I don't believe you," she said again.

"Why would I lie to you?"

"Because you want to hurt me. Along with my mother and that Webster bitch. Won't go away, won't stop hurting me . . ."

Her jaw trembled a little and her eyes were brighter; you could see the violence rippling like a dark current just beneath the surface of her face. The knotted feeling in my groin intensified. Keep her talking, for God's sake, I thought. But don't say anything to provoke her.

"I never wanted to hurt you, Karen. I only wanted to help your uncle."

"No. You were working for Webster all along."

"But I wasn't," I said, and took a careful sidestep toward the couch. The gun did not move in her

hand. "Christine never contacted me. I never met her or talked to her."

"You're lying again. She had your business card. And she *told* me she'd hired you, just before I did it to her."

That did not surprise me. The reason why Christine had lied was obvious: she had been trying desperately to save her life. And the lie explained how Karen had known I was a detective when I arrived at her house on Wednesday morning. I had only given her my name at the door, not my occupation, and by their own testimony Laura Nichols had not told her daughter of her plans to hire an investigator. Yet the first thing Karen had said to me was, "You're that private detective."

"Working for Webster," she said now, "and then right away going to work for my mother. Don't you think I know the real reason *she* hired you?"

"I don't know what you mean. Your mother hired me to watch over your uncle."

"That was just a lie for my benefit. She hired you to investigate *me.*"

"Why would she do that?"

"She hates me, that's why. She suspected I was gay. She suspected I was in love with Bobbie and wanted to hurt the bitch who killed her. She hired you so you could both work against me."

Paranoid psychosis, I thought. Everybody out to harm her, including her mother. Especially her mother. She was the one with all the hatred, not Laura Nichols; and those feelings had to be at the

root of her persecution complex and her need to strike back.

I took another step toward the couch. My nose was running again, dripping down over my upper lip; I sniffled and just let it drip. No use pressing my luck by reaching into the back pocket where my handkerchief was.

"Your mother didn't tell me about you and Bobbie," I said. "She doesn't know you're gay."

"She must have told you. You weren't surprised when I said it just now. You already knew."

"Yes. But I found out another way—"

"*She* told you. Stop lying to me."

Easy, I thought, drop it right there. Because the truth was provocative: it was Karen herself who had told me. On the phone Thursday night she'd said she and some friends had spent the day at Civic Center and I remembered noticing in Friday's paper that at Civic Center on Thursday there had been a big Gay Rights rally. And when I had talked to her Saturday night from Bodega Bay and asked if she knew Bobbie Reid, she'd said, "No. Who's she?" Yet Bobbie, or Bobby, is a far more common male name than a female name; the assumption almost everybody makes the first time they hear it is that it's short for Robert, not Roberta or Barbara. Which indicated Karen *had* known Bobbie Reid. Add those facts together, along with Eberhardt's news that Bobbie had worked for Arthur Brown, the Nichols' family

attorney, and Steve Farmer's admission that Bobbie was gay, and the truth became clear enough.

"Well?" she said. "My mother told you, didn't she?"

"Yes."

"And you think being gay is terrible, don't you? Just like she does."

"No, I don't think it's terrible."

"Are you lying to me again?"

"No. I think every person has the right to be what he wants to be. As long as he doesn't harm anyone else."

"Webster harmed Bobbie. *Killed* her, the bitch."

"How did she do that?"

"With words. Words. Bobbie never told anyone about us; she was confused about being gay. But Webster got it out of her. She told Bobbie it was evil and she was sick and needed help. Kept telling her again and again. Bobbie couldn't take it. She was a sensitive person and she just . . . she couldn't take it. She took those pills, and she called me afterward to say she was sorry, she had to do it, she couldn't cope anymore after what Webster had been telling her. I told her how much I loved her, I begged her not to do it, but she said it was too late. I called the emergency hospital, I drove over there myself, and it was. It was too late. . . ."

Poor Bobbie Reid: emotionally screwed up, unable to come to terms with her life and her sexuality—a probable suicide in any case. Poor Christine Webster: well-meaning, foolish, always trying

to meddle in other people's lives. Victims, just like Jerry Carding. Poor Karen, too: unbalanced, deluded, filled with paranoid hatred for her domineering mother. She was another victim, and I pitied her a little in that moment. But I pitied Jerry and Christine and Bobbie a great deal more.

Karen seemed to be caught up for the moment in memory and grief; the sun was steady but no longer pointing straight at me. I took another step that brought me up next to the couch. But the movement alerted her, made her blink and swing the weapon back dead-center on my chest.

"Don't move," she said. "Why are you moving?"

I stood motionless, watching the gun. "I want to sit down. Is that all right?"

Hesitation. Then, "I don't care. I'm going to do what I have to pretty soon. Like I did with Webster. I wish I could do it to my mother too. But I can't. I want to but I . . . can't. Not yet."

I eased myself down on the arm of the couch, let my right arm dangle down at my side. The closest of the throw pillows was eight or nine inches away: I would have to lean in that direction in order to reach it.

"How did you do it to Webster?" I said. "How did you get her to meet you at Lake Merced?"

"Why do you want to know that?"

"I just do. Will you tell me?"

"I called her on the phone, that's how. Not like the other calls, where I disguised my voice. I said

I knew who was threatening her, but I didn't want to say anything on the phone and I was afraid to come to her apartment because the person might be watching her. I asked her to meet me and she said she would. She thought it was a *man* who wanted to hurt her, you see; she wasn't afraid of me. But I made her afraid. I made her very afraid before I did it to her."

A feeling of nausea formed inside me: her words, tension, suppressed fear. I tipped my body to the right, moved my arm out away from it—one inch, two, three.

"I thought it was all done with then," she said. "Webster did it to Bobbie, I did it to Webster. But then you came. And there were all those lies about Uncle Martin. And Victor Carding was murdered. And I found out Jerry Carding was his son and Webster's boyfriend too. I never knew that before. I never even heard of Jerry Carding. It confused me, I couldn't understand what was happening."

Concidence, that was what had been happening. Martin Talbot and Victor Carding have an accident; Carding's son is Christine Webster's fiance; Talbot's niece is having an affair with Bobbie Reid; Bobbie Reid is a friend of Christine's and used to date a friend of Jerry Carding's; Christine finds out Bobbie is gay and admonishes her for it; Bobbie commits suicide; Karen blames Christine and murders her. And Bobbie works in Arthur Brown's law office; Christine works part-time in the same

building; Brown is Laura Nichols' attorney; I've done some work for Brown and always hand out cards to my clients; Christine gets one of the cards from Brown; Laura Nichols wants to hire a private detective and Brown recommends me. A crazy-quilt of concidence.

But there was no point in saying any of that to Karen; she would not have believed it. I stayed silent and kept leaning toward the throw pillow. Four inches. Five.

"Then I did understand," she said. "It was somebody *else* working against me. Not just you and my mother, but Jerry Carding too. He knew I was the one who hurt Webster and he did it to his own father so Uncle Martin would be blamed. That was his way of hurting me back."

Six. Seven—

*Sound out in the hallway.*

I froze, listening, staring at Karen. She seemed not to have heard it: a footstep, muffled by the carpeting out there. One of the Madisons, the couple who lived in the other flat on this floor?

"If I knew where Jerry Carding was, I'd do it to him too. I'd make him leave me alone."

Behind her a crack opened between the door and jamb; she had not closed the door all the way so there was no click of the latch opening, no sound at all. I straightened away from the pillow, leaned forward instead. Every muscle and nerve in my body felt coiled.

"I'll make everybody leave me alone. I don't

believe you about the police; they don't know yet. Only you and Mother and Jerry Carding know."

The crack widened a little more. A head poked around the edge of the door.

Dennis Litchak.

"You first and then Jerry Carding when I can find him. Then my mother someday. Then I'll be safe—"

The hinges squeaked. She heard the sound this time and her face registered surprise; reflex made her jerk her head around to look behind her, made the gun swing away from me.

I levered up off the couch and threw myself at her.

The damned gun went off, the lamp on the sideboard near the kitchen shattered, the door banged shut, I hit her with my shoulder and sent her reeling back against the wall. She caromed off, crying out in a hurt way, and the gun flew clear of her hand and skittered under the writing desk; she went down and rolled over and lay in a quivering little heap.

I veered away from her, went to one knee beside the desk, and scooped up the gun. When I straightened with it, the tension went out of me all at once, like a balloon deflating, and I had to lean against the desk top to keep from falling down.

Karen stopped quivering and lifted onto her knees. Looked at me with eyes that had gone dull with pain and confusion. "Why did you do that?"

she asked, as if she really did not know. "Why did you hurt me?"

When I didn't say anything she got up slowly, rubbing her arm where I had hit her, and then went over and sat down on the couch. Sat the way she had that first time, in the living room of her mother's house: knees together, back straight, hands folded in her lap, eyes cast down on her hands. She did not move; she did not even seem to be breathing.

Rapping on the door. And from out in the hallway Litchak yelled my name.

I called back, "You can come in now, Dennis, it's all over," and my voice sounded as if it were coming through liquid.

The door opened and he poked his white-maned head around the edge again. Came inside in tentative movements. He looked a little gray and shaken—but not nearly as gray and shaken as I felt.

"God Almighty," he said. He peered at me through his glasses, glanced over at Karen, looked back at me. "What the *hell* is going on?"

"It's a long story." I wanted to push away from the desk, go into the bedroom and get the phone and call Eberhardt; but I did not trust my legs just yet. "Listen, you probably saved my life. Thanks."

"I did?"

"You did. Why'd you come up? You hear me downstairs? Or was it your flat she buzzed to get in?"

"Neither one. I didn't even know you were home. I came up to check on the place again, like you asked me to, and saw the door standing open—"

A laugh popped out of me—sudden, humorless, ironic.

Litchak frowned. "What's funny?"

"Nothing," I said. "It's you showing up when you did."

"Huh?"

"Coincidence, Dennis. Just one more coincidence."

on the Canada border, government funds are confiscated on the strength of a few photographs. Apparently the rest of the men in the launch were lesser cogs—potential witnesses, each hoping for immunity, and guaranteed protection in return for cooperation—and so on.

Item: Gerry Nichols had been charged with the murder of Charlene Weber, and the expected

# ° TWENTY-TWO °

Four days passed. So did my cold, with some medical assistance from Doctor White and forty-eight hours in bed. And so did the worst of the nightmares about guns and water and death.

A number of things happened in those four days.

Item: Andy Greene was apprehended by Washington state officials trying to cross the border into Canada. In the suitcase he had with him were twenty-seven thousand dollars in cash and the Browning 9 mm automatic he had tried to use on me. He refused to talk to anyone except an attorney and was being held for extradition back to California.

Item: The Alcohol and Firearms investigators discovered a case of illicit-whiskey hidden in Gus Kellenbeck's garage, along with certain evidence—nobody told me what it was—which broke the whole bootlegging operation wide open. The distillery turned out to be located on the British Columbia coast, near Prince Rupert; it was

raided by Canadian government agents and six other men were arrested. An eighth arrest was made, by the Federal boys a few miles down the coast from Bodega Bay, of a rancher whose barn had been used by Greene and Kellenbeck for storage. Still more arrests were expected on the trucking and distribution end.

Item: Karen Nichols had been charged with the murder of Christine Webster and the attempted murder of me and was being held in the psychiatric ward at San Francisco General. Neither Eberhardt nor anyone else in the Department had been able to talk to her; she went into a violent paranoid reaction each of the two times they tried.

Item: All charges against Martin Talbot were dropped, but he was still hospitalized for observation and treatment. He had not been told about his niece's arrest, of course; the doctors were afraid the news would destroy all chance for his recovery. But they were not optimistic anyway, according to Donleavy. Neither was I. Even if he did get better, what would he have to come home to, poor bastard?

Item: Laura Nichols was reported to be "in seclusion" with friends outside the city. She had made no effort to see her daughter, Eberhardt told me, nor had she gone back to visit her brother. Mourning for herself, probably, for her own shattered existence. Mourning the fact that insanity really did run in her family.

Item: The media gave me a lot of publicity and

the phone rang several times—reporters asking questions and wanting to set up interviews. One guy said he wanted to do a feature article on me and my pulp collection and what it was like to be a private eye. And would I pose for pictures wearing, you know, a trenchcoat and a slouch hat? I told him I would think about it and that I would have my secretary, Effie Perine, get in touch with him. Literate guy that he was, he said he would look forward to Ms. Perine's call.

Item: I ate Thanksgiving dinner with Dennis Litchak and his wife, and the thanks I gave was that I was still alive. Afterward I told him I was going to buy him a case of Scotch for saving my arse as he had. He said, that wasn't necessary, but I insisted. Make it Johnnie Walker Black Label, he said.

Item: I went down to the office on Friday, my first day out since Tuesday's visit to Doctor White, and cleaned up the wreckage. Gave the slashed chair to Goodwill, along with the gouged and glue-damaged desk. Ordered replacements from a second-hand office-supply outfit. The place depressed me; it just did not feel the same any more. Maybe my CPA neighbor, Hadley, was right. Maybe it *was* time to think about moving out and setting up shop somewhere else.

On Saturday night Eberhardt and Donleavy and I went out for a steak dinner at a restaurant on Van Ness. It was the first chance we had had to get

together—and both of them seemed to feel they owed me a meal.

"There's one thing that keeps gnawing at me," Eberhardt said over the first round of beers. "I can't seem to get it out of my mind."

"What's that?" I asked. "All the coincidence?"

"No, not exactly. It's what happened to those two families after their paths crossed—one of them wiped out completely, the other one just about wiped out in a different way."

"Yeah."

"I mean, Talbot and Victor Carding have an accident and it seems to trigger a chain reaction. Death on the one side, insanity on the other."

"It didn't quite start with the accident," Donleavy reminded him. "Other things happened before and at the same time."

"Sure," Eberhardt said. "That's part of it, too. As if . . . hell, I don't know, as if fate or something was out to get both families. As if all the coincidences weren't really coincidences at all. You know what I mean?"

I had never heard him sound so metaphysical; the thing was really bothering him, all right. But he was not alone. It bothered me a little, and Steve Farmer, judging from what he had said to me at Bodega Bay, and maybe Donleavy too.

"I know what you mean," I said.

"So how do you figure it?"

"You don't," Donleavy said. "You don't even want to try."

Silence for a time.

Eberhardt said finally, "The hell with it," and drained the last of his beer. "Let's have another round before we order."

"I've got a better idea," the last of the lone-wolf private eyes said. "Let's have three or four more rounds."

And we did.

*Turn this book over
for more mystery
and adventure with*

**THE "NAMELESS DETECTIVE"**

We hope you have enjoyed this
KNIGHTSBRIDGE book.

We love good books just as you do,
so you can be assured that the
KNIGHT ON THE HORSE
stands for good reading, every time.

WE HOPE YOU HAVE ENJOYED THIS
KNIGHTSBRIDGE BOOK.

WE LOVE GOOD BOOKS JUST AS YOU DO,
SO YOU CAN BE ASSURED THAT THE
KNIGHT ON THE HORSE
STANDS FOR GOOD READING, EVERY TIME.